Match Made in Paradise

BARBARA DUNLOP

JOVE
New York

A JOVE BOOK
Published by Berkley
An imprint of Penguin Random House LLC
penguinrandomhouse.com

ISBN: 9780593332962

First Edition: May 2021

Printed in the United States of America
1   3   5   7   9   10   8   6   4   2

Book design by George Towne

Match Made in Paradise

Chapter One

MIA WESTBERG HAD DRESSED METICULOUSLY FOR HER husband Alastair Lafayette's funeral. She wore a black silk jersey under-dress that hugged her slim frame. A lace overlay softened the sweetheart neckline and brushed her knees in a sheer, scalloped hem. She added a lariat necklace of black diamonds and put her blond hair up, pinning a puff of black mesh to the wispy braid coronet. She finished with a pair of simple diamond halo onyx studs and slim heeled ankle boots over sheer black tights.

Alastair would have appreciated the ensemble. He'd chosen the dress himself from Lafayette Fashion's new fall Eternity Collection. Knowing his heart condition was worsening, he'd joked that she should wear it before it went out of season. It was dark humor, but that had been his way.

Now Mia and three hundred other mourners were assembled in St. Catherine's Cathedral off Wilshire Boulevard. Mia was on the aisle of the front right-hand pew with Alastair's adult children, Henry and Hannah separating her from his ex-wife, Theresa. None of the trio had looked her way. No surprise there. Henry and Hannah had just turned twenty-five. Mia was twenty-seven, and they'd never forgiven her for that.

The mayor was speaking at the pulpit. His remarks were supposed to be brief, making way for Joseph McKenzie to deliver the eulogy. Joseph was head of the California Fashion Design Council and a longtime friend of Alastair's. He sat across the aisle from Mia right now, notecards in hand, obviously holding back tears.

Mia's emotions were more complicated. She'd loved Alastair for the nine years of their marriage, and fifty was far too young for him to die. But she knew what nobody else did: Alastair's heart condition had made this moment inevitable. It had grown worse over the past six months, causing him intolerable pain and becoming more and more difficult to hide. But he was a proud and private man, and he'd wanted to keep his health a secret right up to the end.

Mia couldn't help but be happy that he'd succeeded. Her husband had lived a gifted life and died on his own terms.

The mayor, who clearly enjoyed the sound of his own voice reverberating from the redwood rafters of the beautifully gilded cathedral, finally ended his speech. People shifted, and a few coughed or whispered as the mayor left the pulpit.

Joseph rose and stepped across the aisle to give Mia's shoulder a comforting squeeze.

She sent him an encouraging smile. Unlike the mayor, Joseph wasn't a fan of public speaking.

But he did both himself and Alastair proud. His voice broke over a few heartfelt passages, and he paused twice to blow his nose. He brought some humor in at the end, and Mia chuckled along with everyone else at the story of Lafayette Fashion's first overseas show. It was long before her time, but anything that could have gone wrong did, and Alastair had eventually seen the humor.

"Did you see that?" Mia heard someone whisper behind her.

"Easy to tell she's not so brokenhearted," someone else whispered back.

Henry looked over at Mia then—well, glared really, but she levelly met his gaze. It was no secret that he and Hannah considered her a gold digger. After reading Alastair's will, they were more convinced of it than ever. As Alastair had predicted, they'd already contested the will in court.

Theresa daintily dabbed her eyes with a lace-edged hankie while Hannah squeezed her mother's hand in a show of support. But having heard Alastair's side of the divorce and having watched Theresa's behavior over the past nine years, Mia knew it was all for show. If Theresa was broken up about anything, it was the lack of an inheritance.

Joseph ended with a heartfelt farewell to Alastair. The priest led the congregation in a prayer then in a hymn where half the people knew the words and half the people obviously didn't. Mia was in the half who didn't. And then everyone rose as the pallbearers escorted the casket down the aisle.

"She couldn't be bothered to shed a tear." Mia heard the voice behind her again.

She could have turned to see who'd uttered the words, but it didn't matter. She lifted her chin, squared her shoulders and fixed her expression, pretending she was on a runway in New York City. It was Alastair who'd fostered the ice-princess persona for Mia's modeling career. He'd want her to carry it off today of all days. He'd be sorely disappointed in her if she turned into a blubbering mess.

And it wasn't that kind of a sendoff. She was proud of Alastair, and he needed her to be strong. They'd often talked about the future, what would happen when she was left to manage things alone. It was time now for her to carry on.

Mourners clustered around Theresa as if she were the grieving widow. But their words of condolence faded as Mia followed behind Alastair's casket. Nobody reached out to her, and she could feel the shuns, the disapproving stares as she made her way to the back of the chapel. Even Lafayette's vice president of marketing, Geraldine Putts, slid her gaze to one side when Mia passed. The action struck Mia as odd, but the moment was over quickly, and then she was outside the cathedral, where a black hearse waited under the hot June sun with a dozen black sedans lined up behind.

There was something terribly final in the way they slid Alastair's casket into the elongated car. Maybe it was knowing the next stop was Sunnydale Cemetery, where they'd put him in the ground and smooth the earth above him to erase his existence. Mia's chest tightened, and she swallowed. She refused to cry.

Someone touched her arm. "You doing okay?"

It was Marnie Anton. Marnie was on the short side. She had a slight frame, glossy auburn hair, a spray of freckles and was wearing a pair of mottled-green oblong glasses over her green eyes. Dressed in skinny jeans and a white French-tucked blouse with a lightweight olive-colored jacket draped over top—interesting choice for a funeral—Marnie didn't look at all like a lawyer. But she was the best.

"I'm doing fine," Mia said, surprised that Marnie had shown up at all but relieved to have a supporter at her side.

"I came as soon as I heard."

"Heard?"

Marnie had known about the funeral arrangements since Monday.

The pallbearers drew away and the hearse driver closed the oversized door. A flock of pigeons flew up from the square. Not doves, but still, maybe it was something. Mia's breath hitched one more time.

Marnie canted her head to where Theresa, Henry and Hannah stood few feet away. She lowered her voice. "That those three just stabbed you in the back."

Theresa started forward then, her nose in the air, holding tight to Henry's and Hannah's hands as she marched straight to the first sedan in the lineup.

"Seriously?" Marnie said, staring after the swish of Theresa's taffeta skirt and the bobble of Hannah's netted little fascinator hat.

Mia wasn't sold on the fascinator's bow and protruding feathers. A British event was really the only place to pull off that look.

"Whatever," she said to Marnie, trying to mean it. But for a flash of a second she considered elbowing Theresa out of the way and diving into the lead sedan. But she could hear Alastair's admonishing voice: *Never let them know you care. You don't.*

"Ride with me?" she asked Marnie.

"You got it."

The driver of the second car solemnly opened the back door for them. Marnie ducked in and slid across the seat to make room for Mia. She set her roomy tan leather tote bag in the middle.

The driver took his place up front, but they didn't move, waiting for the rest of the procession to gather in their cars. Thankfully, the engine was running so they had air into the backseat.

"I just came from the courthouse." Marnie said. "There were five lawyers there from Brettan LaCroix representing the Lafayette kids. They filed an injunction."

"An injunction against what?" They'd already contested the will.

"Against *you* taking charge at Lafayette before the estate is settled," Marnie said.

Mia turned to peer at Marnie in confusion. "That can't work. How can that work? Who'll run the company?"

"The vice presidents in a caretaker capacity—with Henry and Hannah right by their side."

Mia thought back to the way Geraldine Putts's gaze had slid away in the chapel. It all came clear.

"They know," she said. "The vice presidents already know."

"Some of them supported the injunction," Marnie said.

The sedan pulled forward as Mia tried to make sense of the new information. "The vice presidents *want* Henry and Hannah to take charge?"

Alastair's two children had empty titles, meaningless jobs. They'd never been involved in actually running the company.

"They definitely don't want you in charge."

"Why not?" Mia had worked side-by-side with Alastair for years.

Okay, sure, most people thought of her as merely a model and Alastair's wife. But she'd been his trusted adviser. She knew the inner workings of the Lafayette Fashion company. She'd been involved in every significant decision. And, by the way, she *owned* it now.

Marnie gave Mia a pointed look. "You know you know the answer to that."

Yes, Mia knew the answer. And it was colossally unfair. She wasn't just a pretty face in an ad campaign. "Can we fight it?"

"The judge granted the injunction."

"So, we lost? We already lost?"

This wasn't what Alastair had wanted. He couldn't have been any clearer in his final wishes. The company went to Mia. Hannah and Henry got jobs for life with generous perks. And Theresa . . . well, Theresa was on her own. Alastair had been clear about that too.

Marnie was looking down at her phone. "I'll appeal, but this is going to get ugly."

"It's already ugly." The tabloids and social media had not been kind to Mia.

"Uglier," Marnie qualified. She went silent for a moment. "Did you say you had a cousin in Alaska?"

Mia drew back. "I'm not running away."

"Right. Sure. Of course." Marnie paused again. "Thing is, there's already a photo of you at the funeral." She held her screen Mia's way. "They're saying the ice princess didn't cry."

"Alastair didn't want me to cry."

"The social media trolls wanted you to cry."

"*Forget* the social media trolls."

"Yeah, I don't think that's worked for anybody . . . ever."

SILAS BURKE SHOOK THE RAINWATER FROM HIS WEST Slope Aviation ball cap as he entered Galina Expediting's cavernous warehouse in the small town of Paradise, Alaska. Lightning was muted in the storm clouds behind him, masked by the long summer daylight, while the thunder rolled from mountain to mountain across the massive sky.

He knew the storm was wreaking havoc on Galina's delivery schedule, frustrating operations manager Raven Westberg. He guessed that was why his boss, Brodie Seaton, owner of West Slope Aviation, had reached out to him. A flash flood yesterday on the central Alaskan haul road meant supply trucks loaded for Galina Expediting were stuck fifty miles outside town.

Silas followed the marked pathway along the concrete wall toward the back of the warehouse and Raven's office.

"I can't keep a supply chain running under conditions like this," Raven complained to Brodie.

The two were standing next to an empty shelving unit, and Brodie nodded to Silas, acknowledging his arrival. "Looks like we'll have a weather window starting at sixteen-hundred."

"What's up?" Silas asked, halting as he came to them. He'd had a text from Brodie a few minutes ago, saw his truck in the Galina parking lot and swung in. He assumed he'd have some flying to do in the next few hours.

"Hey, Silas," Raven said.

"How can I help?" he asked, looking around the warehouse to see what was under way.

Two aisles over, Kenneth Hines zipped past on a forklift, its electric motor whining through the cavernous building as he headed for the staging area in front of the loading dock. There, AJ and Leon were staging loads of groceries, separating bulk orders manifests and shrink-wrapping product into bricks. The orders would be loaded on a Galina transport truck and taken to the WSA airstrip outside town for final transport by bush plane.

"Viking Mine needs their new fire extinguishers by tomorrow or they'll be out of safety compliance," Raven said, as she scrolled through her tablet. "Mile High Research put a rush on a new backup generator. And the Wildflower Lake Lodge is running critical on Cabernet Sauvignon."

"Priorities," Brodie said with a slow grin.

Silas smiled too.

"You know the guests at Wildflower Lake," Raven said.

"They have expectations," Brodie said.

The two shared an amused look.

They might mock Wildflower Lake Lodge, but Silas knew it was an excellent customer for both Galina Expediting and West Slope Aviation. Owner Cornelia Rusk paid a premium price and expected premium service.

"Xavier and I can take an islander up as soon as the weather breaks," Silas put in. As WSA's chief pilot, he kept current on pilot scheduling and availability. "Viking, Mile High then Wildflower Lake will work. What's the weight on the generator?"

The islander was a stalwart bush plane, with short take-off and landing capability and plenty of room for cargo.

Raven checked the generator specs on her tablet. "Nine-hundred and twenty-two pounds."

"How much wine did they order?"

"Twenty cases."

Silas did a quick calculation inside his head. "All right . . . it's doable."

Raven turned and caught Kenneth's eye, waving him down.

"Three-Zero-Alpha's your best bet," Brodie said. "Unless you know something I don't. The seats are already out."

"What's up, boss?" Kenneth asked Raven.

"As soon as the weather breaks, we can take the generator, Viking's safety stuff and the wine for Wildflower Lake."

"I'll truck it over to WSA." He looked to Silas. "Can you unload okay at Mile High?"

"We'll be fine," Silas said. "Xavier's my copilot."

"Too bad," Kenneth said with a regretful grin. Young, strong and capable, it was no secret he liked coming along on the flights as a swamper to load and unload cargo. He gave Silas a mock salute and hustled back to the forklift.

"I'd like to get the fresh produce out next," Raven said to Brodie. "And the Three Rivers operation needs a fuel haul."

"The fuel will have to wait until tomorrow. We can send the beavers out with the produce—do it in overlapping loops to save time, assuming the weather holds."

The WSA fleet had two beaver airplanes. They took smaller payloads than the islanders, but they'd fly though anything and you could land them anywhere.

Raven's hand-held radio crackled.

"Dixie for Raven," the Galina Expediting bookkeeper's voice came through the speaker.

Raven keyed her radio, looking up to the glassed-in mezzanine, where Dixie was looking down at them. "Raven here."

"Going on a coffee run to the Bear and Bar. You want anything?"

Raven looked at Brodie and Silas, lifting her brow to see if they were in.

"Coffee and a cinnamon bun," Brodie said.

Silas shook his head. He planned to go straight out to the airstrip and help load the islander.

"You share?" Raven asked Brodie.

Bear and Bar cinnamon buns were legendarily huge.

Brodie chuckled and shook his head as if she was being a wimp. "Sure."

Raven keyed the radio again. "Two coffees and a cinnamon bun. Thanks."

"You got it." Dixie gave a thumbs up through the upstairs glass.

"Catch you later," Silas said, turning away.

"Your Fairbanks run tomorrow?" Raven asked, stopping him.

Silas turned back. "I've got drillers going into Three Rivers, why?"

"Can you bring in an extra passenger?"

"To Three Rivers?"

"Here."

He guessed it might be possible. "Is he big? Does he have a lot of cargo?"

The mining drillers knew to pack light, but there were already five of them going in the Navajo plane. There wasn't a lot of extra capacity.

"Small," Raven said. "It's a woman. She's lightweight, maybe with a few days of clothes and toiletries."

"Sure," Silas said, catching an odd expression from Brodie. "What?" he asked his boss.

"Nothing," Brodie said in a tone that said it was something.

Silas looked to Raven for more information.

"It's my cousin. From LA."

"Oh." Silas was a little surprised to learn Raven had a cousin in LA. He knew she'd grown up on a mining property in Alaska with three brothers and a father. This was the first he was hearing about an extended family.

Still, there was nothing odd in a cousin coming to visit

Paradise. Well, maybe a little odd, since the town wasn't exactly a tourist hotspot. Nobody but fishing and mountain climbing enthusiasts would consider it a prime destination. They didn't have a hotel, and the Bear and Bar was pretty much it for restaurants. Paradise residents usually traveled outside to visit friends and family rather than the other way around.

"Is she sporty?" he asked. "Outdoorsy?"

Brodie's mouth twitched as he obviously fought a smile.

"It's a getaway," Raven said vaguely.

Silas didn't know what was going on with Brodie, but whatever. It wasn't his problem. He was just the pilot.

"A vacation in Paradise is definitely getting away," he said easily and left them to it.

IT WAS COMING UP ON TWENTY-TWO-HUNDRED HOURS. The storm clouds had cleared and the sun was still high as Silas and his copilot, Xavier, went short final in the islander bush plane returning to the Paradise airstrip. The West Slope Aviation radio operator gave them wind speed, direction and altimeter.

Xavier was at the controls right now, gaining experience landing the twin engine.

"Full flaps," Silas advised through the headset. "Don't let your airspeed get too slow."

Silas's attention went from the gauges to the ground, checking the minutia of Xavier's landing. "Okay. Looks good down there. Touchdown abeam the windsock. That's the sweet spot, smooth and level."

After a storm, Silas knew to miss the patchy puddles at the west end of the strip. And the windsock was the guide to putting it right on the numbers, just short of the access road to the WSA hangar and office complex, the only infrastructure at the remote airstrip.

Silas saw the airspeed drop.

"Wind sheer," he instantly called out as the plane canted sideways and dropped like a stone to hit the strip and bounce. Rocks clanked up beneath them, one making a loud, definitive twang.

"Max power." Silas closed his hands on the yoke. "I have control."

"You have control," Xavier echoed, letting go.

Silas righted the aircraft, taking them to the center of the airstrip and smoothing it out.

"Sorry, man," Xavier said through the headset.

"It happens," Silas said, relieved to have stayed cockpit side up.

As chief pilot, he tried to give his copilots as many take-offs and landings as he could, because the only way to become a good bush pilot was to practice. Truth was, as a new pilot, you wanted to be tested while there was a captain in the plane to bail you out.

"Was that a prop strike?" Xavier asked, sitting up tall, looking out both sides. Not that he was going to see anything on the spinning props.

"I hope not," Silas said as he turned to taxi to the tie-down area and the West Slope Aviation hangar.

He knew it was a prop strike, but he didn't want to say anything to Xavier just yet. Let him get past the difficult landing first.

"Three-Zero-Alpha closing flight plan," Xavier announced to radio operator Shannon Menzies. "Taxiing for the hangar."

"Three-Zero-Alpha, flight plan closed," Shannon replied.

"Can you get Cobra to meet us?" Silas asked Shannon, referencing the company's aircraft maintenance engineer, their AME.

"Confirming, Cobra to meet," Shannon said back.

Xavier groaned.

"Let's check it out, see what we've got," Silas said to Xavier.

Silas eased the airplane to a stop in front of the hangar and killed the power. He released his harness and draped his headphones around his neck while Xavier worked through the shut-down checklist.

WSA owner Brodie came out of the hangar, ambling toward them with AME Cobra Stanford. Cobra was one of the few guys in town who dwarfed the athletic Brodie. Tall and brawny, he could muscle engine parts into place that normally took a jack or hoist.

"Seriously?" Xavier said in an incredulous voice. "The boss has to be here too?"

"Brodie's going to find out sooner or later. Might as well get it over with."

"It was a prop strike, wasn't it?"

"Sounded like," Silas admitted.

"Am I going to get fired?"

"It was the rock's fault, not yours."

"I messed up the landing. Brodie was here. He saw it. It *is* my fault."

Silas swung his door open. He reached behind the seat for his pack. "You're getting ahead of yourself."

Xavier muttered something as they both climbed out of the aircraft.

Silas felt for the guy. Nobody wanted to be responsible for damaging an airplane. Repairs could be ridiculously expensive.

"Oil pressure stay up?" Cobra asked.

"Pressure's been fine," Silas said. "We kicked up a rock on the landing, sounded like a prop strike."

"Which side?"

"Right."

Cobra moved to the propeller, and Xavier followed him.

"Wind sheer caught us," Silas said to Brodie.

"Xavier took the landing?"

Silas nodded.

"I didn't think that looked like you," Brodie said, the gleam of a tease lurking in his dark eyes.

Silas frowned instead of smiling. He sure hoped his landings didn't look like that.

"There's a ding, all right," Cobra called over to them. "I'll have to measure. Could go either way."

"Either way?" Xavier asked, clearly worried.

Cobra clapped him on the shoulder in a gesture of reassurance and headed inside to get a tool.

Xavier stuck with Cobra, following him in.

Silas couldn't tell whether Xavier was curious about the repair process or afraid to stay out here with Brodie.

"Everything else go okay?" Brodie asked.

"Xavier's coming along fine on the twin. It's good that he's getting lots of hours."

Xavier was young and new to Alaska, but he had good hands and feet, the raw skills needed to make a good bush pilot.

"He's got a future," Brodie said.

Silas nodded to that. He and Brodie generally agreed on pilot assessments.

"Wildflower Lake sent back a bottle of the cabernet." Silas swung his pack from his shoulder and pulled the zipper. "And Cornelia said to tell you thanks."

Brodie chuckled. "You know it's a bribe."

"Hell, yeah, it's a bribe." Silas removed the bottle and handed it over. "And it's a good one. You can double-check with Raven on the price, but that's one expensive bottle of wine."

Brodie stared at the label for a moment. "I've been thinking about fixing her roof."

Silas was confused. "Cornelia's roof?"

"Raven's roof. It's leaking again, and I can't convince her to move into staff housing."

Silas could understand Raven's reluctance. He personally had no problem with the utilitarian camp trailers and central cafeteria, but WSA and Galina were 99 percent men, and she probably wanted a little privacy.

"I can give a hand with that."

Raven was like a sister to the guys at West Slope. She kept Galina Expediting running like a well-oiled machine, making their lives easier and enabling them to maximize flying hours, thereby maximizing their paychecks.

Cobra returned with a set of calipers to evaluate the prop and got to work.

"And?" Brodie asked after a couple of minutes.

"Not good," Cobra said.

Brodie gave a curse under his breath.

"What does that mean?" Xavier asked, looking from Cobra to Silas, skipping over Brodie.

"That means we ship it out for a teardown and inspection," Cobra said.

"The prop?" Xavier sounded like he was in pain.

"The engine," Silas said. It was as bad as he'd feared.

The color drained from Xavier's face.

"The prop goes too," Cobra clarified.

Brodie smacked his flat hand on the fuselage.

Xavier cringed, obviously waiting for Brodie to bring the hammer down.

"Well . . ." Brodie paused. "That's aviation. Better start stripping it out."

Xavier gaped at Brodie, clearly taken aback by his blasé reaction.

"You," Cobra said to Xavier, pointing at him with the calipers, "can help me with that."

"Sure," Xavier said. "Yeah. No problem." He snapped-to beside Cobra.

"Misty Mountain Mine wants the crew picked up in Fairbanks this week," Brodie said to Silas as the other two men headed for the hangar.

"Same as Viking?" Silas guessed. "Until they fix the washout?"

Brodie shook his head. "They're making a permanent change in procedure. Corporate brass wants FBO Fairbanks from now on."

"That'll cost them," Silas said.

"I know."

"Good for us, though."

"Can you set it up?"

"You bet." Silas moved his thinking on to tomorrow morning. "Did you know Raven had a cousin in LA?'

Brodie started for the office. "I did not."

"Odd."

"Odd how?"

"Can you picture a citified version of Raven?" Silas couldn't.

Brodie looked amused again. "No. And apparently Ms. Mia Westberg is accustomed to the finer things in life."

Silas considered that for a second. "Well, she won't find those in Paradise."

Chapter Two

THE FAIRBANKS FBO WASN'T WHAT MIA HAD EXPECTED. She was familiar with fixed base operators, the posh, amenity-rich check-in and lounge areas for private aircraft that some of Lafayette's clients used. But the one Raven had sent her to . . . not so posh.

It was cramped, utilitarian with a tiny coffee, fruit and pastry station in one corner and a small lounge full of worn furniture that was merely an extension of the check-in space. LA's local bus station was fancier than this. The place didn't even have a proper ladies' room; nothing but a single person unisex restroom with an unpredictable lock on the door. It boasted a urinal stall beside the toilet and a free-standing sink with a tiny hanging mirror. Forget about a powder room lounge and proper lighting.

Mia had landed in Anchorage yesterday after a comfortable first-class flight on a wide-body jet. The commuter flight to Fairbanks had been considerably scaled down, but that was fine. The attendants were cheerful, and the seats were small but comfortable.

The Eagle-View Motel last night had been something else entirely. Alastair's assistant, Veronica, had made a last-minute reservation, claiming the big chains had all been booked up.

At first, Mia wondered if Veronica had lost her mind, or if she'd been influenced by Mia's detractors and enemies at Lafayette and this was some form of retribution. If that was the case, as soon as Mia was in charge, Veronica was going to find herself out of a job.

But it hadn't turned out to be the case. Through an excruciatingly slow internet connection last night, Mia discovered the Eagle-View Motel's marketing created a false impression. The website showed clean, spacious, if dated rooms. The property description boasted an extensive breakfast buffet, an indoor pool and a fitness club.

Ha! After a painful night's sleep on a saggy bed, Mia had suffered through a lukewarm shower, dried off with a threadbare towel, skipped breakfast altogether and was genuinely afraid of what might be growing in the indoor pool.

Thankfully, this was the last leg of her trip. In a couple of hours, she'd be in Paradise, Alaska, with her cousin Raven, out of the reach of the protesters and media hounds who'd staked out her house and far enough away that online threats couldn't turn into real threats.

As of yesterday, it was either get out of town for a few weeks or hole up in her house and hire round-the-clock private security. She couldn't even use her patio and pool for fear of photographers' long lenses catching her every move and interpreting her every action and expression as confirmation that she was a gold-digging widow dancing on her husband's grave.

She'd had enough.

Good luck to them finding her in Alaska.

Most of the Fairbanks FBO lounge was taken up by five scruffy men who looked to be in their thirties, slouched and sprawled out in chairs reading dated magazines or scrolling through the screens on their phones. They all had beards, wore scuffed canvas work pants with too many pockets, threadbare shirts of nearly indistinguishable color and steel-toed boots that had clearly seen better days.

One of them gave her a nod.

She wasn't afraid of them, more worried that her white and blue knit top would soak up residual dirt from their clothing.

She'd worn jeans today, knowing Alaska was a more laid-back state. The pair was from the Boyfriend Collection, slim and stylish, but comfortable too, with a slightly lower waist, which was good for long periods of sitting. She'd paired the jeans with tan leather ankle boots, low-heeled and pre-aged for a nice outdoorsy look.

Her shirt was striped, a knit fabric for flexibility. And she'd gone with a simple gold necklace and flat gold stud earrings. She'd even put her hair in a high ponytail, informal but crisp in case she ended up out in the wind. It was low-key casual, and she thought she'd nailed it.

She arranged her burgundy plaid roller-bags, her garment bag and her carry-on in a corner of the lounge and checked out the seat beside them. It looked gritty, so she crossed to the snack bar and pulled a couple of napkins from the dispenser. Then she returned to wipe the seat and dropped the soiled napkins into a trash.

When she turned to sit down, all five of the men were staring at her.

Also staring was a man in an olive-green flight suit with wings on his chest and stripes on his arm. He was standing in the glass doorway that led to the runway.

Magnificent was the first word that came to her mind. If she was casting a model for a rugged, outdoors spread to attract women from far and wide, inspiring them to buy something for their own man from a new Lafayette wilderness clothing line, this would be her guy. There was a hint of irony in his half-smile, a hint of mischief in his blue eyes. He was fit and tall and confident enough to take on the wild. They'd make a fortune.

He looked her over from head to toe. Then he moved his attention to her luggage.

The five men rolled to their feet.

"Hey, Silas," one of them said.

"Ricardo," the man, obviously a pilot, and apparently named Silas, said in return.

"How's it going?" another of the men asked Silas.

"Welcome back to the grind," Silas said.

The other man grinned and nodded.

They all hoisted their backpacks and lifted their compact duffle bags to head for the door.

Silas, the pilot, stepped to one side, out of their way, while Mia sat down to wait.

"I take it you're Mia," Silas said.

She looked up, met his bright blue eyes and felt her chest tighten and her toes tingle in recognition of his sex appeal.

Yeah, she was a woman and she was alive, and he was a perfect specimen of a man.

Then it hit her. He knew her name.

"You're here for me?" she asked. She'd thought he was here for those men.

"I'm from Paradise."

"But?" She looked through the glass to where the five men trooped to a small airplane parked on the tarmac.

He waited.

"What about them?" she asked.

"We're dropping them off." He moved toward her, nodding at her luggage. "Raven didn't tell you to pack light?"

Mia looked at her things. "This is light."

"Lady, we're getting into a Navajo PA-31 with five other passengers who, as you can see, are heavier than the average weight." He picked her bags up one at a time, seeming to test them for weight. "They're my paying cargo. You're a ride-along."

"I'm going with *them*?" Mia was still getting past that information.

Silas pulled her biggest roller-bag to one side. "You have to leave this behind."

"What?" Was he insane?

"Becky?" he called over his shoulder. "Can you store this bag?"

"Sure," the woman named Becky said.

"No!" Mia cried out.

Silas gave her a glare of impatience. "Okay, then these two." He pointed to her garment bag and her carry-on.

"No way." She shook her head. She could not leave her carry-on behind. "I'll put this one on my lap."

"It's a weight issue, not space."

"But . . ."

"Those two?" He pointed to her smaller roller-bag and the garment bag.

That was a bit better but still not doable.

Becky joined them, obviously waiting to see which bags she'd be storing in the FBO.

"There must be some other way?" Mia tried her ice-princess look, the one that usually got her what she expected. When that didn't seem to move Silas, she changed her expression, hoping to appeal to his compassion. "Maybe one of those guys could . . ."

"Those guys are heading to a drilling camp for three weeks. They took exactly what they needed."

Mia didn't have an answer for that.

Silas folded his arms over his chest, his expression implacable. "I am *not* crashing the airplane so you can bring your makeup and evening gowns."

"My . . ." She started to be affronted but then dialed it back. Okay, she *had* brought one dress that could be considered an evening gown. It was a gown, and she could wear it in the evening, not to a super-formal event, but surely to anything that happened in Alaska.

"You coming or not?" He looked fully prepared to leave her behind.

"Fine. But I have to rearrange a few things."

Silas muttered something under her breath.

Before he could tell her no, Mia quickly crouched and unzipped her smaller roller-bag. She pulled out the essentials: panties, bras and nighties. It figured he'd have to get a look at her underwear. But that was the kind of day she was having.

She stuffed them into an outer pocket of her large roller-bag. To hell with wrinkles. She'd steam them later.

She zipped up the bag, stood and righted it. "Those two can stay." She pointed to the small roller-bag and the garment bag. "Thanks," she said to Becky.

"No problem." Becky looked a whole lot more cheerful than Silas.

Silas grabbed the handle of her big roller-bag, lifted her carry-on and headed for the door.

Stuffing her purse under her arm and glancing frantically back at the chair to make sure she hadn't left anything behind, Mia followed.

There was a tiny door into the Navajo.

Silas stowed her bags on top of the others, then secured a net to hold them in. He pointed her up the narrow aisle, and she turned sideways, knocking into the men's shoulders along the way to get to the single vacant seat.

As she sat down, a thought occurred to her. "Uhhh . . . Silas?"

He paused where he was backing out the little aft door. "What?" The exasperation was clear in both his tone and expression.

"Where's the restroom?"

Five sets of eyes from the other passengers swung her

way. One of the men grinned. Another shook his head in apparent despair.

Silas muttered under his breath again and then spoke louder. "Do you *see* a restroom?"

She looked around. "No." Hence her question.

"Did you *visit* the restroom in the FBO?"

She gave a grim little smile and a tiny shake of her head.

He closed his eyes for a second. "Give me strength." Then he stared at her as if she was the bane of his existence. "You have three minutes, or the drillers, your luggage and I leave without you."

Mia sprang from the seat and rushed back up the short aisle.

SILAS TAXIED THE NAVAJO ALONG THE ACCESS ROAD AT the Paradise airstrip, bringing it to a stop outside of the WSA hanger and shutting down the engines.

He'd dropped the drillers off at the exploration camp, so Ms. Mia Westberg was the only person left in the back. It was nearly impossible to believe this uptight princess was related to Raven. A bastion of reliability, Raven knew her way around, well, pretty much everything: the bush, the weather, heavy equipment. She couldn't fly a plane, but she could operate a loader, a snowmobile or a forklift with the best of them.

Silas closed off his flight plan, walked through the shutdown and unbuckled his belt, twisting back to see how Mia was doing.

She'd unbuckled and was stretching in her seat. With her oversized tortoiseshell sunglasses, it was hard to know where she was looking. The best he got was a wink from the crystals on a top corner of the frame.

He left Xavier in the cockpit to finish up and climbed out the pilot door to pull open the rear passenger exit. Stepping up, he leaned inside, unfastened the safety net and retrieved her bags, setting them down on the gravel.

She didn't speak or take his offered hand as she took the three steps down.

He hovered anyway, worried she'd stumble on the unsteady stairs. She wasn't wearing stilettos or anything, but her heeled boots were made for fashion, not practicality.

She didn't stumble. Safe on the ground, she straightened her sweater and gazed around.

The bush was freshly cut back around the access road for safety, bright stumps sticking up, sawdust still scattered. The orange windsock flapped in the breeze back on the strip. There was some heavy equipment away to the east side and a couple more planes parked in the lot, with most of them out for the day. The only other feature was the big rectangular hanger with a red and white WEST SLOPE AVIATION sign hanging against its dusty blue metal siding.

She lifted her chin, pressed her lips together and started for the hanger office, a low offshoot of the main building.

Concluding this was the silent treatment, Silas considered leaving her bags sitting on the gravel. But he decided it would be a jerk move with no point except to annoy her. And she was Raven's cousin, after all. So, he picked them up and followed along, curious to see what she'd do next.

She marched toward the office door, more gracefully than he would have imagined given the rocky terrain. She was tall, maybe five inches shorter than him, with legs that went on forever. Her jeans molded snugly to her hips, and the crisp white-and-blue-striped sweater clung to the indent of her tiny waist. Her ponytail settled into a sexy little swing while she walked.

He stood back to enjoy the view, thinking it was no surprise the woman seemed used to getting everything her own way.

She stopped on the worn concrete patch that served as a porch, and he wondered if she'd turn and ask a question.

Nope. She tried the door handle, finding it open, she pushed it in. The hinges creaked as Silas caught up to her.

She had to have heard him behind her. He wasn't exactly

stealthy on the loose gravel. But she didn't turn, just marched into the office.

It was dim, dusty and empty, as he'd guessed it would be. Operator Shannon Menzies was working in back in the radio room, and Cobra would be somewhere in the bowels of the hangar next door. While Mia set her sunglasses on top of her pretty blond hair and gazed around in a sweeping arc, Silas leaned against the jamb to watch.

She turned back then, hitting him with a deep blue gaze—irises such a stunning cobalt that they looked fake and probably were. "I thought Raven would be here to meet me."

"She speaks."

Mia frowned in a way that told him she was highly disappointed by both his attitude and his tone. It was an impressive feat to put that much into a single glare.

She didn't speak again but pulled out her phone instead.

"I'll give you a ride into town," he said. It was clear he couldn't out-silent treatment her.

"No need," she said, putting her phone to her ear.

"Hang it up," he said.

She drew back in obvious shock at his order.

"Raven's busy working. She doesn't have to drop everything and come all the way out here."

"I'm sure she won't mind."

"She might pretend she doesn't."

Mia glared again and went silent. "Raven, hey, hi." A bright white smile spread on Mia's face, and her tone turned happy, unnaturally so. "I'm here. I've landed. I'm at the airport."

Then her gaze shifted to Silas. "Yes, it was." She half turned away. "I don't—"

"This is ridiculous," Silas said, earning himself a sharp look over Mia's shoulder.

Raven was going to wonder what the heck was wrong with him.

He moved closer, talking loud enough that Raven was sure to overhear. "I can give you a lift."

His reward was another frigid glare.

"I will," Mia then said to Raven. "You bet." She ended the call.

He widened his stance and crossed his arms over his chest, growing tired of this silly game. "Tell me she's not coming all the way out here."

"She said to ask you for a ride."

"Was that so hard?"

"I don't normally accept rides from strangers."

"Strangers? Seriously? There are no *strangers* in Paradise. Everybody knows everybody else."

She tossed her hair—or would have tossed her hair if it hadn't been fastened in a ponytail. "*I* don't know anyone here."

"I'm not going to make a pass at you."

"I never—"

"I'm not even going to flirt with you." He realized how egotistical that sounded, like she'd be angling to have a guy like him flirt with a woman like her. Not in his dreams.

"Can we stop this?" she asked.

"Sure." It sure wasn't his finest moment. "I'll put your stuff in my truck, and we can get going."

"Hey, Silas?" Xavier called from outside.

Silas moved to the open door so Xavier could see him. "Yeah?"

"Navajo's tied down. I'm going to see if Cobra needs any help."

"Sounds good. You on deck for the Viking Mines fuel haul at six?"

"I'm taking Zeke along as a swamper."

"That'll work. Thanks."

"Catch you later." Xavier gave a wave as he headed for the hangar.

Silas gestured to the door, waiting for Mia to go first.

She squared her shoulders and brushed past him.

"Take a left," he told her as he came outside and lifted the suitcases. "The blue extended cab beside the picnic table. You'll want to give the fuel barrels a wide berth."

She gazed suspiciously at the parking lot. "Why?"

"The ground's soft on that side. Your boots will get muddy."

She blinked at him for a moment. "Oh. Thanks." She started walking.

He fell into step. "Surprised that I'd warn you?"

"No."

"You sounded surprised."

"It seems out of character."

Well, that was a bold statement. "You already think you know my character?"

She cast a pointed look his way. "You already think you know mine."

He'd give her that one. But the difference between them was, he was pretty sure he did.

MIA WASN'T ABOUT TO COWER UNDER SILAS'S MOCK-ing and misjudgment. She'd been through worse. In fact, she'd been through worse in the past week. She'd been mocked and misjudged by the entire Lafayette Fashion company, most of the fashion industry and what felt like every social media user in Southern California. Silas might be a bad-ass Alaskan bush pilot, but where it came to disdain, he had nothing on the internet trolls.

They zipped along a well-worn gravel road, dodging most potholes, hitting others so that her chest jerked against her seatbelt. The thick forest encroached on both sides, a bent branch occasionally brushing the side of the truck. They were the only traffic. They didn't pass a single vehicle coming the other way.

If not for Raven telling her to get in the truck with Silas, this situation would have had Mia on high alert. She was alone—it felt like alone in the world—with a scowling, silent man who clearly didn't like her much and looked like he could break a tree trunk with his bare hands.

He took a sudden and unexpected right turn onto a rutted dirt road. Their speed slowed, but that didn't stop them from bouncing over a crisscrossed mesh of tree roots from the tall cedars on either side with overhead branches that gave a horror flick–like gloom to the air.

Then they rounded a bend and came to a house—a shack, really, dilapidated and deserted-looking with a sagging porch and a moss-covered roof. Mia's danger meter spiked even higher. For a crazy second, she thought about jumping from the truck.

She glanced Silas's way, gauging her chances of success at escaping on foot. But he looked strong and incredibly fit. Her chances of outrunning him were obviously slim.

He rocked the truck to a stop and shifted it into park.

She stilled, her hands curling into fists against the worn fabric on the bench seat as she waited to see what he was going to do.

She'd have given anything for the can of mace she normally carried in her purse, but it was prohibited on the plane to Anchorage. So, she'd left it at home, thinking she was unlikely to get mugged in a small Alaska town. That might have been a mistake.

Her brain began clicking through scenarios as her mounting unease edged its way toward panic. Forget being mugged; what about being assaulted and murdered, her body dumped deep in the Alaskan bush where nobody would ever find it? She supposed Theresa and the twins would be relieved to be rid of her, not to mention most of greater LA.

"I'll put your stuff away," he said, exiting the truck and leaving the door standing open.

He hoisted her suitcases from the box of the truck and

started for the shack. As he walked away with her belongings, the isolation closed in tighter than ever.

The keys still dangled in the ignition.

This was it, her chance to escape—maybe her only chance to escape. Her pulse sounded in her ears, all of her instincts telling her to flee. In a situation like this, a woman had to trust her instincts. All the psychologists said so.

She quietly unbuckled her seatbelt and slid across the bench seat. As Silas stepped onto the porch, she quietly shut the driver's door and eased the truck in reverse. She had to give up the element of stealth then, so with her heart beating against her chest and entire body tense, she cranked the wheel and stepped on the gas.

He turned at the sound, gaping at her in complete astonishment.

His lips moved, but she couldn't hear what he said. It was probably just as well.

She hit the brake, but she wasn't fast enough. The rear bumper crunched against a tree.

He dropped the suitcases and sprinted for the truck.

She fumbled with the shifter, putting it back into drive and stepping on the gas. The tires spun, and Silas wrenched open the driver's door.

"What in the hell!" He hopped up on the running boards and grabbed the steering wheel.

Kicking herself for being stupid enough to leave the door unlocked, she battered his hand.

"What is *wrong* with you?" he demanded, unceremoniously shoving her across the seat.

The engine speed died and the truck rocked to still on the uneven ground.

She backed herself up against the passenger door, frantically looking for something to use as a weapon.

He stared at her, breathing hard.

"Don't you dare touch me," she said.

"*What?*" he roared, a flush of anger coloring his face.

She wrapped her hand around her purse. It wasn't much, but she could at least throw it at him, maybe distract him for a second, then jump out and make a run for it.

"Why did you do that?" He looked more baffled than angry now. He didn't move, didn't reach for her, just waited for an answer.

"I'm not going in there," she said, voice shaking as she stared at the spooky-looking house.

"Raven's place? Why not?"

Raven's place? Mia swallowed against a paper dry throat. Had he just said this was Raven's house?

"Are you afraid of mice?" Silas asked. "I think she got rid of them all last year."

Mice? Mia fought back a bubble of hysterical laugh.

"Raven didn't tell me you were nuts," Silas said.

She straightened up to a proper sitting position. "I'm not."

He stared at her as if he was trying to figure her out. Then he seemed to give up. He turned off the engine, pulled the key. "Then quit acting like you are." He left the truck.

Mia all but quaked with relief. They'd stopped at Raven's place, not at some secret deserted lair where Silas the serial killer brought his victims. It was her cousin's . . . cabin?

Curious, Mia unlatched the door and stepped out of the truck. Raven lived *here*? Worse, Mia was going to stay here?

Like she was approaching a train wreck, she moved in for closer look.

The cabin was small, that was for sure; small and old. The wood siding was weathered to gray. The stone chimney going up a side wall didn't look all that secure. The roof didn't look particularly weatherproof and—Mia glanced around—it was completely isolated in the middle of a forest.

She didn't know what kinds of animals were out here, but her imagination ran wild as she stopped to listen. Something rustled in the thick underbrush. Anything could be hiding there.

She had a choice of risking whatever had made that noise, hopping back into the truck or getting inside the cabin. The cabin was closer. Plus, Silas was in there— possible protection, all things considered. She was curious to see where Raven lived, so she made a quick dash for the cabin.

The door hinges squeaked predictably as she pushed it open. Silas turned from where he'd set down her suitcases next to a faded red brocade sofa in a tiny living room alcove with two armchairs arranged around a battered coffee table and a black woodstove.

Along a windowed wall beside her was a raw wooden countertop and a single stainless steel sink with a drain rack holding two plates and two glasses. Tea towels hung from hooks on the wall next to open shelves that held dishes and dry goods.

"You change your mind?" he asked. He didn't look so scary anymore; a little intimidating still, but she realized she'd let her imagination run very far away. To be fair, it had been egged on by the setting. It would be easy to stage a murder mystery in a place like this.

"I need to use the restroom," she told him.

"On your left."

She looked to find a small white door against the entry wall. It opened to an airline-sized bathroom—coach, not first-class. There was a cracked pedestal sink beside the door, an odd-looking toilet next to the sink and across from a white tin shower stall with a plastic curtain.

She had to shimmy around the door to close it.

She sat gingerly down on the toilet then needed to hunt for toilet paper, finding it up above her on a window ledge. The roll felt slightly damp from condensation but did the job.

Then she stood and looked to flush.

There was no handle.

She looked around the back then on the wall, closing the lid, then opening it again.

She finally gave up.

On an overall humiliating day, this was the worst.

She moved to the door. "Silas?"

Nothing.

"Silas!" she called louder.

His footsteps sounded approaching the bathroom door. "You okay?"

There was nothing to do but come right out and ask. "How do you flush?"

"Foot pedal," he said. "Down front. It's black."

She looked. "I see it."

"Scoop some water from the bucket. It's under the sink."

She looked and found the metal bucket. Half full of water, it had a dipper hanging out the side.

"Seriously?" she muttered to herself. "*Seriously?*"

But it worked. She scooped some water into the bowl and stepped on the pedal; the hatch opened and all was well. At least, all was well until she tried to wash her hands.

The taps on the sink turned out to be decorative. So, she used the scoop again along with a sliver of soap on the edge of the sink. Then she dried off on a white and pink floral towel that hung above.

She came out of the bathroom feeling somewhat shell-shocked and gazed around the cabin again, wondering if she was being pranked. Did the citizens of Paradise bring all their visitors here as a joke and pretend it was where they'd be staying?

Cast iron pans dangled from hooks attached to the bare rafters. Another three metal buckets were stacked beneath the open sink. A row of white porcelain canisters lined the back of the counter, decreasing in size, and labeled FLOUR, SUGAR, OATMEAL and COFFEE.

Maybe this was a museum.

Silas came her way, and the place got smaller still. "You ready?"

She waited a moment, hoping he'd laugh and let her in on the joke.

He didn't.

"Yes," she said, glancing past him in lingering disbelief.

"Good. Let's go see Raven."

Chapter Three

MIA FOLLOWED SILAS PAST THE YAWNING GALINA loading dock, feeling dwarfed by a silent semi truck and trailer parked there. They crossed into a noisy warehouse and gave a forklift a wide berth as they wound their way among stacks of wood pallets to parallel a concrete wall.

She gazed around at the cavernous space, taking in crates and pallets, shelves and equipment. Another forklift whizzed past, startling her at how close it came. Then she flinched at a loud metallic clang in the distance, followed by some shouted instructions.

Raven appeared around the corner of a shelving unit dressed in sturdy boots and a bright orange vest, a yellow hardhat perched on her head. She spotted them, ditched the hat on a shelf and smiled as she sped up.

Mia rushed forward to meet her. "Raven, hi!"

It felt good to hug her cousin for the first time in years.

Silas hung back, obviously meaning to give them privacy.

"I am so sorry about Alastair," Raven whispered into her ear.

"Thank you."

"You must miss him."

"I do."

"Tell me how I can help."

Mia appreciated the sympathy, but she wasn't a fragile grieving widow. "I did have some time to prepare for it. We both did."

Raven drew back and tilted her head, looking slightly perplexed. "You did? I know he was older than you, but . . ."

"He was fifty. It was his heart. And we'd known about his condition for quite a long time."

Raven smoothed Mia's shoulder. "That must have been a terrible ordeal."

Mia didn't like to frame it as an *ordeal*. Alastair hadn't. He'd accepted it and made the best of the time he had. She wanted to respect that.

"He was at peace with it in the end," she said. "And so was I. So am I."

Raven considered Mia's expression for a second. "You're strong. Good for you."

Mia wouldn't describe herself as strong. But she was focused on the future. "It's good to finally be here." She took in Raven's fit-looking form, clear eyes and healthy skin. "And *you* look fantastic. You haven't changed a bit."

Raven scoffed out a laugh. "Well, I changed my clothes, that's for sure." She gestured to her work pants, gray T-shirt and steel-toed boots. "Last time we were together was at that Hollywood party. We were fresh from the hair salon and makeup artists, wearing the Lafayette collection."

Mia remembered. It had been loads of fun for them as teenagers. She and Raven had clicked on that visit, and she'd felt a closeness to her ever since, even though their lives had gone in very different directions.

"How was the flight?" Raven asked, then added to Silas in a louder tone, "Thanks for bringing her in."

"No problem." He moved closer now, and Mia tried to decide if there was some irony in his voice.

"The flight was good," Mia put in. She'd appreciated his effort, if not so much his attitude. Now she looked around. "So *this* is where you work?"

"This is it." Raven gestured around the massive space.

There was another metallic clang on the far side of the room.

"It's loud," Mia said as the jangle reverberated in her eardrums.

"We have hearing protection. You want a pair of earplugs?"

"I'm okay."

"I'll just go grab my things, then," Raven said.

"Can I help out at all?" Silas asked Raven.

"The Viking manifest flagged dangerous goods. Can you double-check the permits and packaging?"

"On it."

"Thanks, Silas."

"He works here too?" Mia asked, confused by the exchange.

"Silas? No. He's a full-time pilot."

"I don't understand." Mia watched Silas walk away.

"WSA crew pitches in where they can. Galina ships goods into town by truck then WSA flies the last leg to the customer. Brodie, the owner of WSA, encourages collaboration, and Silas is his number-one guy."

"Really?" Mia had a hard time picturing Silas as Mr. Good Attitude.

A forklift cruised to a stop beside them and a worker peeled off his hardhat and earmuffs as he hopped out, tablet in his hand. "Can you sign off on the Wildflower Lake order?" he asked Raven.

"Everything accounted for?" Raven asked as she looked something up on her own tablet.

The man's gaze flicked to Mia a couple times. "Looks

good. Mostly groceries and cleaning supplies. Nothing's back-ordered."

Raven scanned the screen and looked up at him. "Rocks?"

"That's what *I* asked," he said, sounding as though he felt vindicated. "Giallo marble. They're redecorating something in the lodge. Crazy rich people."

Raven shook her head and grinned. "Rocks it is."

"Giallo's nice," Mia chimed in. One of her neighbors had recently used it when they renovated their entryway. "Gold, very lustrous."

The worker's gaze stayed on her this time.

"Looks like they made a good choice," Raven said. "Leon, this is my cousin Mia Westberg. Mia, Leon. He's one of our shippers at Galina Expediting."

"Nice to meet you, Leon." Mia offered her hand.

Leon fumbled as he peeled off his leather glove to close his hand over hers. "Welcome to Paradise."

He seemed flustered, so Mia tried to put him at ease. "Thank you. It looks like you're all busy around here."

"Really busy." Leon spoke in a rush. "Late trucks today and more coming in early tomorrow. We'll be loading up every plane Brodie's got. Are you staying long?"

"I don't know for sure," Mia said. She glanced down to where Leon was still pumping her hand, hoping to prompt him to let go.

He quickly did and pulled back. "Well . . . Uh . . ."

Raven lifted her brow in Leon's direction. "You going to load up the Wildflower Lake order?"

"Yeah." Looking sheepish, he quickly stuffed the tablet under his arm. "Bye, Mia." He backed up a couple of steps before turning.

The radio on Raven's chest crackled and a voice came through. "Kenneth for Raven."

Raven pressed a button. "Raven here. Go ahead, Kenneth."

"Brodie says they can do Viking tonight if we're ready in an hour."

"Can you make it?" she asked.

"It'll be tight."

"You need my help?"

"Silas is here to help. Can I keep AJ?"

"You bet."

"Thanks. Kenneth out."

"Am I in the way?" Mia asked, feeling awkward and out of place with so much going on around her.

Raven swiftly shook her head. "No, you're good."

But Mia wasn't convinced. "Are you sure? Because I can—" She pointed back behind them, thinking she could find somewhere to wait outside.

"No," Raven repeated emphatically. "I was about to ask Kenneth to take over so we could get out of here."

She extracted her cell phone and dialed, waiting a moment as the call rang through. "I'm taking off early today. Can you take care of things here?"

She paused.

"Because my cousin just got to town. I'll catch up on everything in the morning. I'll be available by phone if you need anything tonight."

Mia moved into Raven's line of sight. Still worried, she whispered. "I can just—"

"We're good," Raven said with a nod of reassurance that looked sincere. Into the phone she said, "Thanks, Kenneth. I appreciate that."

She pocketed her phone and gave Mia a bright smile. "Let's go."

On the way out, Raven was stopped several times for questions and instructions. People seemed like they were in a rush to get her input before she left.

"Are your bags in Silas's truck?" Raven asked as they finally passed through the exit door into the much quieter in the parking lot.

"Silas dropped my bags off at your place."

"Oh good. That was nice of him. Careful of the puddles." Like Silas back at the airstrip, Raven didn't seem to trust Mia's boots.

Mia wasn't sure why. Then again, it had never occurred to her to wonder if they were waterproof.

She caught sight of Silas striding their way.

"Heading home?" he asked Raven, falling into step with them.

"We're going to get Mia settled in. You? Flight tonight?"

He nodded. "As many as we can while the weather holds. I'm heading for the Bear and Bar first, grabbing a burger to take along."

"Sounds good, just let me know if—" Raven stopped short, staring at the damaged bumper on Silas's truck.

Mia's heart sank at the extent of it—a rather large U-shaped dent that still trailed a pine branch.

"What happened here?" Raven sounded and looked amused.

Silas gaze met Mia's, obviously expecting her to speak up.

She didn't mind taking responsibility for the dent, but she was embarrassed by why it had happened.

"What?" Raven asked, glancing back and forth between the two of them.

Silas waited, while Mia struggled to compose a reasonable answer.

Then he spoke up. "Not a huge problem. Mia misjudged a turnaround."

"Mia misjudged—" Raven looked baffled.

"I've never driven a truck," Mia added, appreciating that Silas had glossed over her behavior. "Alastair liked having a driver most of the time," she explained. "I sometimes drove the BMW to the club or up the coast to meet the girls. But nothing as big as a pickup truck."

"You drove Silas's truck?" Raven looked baffled.

"No big deal," Silas said, pulling the tree branch from

the dent and tossing it over the fence. "Cobra will pound it out for me."

"Maybe I should learn more about trucks," Mia said. "You know, when in Rome."

Raven stared at her in perplexed silence.

"Well, Milan mostly," Mia kept talking, not knowing what else to do. "We only went down to Rome once. It's not all it's cracked up to be, unless you like really old, crumbling buildings."

Catching sight of Raven's and Silas's bewildered expressions, she stopped talking and silence took over.

"I guess I'll go get that burger," Silas said.

Mia didn't wait for Raven's response before heading for the passenger seat of the truck, face warm with embarrassment.

After a pause, Raven headed for the other door. "What was that all about?" she asked as she climbed into the driver's seat.

"It was just a tiny misunderstanding," Mia said.

Raven waited a moment. "And?"

Mia struggled to pull out the seatbelt, but it wouldn't budge.

"You don't really need one around here," Raven told her.

Mia gave up on it, sitting up straight, crossing her legs and looking out the windshield, hoping Raven would simply move on.

Thankfully, she started the engine. "Are you that embarrassed about hitting a tree?"

Mia heaved a sigh, giving up on the pretense, not liking that she was holding information back from Raven. "I tried to steal his truck, okay."

"You *what*?" Raven sounded thoroughly shocked. "Why would you do that?"

Mia curled her hands in her lap.

"Why?" Raven repeated.

"You can't tell him. You have to swear here and now

on . . . on something important . . . that you'll never tell him why."

"I swear on my . . . job."

"Your *job*?"

"It's important to me."

"Fine. I thought he was a serial killer."

"*Silas?*"

"It sounds silly now." Mia knew that.

"Now?" Raven asked. "Was there a point where it *didn't* sound silly?"

Mia tried to explain. "He drove me to your house. He didn't even tell me it was your house, and—" She hated to be blunt, but she wanted her cousin to understand. "No offense, Raven, but it looked more like a creepy killer's lair than my cousin's home."

Raven rubbed her hands on the steering wheel for a moment. "Okay, fair enough; the place does need a little maintenance, I'll admit." She looked embarrassed and Mia felt bad about being judgmental.

She quickly moved on. "Silas left the keys in the ignition. So, when he took the suitcases inside, I tried to escape."

"But, you didn't."

"He caught me."

"On foot?"

Mia wasn't wild about the note of respect in Raven's voice and felt the need to defend herself. "Hitting the tree slowed me down."

A laugh erupted from Raven. "What did you tell him?"

"He assumed I was afraid of mice."

"I don't have mice."

"I know. That's what Silas said."

"That's hilarious."

"You can't tell *anyone, ever.*"

"All right." Raven put the truck into reverse and backed out of the spot. "Silas is harmless, you know. He doesn't even like to fish."

"He doesn't look harmless."

"You think?"

"He looks hard and dangerous. Especially when you're on a deserted lonely road, and he's a stranger, and he pulls up to a dilapidated shack without an explanation." Mia hesitated. "I'm sorry. I didn't mean to insult your house again."

"I'm the one's who's sorry. I shouldn't be laughing at you. You came here to heal."

"Not to heal." That wasn't what this was all about.

Raven turned to look questioningly at Mia.

"I came here to hide."

THE WEST SLOPE AVIATION OFFICE OFTEN WENT FROM frantic in the morning, when most loads were readied and planes got off the ground, to a quiet lull during the day, when everyone was flying. Then it got busier in the evening, when most pilots and crew came back again and were looking to debrief on the day and shoot the breeze.

As a freight operation, it was a casual place built for function, not beauty. The few passengers who boarded or offloaded in Paradise were the workers and scientists who knew the drill, or fishing enthusiasts headed for a river camp during the salmon run. The high-end tourists destined for places like Wildflower Lake were shuttled straight from Fairbanks in plush, luxuriously appointed Barons or 310s.

Nice planes, but Silas couldn't say he envied those pilots dealing with high-maintenance walk-on cargo. Case in point, Mia Westberg.

Silas and Brodie had parked themselves at one of three mismatched tables tucked in the room behind the front office to have a beer at the end of the day.

"What did you think of the cousin?" Brodie asked, opening the topic that was on a lot of guys' minds after a few of them got a look at Mia down at the warehouse and spread the word.

Silas was honest. "Big-city, entitled, the antithesis of Raven. Raven's got her hands full, that's for sure."

Brodie took a swig of his beer, Amber Ice from a local Alaskan brewery. "This ought to be interesting."

"How long's she planning to stay?" Silas pushed at the corner of the foil label with his thumb.

Brodie shrugged. "Raven only knew she was arriving today."

"She won't last long." Silas would put a fair bit of money on that. "We stopped at Raven's to drop her bags. I got the impression Paradise isn't what she expected."

"I told Raven a dozen times to move into staff housing." Brodie had clearly missed the broader point.

"There's nothing wrong with Raven's cabin," Silas said.

"The roof leaks," Brodie pointed out. "And her solution is a bucket on the floor."

"We can fix that. What I mean is Mia is obviously used to much finer things than what we have to offer here in Paradise."

"Word is she's a famous model," Brodie said. "A couple of the guys were burning up the internet connection checking her out."

"Well, I've never heard of her."

Brodie chuckled. "Pay a lot of attention to Fashion Week, do you?"

Silas lifted his beer bottle in a silent touché. "Must have missed last season."

Brodie rocked back and grinned. "I hope Raven doesn't regret inviting her."

"I'm willing to bet Mia invited herself. She seems like the type."

The front door squeaked open and Cobra appeared. "I heard you flew in a supermodel," he said as he grabbed himself a beer from the battered gold fridge that was older than Silas.

"Is that what she calls herself?" Silas asked.

Cobra pulled up a wooden chair and plunked himself down. He'd stripped off his gray coveralls and now wore jeans and a T-shirt. "That's what Xavier calls her. And he said the drillers were drooling all the way into camp."

Silas hadn't seen that. If it was true, he didn't like it, no matter what his impression of Mia. "I hope she froze them into blocks of ice."

Both Brodie and Cobra gave him a quizzical look.

"Because she's a paying . . ." Silas realized he had that wrong. "She's a WSA passenger. She deserves peace while she flies with us. No matter how entitled she acts."

"A guy can look," Cobra said.

"Blocks of ice?" Brodie asked with a lift of his brow.

"She's got these glacier-blue eyes," Silas said. "She tried it on me when I said her luggage was overweight."

Cobra laughed.

"Who won?" Brodie asked.

"*Please,*" Silas said. Like he was going to let some spoiled city girl compromise the weight and balance of his aircraft.

Cobra twisted the cap off his bottle. "Xavier said she was smokin'."

Both men looked to Silas for confirmation.

"Depends on your taste, I suppose." Physical beauty wasn't his problem with Mia.

"Tall, blond and gorgeous is pretty much everyone's type," Cobra said.

"She's got it in the looks department," Silas agreed.

"You didn't like her?" Brodie asked, dropping his joking tone.

"I don't know her." Silas remembered her cutting remark that he thought he knew her character. In retrospect, it was a reasonable point. He might know her type, but he didn't know her.

"First impression?" Cobra asked.

"Never used an outhouse."

"I'd call that a plus," Cobra said.

"I wonder how Raven's holding up," Brodie mused into his beer. "She's such a loner."

"You think?" Cobra asked.

Silas wondered the same thing as Cobra. Raven was perfectly friendly to the guys, not at all standoffish. She'd known a lot of them for years and could hold her own in any conversation.

"She likes her space," Brodie said as if he knew.

"She told you that?" Silas asked.

Brodie shrugged. "She lives halfway out in the bush. She won't move into staff housing even though her roof leaks. She burns ten cords of wood a year keeping that place warm. You'd think she'd prefer oil heat."

"I suppose," Cobra said, obviously accepting Brodie's logic.

"She might not want to live with twenty pilots and all the rampies," Silas ventured.

Staff housing was fine. The beds were comfortable, and the food was good. But it was close quarters, and in addition to the pilots—only one of whom was a woman—the ground crew was 90 percent men.

"Maybe," Brodie agreed. "But would you want Mia the big-city high-maintenance cousin living with you?"

Cobra raised his hand. "I'm going with a yes on that."

RAVEN'S SCREENED-IN SUNPORCH MADE A WHOLE LOT of sense to Mia as the evening bugs arrived. They were giant-sized: wasps, mosquitoes, three species of flies and other spindly black buzzing things that she couldn't identify.

Raven had grilled burgers on the sunporch, slathered a fresh-looking white bun with mustard, ketchup and mayo, then added a rather tragic-looking tomato and some wilted lettuce to create their dinner. She squirted them each a glass of merlot from a cardboard box, then they'd brought it all back out to the porch, where they settled into deep Adirondack chairs covered in faded plastic cushions.

The two chairs were angled toward each other but also facing a view of the forest at the side of the house. There was nothing but trees and blue sky in their view. And the only sounds were the insects and the faint rustle of the wind blowing through the poplar leaves.

Mia guessed it had been years since she'd eaten anything on white bread. And it was the first time she'd tried wine from a box. But she was starving, and Raven had worked hard in the kitchen, so she wasn't about to complain.

"No phone service at all?" she asked as she set her wineglass down on a small wood-slated side table. It wiggled a little but then settled with three of its legs touching the warped floor.

"If you climb up to the cache, you can usually get a bar. It's spotty, but if you're in a pinch . . ."

Mia found it almost impossible to believe a person could live without cell service or wireless. "And if somebody wants to get hold of you?"

"They come over. It's only a few miles into town, and I can use the Galina wireless when I'm at work. Or the Bear and Bar will sell you a package. It's slow and expensive, but it works."

"No streaming services, I guess."

Raven shook her head. "I've got a basic satellite dish and a DVD player."

"I'm off the grid," Mia said in amazement as she took a bite of the burger.

"You did say you wanted to hide out. They sure won't find you here."

The bun was fresh and delicious. The charred meat was crisp and flavorful. Mia barely even noticed that the vegetables were lacking. "This is *delicious*."

Raven smiled. "I'm glad you like it."

"What's your secret?"

Raven shrugged. "No secret. Burgers, heat, buns."

"I've never tasted a bun like this." The texture was dense and soft at the same time, with an interesting smoky sweetness.

"It's sourdough from the Bear and Bar, made with fireweed honey instead of sugar."

"Wow," Mia said and took another bite. "This is dangerously good."

"You're probably starving," Raven said, taking a sip of her wine. "WSA isn't known for its stellar in-flight service."

Mia smiled at that. "They didn't even have a bathroom." She remembered the hard green seats and the gritty floor. It was a far, far cry from her first-class leg out of Los Angeles.

Raven grinned along with her. "You learn to go before you get into a small plane around here, that's for sure."

"I almost didn't." Mia recalled Silas's expression when she'd had to bail out for the restroom before takeoff. She took a sip of wine to forget and discovered the merlot wasn't nearly as bad as she'd feared.

"How long will you need to stick around?" Raven asked.

Mia was hit with a sinking feeling. "Is having me here a problem?"

"No, no. That's not what I meant at all." Raven gestured around. "I was thinking this must be quite the downgrade from your mansion."

"That doesn't mean I don't appreciate it." Mia hoped she hadn't done anything to give away her dismay at some of the amenities.

"It can't be much fun for you," Raven said.

Mia watched her cousin's expression, trying to figure out if she was welcome or not. "It's better than the threats."

"Threats?"

"You know, the trolls on social media, and the people at

the end of my driveway accusing me of dancing on Alastair's grave, of stealing his company, of murdering him. Some of them want revenge." Mia took a larger swig of her wine.

Raven looked genuinely shocked.

"You're really not on social media, are you?" Mia asked.

Raven shook her head.

It hadn't occurred to Mia that Raven wouldn't know the broad stokes of her situation. She'd been bombarded with it so steadily herself, it felt as though everyone in the world had sided with Henry and Hannah and developed a morbid interest in waiting on Mia's eventual comeuppance.

"Alastair's children have taken me to court over the will. It's their mother pulling the strings. I'm sure of it. She was such a witch to Alastair during the divorce."

"I didn't remember Alastair had kids."

Mia knew she'd never mentioned them. "They're twenty-five now; twins, Henry and Hannah. They've lived with their mother since they were seven, and she systematically turned them against him."

"So, they're . . . *our* age?"

"You can imagine how well that went over. Everyone decided I married him for his money. That's the furthest thing from the truth." It was important that Raven believe her.

"I never thought you did. I mean, why would you? You were already a successful model. And who needs that much money anyway?"

Money was obviously not important to Raven. That was both admirable and refreshing.

"His kids want it now," Mia said. "And they're going to fight hard."

"All of it? Can't you just split it up?"

"They're after the company. He left Lafayette Fashion to me so I could continue the legacy, run it just like he has all these years. But people don't know that part, or they don't want to know that part." Mia polished off her wine.

"Don't know what part?" Raven finished her own glass and reached out for Mia's empty.

"How much I helped him run it over the years. It's what we did. We collaborated. We talked through everything. I wasn't just a face of the company, I was behind the strategy too."

When Raven got to her feet, Mia followed her into the kitchen.

"Virtually every night," Mia continued, "we'd have dinner, wine or a cocktail; review the day; talk about upcoming lines and shows, fabrics, marketing campaigns. I had input on everything."

Raven pressed the spigot on the wine box and refilled Mia's glass.

Mia pictured Alistair's battery cork remover, the expensive bottles he so lovingly pulled out of the big wine cellar then told short stories about their vintage and his expectations. Even when his heart condition meant he couldn't drink wine, he'd still open a bottle for Mia, saying he loved watching her enjoy it.

She'd never given a thought to how much of the bottle got wasted. But she gave it a thought now, wondering if anyone on the housekeeping or cooking staff had thought to take it home or share it among themselves. She hoped they had.

She accepted the glass from Raven, taking a sip and banishing her memories. This wine was perfectly acceptable. She didn't need to be a princess every minute of every day.

"So who are you hiding from? Shouldn't you be running the company?"

"The twins got an injunction against me. The vice presidents are running it until the estate is settled."

Raven sat down. "Then shouldn't you be in court fighting them?"

Mia returned to her own unexpectedly comfortable chair. "Marnie, my lawyer—she's also a good friend, and she's beyond awesome—is appealing the injunction. But I had to get away. I was . . ." Mia hesitated, embarrassed to admit it, especially after the Silas incident today. "Scared."

Raven shifted in her chair, sitting up straighter. "It was that bad?"

"Most of it was just trash talk . . . gold-digger, evil stepmother, blah, blah, blah. But some of the threats had the police worried."

"The *police* were involved?"

"Just the local ones, not the FBI or anything."

The sun's slanted rays were warm against her, a wildflower-scented breeze wafted in and some birds chirped outside in the trees. Mia suddenly felt safe, and she realized she hadn't felt this way in a very, very long time.

"I got scared," she repeated, relieved to be able to be honest. "A couple of the trolls threatened to kill me; one wanted to strangle me with my own evening gown. Oddly specific, I thought. Another threatened to assault me before throwing me off the penthouse balcony. We don't even live in a penthouse."

"That's horrible." Raven's face had gone pale.

Mia didn't disagree. She took another sip of her wine. "It got so I had to drive through people holding signs and cameras and all screaming at me and banging on the car windows whenever I wanted to leave the property."

"I'm glad you came," Raven said.

"I'm glad you let me."

"Of *course* I let you." Raven gestured around them once again. "I know it's not much, but I have twelve-gauge and a thirty-thirty in the closet, and you're welcome to stay just as long as you like."

Chapter Four

RAVEN HAD OFFERED MIA A CHOICE FOR THE NEXT morning: get up early to drop her off at work, or sleep in and stay at the cabin without a vehicle. When Mia learned just how *early* "early" was, she opted to stay stranded, at least for the first day. She and Alastair had never been early risers. There were too many evening engagements in their lives, too many lengthy business dinners and too many late-night discussions on the state of the industry.

Mia was a brunch rather than a breakfast person: a tropical fruit salad, some grainy bread, maybe a little yogurt or a smoothie. She usually hit the gym in the morning, either the Blue Star Club on Abby Drive or just down in the basement to work out on the elliptical and the rowing machines. Nothing fancy, just a bit of cardio and toning. Her shower, hair and makeup didn't take too long, and then she was ready for whatever meetings Dara-Leigh, her personal assistant, had put on the schedule.

Today was much different. The options in Raven's kitchen included white bread and strawberry jam, and no

yogurt in sight, but Mia did find a little block of aged cheddar cheese. She wasn't ready to brave Raven's shower—an
odd contraption that needed two kettles of hot water and
the use of a battery-powered suction hose to draw the warm
water out of a bucket and through the nozzle to rain down
in the little tin shower stall. Mia decided to save that excitement until later in the day.

At least the bed had been comfortable if a bit small.
Raven's open loft above the living room had two twin beds
placed at opposite ends. It reminded Mia of summer
camp—not that she'd ever been to a summer camp. But
she'd seen them in the movies, and they looked a lot like
Raven's loft.

After breakfast, Mia combed out her hair, did a quick
makeup job then changed into a pair of mottled peach and
turquoise workout pants topped with a peach tank top. Raven had said she could sometimes get a bar on her cell
phone from the cache in the yard. Mia didn't know where
the cache would be, so she wandered around the wooded
yard for half an hour trying to get a signal.

With no luck in the yard, she walked the long driveway
to the road. But couldn't get a signal there either.

By the middle of the afternoon, boredom set in. Since
she hadn't had any exercise in two days, she decided a run
into town would kill two birds. She'd get in some cardio
and find herself a cell signal. Maybe she'd stop at the Bear
and Bar and see about a data package too. It would be good
to check her email—her private email, not the corporate
account the spammers had found and filled with hate mail.
And she wasn't going anywhere near her social media ac-
counts until she got the all-clear. Marnie had arranged for
a security firm to monitor those and forward anything that
seemed personal.

Mind made up, Mia twisted her hair into a quick French
braid and pulled out her running shoes. She'd already discovered Raven's cabin door didn't have a lock. She sup-

posed there wasn't anything here worth stealing, although Raven seemed to think the entire town was trustworthy anyway. Mia supposed if everybody knew everybody else, you couldn't exactly fence your stolen goods.

She started at an easy pace down the driveway, avoiding the tire ruts, potholes and tree roots but appreciating the shade from the overhanging limbs. When she got to the road, she discovered the packed dirt at the edge made a nice spongy running surface. She still had to watch her footing, but her idea was turning out rather well.

Fifteen minutes in, after crossing the Paradise River bridge, she checked her phone and found a single bar. She was ridiculously thrilled by the first sign of civilization. By the time she got to town, she'd probably have two bars, maybe three. She could call Marnie and check in. It had only been a day, but Marnie was trying to nail down a court date. The date would tell Mia how long she'd be stuck in Alaska.

Not that she hated Alaska so far. Mostly, it seemed peculiarly idiosyncratic, and so slow-paced it was like beaming back in time. She'd been running for nearly half an hour and not a single vehicle had passed.

No sooner had the thought surfaced than she heard an engine. She smiled to herself. Speak of the devil. She hoped the vehicle didn't kick up too much dust. She'd been enjoying the sensation of drawing the pure air into her lungs. If she could package *that* and take it back to LA, she'd make a fortune.

The truck slowed as it approached; very considerate. It was a blue pickup, and she wondered if anyone drove anything besides pickup trucks around here. She hadn't seen much of the town yesterday, but she didn't recall any cars, just trucks and a couple of older SUVs.

The truck rolled to a stop and she recognized Silas in the driver's seat.

He unrolled his window. "You headed for town?"

She nodded.

"You need a ride?"

Mia began jogging in place to stay warm. "No, thanks."

"You're exercising?"

"A run into town."

He looked up and down the road. "Raven know you're doing this?"

Mia shook her head. Why would Raven care if she went for a run?

He looked her over. "You have bear spray on you?"

Raven had a shelf full of various bug repellants but nothing that mentioned bears. Was Silas messing with her?

"Is that a joke?" Mia asked.

He put the truck in park and opened the door.

"Are you mocking me again?" she asked.

"I'm not mocking you." He got out and reached into the truck box, pulling out a black utility belt. "You can borrow mine." He marched toward her.

"What are you doing?" She took a step backward as he advanced. She wasn't afraid of him this time, but he sure had a way of acting suspicious.

"Lending you some bear spray."

Looking closer, she could see a canister dangling from the belt.

"That's really a thing?" she asked.

He stopped in front of her. "It's really a thing."

"I don't . . . what?" She stiffened as he reached around her waist to loop the belt.

He was tall.

She was nearly as tall as most men, a few inches taller than Alastair, but she wasn't anywhere near Silas's height.

He was broad too, big shoulders, sinewy arms, wide chest, woodsy scent, and oh what a handsome face.

She thought again that he'd make a good outdoors model.

He snugged the belt with a tug, one hand bracing her hip

MATCH MADE IN PARADISE 55

while the other fastened the catch. Her exercise pants and top were thin, and his hands were warm where they touched her.

His breath puffed her forehead, calling attention to his lips. They were full, balanced, soft-looking, slightly parted.

She thought about kissing him and felt dormant emotions surge up inside. She hadn't kissed a man since Alastair, had barely kissed Alastair in many, many months. His heart condition had made lovemaking impossible, so it had been years since they'd been intimate, years where she was more a caretaker than a wife. Years where she'd repressed her sexuality in favor of work and caregiving.

And now it was back, all at once, all in a rush.

"I'll show you how," Silas said.

Her passion surged, ready for anything.

But he pulled a flap on the belt, and the sound of the Velcro strip cut through the air. Then he tugged the canister free. "You pull back the orange tab," he said, demonstrating the motion with his thumb.

Mia blinked, bringing herself sharply back to reality, struggling to suppress her embarrassing hormonal reaction to a healthy male standing way too close.

"That's the trigger guard. The nozzle is this little white square here. Point it away from you. Are you looking?"

She wasn't. "Yes." She focused her attention.

"You have to wait until the bear gets really close. I mean *really* close, like under ten feet."

"Do they"—she swallowed, thinking about it—"get that close?"

"They can. If they're mad, or if you startle them. That's when they're a problem. Some of the spray might blow back. It usually does, and it'll sting your eyes, so don't let that rattle you."

"You're serious," she said.

He looked and sounded deadly serious, the same way he had giving the safety briefing on the airplane yesterday.

"You think pepper spray is a joke?" He was clearly aggravated by her question.

"No. I mean, I'd never heard of it before. I thought you might be messing with me. You know, new kid in town and all that."

"I'm not going to joke about bear safety, Mia."

"Clearly."

He heaved a sigh of obvious frustration. "Point it away from you." He demonstrated. "With the orange trigger guard removed, hold it at arm's length, wait until the last possible second and only if you're being seriously charged, then spray it in the bear's face. Got it?"

"Got it." She understood the concept, but it was hard to imagine a bear out here on the road; harder still to imagine one charging her.

"Good." He wiggled the canister back into the holder and refastened the Velcro strap.

"You can keep this. I've got others." He was still close, still handsome, still powerful and sexy.

"Thanks." She wanted him to kiss her . . . or something. She wanted him to at least look like he wanted to kiss her.

"Catch you later," he said instead, turning away.

His truck was still running. He took one step, then two, then three and four.

She glanced around at the thick bush, realizing that when he drove away it was going to be completely silent and completely empty all around her. She hadn't been nervous until now, because she'd thought of the forest as a great big park.

It didn't look like a park anymore.

He put his hand on the driver's door, and she took a couple of quick steps his way. "Uh, Silas?"

He looked over his shoulder.

She paced quickly toward him. "I was wondering . . ."

"You want to catch a lift into town?"

She gave a rapid nod.

To his credit he didn't grin or roll his eyes or otherwise mock her fear. Instead, he came her way and reached for the belt at her waist.

A vivid kiss fantasy bloomed in her mind again, and she tipped her chin ever so slightly his way.

"Can't take this inside a cab," he said, unfastening the black belt. "If the spray accidentally deploys, it'll blind the driver. We'd crash."

She pressed her lips together, struggling once again with the embarrassing rush of longing that heated every corner of her body.

Silas was all business, while she was melting into a pool of sexual desire.

MIA WAS HOT WITH A CAPITAL *H*. SHE WAS ALSO BIG-eyed, charming and disarmingly vulnerable.

Vulnerable women irritated Silas.

Oh, it might be sexy in a midnight fantasy kind of way. But in the real world, vulnerable women were usually weak women and often manipulative women, all sweet, simpering helplessness that cut a man to the core.

He'd known some of them well, met others in passing. He knew the drill.

It didn't mean he wanted Mia to get mauled by a bear. Odds were, she'd have been fine jogging her way into town. But Paradise was bear country, grizzly country and at a high enough altitude to be part of the bears' summer range.

"Where do you want me to drop you?" he asked as they entered the north end of Paradise. He was due to take off on a flight to Viking Mine in thirty minutes. He could still make it on time, if barely.

"I don't know," she peered around at the buildings on Main Street: businesses like Bill's Hardware, the Butterfly Boutique, Caldwell Corner Gas and Repair Shop, and the Co-op Grocery Store. There were private homes at the

north end of town and more at the south end of Main near
the river. It was prettier over there, with the white water
rushing past and a clear view out everyone's door of the
glacier peaks.

West down Red Avenue was Silas's place in WSA staff
housing, which was made up of modular units with the ba-
sics: single beds, desks and compact bathrooms. On the
opposite side of Red Avenue, Galina Expediting had taken
over an old army bunkhouse. It was dormitory-style ac-
commodations, with bathroom facilities at the end of the
hall. The guys living there shared the WSA cafeteria and
lounge. On the east side of town was Blue Crescent leading
to the WSA warehouse and depot. Besides the medical
clinic, the Baptist Church and the school, that was about it
for Paradise.

"Raven mentioned the Bear and Bar," Mia said. "You
could drop me there."

"How are you planning to get home?" Silas couldn't
help her with that. He'd be at the Viking Mine until later in
the evening.

Mia pulled out her phone. "I'll call Raven and see when
she's ready. I've got three bars now."

"Raven's cabin is in a dead spot." Silas brought the truck
to a stop beside a section of raised wooden sidewalk. If it
were him, he'd have put in a signal booster by now. Then
again, if it were him, he wouldn't be fixing his leaking roof
with a bucket either.

Maybe once he and Brodie fixed the roof, they could
talk to Raven about upgrading her Wi-Fi. For safety alone
it would be a good idea.

"She said something about the cache," Mia said. "That
she could get one bar up in the cache if she needed to make
a call. I tried before I left, but I couldn't get a signal anywhere."

"You climbed the cottonwood tree?"

"*Climbed?*" Clearly, she hadn't.

"It's the old food cache from when Hugh Oberg first built the place. It's up in a tree to keep the bears away. There are wooden rungs nailed to the trunk. If you ever need to get up there, a trapdoor pushes open from underneath the floor."

She was staring at him like he was explaining cutting edge theoretical propulsion systems. "A tree?"

"It gets you up high enough for the signal."

"I'm not climbing a tree."

He couldn't stop himself from cracking a smile.

"You're laughing at me."

He was. "You're funny."

She wrenched open the door. "And you're a jerk."

"Yeah, I am." He knew he was having fun at her expense.

"Thanks for the ride," she said tartly, sliding from the high seat onto the sidewalk.

"You want to take the bear spray?" he asked.

"I don't expect to need it. If I do, I'll buy my own."

"Over at Bill's Hardware," Silas said as she shut the door behind herself.

He watched for a minute while she walked toward the front of the Bear and Bar. Two of the Galina warehouse guys were coming out the other way, and they held the door, their gazes glued to her as she smiled her thanks.

Xavier came out behind them and hailed Silas.

Silas rolled down the passenger window. "Hey, Xavier."

Xavier walked over. "You heading out to the strip?"

Silas nodded. "Got a Viking run this afternoon."

Xavier opened the door and hopped in. "Great. I told Cobra I'd give him a hand."

"You planning to become an AME instead of a pilot?"

Xavier stretched his arm along the back of the seat. "Any reason I can't be both?"

"Not a one," Silas said as he pulled away.

"She's a hottie," Xavier said.

"She is," Silas agreed.

"She's going to be trouble."

Silas thought that might be going too far. "We have women in town all the time."

Sure, Mia was more glamorous than most, but that would wear off. He couldn't see her keeping up that fluffy hair, the perfect makeup and that fashion parade way out here.

"*Dude,*" Xavier intoned.

"What?" Silas upped his speed as they cleared town.

"We don't get women like *that* here." There was an undercurrent of excitement in Xavier's voice, and Silas realized he'd misunderstood what Xavier meant by trouble.

"I'd give her a wide berth," Silas advised.

"Why? If she'll give me the time of day, I'm taking it."

"She's just visiting." Xavier was a decent guy, but Silas couldn't see Mia being interested in him—or in anyone else from Paradise, for that matter. The men here were ordinary, hard-working, two-feet-firmly-planted-on-the-ground types.

Mia was a high-fashion model, and her late husband had been a millionaire industry mogul who probably jetted her off to New York, London and Milan to stay at five-star hotels and attend A-list parties. Paradise had nothing that could compete with that.

"I'm not planning to marry her," Xavier said. "Maybe a date."

Silas thought Xavier was dreaming in Technicolor. "To the Bear and Bar?"

"I don't know. A flight-seeing tour of the Pedestal Glacier? People pay big money for that."

"You think Brodie's going to lend you a plane?"

"Maybe."

"Maybe not. We're wall to wall."

"I suppose," Xavier said. "I'll think of something else."

It was far too easy for Silas to picture Mia on a flight-seeing tour of the Pedestal Glacier, her bright white smile in awe the blue fissures at Right Ridge, her gasp of amazement at Briar Falls. The image warmed him, and he didn't like that, especially since he was picturing himself as the pilot.

He pressed harder on the accelerator, churning up a spray of gravel behind them.

WITH A PHONE CALL FROM THE BEAR AND BAR, MIA learned Marnie had nothing new to report. No surprise there. It had barely been a day since Mia left LA. Still, she couldn't help be impatient. They hadn't even set a court date to hear the appeal to the injunction, never mind a court date on the will itself.

She'd also talked to Raven, who had estimated she'd be finished with work around seven o'clock.

Mia was surprised by the long workday. She'd been told summer was the high season in Alaska, but thirteen hours? She hoped Raven made a lot of money as Galina Expediting's operations manager. Although judging by her house, she couldn't be doing all that well. Who didn't have proper plumbing in their bathroom?

Coming up on seven, Mia crossed the noisy crowded Galina parking lot, winding her way through pickups and alongside a red semi truck.

"Hey, lady!" the driver called out his window, shouting above the rumble of the diesel engine.

She stopped and looked up. "What?" She'd normally ignore a strange man's shout, assuming it was a cat-call or a brash proposition. But this guy didn't sound like he was trying to pick her up.

"*Blind spot*," the scruffy, portly fifty-ish man said with his arm raised in frustration.

She looked behind herself.

"You're *in* my blind spot. Get out if you don't want to get run over."

"No need to be rude," she said, but she skittered ahead. She didn't know what he was on about, but she'd get out of his way to keep him happy.

He muttered a swear word, and the truck let out a booming hiss and belched some black smoke as a piercing intermittent alarm engaged. The big rig jerked a couple of times on its oversized tires and gradually eased backward.

"Hard hat! High vis!" the driver called out his window for good measure.

She wasn't sure how that was an insult. But it sounded like an insult. She hurried through the big warehouse door and left him and his anger behind.

"You're looking for Raven?" A twenty-something man briskly approached her. He was fresh-faced, tall and lanky, and he sounded eagerly friendly.

That was more like it. "Yes, I am. Thank you."

"Bert can be a jerk," he said.

She assumed Bert was the truck driver.

"But you were in his blind spot," the younger man said.

"I didn't mean to be."

The young man pointed back behind her. "If you take the gravel walkway around the corner instead of cutting straight through the loading dock, you'll be safer."

"Thanks." She'd do that in the future.

"I'm AJ Barns. I'd shake." He self-consciously wiped his hands down the front of his coveralls. "But you probably don't want to get your hands dirty."

"I'm Mia Westberg."

He started to walk beside a long wall. "I know. Raven's cousin from LA."

She went along with him. "That's right."

The noise from the backing semi was replaced by the sound of a forklift and the clatter of crates being moved from one place to the other.

"We don't get many ba—I mean, girls." His brow furrowed. "I mean women here in Paradise."

"It does seem to be mostly men," Mia said.

"There's Raven, of course. But she's . . . well . . . Raven, you know?"

Mia didn't know, but he didn't seem to be looking for an answer.

He kept right on talking "And Dixi. She's older than my grandma, like Mrs. France at the Bear and Bar. Hailey's a girl pilot over at WSA, but you don't want to mess with her. I mean." AJ chuckled. "If she didn't kill you, Silas or Brodie would."

"Silas?" Mia asked, partly from curiosity about Silas's relationship with Hailey the pilot, and partly to stop AJ from listing every woman in town.

"He's the chief pilot over at WSA. Next to Brodie, Silas is the head honcho."

"He'd defend Hailey's honor?"

AJ's head bobbed up and down. "Yes, he would."

"Why?"

AJ looked confused. "He takes care of all his pilots. I mean, not that the guys need someone to defend them. Neither does Hailey, really. But she is one of the few girls here and has to deal with all these guys, and he don't take no guff."

Mia could see that in Silas. He did not seem to be a guff-taking kind of guy.

"Raven's right up those stairs, around at the end. Don't cut across the red line to get there. You need a hardhat for that."

Mia remembered the way, but she hadn't known about crossing the red line.

"All right. Thank you, AJ." She held out her hand; to hell with the dirt. She appreciated him walking her back here.

"You sure?" he asked.

"I'm willing to brave it if you are."

A little flush came up on his cheek and his grin went wide. "Nice to meet you, Mia." He shook her hand, a little too vigorously and a little too long.

"Nice to meet you too, AJ. Thanks for the help."

"No problem." His head bobbed again. "Anytime."

Mia stuck to the red line until she came to the stairs. She found Raven on the phone behind a little desk in a small room crowded in by filing cabinets, a credenza and about a three dozen manuals overflowing a bookshelf.

Raven grinned and pointed to a torn green leather guest chair.

Mia's pants were pale turquoise and peach, and it was impossible to know if the dark-colored chair was clean or dirty. She took a breath, hoped for clean and perched herself on the edge. She didn't want to guess what Raven might have for laundry facilities in her cabin. Whatever they were, she doubted they'd take grease or oil out of Malaysian bamboo.

"I understand the governor is busy," Raven was saying. "It doesn't have to be the governor. Just give me the number of whoever's in charge of road maintenance." She paused and pulled an expression of exasperation, clearly aimed at the person on the other end of the line. "I know we've had a lot of rain this summer. It's been falling on our heads." She waited again. "Brodie could do a fly-by of the capitol building. Would that get his attention?" Then she grinned. "I thought so. Yeah, I've got a pen."

She jotted down a number and ended the call.

"The governor?" Mia asked.

She'd met the governor of California once. As head of the California Fashion Design Council, Alastair's friend Joseph McKenzie knew most of the movers and shakers in the state, and he'd introduced Mia to the governor at a party.

"The road problems keep compounding." Raven had talked about the flooding to Mia last night.

"It didn't rain today."

"Not here, but it rained up in the mountains. Runoff hits the tributaries, tributaries hit the rivers, and the permafrost can't absorb the moisture."

"And water runs downhill."

"Exactly, right onto the haul road. The washout they fixed yesterday got un-fixed last night. They need to put in some culverts and use better material, even if it does cost more." Raven straightened a stack of papers on the top of her organized desk. "How was your day?"

"Good." Mia had maxed out her data allotment, but Breena France, a waitress at the Bear and Bar, granddaughter of the owner, had been very friendly and sat with Mia during the afternoon lull. Breena had grown up in Paradise and was home for the summer from the University of Anchorage, where she was studying computer science.

Raven rose. "Brodie told me Silas gave you a ride in?"

Mia gave a hollow chuckle as she remembered the experience. "He told me all about bears. At first, I thought he was joking; you know, messing with me because I was new in town."

"He wasn't joking." Raven looked deadly serious.

"I got that."

"I'll give you some pointers." Raven slung a small, battered backpack over one shoulder. "I should have done that last night."

"Was I crazy to go running?" Mia asked, following Raven out the office doorway.

"Not crazy, but—"

"Are the bears just roaming around out there, like by the hundreds or something?"

Silas had acted like it was inevitable she'd run into one.

"Well, yeah, by the thousands, really. But it's a big state, and they're not all in the vicinity of Paradise."

Mia shuddered at the idea she'd put herself in danger. "I guess I won't be running again anytime soon."

They made their way down the stairs and back along the warehouse wall, keeping to the right side of the red line. At least Mia knew that rule now.

"You need to take a friend along—well, friends, plural. Bears almost never bother groups of three or more."

"*Almost* never?"

"You massively decrease your chances of having a problem. It's like getting mugged in LA. The bigger the group, the safer you are."

"I know which neighborhoods to avoid in LA. And the muggers don't have sharp teeth and claws and weigh . . . what . . . five hundred pounds?"

"It can be closer to eight hundred."

Mia let out a little *eek* as they left the building.

The parking lot was quieter now, no semis idling, no backup alarms, no drivers yelling at her. They crossed the wide swath of gravel to Raven's green truck.

"You mind if we make a stop?" Raven asked as they climbed inside.

"Not at all. Where're we going?"

"I have to talk to Brodie about the governor."

Mia remembered Raven's telephone conversation. "Would Brodie really buzz the governor's mansion?"

Raven laughed as she started the engine. "Juneau's a long way from here. But it would sure make our point, *and* get some media attention on the problem."

"Can I help?" Mia asked.

Raven glanced over at her, obviously puzzled.

"Some of Alastair's friends know important people. I once met the governor of California."

"I don't think we need to go interstate quite yet."

Mia couldn't tell if Raven thought she had the problem under control, or if she couldn't imagine a way a mere fashion model might be able to help with a real-world problem. Mia tried not to let the dismissive reaction hurt her feelings.

Joseph McKenzie would help her if she asked. She was

sure of that. At least, she was fairly sure he'd still take her call now that Alastair was gone. Joseph wasn't one of the people who'd shunned her at the funeral.

It was a short drive across Main Street to the unimaginatively named Red Avenue. Red Avenue and Blue Crescent; she couldn't help but wonder if there was a Green Parkway somewhere in town. Could they at least have gone with Scarlet, Indigo or maybe Chartreuse?

Raven nosed the truck into a long strip of street parking alongside about thirty other pickup trucks of varying colors, ages and rust-patch sizes.

"That side is the Galina barracks." She pointed her thumb behind them. "This side is WSA housing. The big, flat building down at the end is the WSA cafeteria."

"Could you live in the Galina barracks?" Mia couldn't help but think it would be nicer to be in town; maybe safer from marauding bears too.

"And share washroom facilities with all those guys? No thanks." Raven opened the door.

"Keys," Mia called out, seeing them still dangling from the ignition.

"They're fine." Raven climbed out of the truck.

Mia followed suit. So, too dangerous to jog alone on the road, but leaving your truck keys in the ignition was perfectly safe. She couldn't help but smile at the irony, thinking she wasn't in LA anymore.

They followed a raw-wood raised sidewalk and entered a set of double metal doors into the big, square building that was obviously the facility's cafeteria.

Mia could smell the grease, the salt and the grilled beef as soon as they stepped inside. She wasn't generally a fast food person. Then again, she wasn't generally a cinnamon bun person either, but she'd tasted one at the Bear and Bar today, and it was delicious.

The building was a big, open square room; well, two rooms if you counted the pass-through kitchen. She could see two men back there in white aprons and white hats busily putting together food orders.

There were ten picnic tables in two rows of five. Each was covered in a different patterned plastic tablecloth, very colorful. About thirty men were distributed around the picnic tables, with four others at a round table in what looked like a lounge area. The four were playing cards while two others stood back to watch.

Curious glances turned her and Raven's way.

Raven made a move, and Mia looked ahead to see Silas. He was sitting at one of the picnic tables, a burger and fries on a plate in front of him.

The man across from him spotted Raven approaching and smiled.

"What's going on?" the man asked. It was clear from his expression that Raven's appearance was welcome but unexpected.

"I tried for the governor again," she said, climbing in to sit next to him. "This is my cousin Mia. Mia, this is Brodie."

At the mention of her name, Silas looked up at Mia. His eyes narrowed, but otherwise his expression was unreadable.

"Nice to meet you, Mia," Brodie said. "Saw you were at the Bear and Bar earlier."

It seemed awkward to lean across their dinner to shake his hand, so she settled for a smile. She could feel interested stares at her back, so she sat down next to Silas across from Raven.

Silas bit down on a fry.

"How'd you do with the governor?" Brodie asked Raven. The amused glint in his eyes said he expected her attempt had failed.

"Got the commissioner's direct number." She pulled a folded piece of paper from the breast pocket of her denim shirt.

"No kidding." Now Brodie looked impressed.

"You want to call?" she asked.

"You don't want to do it?"

"A deeper voice is usually most effective."

"That's sexist," Mia couldn't help but observe.

They both looked at her.

"You shouldn't have to be a man to get things done."

"Way of the world," Silas said.

She turned to rebuke him with a look. "That doesn't make it right."

"I agree with you," Raven said to Mia.

Mia couldn't tell if Raven saw her point or if she was placating her for the sake of conversational harmony.

"But," Raven continued, "I'm more interested in getting the haul road fixed right now than chalking up a win for the sisterhood." She pushed the paper Brodie's way.

Brodie cleared his throat. "Happy to be of assistance," he rumbled in a ridiculously low bass voice.

Silas cracked a smile as he popped another French fry.

A man appeared in Mia's peripheral vision and the table shifted as he sat down on the bench with a tray of food. "Nice to see you again, Mia."

She recognized Xavier as the copilot who'd flown with Silas yesterday. She'd also said hello to him as he left the Bear and Bar this morning.

"Hi, Xavier."

"Mia, is it?" Another man joined them, sitting next to Raven and across from Xavier. "I'm Zeke Podeswa, ground crew with WSA."

"Nice to meet you, Zeke," she said, and he gave her a friendly grin.

He glanced down at his burger. "Are you hungry? Can I get you something? Thirsty?"

She looked to Raven, thinking they likely weren't here to eat, but Raven's attention was on Brodie.

"Thanks, but no," Mia said to Zeke.

He looked disappointed.

"I had a cinnamon bun earlier," she said to soften her refusal.

The answer seemed to make him feel better. "Oh, at the Bear and Bar? Those are fantastic!"

"It was delicious," she said. She'd eaten less than a quarter of the giant concoction, but she'd have happily indulged in more.

The way food was served around here, she'd have to find a replacement for her gym workouts, and fast. Once she took over Lafayette Fashion, she wasn't planning to continue modeling, but she'd still want to keep her form for the new styles.

AJ stopped at the end of the table, a dinner tray in his hands. There was clearly nowhere for him to sit down.

"Hi, Mia. I see you found Raven okay."

"Hi, AJ. Thanks again for your help."

AJ glanced around the table, obviously wishing he could join the group.

Silas abruptly came to his feet. "I'll give you some room," he muttered.

Mia looked up, intending to tell him to stay and offer to make room herself. She and Raven had obviously broken up his conversation with Brodie.

"I didn't mean to—"

But he was gone, walking away, shoulders square, stride determined.

Mia looked at Brodie to see if he was annoyed by the turn of events, but he seemed engrossed by Raven's description of the haul road problems.

AJ took Silas's spot.

"Are you hungry?" he asked Mia.

Chapter Five

TWO NIGHTS LATER, THE CAFETERIA POKER GAME seemed more intense than usual.

Silas balanced a slice of deep-dish pizza and took a glass of water from the kitchen pass-through and headed over to the game table, where Zeke, AJ and four other guys were playing around stacks of red, blue and green chips.

"What's going on?" he asked Xavier who was part of the standing crowd.

"Whoa," a collective exclamation went up as Zeke raised the pot by one hundred dollars.

Since these were friendly games using fake money, and Brodie had a rule against gambling for anything more than a bottle of bourbon, the level of excitement didn't make sense.

Silas took a bite of the hot, crispy pizza.

"Zeke's bound and determined," Xavier said in an undertone.

Silas swallowed. "To what?"

"Win."

"Why?" Silas wondered if the Co-op had brought in some particularly fine bourbon.

"To be the first to ask Mia out." Xavier seemed surprised he had to spell it out for Silas.

"*What?*" Silas stared at Xavier then at the game, half stupefied, half angry, with the angry half quickly taking over.

"Everyone wants a date with her, and this seemed like the fairest way to decide. We don't want to be jerks and bombard her all at once."

"So, you made her a prize? *That* was your solution?"

"She's not a prize. You don't *win* her. You just get first crack at asking her out."

"That's splitting hairs. Does Brodie know about this?"

Xavier shrugged. "I didn't tell him. But it's not a secret."

Silas polished off the water and abandoned his pizza, his appetite gone.

"You going to tell him?" Xavier asked.

Silas shot back a look that said it was none of Xavier's business. Then he left the cafeteria, fired up his pickup and headed out of town.

He was at Raven's in under ten minutes, slamming his truck door behind him. He heard their voices on the screen porch, so he cut around to the side of the cabin.

"Hey, Silas," Raven called out from a chair facing his way, giving him a smile.

Mia twisted in her seat to look at him, her expression staying neutral.

Silas slowed himself down and tamped his anger since Raven and Mia had nothing to do with the absurd poker game. Well, Mia did, he supposed. But all she'd done was exist around lonely men. He couldn't fault her for that.

"Hi," he said, keeping his voice calm and easy.

The outside entrance to the screen porch was around the back, and he went that way.

"Wine?" Raven asked as he came up the steps and opened the rickety screen door.

"I'm good."

"Not a social call?" Mia asked, tipping her head, looking like she saw through his façade.

"On second thought, wine sounds good," he said to Raven. He made a move for the kitchen, but Raven was already on her feet.

"Pull up a chair," she said as she headed inside.

He moved a third wooden chair from the far corner, parking it next to Mia.

Raven came back. "I hope you don't mind." She handed him a clear acrylic glass decorated with colored umbrellas. "We got the last of the clean wineglasses."

Raven and Mia had proper wineglasses, although they didn't match.

"No problem," he said, accepting the drink. He wasn't fussy.

"Something going on?" Raven asked, looking expectantly from him to Mia and back again.

Clearly, she thought he was here on some pretext to cozy up to Mia. She thought he was just like the rest of the yahoos. He wasn't.

"I wanted to warn Mia," he said, deciding to come right out with it. The last thing he wanted was for Raven to sit there waiting for him to make a pass at her cousin.

Mia's expression paled, and she quickly set down her wine, coming to attention. "Did someone show up in town? Did they find me?"

Too late, he remembered what Brodie had told him about her being harassed back home.

"Nobody's here," he quickly said, regretting that he'd made her worry. "It's not that bad. I mean, it's not dangerous in any way. It's . . ." He wanted to call it insulting but decided the best route was to go with the facts, awkward as it was to broach this topic. He rubbed the back of his neck, before coming out with it. "It won't surprise you to know that most of the guys here in town want to date you."

"What makes you think that won't surprise me?"

He wanted to call her on the false modesty. It had to have happened before, because she was the kind of woman all guys wanted to date wherever she showed up.

"Because you're new in town," Raven put in before Silas could say anything more.

It looked like they were all going to pretend here. Whatever.

"They couldn't decide who should ask you first," he said. "So, somebody came up with the brilliant idea to have a poker game." He waited for the revelation to sink in.

Mia and Raven both looked confused.

"To decide," he added.

Nothing.

"By who won." It looked like he was going to have to spell it out completely. "The winner gets you—well, the chance to be the first to ask you on a date."

Mia surprised him by laughing.

Raven didn't seem to see the amusement, but she didn't look angry either.

"You think it's funny?" he asked Mia in astonishment.

She picked up her wineglass again. "Hey, I've been a prize before."

"In a poker game?" He tried not to sound horrified. What kind of a woman allowed for that?

"No," she said. "It was more of an auction."

Silas sat back dumbfounded by her blasé attitude.

"*Really?*" she asked him, taking in his expression. "Your brain went there?"

"My brain didn't go anywhere." But it had. He'd immediately picture a raunchy auction with scantily-clad women and leering men.

"For *charity*," she enunciated like he was daft. Then she included Raven in her answer. "People bid on lunch with a

Lafayette model. A bunch of us did it. We made a lot of money for the local hospital." She slid her gaze back to Silas. "Pervert."

Raven laughed.

"I'm—" He realized that protesting would only make it worse. He took a swallow of the wine. "I just thought you should know," he said.

"Thank you," Raven said.

"I'll play along," Mia said.

"You don't have to," Raven told her, and Silas thought he was finally hearing a voice of reason.

Mia shrugged. "No big deal. I'm assuming you'll know the winner."

"For sure," Raven said.

Mia looked to Silas with a challenge in her eyes. "I take it you're not playing?"

"*No.*"

Mia shrugged. "Just asking."

"I can't believe you're going to encourage them."

"I can't believe you're such a stick in the mud."

"So, you think I should gamble for you?" Exactly how much adoration did this woman need?

"I think you should chill."

"I am—" Silas gave up. He'd done his duty. He polished off the wine and came to his feet. "Thanks for the drink," he said to Raven.

"Thanks for the warning," Raven said.

"Yes," Mia put in belatedly, as if it had only just occurred to her. "Thanks for letting me know."

"Sure," Silas said without looking back at her. He headed out the screen door. He might have banged it shut, but it was rickety enough already, and he didn't want to do damage. Raven had enough of challenge keeping this old place up without him making it worse.

He paced his way back to his pickup.

"Silas?" Mia's voice surprised him from behind.

He paused, realizing she'd followed him.

"Wait a second," she said.

He turned, not feeling particularly charitable toward her, and he let it show in his voice. "What?"

"I'm sorry."

"For what?"

She gave a wave behind herself as she came to a halt in front of him. "For that, back there. I know you were only trying to be nice." She hit him with what had to be a patented vulnerable look.

He wasn't going to react to it. "Did Raven point that out to you?"

"No. Okay, yes." She bit her bottom lip, looking genuinely sorry.

He kept the hard edge to his voice, hating that her act was working on him and hating that he wished he'd entered the poker game and won. "I wasn't trying to be nice."

"Trying to be noble then."

"I'm not noble." He wasn't. He was just a guy trying to be decent, and wasting his time on the effort.

"I don't want to get in the way of their fun," she said.

"Do you want to *be* their fun?"

"You know what they found online about me, don't you?"

"Videos on the catwalk," he guessed. "Probably details of your rich husband and his estate."

"That I'm cold and unfeeling, a predatory gold-digging ice-princess."

He stared at her in silence, trying to take in what she was saying. It that how the world saw her? Is that how she saw herself?

"I don't want them to think that. I don't know how long I'm staying, but while I'm here, I want them to think I'm a regular person."

"You're not a regular person."

She was about as far from being a regular person as anyone could get. She was rich and famous, or maybe it was infamous, but pampered and entitled too. The world—especially the male world—would lay down the red carpet for her if she so much as looked their way.

Well, not him.

"Do whatever you want," he said. "It's none of my business."

Her shoulders drooped, and her eyes clouded with hurt that didn't look like an act.

Damn. How had he turned into the bad guy?

"Fine," she said, breaking eye contact, gazing past his temple into the darkening blue of the sky.

"I didn't mean—" He cut himself off, not sure where he was going with that.

She gave her hair a little toss. "You think you know me. You think what the world thinks of me is true."

"I don't think anything." Truth was, the more he saw her, the more baffled he became.

Her gaze turned brittle on him. "If you were right, I wouldn't care what you or anyone else here thought of me."

Her words made a complicated kind of sense.

She pivoted to walk away, but he reached out, gently touching her shoulder.

"Mia."

She paused.

He closed the gap between them, wishing he could press himself against her back, desperate to feel her warm body against his own. But he stopped short. "I don't think I know you."

She was silent for a minute, and he willed her to turn around, turn into his arms and hold him close, kiss him like he'd wanted for hours now, days now, ever since he saw her sitting in the FBO surrounded by her snooty luggage.

"Your loss," she said and shrugged his hand off to walk away.

Regret hit him hard, and he leaned back against the driver's door, questioning his own sanity.

* * *

ALTHOUGH SHE KNEW BOTH SILAS AND BRODIE WERE
dead-set against the idea, Mia had said yes to the date with
Zeke. He seemed like a nice guy, if a bit talkative. Raven
had confirmed he was honorable and honest, well-liked by
the people of Paradise. Not that Mia had come across any
jerks in the town—even if Silas did have his moments. It
seemed to be full of friendly, hard-working people who
liked an unpretentious lifestyle.

So, she'd met Zeke in town on Friday evening, driving
Raven's clunky truck to park it in front of the WSA housing,
around the corner from the Bear and Bar. Zeke had offered
to pick her up at Raven's, but Mia wanted to avoid any awkwardness at the end of the evening. She might change her
mind, but she didn't see a good-night kiss in their future.

There wasn't much for night life in Paradise, but Zeke had
taken her on a steep, bumpy four-wheel drive journey to a
lookout over the Paradise Valley. It was a stunning view,
miles upon miles of forest, river and mountains, and not a
house, a farm or a telephone pole as far as the eye could see.
It made her feel small. Oddly, it also made her feel safe, since
the outside world was so far, far away.

They trundled back down the mountainside to the Bear
and Bar for dinner. The place was hopping with Galina and
WSA staff, plus a few local families. Mia had learned there
were almost forty children in town, about thirty of them
attending the Paradise School out on—and she could barely
believe it—Yellow Road.

She and Zeke sat at a table beside the wall, and Breena
had taken their order. Zeke went with a burger and fries.
Mia had learned it was the specialty of the house and very
popular. But since Breena told her a fresh produce order
had arrived Friday, Mia decided on the house salad. There
was only so much starch and sugar she could safely eat and
still fit into the few clothes she brought.

She'd found over the years that she had more flexibility than most women in her profession when it came to caloric or carbohydrate intake, but she still had to keep it reasonable. So, when Zeke ordered chocolate cake for dessert, adding the optional whipped cream, she stayed strong and asked for a cup of coffee.

Halfway through dessert, Silas walked through the door. His gaze seemed to zero in on Mia, then it switched to Zeke. He frowned and looked away. He offered a smile to Mrs. France, nodded to a couple of other people, then turned and left.

Later, as Zeke paid the check, his friends called to him from where they surrounded the pool table on the lounge side of the building. He invited Mia to join the fun, but she saw a perfect opportunity for a graceful exit. She brushed away his offer to walk her to her truck—it was exactly half a block away with plenty of daylight even this late in the evening, although dark clouds were moving across the sun. She shooed him toward his friends and left with a cheery wave, feeling a sense of relief when she made it to the sidewalk.

There was nothing wrong with Zeke, but during the date she'd felt like she was back at her old job, schmoozing with contacts at an industry party, or chatting up Lafayette clients after a runway show. She'd forgotten how tiring it was to be "on" for an entire evening.

She turned toward WSA housing and rounded the corner. Raven's truck was just three spaces down the road, and she pulled the keys from her purse, smiling at the whimsical fob that was a goofy cartoon leather moose head. It was adorable, and not at all Raven's style.

She pushed the key into the driver's door and turned the lock. She pulled on the door handle, but nothing happened. Frowning, she reinserted the key, twisting it both ways, listening for the click of the lock. Nothing happened.

"Problem?" a deep male voice asked from behind her.

Silas, of course. He always seemed to be there when things went sideways.

She was glad of the help but not so glad that it had to be him. "Something's wrong with the lock." She wiggled it back and forth.

"You locked it?"

"Yes."

"Why?"

"To keep—" She remembered Raven leaving the keys in the ignition. It was a safe bet she never locked her truck doors. "Habit." She turned to face him, feeling a sense of defeat. "Can you try?"

"It probably doesn't work," he said as he stepped up.

"Brilliant diagnosis," she muttered.

"You just can't keep it to yourself, can you?" he asked as he took the key from her. He was gentle as he eased it back and forth in the lock.

"No," she admitted, peering around his shoulder. Why did he have to be both so annoying and so sexy at the same time?

"This isn't going to work," he said.

"Maybe the other door?" she suggested.

"I'm guessing you locked it too?"

"What would be the point of locking one and not the other?"

"They freeze in the winter. The locks do. That's why nobody uses them."

"It's summer."

"Keeps us in the habit." There was a smile in his voice.

She was amusing him. Great. "You just won't let up, will you?"

"Let up on?" He turned.

"One-upping me. Mocking me. Making me feel like I don't belong."

"You don't belong."

She was too surprised by that answer to respond. She'd

expected him to argue, to reassure her that he hadn't meant to come across that way, he hadn't meant to make her feel bad about being here. At least that's what a normal person would have done.

"Why would you want to belong here?" he continued, looking her up and down. "If there was ever anyone who *wasn't* your average Paradise resident, it's you."

It was an insult. She was sure of that. But she couldn't quite put her finger on the right rebuttal.

She switched focus. "So, you mock me?"

"I'm not mocking you."

She wasn't about to let him get away with that one. "At least own it, Silas."

He held her gaze for a long moment. "Maybe I'm having a little bit of fun with you." He made a small space between his thumb and forefinger. "Little bit."

She socked him in the arm, her knuckles coming up against sinewy muscle. "It's not funny."

"You're the new kid in town. Own it."

"So, you bully me?"

His expression turned more serious. "Is that what you think? Really?"

She didn't, and she wasn't going to lie. "No."

Thunder rumbled overtop of them. There'd be lightning flashing in the sky as well, but they couldn't see it since the sun was still up.

"How was your date?" he asked.

"Fine."

"Fine? Really? Not disappointing or bad or dull?"

"Why would you ask that?" A drop of rain pinged the roof of the truck.

"Because you're out here, and he's in there, and it's only ten o'clock."

"He wanted to play pool with his friends."

"Instead of seeing you safely to your truck?"

"It was half a block." She could tell Silas she'd insisted

on coming out alone, but that would give away the fact that the date had been dull.

"Yet, you ran into trouble all the same." He sounded both self-satisfied and amused.

"It seems to be my special talent."

He smiled. "Doesn't it just."

Her back went up again at his attitude, and she fought an urge to point out her successes. A modeling career for one, plus she'd helped Alastair run a mid-sized corporation. They'd succeeded in the international fashion industry, one of the mostly competitive spaces there was.

But another drop of rain hit, then another and another, a couple of them landing on her head.

"We should try the other door," he said, extracting the key.

"I can do it," she said, reaching for it.

Instead of giving up the key, he headed around the hood of the truck. "Unlike Zeke, I'm not about to leave you stranded."

"I'm not stranded." She followed, trying not to notice the way he walked. His gait was smooth, not quite graceful but contained and easy, his strides balanced, shoulders set square, arms moving slightly.

Her gaze dropped from his broad shoulders to the fit of his jeans. She wasn't proud of her reaction, but he'd never know, so she indulged until he stopped and turned to the passenger-door lock. She raised her gaze, noting his profile was gorgeous too, nose straight, chin strong, chest deep.

The rain came harder and faster, heavy drops out of the thunderclouds, wetting his dark hair, plastering his T-shirt to his chest, highlighting the definition of his biceps and pecs, making her heart beat more deeply in the hollow of her chest.

"Bingo," he said and pulled on the handle. With a satisfied grin, he opened it wide.

"You saved me again," she said, admitting her appreciation.

He gestured to the inside, and she moved past him, turning at the last second before climbing in.

"Thank you," she said.

He'd brought his hand to rest on the corner of the open door, so she was surrounded by him. It wasn't a hug, nowhere near that, but she liked it anyway.

"No problem." His voice was deep, his eyes intense. Now *this* would be a worthy good-night kiss.

She told herself to move, to turn away, to climb in, up on the seat and out of his reach.

"Here you go," he said.

She braced herself, tipped her chin, closed her eyes. Here they went . . .

"Mia?"

"Yes?"

"Your keys."

She opened her eyes to see them dangling in front of her.

"Right. Thanks." Mortified, she took them.

She turned and climbed into the truck then, realizing she was soaked to the skin. She told herself he hadn't noticed her intention, hadn't guessed what she was feeling, what she was expecting from him, hoping for from him.

But there was no way he'd misunderstood, and she'd just made a complete fool of herself all over again. She quickly shifted across the bench seat. She concentrated on inserting the ignition key, steadfastly refusing to look back at him. Then she put her foot on the brake and started the engine.

"All good?" he asked.

She gave a jerky nod, far too embarrassed to even look at him, and he finally shut the door.

SILAS KNEW HE SHOULD HAVE KISSED HER. MIA HAD been right there, practically in his arms, looking up at him both sweet and sexy.

Sweet. He laughed at himself for that thought. Mia wasn't sweet. Saucy, yes, but not sweet.

"You going to take the shot?" Cobra asked him from across the pool table in the Bear and Bar Lounge.

Silas pulled back on his cue and sent the nine ball straight into the right-side pocket.

"Yeah, like that," Cobra muttered, moving to a nearby table to take a drink of his cola.

It was coming up on eleven, and Silas didn't have a flight until three o'clock that afternoon. Cobra was taking a rare day off, nursing a gash on his arm from the jagged edge of some sheet metal. He had seven stitches and an order to wait twenty-four hours before going back to work.

Silas checked out the table for his next shot.

The café door opened and caught his attention.

It might have been her image in his peripheral vision or a whiff of her perfume, or maybe a change in the energy of the room, but he instantly knew it was Mia.

He straightened to look, and her gaze met his.

She stilled.

"Mornin'," he said easily, wondering how she remembered their parting from last night.

She gave him a nod and a casual smile.

That little smile transported him back to last night, her eyes darkening blue, her lips ripe and luscious, her face wet from the rain, and her chin tipped at the perfect angle. Man, he was losing his mind.

"Do we need a shot clock?" Cobra interrupted his thoughts.

"Hey, Mia," Breena's greeting was warm and enthusiastic as she scooted out from behind the bar. "I was hoping you'd come by today."

Mia turned Breena's way then, breaking her gaze on Silas. "I'm mobile this morning. I've got Raven's truck."

Silas dutifully looked back to the lay of the table, but his thoughts were still on Mia. He blew his next shot on the five, rebounding the cue ball, leaving the table in great shape for Cobra.

"Dude," Cobra said, shaking his head in mild disgust as he chalked his cue.

Silas didn't particularly care that he'd screwed up. There was nothing more than a burger riding on the game of eight ball.

Sure enough, Cobra made his last two shots and sank the eight ball. But more significantly, Mia and Breena were coming their way.

"Doubles?" Breena asked them. "Cobra, have you met Mia?"

"Hey, Mia." Cobra moved to offer her his hand. "I heard you were visiting Raven."

Silas found himself watching closely, gauging Cobra's level of interest, checking for a sparkle in her eyes that could indicate something reciprocal.

Women liked Cobra. There was something about his size, strength and rugged looks that interested them. He was quiet, mostly a loner, and he didn't pay much attention to their obvious flirting.

"Nice to meet you, Cobra." Mia's tone was even. It didn't sound flirty at all.

"You play eight ball?" Silas asked her, trying to sound inviting, hoping to keep her around for a while.

"I know the rules," Mia said, finally looking his way. "But I've never played much of—"

"I'll take Breena," Cobra said with a laugh.

Breena had played eight ball with them since she was a kid. She was good.

"Fine by me." Silas would rather partner up with Mia than win the game.

It was also good to know Cobra was more realistic than Xavier. He might recognize that Mia was gorgeous, but he knew he didn't have a chance. Not that Silas had a chance. Not that Silas wanted a chance.

He had to put kissing her out of his mind. But he did take the opportunity to sidle up to her. "Let me know if you need any pointers."

"I think I'm okay."

"Lag for break?" Cobra asked Breena, knowing she was good at placing a ball.

"Sure." Breena stepped up to the end of the table.

Silas moved to stand next to her at the end of the table, placing a ball for himself and crouching for the shot.

"You're not even going to offer it to me?" Mia asked.

Silas turned to give her a baleful look. "You want to take it?"

"No." She raked her shimmering blond hair back into a messy ponytail. "A girl just likes to be asked is all."

He fought a smile. "I'll keep that in mind."

"Thank you." She seemed satisfied with his answer.

Breena won the break and made her first two shots.

Silas courteously asked Mia if she wanted to go first, and she accepted the offer.

He stood ready to help her with her form while Cobra rechalked his cue in anticipation of her miss.

Mia lined up for a logical but difficult shot.

"You might want to try for the six ball first," he suggested.

She gave him a censorious look, eyes narrowed, brows knit together.

He took a step back in surrender, realizing her form looked just fine. "Never mind. Carry on."

"Thank you," she said tartly.

She tapped the cue ball, kissed the two at just the right angle and sent it dribbling into the corner pocket.

"Nice," Breena said.

Mia flashed a grin. She sized up the table for a moment then waltzed around to the far end.

Silas tried to figure out what she had in mind. When she adjusted her stance, he saw she intended to bank the cue ball and put the six in the side pocket.

He straightened, moving to better see the angle. "Are you sure you—" He caught her stern look on him again.

It wasn't exactly a glare. In fact, she looked mostly amused.

"Can you make that?" Breena asked on a note of awe. She'd moved too for a better angle.

Even Cobra was watching closely.

Everyone went quiet as Mia shot the ball.

The bank looked good. She clipped the six. It hit the pocket. And before Silas could even react, the cue ball hit the ten and sank it as well.

Mia repositioned her cue, smiling in satisfaction.

"We've been hustled," Cobra said, shaking his head in amazement.

Mia moved around the table, sizing up another shot. "I haven't played much eight ball," she repeated. "But Alastair liked billiards. We have a table in the basement."

Breena burst out laughing.

"Did you know?" Cobra asked her.

Breena shook her head, while Mia neatly sank the four ball.

"That's my partner," Silas said, impulsively giving her a one-armed hug before realizing what he was doing. He quickly dropped his arm and moved on. "What were we playing for again?"

"Burgers," Cobra answered.

"We should have put some money on it," he said to Mia. "We could have gotten odds."

She slid her bright blue gaze his way. "You really want me to hustle your friends?"

"Yes. No. Cobra, sure. It'd take a lot more than losing a game of pool to rattle him."

She quickly finished off the game.

As Cobra pulled the balls from the pockets, some lunch customers came through the door and Breena went to serve them.

"You're really good," Silas said to Mia. "If that super-model thing doesn't work out for you . . ."

"I can schlep from town to town picking up pool winnings?"

"I've got a plane," he joked. "I'd fly you."

"We'd have to bet big to cover the cost of fuel."

"How about Vegas? High stakes down there in Vegas."

"Even been to Vegas?" she asked curiously.

"No. You?"

"We did a show there once. It's big. Everything there is big. We walked and walked and walked."

"I would have thought you'd take a limo." He could easily picture her in something low-cut and glamorous under the bright lights of the Strip.

"Sadly, they don't let them drive inside those huge hotels."

"Funny," he said.

Her gaze stayed on his for a moment. "If not Vegas, where have you been?"

"Colorado. I grew up in the mountains."

She drew back, making a show of checking him out. "I can see that. You have a practical earthy aura, straightforward and unpretentious."

He wasn't sure how to take that.

"I've known a lot of slick, urbane guys," she continued. "They talk a good game, but no soul."

"Play again?" Cobra asked her, moving closer.

Silas wanted Mia to elaborate. Was she saying he had a soul? Did she like a guy with a soul?

"You sure you want to take me on?" she asked Cobra lightheartedly.

"I don't mind losing," he said. "And it's fun to watch you play."

"Okay." She moved back to the table, her tone teasing. "But I don't know how many burgers I can possibly eat."

Chapter Six

SILAS WAS WITH BRODIE ON SUNDAY MORNING, RIDING in the passenger seat of the newest West Slope Aviation pickup truck, his bare arm bent out the open window. The truck was a painted bold blue with the white company logo—the letters WSA and a stylized swooping airplane—stenciled on each of the doors. It was by far the nicest vehicle in town.

The full-sized back seat could carry additional aircrew, but Brodie and Silas were alone today with a ladder, two stacks of roof shingles, carpentry tools and their leather tool belts stored in the box as they zipped their way down the road from town to Raven's cabin.

"And now there's talk of *another* poker game." It was clear from Brodie's tone that he wasn't about to let that happen.

Silas was glad of that. He'd have been tempted to shut it down himself this time. "She'd beat them all at pool. As I'm sure you heard."

"That made her even sexier," Brodie said, taking a

curve, the back tires doing a controlled slide over the loose gravel, the long wheelbase keeping things smooth.

Silas clamped his jaw. He sure couldn't disagree with that. In any other universe, he'd be vying for a date with her himself.

"It's stupidly distracting," Brodie said.

"So, shut it down." If Brodie didn't, Silas might do it himself.

"I am. I will. Tonight."

"Good."

They rounded the final bend before Raven's driveway.

"Know any details about the roof?" Silas told himself to focus on their job at Raven's cabin instead of fixating on the fact that Mia would be there in all her enticing beauty.

"Raven wasn't big on details."

"When I dropped Mia's bags off I saw four buckets catching drips."

"*Four?*"

"Maybe more. I didn't go upstairs."

Brodie swung the truck left into the driveway. "She made it sound like it was minor."

"Maybe it is, to her. In five years, she hasn't properly plumbed the bathroom."

"I don't get her." Brodie parked the truck.

"What's to get?"

Raven was great, a huge asset to the town. She did her job and kept Galina Expediting running with model efficiency, and he told Brodie as much. They could fix her roof and improve her life without psychoanalyzing her.

"I suppose," Brodie said as they climbed out of the cab.

Both of them strapped on a tool belt and loaded it up with hammers and roofing nails.

Silas lifted the ladder, while Brodie hoisted the two stacks of asphalt shingles.

As they walked toward the house, Raven appeared on the porch. "Today's the day?" she asked, looking them over.

"Coffee on?" Silas asked, since the answer to her question was obvious.

He'd assumed Brodie had given her a heads up they were coming, but Raven seemed surprised to see them. He planted the extension ladder on the ground and leaned it against the side wall.

"I'll get you each a cup." She was dressed in blue jeans and a bulky sky-blue sweater. Her hair was pulled up in a messy bun. Since she never wore makeup, it was hard to tell if she'd just rolled out of bed or had been up for hours.

Brodie's gaze followed her as she walked inside.

"Just going to stand there?" Silas asked him, mounting the stairs. They had to go inside to assess the leaks, plus he didn't expect Raven to haul their coffee outside like a café waitress.

It took Brodie a second to react. "Yeah. Sure."

Silas mounted the front stairs.

Even on a sunny day it was dim inside the cabin. It had been built sometime in the fifties, when window size was not a priority. There were at total of five small windows in the U-shaped kitchen and living room, which wrapped around the staircase that led to the loft.

Raven poured coffee from a battered pot into two white ceramic cups.

Silas went for them, handing one to Brodie as he took a sip from the other. It was hot, and it was good. The amenities of Raven's cabin might be archaic, but they produced a great cup of coffee.

Brodie wandered into the living room. "Four leaks?" he asked Raven, looking around at the bucket locations.

"Two more upstairs," Raven said.

"So, six?" Brodie sounded judgmental.

"We've had a lot of rain lately," Raven said in her own defense.

"And *how* long have you known about them?" Brodie asked.

Silas moved through the living room toward the staircase, deciding to check on the upstairs leaks and leave Brodie and Raven to duke it out over blame.

As he pivoted to head up, he nearly crashed into Mia coming down.

She stared at him in shock.

He gaped at her outfit, a purple silk negligee with spaghetti straps over smooth rounded shoulders and a white lace cover-up drooping down her arms. The thin silk clung to her perky breasts, and her legs were bare from mid-thigh down. Her toenails were polished the same color as the negligee.

She slowly pulled a set of earbuds from her ears. "Hi."

Silas tried to respond, but he had to clear his throat first. "We're here to fix the roof."

"I didn't know you were coming."

He couldn't stop staring because Mia most *definitely* looked like she'd just rolled out of bed, warm from the covers, soft and supple. His gaze went involuntarily back to her breasts, pert and round beneath the thin silk.

Man, oh man, he was feeling an itch to play poker now—and not just to play, but to win at poker so he could take Mia out on a date somewhere secluded and romantic. Forget shutting the game down. He'd changed his mind about that.

Her hair was up, messy around her face. She wasn't wearing makeup, but it didn't matter. Her eyelashes were thick and dark, her blue eyes sparkling, her skin so perfect and so smooth. He wondered if fashion models received secret face treatments.

She was staring back, taking in his faded green T-shirt, scuffed canvas work pants, tool belt and his steel-toed work boots. He hoped she was thinking he had a good soul.

She glanced past him and gave a little nod.

Okay, maybe she wasn't thinking about his soul. She was probably wondering why he was standing here like an idiot instead of getting out of her way.

"Brodie's here too," he said, warning her, even though he'd just stood for a full thirty seconds taking an eyeful.

"Hi, Brodie," she called out.

"Hi, Mia," came his reply.

Silas waited for her to turn and head back upstairs to get dressed now that she knew Raven had company.

"I was on my way to the bathroom," Mia said, taking another step down, clearly expecting Silas to get out of the way.

The idea of her walking blithely through the cabin like this unsettled him. He supposed she wore outfits like this on the runway all the time in front of audiences in the fashion capitals of the world. But this wasn't a fashion show. Bad enough that Xavier was hot for her, and that Cobra had laughed and joked with her over the pool game. She'd been wearing jeans and a scoop-necked sweater then, nothing close to what she was wearing now.

Her bedroom outfit was going to make Brodie's eyes pop.

"You don't want to change?" Silas asked.

She took another step then looked down at herself. "Why? You don't like this?"

It took him a second to find his voice. "Don't be ridiculous."

She was closer now, only one step above him, and they were eye to eye. She pulled the two edges of lace cover-up together. Somehow that made it worse.

There was mischief in her eyes. "You've seen all you're going to see, Silas."

"I was thinking about Brodie."

"Brodie doesn't care what I'm wearing."

Silas couldn't stop himself from looking down at the lace and silk between them. "All guys care when you're dressed like that."

"Brodie's only interested in Raven."

Raven? That was news to him. "They have a business relationship."

"You think it's all business?' she asked, arching a perfectly sculpted brow. "Watch this. Observe how spectacularly unsuccessful I am at attracting his attention."

She squeezed her way past Silas, and it was all he could do not to reach out, wrap his hands around her tiny waist, feel the satin slip through his fingertips, close his palms on her warm skin and pull her into his arms for a kiss.

He gave his head a sharp shake to get rid of the feeling. Then he blinked, focusing on her as she walked. The lace billowed slightly from her slender shoulders. Her neck was long and graceful. The swing of her arms and the length of her legs were miles and miles of sexy. And the back view was exquisite. The purple silk molded to her hips, cascading over the curve of her rear.

She was across the room now, but his hands still itched to reach out. He could almost feel her curves under his fingertips.

She turned then, giving him a smile that seemed to say she'd proven her point.

Silas doubted she would have proven her point, but he had no way of knowing for sure. He hadn't so much as glanced Brodie's way while she crossed the floor, never mind analyzed his reaction to Mia's outfit.

What she had proven was that Silas couldn't keep his eyes off her. He told himself it wasn't his fault. There was a science to female beauty and perfection, and Mia had the formula. It was the reason they paid her to model expensive clothes.

MIA HAD OFFERED TO HELP OUT WITH THE ROOF REpair, but Brodie quickly waved her off and had Raven back him up. Raven said it was too dangerous, while Brodie's expression left Mia feeling she was an interloper and not welcome to join them. She couldn't help but wonder if he was still annoyed about her date with Zeke.

She couldn't really argue back, since she'd never used a hand tool, never mind a power tool. Raven's bizarre shower setup was the first time Mia had even seen a water pump. Truth was, she'd never changed a lightbulb.

While the three of them hammered away up there, she reminded herself that she had other skills. The pool game at the Bear and Bar, for example. It had been satisfying to surprise Silas—in a good way for once. It was a little thing, but she couldn't help but feel good that she'd impressed him.

He'd liked her sleepwear too. She'd seen the heat in his eyes, and it made her feel incredibly sexy. For a minute, she thought he might say something or do something like touch her or kiss her.

Not that the purple two-piece outfit was particularly revealing. She had cocktail dresses that fit more snugly. There wasn't even any lace on the nightgown, no peekaboo this or that. And the cover-up sleeves came halfway down her arms.

Its main attraction was that it was soft and comfortable. She'd had it for years.

Raven shouted something over the sound of the hammers above Mia's head. Her words were unintelligible from inside the cabin, but Brodie answered, and then Silas chimed in. They all laughed, and Mia tried hard not to feel left out.

She'd changed into a pair of jeans and a jade-green top and wore a borrowed pair of knit socks from Raven as slippers. Now she poured herself coffee and moved to the screened porch. She couldn't download any new emails, so she reread the one Marnie had sent on Friday, wanting the comfort of a connection to a friend.

The email was upbeat and chatty, and Mia smiled at the part about Alastair's ex-wife, Theresa, trying to charm the judge. It hadn't worked. The judge was having none of it. Still, he hadn't granted Marnie's request for an expedited hearing either. So, they were likely still weeks away from a court date.

Marnie had also been in contact with the security firm monitoring Mia's social media. There were no recent red alerts, but there were still plenty of taunts and insults coming her way.

Mia knew she wasn't going to feel less lonely focusing on home and Lafayette, without Alastair and where her colleagues all seemed to have abandoned her. Still, she scrolled backward, rereading messages that reminded her of her old life, the time when she still felt part of the Lafayette Fashion team, when people kept her informed and appreciated her input.

But as she read further, she couldn't help seeing the messages in a different light. It was clear to her now that people been writing to Mrs. Alastair Lafayette, not to Mia Westberg. They mostly seemed to be humoring her with simplistic answers, clearly assuming she knew nothing about the business. It was odd that she'd never noticed that before. Now, it was yet another blow to her confidence.

The front door banged open and she realized the noise on the roof had stopped.

"—plus I'm not liking the weather forecast for tomorrow," Raven was saying.

"We'll work as long as we have daylight," Silas said.

"There's nothing pressing so far at WSA," Brodie said.

Mia came to her feet and went back into the house, putting on a smile, telling herself that even if she wasn't a natural fit in Paradise, Raven was family. Family was important. Family was there for her.

Raven had the fridge open and was pulling out some ham and cheese.

"How's it going up there?" Mia asked.

"Good," Raven quickly said with a nod.

"About halfway done," Brodie said as he pulled three soft drinks from the fridge. Then he glanced guiltily at Mia and went back for a fourth. He clearly didn't consider Mia part of the crew.

Silas seemed unnaturally focused on washing his hands at the kitchen sink, while Raven lifted a heavy cast iron frying pan from a ceiling hook. Brodie saw what she was doing and caught it halfway down, setting it on the propane stove.

Silas dried his hands, while Raven and Brodie gathered supplies from the fridge.

Then Silas held up a loaf of bread. "This one?" he asked Raven.

"That'll work."

His gaze finally met Mia's and held there for a second. Then he took in her outfit, and she wondered what he was thinking—that he preferred this morning's look or that she fit in better here dressed like this?

Before she could guess his thoughts, he took the wooden cutting board from behind the canisters, pulled a knife from the butcher's block and started efficiently slicing the bread.

Mia envied their easy comradery. She wished she could spot something to just pick up and do the way the rest of them had. But everything seemed to be under control, and the small kitchen was already overcrowded with three people in it. Even if she could see a way to help, she'd only be in the way.

She hung back, and in what seemed like only minutes, they were gathered around the tiny kitchen table in front of grilled ham, cheese and tomato sandwiches.

"I talked to the commissioner yesterday," Brodie casually tossed out, his gaze surreptitiously on Raven, seeming to watch for her reaction as he spoke.

Raven sat up straight, her interest clearly perking up. "You *did*?"

Brodie nodded as he chewed and swallowed.

"On a Saturday?" she asked.

"The number you scored was for his personal cell."

"Really?" She looked happily surprised. "I thought it was the direct line for his office."

"Nicely done." Brodie gave her a smile and a brow wag of admiration.

"I threatened them with you," she said. "That's what worked."

Mia glanced at Silas, wondering if he was seeing the same thing she was. It was so obvious that Brodie and Raven lit up around each other.

She nudged Silas under the table, and he looked her way.

She cocked her head toward Raven and Brodie, putting on her best see-what-I-mean expression.

"What?" Silas asked her out loud.

Raven and Brodie looked expectantly her way.

Silent conversations were obviously not Silas's strong suit. She didn't know why she thought they'd be on the same wavelength.

"Uh . . . great news." She beamed at Raven and Brodie to cover up her misstep. "About the commissioner, I mean."

Everyone looked puzzled, and she felt more like an outsider than ever.

But then Raven gave her a compassionate smile. "I sure hope it's good news." Her attention went back to Brodie. "What exactly did he say?"

"He's calling the foreman and requesting they upgrade the road material and put in culverts at Grant Creek and on the bend of the river, plus a couple more."

The explanation meant nothing to Mia, and she fell silent, eating her way through the crispy sandwich.

The other three ate and drank more quickly than she did, and Silas was the first to rise from the table. He lifted his and Raven's empty plates. "You guys head on up. I'll take care of these."

"You sure?" Raven asked.

"Sounds good," Brodie said. "We'll start ripping that rotten patch on the north side. We might need to replace the sheathing."

Feeling slow and out of step, Mia dug in on the second half of her sandwich.

"Will they have sheathing at the hardware store?" Raven asked as she came to her feet.

Brodie polished off his soda and stood beside her. "If we're lucky."

"Please tell me we're not going backward on this."

Brodie smiled. "Don't be a pessimist."

As the two of them chatted their way out the door, Silas turned the heat on under a kettle of water and efficiently moved the dishes from the table to the counter beside the sink.

Quickly finishing her sandwich, Mia joined Silas in the kitchen.

"There must be something I can do," she said. She didn't like admitting her insecurity to him of all people, but she hated feeling this way.

"Do about what?" he asked, running some cold water into the dishpan and squirting in a stream of soap.

"Up there." She pointed to the roof. "I really would like to help."

He paused and braced the heels of his hands on the lip of the counter. "Have you done any roofing before?"

"You know I haven't."

"Ever climbed a ladder?"

"No."

"Pounded a nail?"

"Are you making this painful on purpose?"

"I'm not trying to make it painful. I'm making it realistic. It's dangerous for you up there."

"I'm not a toddler. I won't wander too close to the edge."

His lips twitched as he clearly fought a smile.

"Don't," she said.

The kettle whistled and he shut the heat off beneath it. "Sorry."

"I don't laugh at you." She hit him with a reproachful glare.

"You might." He poured the hot water into the sink. "If we were at some snooty fashion event in LA and I showed up in my cargo pants and work boots."

A comical picture formed in her mind. "Your work boots?"

"You'd laugh at me then."

"I would not. Besides, you'd know what to wear."

"What? My good suit? I haven't owned a good suit in years."

"Nobody gets married around here?"

He washed the first plate, setting it in the drying rack. "Not in a formal ceremony, they don't. They usually travel outside if they're going to have a big wedding. We've had a few locally in the clearing by the river, dance afterward outside at the Bear and Bar. They were nice but pretty casual. No suit required."

"Back to me," she said, realizing they'd wandered from the subject.

He grinned. "Used to having all the attention, are you?"

"I didn't mean it like that. I meant me and the roof."

"There is no *you and the roof.* Because we're fine without you, and we don't want anything bad to happen. We like you, Mia."

"Brodie doesn't."

"You're imagining things."

She realized they'd wandered off topic again. "I *want* to help. I hate feeling like . . . like the annoying little sister you have to take along to the park."

He lifted a brow. "My annoying little sister?"

"You know what I mean, the person nobody wants there and who ruins the game."

His gaze and his tone softened together. "Mia, the last game we played was pool. You definitely didn't ruin it."

"You're deliberately missing my point."

"What's your point?"

"That I want to help."

"You do?"

"Yes."

"Then grab a dish towel and start drying."

The suggestion threw her off balance. She looked at the four plates and two glasses standing in the rack and realized it was ridiculously obvious. She quickly grabbed the green-and-white-checkerboard dish towel and started to dry.

"Most of the time you can just jump in," he said. "You usually don't need permission to help."

Mia thought back to the almost choreographed way Silas, Raven and Brodie had made their lunch. She cast her gaze to the ceiling. "So, I can just climb right on up there and start pounding nails?"

"No, not that."

"Then what? It seems like you're making up the rules as you go along." She set the little stack of dried plates back on the shelf. "I want to be on the team, the Paradise team."

"Why not think of this as a vacation?"

"Because a vacation is only fun when everyone else is relaxing too."

He looked like she had him stumped. "That's a reasonable point."

"Thank you."

"You're welcome."

They worked in silence for a few minutes.

"What about Galina?" she asked, casting around for ideas.

"What about it?"

"I could do something there."

He looked her over. "You own a hardhat, steel-toed boots and a high-vis vest?"

She was warming up to the idea. "Is that what I need to work there?"

"Warehouses are dangerous places too."

"Will you stop with that? Everything in the world can't be too dangerous for me." She pressed her lips together, staring up at him, daring him to argue back.

Instead of arguing, he smiled and she felt it right to her toes. He took the dish towel from her hands and eased in. "All right."

"So, you think it's a good idea?" For some reason, it warmed her to have his approval.

"I think, Mia, that you're smart enough to do whatever you set your mind to doing."

She liked the authenticity in his eyes. It made her feel secure. It made her feel bold and senselessly happy.

His eyes darkened then and he narrowed the gap between them.

Her pulse jumped a beat, settling into a faster rhythm. Wavelets of energy teased her skin, intoxicating energy that lit up her hormones. She wanted to reach out and touch him to get a bigger dose, but she settled for inching in, trying to capture by osmosis whatever it was he was giving off.

"Mia." Her name was breathy on his lips.

It wasn't a question, so she didn't answer.

He brought his head down a few inches. Then he paused. His lips seemed to part, but he was out of focus now, so she couldn't be sure. His warm hand closed gently around her waist.

She tipped her chin and stretched up, wondering if this was going to end the same as last time, with him pulling away and frustration chilling her for long minutes afterward.

But his lips touched hers, and the circuit was complete. His heat, his taste and his energy engulfed her. She stepped forward, her body brushing his. Then his arms snaked around her, pulling her close, enveloping her in a strong, sexy embrace.

Now *this* was a kiss, a throw-caution-to-the-wind, tear-off-your-clothes, run-to-the-nearest bed kiss. She'd never felt anything like it.

He braced the small of her back and bent her backward. She wound her arms around his neck, holding him tight, sliding her fingertips across his skin, dipping into his hairline.

He dropped his hand, cupping her rear, pulling her tight against the vee of his thighs.

"Yes," she whispered.

He stilled, going tense.

She knew what that meant. She could feel the shift in his stance, the change in his energy. She wanted to rage at the unfairness of what he'd done to her. How could he stop like that? How could he tease her with paradise and then back off?

His arms slackened, loosening the embrace.

She firmed her knees beneath her.

He drew back, his lungs expanding his chest, hands still resting on the top of her hips. "I shouldn't have done that."

"You didn't do it alone." She'd been an enthusiastic participant, still was. His kisses left her warm and alive, feeling like she could do anything.

"This is too complicated." He tilted his head upward for a minute like he was gathering his strength. Then he smoothed her hair back from her temple.

"Everything's complicated." She wanted to feel it all again. She looked up at him, inviting him for another kiss.

"We need to leave it alone." He slipped sideways, breaking their contact.

She felt the loss like a bucket of cold water. Did he mean now? Did he mean forever? Had the kiss not blown him away like it had her?

"Brodie and Raven need my help."

"Right," she said, feeling hypersensitive. "Because you're skilled and useful."

"Because it's going to rain tomorrow."

She steeled herself and waved him away. "Go be useful. I'll just stay here and be . . . I don't know . . . decorative and useless."

"Nobody's saying that."

But they were. And she wasn't in the mood to defend herself anymore. She turned pointedly away and latched onto the first thing she spotted, the dish towel. She folded it in half then in half again as she heard the door shut behind her.

MIA WOKE UP DETERMINED.

Neither Silas nor anybody else was going to dissuade her from helping Raven. He'd said one brilliant thing yesterday, before he'd blown it all by kissing her into oblivion then walking away. He'd said she should just jump in. Well, this was her jumping.

She got up early, got dressed and was cooking breakfast before Raven as came down the stairs.

"Can I borrow some of your old clothes?" she called out, stirring the pan of scrambled eggs. She didn't normally eat eggs, but she knew they were Raven's favorite.

The toaster popped, and she crossed the kitchen to spread the slices with butter.

"What are you doing?" Raven looked slightly horrified at the sight of all the breakfast fixings scattered across the counter.

Mia realized then that she'd gotten a little messy, but she would clean it up, no problem. "Making breakfast."

"Why?"

"I know you like a good breakfast before work."

"I do." Raven rinsed the dishcloth and wiped some toast crumbs and a smear of butter from the counter.

"I can take care of that. This is almost ready."

Raven backed out of the way as Mia—feeling very efficient—crossed the kitchen and retrieved two plates.

"Why did you get up so early?" Raven asked.

"I have a plan."

"Okay." Raven returned to the sink and filled the kettle with water.

"I know I need to help out more."

"This is nice, and I really appreciate it, but I can make my own breakfast," Raven reassured her.

"I'm not on vacation, and you're so busy."

"It's no different than any other year. Summer is our busiest season."

"But you have me here now. At least for a while. Maybe a long while, according to Marnie."

Raven's brow furrowed for a moment. "I see."

Mia spooned the scrambled eggs onto the plates. "So, you see that I need to be useful. I was thinking I could start with some of those work pants. Do you have an older pair you aren't wearing anymore? And you have special shoes for work, right?"

"You mean steel-toed boots?"

"Yeah, those. Got an old pair of those hanging around?"

"Why do you want steel-toed boots?" Raven frowned with concern. "What are you doing?"

Mia covered the slices of toast with a layer of peanut butter. She started to put the knife down on the counter, but on second thought she put it directly into the sink. She could tell her haphazard cooking style was making Raven jumpy.

"I thought you didn't like peanut butter," Raven said. "Or eggs. What happened to your fruit and yogurt?"

"You said protein sticks to your ribs when you're working."

"You don't have to eat what I eat."

She added jam to the toast, then held one plate out to Raven. "There."

"Looks . . ." Raven hesitated for a beat. "Great."

Mia knew she hadn't done as good a job as Raven would

have. But she'd get better. She just needed some more practice.

"Orange juice or coffee?" she asked.

"I'll take both."

Mia went for the juice and Raven poured two cups of coffee.

Then they both settled at the table.

"I can start slowly," Mia said. "I don't have experience, but I learn fast and I'm a hard worker. I want to be on the team."

Raven stopped with a slice of toast halfway to her mouth. "What team?"

"Galina. Extra set of hands." Mia held hers up to make her point.

Raven hesitated longer now. "We have a full staff."

"You can give me something simple. I can lift boxes and things. It's not like I have to run power tools or climb up on a roof." Mia gave a little laugh at her own joke.

Raven took a bite of the toast and chewed like she was contemplating.

Mia waited. "Please let me try. All I want is a chance."

Raven swallowed. "Uh . . ."

Mia sat forward and gave an eager smile meant to look like she'd give it her all.

Raven set down her toast. "Have you ever driven an electric vehicle or a four-wheeler?"

"A golf-cart at the country club." Mia had had plenty of practice at that.

Raven rocked her head back and forth as if she was thinking it through. "We do have a steady stream of grocery orders to assemble."

"I have plenty of experience shopping."

Raven gave her head a slow shake, even as a smile crossed her lips. "I suppose you have." She took another bite of her breakfast.

Mia raised her coffee cup for a sip, hoping that answer

was a yes, and Mia dug into her breakfast. "Most people don't know it, but modeling is really hard work."

"Jobs that look like fun are usually really hard," Raven agreed.

"Exactly." Mia was gratified that she'd accepted the point.

"Brodie tells me that about flying. People think it looks fun and exciting, cruising around in the skies, but pilots make complex calculations on everything from mechanics to weather to weight and balance, never mind always thinking five, ten and fifty miles ahead and having contingency plans for everything."

Mia couldn't help but think of Silas. He seemed to worry a lot about risk. Raven's description helped explain why.

"And I know what it's like to be underestimated," Raven said, a thoughtful expression shadowing her eyes.

"I can't imagine anyone underestimating you," Mia said, surprised Raven would ever think that.

Raven gave a laugh.

"You look so capable and smart," Mia continued. "It's something about your eyes. Or maybe your expression, the way you always look so thoughtful but confident, like it doesn't matter what anybody says, no matter how complex, you look like you understand exactly what they're getting at and what needs to happen next. And don't get me started on when you open your mouth. When you open your mouth and say smart things, it's game over."

"I . . . wow." Raven looked touched.

"Wow is definitely the way I feel about you." Mia drank the last of her coffee, rising from her chair. "So, is it time for us to get to work?"

Chapter Seven

THE STEEL-TOED BOOTS WERE CLUNKY ON MIA'S FEET. The workpants she was wearing felt stiff. It was tricky to balance her hardhat, and she kept getting flashes of the bright orange vest in her peripheral vision. It was an interesting concept, clothing for protection instead of decoration. She'd never thought about it that way.

"This is representative of the fleet," Kenneth said, pointing to a short line of vehicles angle parked against the outside wall of the warehouse.

They were around the corner where it was quiet, away from the loading dock traffic. Dust rose under their feet, and a few mosquitoes buzzed around her ears. But the pests weren't getting through her canvas pants or the nylon vest, so the only things she had to protect were her face and neck by waving them off with her hands.

"Except for the forklift," Kenneth said. "You won't be driving the forklift."

"Is it harder to drive?" She was warming to Kenneth. He was thirtyish, tall and lanky, polite and no-nonsense.

"It's more dangerous, heavy, tons of torque. And it's easy to unbalance a load when you're lifting with it. Nobody gets near the forklift without the thorough training course."

"Okay by me," Mia said. "This looks less intimidating."

She checked out the four-wheel ATV and what looked like an oversized golf cart with a long flatbed sticking out the back. The two were parked next to a mini front-end loader with a scoop bucket. The loader looked like it might be fun.

A pickup truck came to a stop on the gravel behind them and AJ hopped out. "What's going on?" he asked, striding over.

"I'm learning to drive," Mia answered.

AJ looked perplexed. "You don't drive?"

"I have golf cart experience."

"Utility vehicle," Kenneth corrected her.

"I guess we won't be golfing," she joked.

"Let's start with that," Kenneth said, setting his hand on the roof of the vehicle. "Hop in."

She stepped gamely into the driver's seat, stumbling slightly when her clunky work boot hit the running board and landing hard on the black vinyl seat. She straightened herself and settled.

"Seatbelt," Kenneth said, demonstrating it. "Start and stop." He pointed. "Accelerator and brake. Use your signals. Turn on the four ways if you're stopping somewhere."

Mia nodded. It seemed straightforward so far.

"Remember, you're longer than usual in this. So you have to take the corners wide. And be particularly careful driving in the center part of the warehouse, because some of the spaces are tight there when the shelves are full."

Mia took a bracing breath at the thought of maneuvering between the warehouse shelves. She couldn't imagine zipping along as fast as she'd seen some of the guys driving.

"I *thought* that was you." Breena's cheerful voice reached her. "What's going on here?"

Mia turned her head and smiled. "I'm learning. Where'd you come from?"

"I'm on my way into work."

"You walk?"

"Yup." Breena looked her over. "Wow. You even make safety gear work. You have a gift."

"Ready to take it for a spin?" Kenneth asked.

Mia hadn't expected the orientation to be that short, but she was game. "You want me to take it inside?"

"We'll practice out here. How about around the end of the building to start?" Kenneth said.

"I'll come along." Breena quickly hopped into the passenger seat.

Kenneth looked hesitant, but then he patted the roof. "Okay. Go up to the east end, around the back, but then turn and come back this way. I don't want you crossing the loading dock."

"Got it," Mia said as Kenneth stepped back.

"Girls' road trip," Breena called out. Her lightheartedness eased a bit of Mia's nerves.

"No messing around," Kenneth said.

"No, sir," Mia said, completely prepared to take this seriously.

She switched on the vehicle then put it into reverse.

Her heavy boot slipped as she pressed the accelerator, and the cart leapt backward.

Kenneth cried out. "Watch out for the—"

She hit the brakes and stopped them short.

"Truck," Kenneth finished.

"It's peppy," Mia said, trying to mask her shock.

AJ was already dashing back to the pickup truck to move it out of the way.

"Take it easy," Kenneth told her.

"Will do," Mia said, taking another breath before gingerly touching the accelerator. They inched backward a few feet before she remembered to put it into forward.

"Relax," Breena said.

"I am. I am."

"You got this."

Mia eased the vehicle forward, and it went much better this time. They puttered across the gravel beside the high concrete wall.

"Are you doing this for fun?" Breena asked.

"I'm going to do some work," Mia said. "Help out. Raven's so busy."

"Wow." Breena seemed to ponder for a moment. "I bet it'll be different than your regular job."

"A change is as good as a rest," Mia said.

"I agree with that. I'm resting right now."

"At the Bear and Bar?" Mia had seen how hard Breena worked waitressing.

"Resting my brain. My program skips the summer term, so I come home and go through a little culture shock. For months, I'm studying coding, straining to learn new concepts. Then suddenly I'm back to serving coffee and burgers—physically draining but not so mentally demanding. It helps me recharge."

"So, you like the variety?"

"It's good." Breena went quiet for a minute. "A couple more years and I'll be permanently out of here. I'll mostly be glad to go, but I'll miss a few things."

"So, you're not planning to live in Paradise after school?" Mia kept the utility vehicle moving in a straight line toward the back corner of the warehouse, where the forest bordered the Galina property.

Breena shook her head. "Not a chance."

Mia understood Breena wanting to spread her wings. "Where do you want to live after you graduate?"

"Not Alaska, please. Down south." There was a lilt in Breena's voice as she spoke. "A big city. The bigger the better, maybe New York or Chicago."

"You already know someone in LA," Mia said, giving her a warm smile.

"I like the idea of all that sunshine. But a software engineer in Silicon Valley is almost a cliché. You grew up there, right?"

Mia nodded as they rounded the corner to the back of the warehouse. "Born and raised."

"Did you ever have an urge to leave?"

"Alastair and I traveled quite a bit, so I got to see different places without moving."

"That appeals to me. Maybe I should try for a job in the travel industry, a cruise ship or a hotel chain with resorts all over the world."

"I'd be careful with work travel." The space around the back of the warehouse was much narrower than the side, so Mia slowed down and steered the vehicle tight to the wall to give herself room for the turn.

They bumped over a rock, canting slightly sideways, and the mirror barely missed scraping the concrete.

"Whoops," Mia said, cringing.

"Nice miss," Breena said, looking back behind them.

Mia cranked the wheel and took a slow turn. She didn't quite make it all the way around, so she switched to reverse, carefully backing toward the wall to give herself enough space.

When she finished, she realized her hands were sweating.

"Nice recovery," Breena said in a congratulatory tone.

"This thing is long," Mia said, glancing in the mirror at the flatbed sticking out the back.

"So, what's the problem with work travel?" Breena asked.

"You end up in all these iconic exotic places, but you don't get to see them."

"I suppose that would be frustrating."

"If you can take a few days before and after the trip, it's nice. Lots of the other models worked that out. But Alastair and I were always in a rush."

They came around the corner to see Kenneth and AJ were waiting in the distance.

"Do you miss him a lot?" Breena asked.

"I do. I mostly miss his company though." Mia didn't feel like she deserved the same kind of sympathy as a regular widow.

Breena turned slightly in her seat. "I don't understand what that means."

"It means our relationship had evolved over the years. When his health went downhill, companionship became more important than intimacy."

"This might be too personal." Breena paused.

"Go for it."

"Was he happy with that?"

"I think he was." There were times Mia thought he preferred their platonic friendship, times when she thought that was what he'd wanted all along.

She slowed the vehicle to a stop.

"How'd that feel?" Kenneth asked, coming up on the driver's side.

"She's a natural," Breena said with a bright grin.

"Great," Kenneth said. "ATV next, then we try the mini loader."

It took Mia a while to catch on to the ATV. It was clunky and bouncy with its big tires, and the handlebars were awkwardly far apart for her. But at least it was shorter than the utility vehicle, and that made it easier to maneuver around corners.

The mini loader was an entirely different story. Although she spent most of the morning trying, she just couldn't catch on. It was run by two joysticks instead of a steering wheel, and she kept mixing them up. The engine speed was variable, plus there was boom up, bucket down, scoop, dump, and curl.

She kept turning left when she meant to raise the boom

or raise the boom when she meant to curl the bucket. Or curl the bucket when she meant to back up.

Kenneth jumped out of the way as she showered them both with sand . . . again.

Mia waved her hand in front of her face to dissipate the dust. She coughed, and squeezed her eyes shut as they watered.

"*What* are you doing?" Raven asked, appearing beside them surprise in her tone.

Mia blinked her cousin into focus.

"The loader's not going so well," Kenneth admitted.

"Why is Mia running the loader?"

Kenneth paused for a second. "You asked me to give her the vehicle orientation." He paused. "Right?"

"To the ATV and the utility," Raven said. She gestured to the Mia and the mini loader. "Not this."

"Oh," Kenneth said with obvious regret.

Mia let go of the joysticks and shut the machine off. She at least knew how to do that much.

Raven took in her appearance and clearly stifled a grin.

Mia touched her check and felt a layer of grime. She might have been struggling, but she would have kept trying. She wouldn't even mind taking another run at it someday.

For now, she unbuckled her seatbelt to clamber out of the loader. She dusted her clothes and pulled off the hardhat to shake her hair, refusing to be deterred. "All right. What's next?"

SILAS WAS DRIVING, BRODIE IN THE PASSENGER SEAT, his window unrolled, elbow hooked out into the muggy air.

"What is *that*?" Silas asked, looking out his side window and doing a double-take at the Galina parking lot.

"We're going to lose the weather," Brodie answered, looking skyward.

"Not the sky," Silas said, slowing and pointing to where a dusty-looking Mia stood with a hardhat in her hand. "Is that Mia?"

Brodie looked over. "I'd say yes."

"They had her in the loader?" Silas could barely believe it.

"Raven looks frustrated," Brodie observed.

"Have they lost their minds?" Silas didn't expect an answer, but he couldn't hold back his astonishment either.

"Did you check the four o'clock forecast?" Brodie asked, moving his attention east and frowning.

"Should we stop?" Silas asked.

"Stop for what?"

"To find out what's going on there." Silas could see the danger of the situation, even if Raven couldn't.

"I'm a lot more interested in the storm that's rolling in," Brodie said.

Silas didn't like it, but he understood Brodie's standpoint. Galina was Raven's domain, and Mia was her cousin. And he had checked the latest forecast. "The sixteen-hundred update showed high and broken clouds through twenty-one-hundred."

"That's not going to hold."

Eying the clouds towering over the peaks, Silas agreed. The approaching storm had obviously picked up speed.

"Who's still out flying?" Silas asked.

"Xavier and Dean are bringing Delta-Romeo in after the Misty Mountain crew change. They're coming in from the north, so they'll have no trouble. Tristen and Tobias took that big load of lumber in Niner-Quebec to Wildfire Lake. They can stay put. Hailey will have to follow the river to stay below the ceiling." Brodie pressed a button on his phone, and Silas knew he was contacting the WSA radio operator. "I'll make sure Shannon's had an update on everyone's position."

The erratic weather wouldn't leave them alone.

"She's not answering," Brodie said. He dialed again and waited while it rang. Then he shook his head.

"Want to try Cobra in the hangar?" Silas asked.

"He's in town at Caldwell's."

"Should we head out there to check?"

Brodie tried one more time, his frown telling Silas there was no answer.

"We'd better go," Silas said, taking a sharp right to head for the airstrip.

Brodie redialed, knowing they'd lose service in just a few minutes.

"Still nothing?" Silas asked as Brodie let his hand drop to his lap.

"She might be *on* the radio," Silas said. It was a distinct possibility that Shannon was on a call with one of the planes.

"Maybe," Brodie said. The timbre of his tone told Silas he was worried.

Silas understood why. Even if Shannon was on the radio with a plane, she'd take Brodie's call, especially if he tried multiple times.

When Shannon missed the fifth time, Silas sped up, worried she might have had a medical issue.

Shannon was in her late fifties, and she wasn't the fittest person in the world. He knew she had diabetes, and she was open about struggling with her blood pressure.

"Can you go faster?" Brodie asked.

Silas upped the speed as much as he dared. He and Brodie both had first-aid training. All the WSA pilots did.

It seemed like forever, but it was only a few more minutes until they zoomed into the parking lot. Silas skidded to a halt in front of the WSA office and Brodie jumped out, leaving the door wide open.

Silas followed, rushing inside, immensely relieved to

hear Shannon's voice coming from the back room. But as he walked forward, her words came clear.

"I've got you on tracking," she was saying. "We're going to know exactly where you go down."

"Brodie here." Brodie had obviously taken the microphone. "Hailey, can you estimate your airspeed?"

Silas breath caught in his throat as he squeezed into the compact radio room.

"Bringing it down. I'll go almost to stall," Hailey said, sounding calm.

Silas raised his brow to Shannon, wanting to know what was wrong, but knowing better than to interrupt whatever was going on.

Shannon left her seat and moved close to him. "Engine failure," she whispered so as not to disturb Brodie.

"Where is she?"

"She's trying for Slim Meadow."

Silas swore under his breath. No one had ever landed a beaver at Slim Meadow. Brodie once put a Super Cub down there, but you could land a Super Cub on a flatbed trailer if you had to.

The grass was long, and the brush was thick, and she'd have no way of knowing what the ground looked like underneath.

"Three hundred," Hailey said.

Silas's hands curled into fists, mentally going through what Hailey had to be experiencing.

"Two hundred."

"We're going to lose transmission," Shannon said.

The radio crackled and went silent.

Brodie slammed the end of his fist on the table. He turned to Silas. "Can you get up the trail on an ATV?"

"I'll make it work," Silas said. He grabbed the compact first-aid kit from where it hung on the wall. "Give me all the supplies you can," he called to Shannon, heading out the door for the door to the hangar to load up a company ATV.

He saw another truck pull into the parking lot. "Cobra's back," he shouted to Brodie.

"Get him to follow you up," Brodie answered. "Let's hope you can fly it out."

Silas could hear the edge to Brodie's voice. First priority was Hailey, but if she'd saved the airplane, they'd try to bring it home.

"Can you call in a chopper?" Shannon called from the front office, where she was pulling out the larger first-aid kit from below the counter.

"They won't make it here before the storm," Brodie said.

He was right. If Silas couldn't make it up the hiking trail, Hailey would be stuck there alone until the storm cleared, possibly until morning.

Cobra got out of his truck.

"Need your help," Silas called through the rain to Cobra.

Cobra was behind him in seconds entering the cavernous hanger. "What's up?"

"Hailey had to put the Papa X-Ray down in Slim Meadow."

Cobra's expression revealed his horror. "She okay?"

"We lost transmission at two hundred feet."

Cobra swore. "What's the plan?"

"You and me take two ATVs. I'll got first with medical. You follow with a trailer and a toolkit."

Cobra was already moving to the workbench and his travel toolkit.

Silas took the closest ATV, strapped two fuel cans on the back rack, fired it up, checked the fuel in the tank, then pulled out to the front of the office. Cobra would follow as soon as he could, and the trailer would slow him down, so Silas wasn't waiting.

Shannon and Brodie were ready outside the door. Brodie strapped three first-aid kits onto the front rack while Shan-

non handed Silas a windbreaker, goggles and a baseball cap.

"I'm going to call about a chopper," Brodie said. "Just in
case they're an option."

"Good." If the trail had turned to mud, Silas might get
stuck partway to the meadow. The chopper might be a long
shot, but it was one they should take.

Brodie clapped him on the shoulder. "Good luck."

SILAS HEADED DOWN A LITTLE USED ROAD PAST THE
airstrip. When that petered out, he turned onto a hiking and
snowmobiling trail.

The first few miles were fine, but then the rain came
down hard, and the narrow dirt trail turned to mud.

It took him nearly three hours to slog his way up to Slim
Meadow, rocking through puddles and bouncing off logs.
The rain was driving hard when he arrived, but he could
make out the beaver at the far end of the meadow. It hadn't
caught fire and it looked to be right-side up. He breathed a
huge sigh of relief.

He sped up on the open ground, the ATV bouncing hard
on the uneven meadow. He avoided clumps of brush, sticking to the grass and moss cover as much as possible.

And then he saw her. Hailey was standing about a hundred feet in front of the airplane that had come to a halt
short of a small rise. She was waving her arms to get his
attention.

He zipped her way, stopping close and leaping off the seat,
and she rushed forward and threw herself into his arms.

For a moment, he just hugged her, feeling her shaking a
little, whether with fear or with cold, he didn't know. She
was soaking wet.

"You okay?" he asked, stripping off his smeared goggles,
scanning her face, then her head, then her arms and torso.

But she was nodding. "Rough landing, but I think everything's intact. Well, except for the engine. But I don't think I bent the gear or anything."

He kept his hands on her shoulders, not sure if she needed steadying. "Cobra's behind me."

She looked past Silas. "He is? That's great news." Then she took a step back and wiped her wet copper-toned hair back from her forehead.

"You sure you're okay? I brought first aid. Does anything hurt? You should sit down." He nodded back to the ATV. The seat was comfortable, if wet from the rain.

"I think I'm good," she said.

"*Think* isn't enough."

"Maybe these." She held out her hands, and he could see they were smeared with dirt, scratched, scraped and bleeding. "I cleared away some of the rocks and brush, hoping we could get a runway."

"Ouch," he said softly.

She glanced down. "I didn't really notice it while I was working." Then she pointed down the length of the meadow. "It's socked in right now. But I hoped I'd be able to take off northwest toward the granite peak. I can't tell if there's enough room."

"Your hands first," he said, moving to the ATV and pointing to the seat. He took off his cap and covered her head with it against the persistent rain. "Do you have a jacket?"

"It's underneath." She pointed to her wet flight suit as she sat down.

She was slim, so it was hard to tell she'd layered up.

He opened the top first-aid kit. The rain made it frustrating, but he disinfected her hands and gently wrapped them in gauze.

As he worked, Cobra's ATV sounded in the distance, pulling up beside them few minutes later. He hit the kill switch and pulled off his hat and goggles. "Wow. Great to see you're okay, Hailey."

"Came down a little hard," she said gamely, coming to her feet. "But I didn't hear anything break."

"I'll go have a look." Cobra restarted the ATV and moved it closer to the plane.

They followed Cobra back to the beaver. Thankfully, the rain had slowed some, although the clouds were still dark, and the wind buffeted them in the open meadow.

"Hear anything before it quit?" Cobra asked, pacing around, eyeballing the overall condition of the plane. "Smell anything? See smoke?"

In situations like this, Silas had to admit it was handy to have a super-fit, uber-powerful AME. Cobra could do a lot more in the field than most technicians.

"Nothing," Hailey said. "It just stopped."

"You switched tanks?" Silas asked, though he'd have been surprised if that wasn't her first move after the engine quit.

"Yes. I tried the boost pump, but it didn't get me anything."

"I'll check the filter," he said.

"You warm enough?" Silas asked Hailey.

Her cheeks were pale, and that could be a sign of shock. Then again, she had a light complexion sprinkled with freckles on her upper cheeks. He'd always guessed she must be Irish, with her light, almost red-tinted hair. But she didn't talk much about her past.

"I'm fine." She craned her neck to watch what Cobra was doing. "Need any light in there?"

Cobra grabbed a few tools and climbed under the engine. "I'm good."

Silas and Hailey settled back to wait in the rain.

"The fuel had to be contaminated," Cobra said, climbing back out half an hour later. "I cleaned and serviced the filter. Do you have a tank with WSA fuel only?"

"Rear tank," Hailey said.

"Good. Switch to that one and give it a shot."

Silas opened the door and left it that way as he climbed inside.

"Fire it up," Cobra called out, watching carefully.

"Clear," Silas called, and both Hailey and Cobra took a reflexive step back.

Silas set the throttle slightly open, counted the blade rotations then turned the mags on. The engine coughed then fired, then started to run. He adjusted the throttle to idle and looked over to see Cobra's thumbs up.

After a few minutes, Silas shut it down and climbed out of the cockpit.

Cobra began checking the gear, while Silas made his way around the wings. Hailey went to the tail as they checked the control surfaces.

"What do you think?" Silas asked Cobra.

"Up to you," Cobra said. "I don't see any reason it won't fly." He turned his attention to the meadow stretching off to the north. "Figure you've got room?"

"I'll have to pace it off." Silas started to walk.

They came to the drop-off and peered down.

"I make it five hundred feet to the edge here," Silas said.

"That's too short." Hailey said, worried.

"Super tight," Cobra said.

Silas peered into the valley. "Unless."

Hailey moved up and peered over with him. "Are you kidding me?"

"Theoretically, it should work." Considering the weight of the load and the meadow surface, if Silas had even the slightest north wind, he could probably get the beaver flying by here. And so long as he was almost flying when he went over the edge, he could point the nose down and gain airspeed.

Cobra came up on his other side to look over. "Theoretically."

"I can get into ground effect." Silas was confident of that. "I'll lose altitude after I go over." He looked up the valley. "But I'm going to gain airspeed. And the valley's wide. I won't get boxed in."

"You're slightly nuts," Cobra said.

"It's a plan," Hailey said, looking hopeful. "Ever done it before?"

"No, but I've heard tell . . ."

"You're more than slightly nuts," Cobra said.

"You guys head for home. Let Brodie know what's going on. I'll sit tight until the weather clears, then I'll see you back at the strip."

"I hate that I screwed up," Hailey said as she gazed off at the muted lightning.

"You didn't screw up. You made an impressive dead-stick landing on rough terrain without breaking your airplane. You'll have stories to tell."

"It happened so fast. I don't even remember most of it."

Silas grinned. "So, make something up. Make it exciting."

She scoffed out a laugh.

"You've earned it," he said.

She shifted her gaze to the plane. "You think you'll be here all night?"

"Probably." He wasn't looking forward to huddling his wet self in the cold airplane all night long. He was also starting to wish he'd eaten a bigger breakfast.

Chapter Eight

EVERYONE IN THE BEAR AND BAR WAS EATING AND
drinking and celebrating Hailey's safe return. Word of the
hard landing had traveled fast last night, and Mia, along
with most of the town, had been worried into the wee
morning hours that Hailey might have been seriously hurt
or killed. Now, after dutifully completing their workday,
most of the community had gathered at the lounge and restaurant to have a drink in her honor.

Conversation was loud and lively through the restaurant.
People were shoulder to shoulder and the in-house sound
system was cranked up, competing with their chatter. The
music had a country flare with a catchy beat. The air was
warm and close with the aromas of deep-fried savories and
grilled meats seeping from the kitchen.

Sitting at a crowded little window table wedged between
Raven and Dixi with a few others across from them, Mia
felt a little bit more like she belonged in Paradise. She'd
spent two full days working at Galina. Once she got past

the mini loader debacle, she thought she was getting the hang of it. Well, the hang of some things, anyway.

The guys there had all been super helpful about showing her the ropes, and she was learning from her mistakes. She did worry she was pulling them from their duties sometimes, because they were all super quick to rush to her aid if she struggled with a heavy box or had to get something down from a high shelf.

The experience had left her in awe of Raven. Her cousin seemed to be everywhere doing everything all at once. It was clear the staff respected her, and she had an uncanny ability to stay calm no matter what was happening around them. Mia had appreciated that when she took a corner too tight in the utility vehicle and knocked over a stack of packing boxes, several of them breaking open and spewing their contents across the concrete floor.

A sudden cheer went up from the Bear and Bar crowd as Silas walked through the front door. Everyone had wanted to hear about Hailey's emergency landing in the beaver, but she'd mostly talked about Silas rescuing both her and plane. He'd apparently flown the beaver off a cliff and back to Paradise this morning, so he was a hero now too.

He grinned and waved at everyone, accepting a handshake from Xavier then disappearing as people crowded around him.

A loud bong sounded above the din, and the room suddenly went quiet around a Blake Shelton tune that was still playing through the speakers.

Brodie stood next to the big copper gong that hung at the end of the bar. Everyone cheered even more loudly. A few people close to Brodie gave him a high-five.

"Why'd he do that?" Mia was surprised Brodie would draw the attention away from Silas. That didn't seem like what she knew of him.

"It's like a bar bell. Brodie just bought a round of drinks."

"For the house?" Mia glanced around. There had to be more than fifty people crowded inside.

"He's committed now," Raven said with a delighted grin.

Breena, who had been serving tables, moved behind the bar to help her grandmother and Badger the bartender fill the rush of orders as the crowd surged their way.

Brodie made his way toward Raven and Mia's table, his attention clearly focused on Raven. "What are you all drinking?"

"While I have everyone's attention!" Mrs. France's voice boomed out from behind the bar.

Mia turned to see Mrs. France standing taller than everyone else, Badger steadying her on something—a stool or a chair.

There was more cheering, and she gave a mock bow. Then she held up her hand for quiet. "While I have everyone's attention. You should know Badger saw a grizzly sow and two cubs in the meadow berry patch earlier today. If anyone needs bear spray or company for the walk home, come and see me." She waved a red can of bear spray while Badger reached a hand up to help her down.

"Is that close by?" Mia asked Raven. "The meadow berry patch?"

"Drinks?" Brodie repeated, putting his hand on Raven's shoulder.

Raven pointed to her glass. "Old-fashioned."

Brodie looked to Mia next, and she was sure it was only because she was with Raven. He was perfectly polite to her; overly polite, really. She sure didn't get a warm feeling. Maybe that was why Silas had backed off on their kiss. Maybe he cared too much about what Brodie thought.

"I'm fine," she said. She was only halfway through her glass of Chardonnay anyway.

Raven gave her a look of disgust. "Chardonnay," she said to Brodie. "Make it bear-sized."

"Coming right up," Brodie said.

"Bear-sized?" Mia asked, realizing that protesting further would be silly.

"Bigger," Raven said. "Don't let him off the hook like that. He offers to pay, you let him pay."

"Okay."

"How come you two get preferential table service?" Dixi asked in a mock huff at Mia's left-hand side.

"Brodie's only got so many hands," Raven sang back.

Brodie paused halfway across the room to talk to Silas. They stood close, and Brodie spoke into Silas's ear above the music and the ambient conversation. Silas answered back, and they both laughed. Brodie brought a hand down to Silas's shoulder and said one more thing before continuing toward the bar.

Then Silas gaze caught Mia's gaze. Their kiss bloomed in her mind, followed by humiliation from the way he'd backed off.

He moved her way, and with every step he seemed to grow more powerful and attractive. It was hard not to think of him as a superhero while people kept stopping him to offer congratulations. He was friendly but brief in each of the chats. He kept steadily coming her way, looking determined, like a man on a mission.

"Nicely done, you!" Raven jumped up from her chair when Silas was only a few paces away. She wiggled between the crowded chairs to give him a quick hug. "Brodie was impressed."

"It wasn't a big deal. I had a good ten feet to spare on the takeoff."

"Ten feet," she mocked with an eye-roll. "You know you saved him a fortune. You should be the one we're thanking for the free drinks."

"I'll tell him you said so."

"Want to sit down?" She gestured to the chair next to Mia, and Mia's stomach clenched.

"I'm not taking your seat. Look, your drinks are here." Silas shifted to one side so Brodie could squeeze past.

Mia remembered she still had half a glass of wine left and took a swallow. Then she took another one, deciding a hit of alcohol might blunt her unwelcome attraction to Silas. Whatever he'd thought of their kiss, she couldn't get it out of her mind.

"Mia?" Another voice came from behind her.

She turned to see Zeke had wound his way close to their table. His glance flicked to Silas and Raven before settling back on her.

She gave him a bright smile. In the short time she'd been in town, she'd seen there was a hierarchy at WSA. It wasn't overt, but the pilots were top dogs, while Zeke was lower down the ladder because he was on the ground crew. Raven was also up there because she was in charge at Galina, plus she was tight with Brodie and Silas.

"Take a seat," Mia said to Zeke, not wanting to buy into all that. But she could tell by his expression there was no way in the world he was taking Raven's chair.

"Do you want to dance?" he asked, looking hopeful.

Mia looked around the rollicking room. There wasn't a square inch of spare space. "Where?"

He cocked his head. "Out back on the deck. That's where the music's loudest."

"Okay. Sure." She couldn't stop herself from looking Silas's way, but he was occupied with Raven and a couple of other people who seemed to be congratulating Silas on his feat.

Mia came to her feet, and Silas looked at her then. Giving him a carefree little wave to show she was unaffected by his presence, she fell into step behind Zeke, following him through the crowd to an open set of double doors and a wooden patio surrounded by a low rail.

Several couples were already outside, cheerfully gyrating to the fast beat of the country tune. Mia and Zeke joined in. The music was definitely louder outside than in, and as the song ended, AJ asked her to dance.

It was a bit of a silly formality since people weren't really dancing in couples. It was more of a free-for-all, but she was game, and AJ seemed to be having a great time. After AJ, another guy asked her, calling out that his name was Hank.

Soon she was lost in a whirl of dances and a whirl of partners, until she was exhausted.

She turned Zeke down when he asked her again, giving him a pat on the shoulder as she apologized. Then she turned and all but ran into Silas who was standing in the double doorway.

"Oh, hey," she said, bringing herself to a screeching halt, telling herself to be cool and keep it together, and not, *not* think about the kiss.

He held up a glass of white wine. "Are you looking for this?"

"Is that mine?"

"It is."

She drew a bracing breath and accepted the glass. "Thanks."

He held a highball glass of something amber in his other hand. "Want to get out of the noise?"

"Sure." She was still playing it cool, plus her eardrums could use a rest.

He led her to the edge of the deck and opened a little gate at one side.

She followed him three steps down to the wooden sidewalk and down a ways where the wall of the restaurant blocked the noise. The Bear and Bar was painted white with green trim, two stories high. The sidewalk was worn beneath her feet, built up from the gravel street.

The sidewalk was dry, so she sat down and planted her low-heeled boots on the gravel. They were the boots she'd worn the day she met Silas in Fairbanks, and she couldn't help thinking so much had changed in such a short time.

He sat down beside her and took a sip of his drink. "I hear you started working at Galina."

Mia nodded at the safe topic. "I think it's going well."

"Oh?"

"Except for the mini loader." She took a drink. "That didn't go so well. But I found a manual, and I'm going to study up and have another go."

"There must be plenty of other things to do there besides drive a loader."

"Sure, there are. But I don't want to be defeated. I'm learning new things, taking new chances."

"So long as you're safe."

She coughed out a laugh at that. "I've never seen a place more obsessed with safety."

He fell silent and twisted his glass in his hands, staring down at it. "I hope you didn't misunderstand me the other day."

"Misunderstand what?" she asked, turning to take in his profile, tucking her hair behind one ear and pretending she didn't have any idea what he meant.

He gave a self-conscious smile. "When I backed off."

She gave a shrug. "It's fine."

"I was trying to be respectful."

"Of Brodie." She could understand that. Brodie was Silas's boss after all.

"No." Silas seemed surprised by her answer. "Of you. You're only in town for five minutes, and you've just lost someone."

"You mean Alastair."

"Yes, Alastair, your husband."

Mia thought about letting the subject drop, letting Silas feel noble and forget about the attraction she'd felt for him and the mind-blowing hormone rush she'd gotten from his kiss. It was the smart thing to do, the right thing to do.

Instead, she took a sip of her chardonnay. "I was eighteen when my parents died." Nobody but Marnie knew the real story, but Mia wanted to tell it now.

She focused on the detail of the gravel road in front of her. "I'd been under contract to Lafayette for a couple of years by then and my career was flourishing. Alastair worried about me being left alone and took me under his wing. It might have been part self-interest, but he helped me through the grief. He was already divorced by then. He was steady, stable, smart and funny, with extravagant plans and brilliant ideas. The younger guys all paled in comparison."

"You know you don't have to explain to me."

"I want you to have an accurate picture. I was more a protégé than a lover, more a companion than a wife, then more a caregiver in the end. It got even more complicated when—" A flash of movement in the intersection caught her eye.

It was a black shape moving. No, two black shapes. No, *three* black shapes lumbering across the street toward Blue Crescent. The biggest one put its nose in the air.

She grasped Silas's arm. Her voice came out hoarse. "Bears."

"Where?"

She pointed.

He turned his head to look, but his tone stayed astonishingly calm. "Good spotting."

Adrenaline rushed through her, and her grip tightened. "Shouldn't we do something?"

"Like what?"

"Go back inside?"

"Sure, if they come this way," he said. "But the music will likely keep them at a distance. And they look like they're heading out of town anyway."

"Shouldn't we warn people?"

"Mrs. France already did. Word's spreading. Everyone will be on alert."

"So, we're just going to sit here and watch?" Mia tried to take another swallow of her wine and realized she'd finished the glass. That might be why she wasn't flat-out panicking.

"They're an impressive animal," he said as the bears stopped under the sole streetlight. The sow turned her head toward them, sniffing the air again.

One of the cubs plopped down, and the other nuzzled its sibling's head.

"Impressive," she agreed. She inched a little closer to Silas, pressing her shoulder to his.

"Scared?" he asked.

"A little."

"We can go inside if you want."

"It's okay." The bears were a good hundred yards away. Mia calculated she could make it back into the Bear and Bar in about five seconds. It seemed unlikely the bears could run a hundred yards in under five seconds.

"Silas Burke, ace pilot," a voice boomed behind them.

The mama bear looked over her shoulder at the sound.

Silas hopped to his feet. "Hey, guys."

He offered his hand to Mia to help her up.

She took it, and he drew her to standing as the bears decided to lope away down Blue Crescent.

The two men were obviously brothers, tall and broad-shouldered, Nordic-looking, one with tight-clipped blond hair and the other with a shaggier cut.

"Mia, this is Tristan and Tobias. We call them T and T-two."

"Excuse me?" Mia asked.

"Tristan came to town first," Silas said, indicating the man with short hair. "Joined up with WSA a couple of years ago. T-two followed."

Tobias flashed a bright smile and offered his hand to Mia. "I like to point out I was only a month behind Tristan in moving to town."

"Were you second-born?" Mia asked curiously.

Tobias shook his head.

"So, the nickname is a demotion."

"That's why Tristan made sure it stuck."

Tristan grinned. "Busted."

"They're both excellent pilots," Silas said, and Mia realized he was still holding her hand. She could have let go, but she didn't.

"We've got nothing on this guy," Tobias said to Mia.

"It wasn't as dramatic as it sounds," Silas said, and Mia realized she hadn't even asked him about the rescue and his daredevil takeoff.

"You took off over a cliff," Tristen said, awe in his tone. "That's bad-ass."

Mia's hand contracted around Silas's. People hadn't talked like it was dangerous, but it must have been for Tristen to make such a big deal out of it.

"I was all but airborne before I flew over," Silas said. "Other guys have done it, and it works perfectly well."

"One for the record books," Tobias said.

"We just wanted to say congratulations," Tristen said. "Nice to meet you, Mia."

"Welcome to Paradise," Tobias said to her.

"Thanks." She smiled as both men turned to go. She liked them.

Brodie seemed to have put together a great team of pilots. It made her think he was a good judge of character.

She slipped her hand from Silas's, wondering what it was Brodie saw in her that he didn't admire.

THE SITUATION SILAS SPOTTED ON THE GALINA WAREhouse to the loading dock was pretty self-explanatory. A regretful-looking Mia was standing with Kenneth, AJ, Leon and Billy Leland, and they were all staring at a slashed and flattened left rear trailer tire. The mini loader was parked a few feet away.

"—and a repair might get me back to Fairbanks," Billy was saying to Kenneth. "But I'm going to have to replace it when I get there."

Raven and Brodie arrived then, surveying the damage.

Silas felt annoyed on Mia's behalf. Why would they have put her back on the mini loader? What were they thinking?

"It's my fault," Leon was quick to acknowledge to Raven, earning Silas's ire.

"I think I hit a button," Mia added. "Accidentally. Maybe with my thumb. I was turning, and—"

"We thought she had it," AJ said.

"I'll pay for the tire," Mia said.

"Galina will pay for the tire," Raven jumped in.

"As long as somebody pays," Billy said.

"Was anybody hurt?" Silas asked. They were missing the important question, as far as he was concerned. He looked Mia over from head to toe.

"She's not hurt," Leon said, and Silas shot him a stern frown. The man had no business putting her in that situation.

He tried to catch Mia's eye to give a little moral support, but she wasn't looking his way. She had to feel terrible. Nobody wanted to be the person who caused damage. He'd done it a time or two on an airplane, and it sucked.

Kenneth ended a phone call. "Caldwell can patch it," he said to everyone. "He's on his way over."

"Good," Raven said, moving closer to Mia and rubbing her arm in sympathy. But there was tension around her eyes.

Silas knew it wouldn't be the cost of the tire. That was negligible. Raven was probably worried about Mia's safety. Or maybe she was worried about disruptions in the busiest season of the year. She couldn't be happy that half the crew was standing out here doing nothing.

"Can we all get back to work now?" she asked, looking around the circle.

Everyone muttered agreement, and the group began to disperse.

"It was that little button," Mia said to Raven. "My turn was a bit jerky, but I was going really slow, and—"

"Don't worry about it," Raven said, but Silas could see Raven's strain even more clearly now.

He didn't like the way things were going. There was genuine danger to a rookie in a busy warehouse, and Raven didn't need any extra headaches. Since he'd prompted Mia to step up in the first place, it was partly his fault. He sifted things in his brain until he landed on a solution—temporary, but at least it was something.

"Hey, Brodie," he called out. "Got a minute?"

Brodie gave him a nod and Silas walked over. "She's making Raven nuts," Brodie confided in a lowered tone.

"I think I can get her out of the way for a while," Silas offered.

Brodie raised his eyebrows.

"I'm going on a run to Wildflower Lake in Papa-X-ray. I can take her along, give her a tour, keep her out of town for the rest of the day."

Brodie clapped Silas firmly on the shoulder. "Yes. Yes. Do it. You're the one guy I can trust to keep his mind on business and off the supermodel."

Nothing in the world would keep Silas's mind off Mia. But she wouldn't impact his performance as a pilot, and there was no way in hell he was going to tell Brodie about their kiss. So he simply nodded in agreement and strode back to Mia to close the deal.

"Hey, Mia," he opened. "Busy this afternoon?"

She seemed taken aback by the question.

"I'm doing a run up to the Wildflower Lake Lodge," he continued smoothly. "You should hop in the copilot's seat and take a tour."

Raven hit him with an instant look of gratitude, jumping in immediately, her tone openly enthusiastic. "That's a *great* idea. They've got a really nice setup out there, Mia. You'll love it."

"But—" Mia looked around, obviously not wanting to leave in the middle of her own mess.

He understood, even admired her hesitation. But she couldn't fix a flat tire, and right now she was causing more harm than good.

"My truck's right out there by the road," he said, pointing with a jab of his thumb.

Raven gave her cousin a swift one-armed hug. "You should go. It's a perfect day for a little sight-seeing."

"You're sure?" Mia asked.

"Absolutely. You need to have some fun while you're here. Go see a few things, kick back, pretend you're a tourist for the afternoon."

"Let's do it," Silas said. "It's a super-light load, and it's ready to go."

Mia hesitated a final second while Silas gave her an encouraging smile.

"Okay," she finally agreed.

Silas shared a parting look with Raven, and she mouthed a "Thank you" as he and Mia set off in the direction of his truck.

He played tour guide on the drive to the airport, talking up the state and describing some of the features he'd show her on the flight. Then after the safety briefing and takeoff, he took up the role again, naming the rivers and mountains along the way, swooping low on the peaks for a view of a mountain sheep herd, then down into the valley to see a moose in the shallows and a small pack of wolves running along a worn trail. As the airplane gained altitude again, Wildflower Lake Lodge came into view.

"Are those wolves dangerous?" Mia asked, craning to look back over her shoulder. "They seem awfully close to the lodge."

"They're thirty miles back and over a mountain pass. They won't bother anyone there."

"So long as you're sure about that." She peered out the side window then at multiple red roofs gleaming boldly in the sunlight against the emerald forest next to the crystal-blue lake.

"I'm sure."

"We're a long way from anything, aren't we?"

"Paradise is the closest town."

She went quiet as he circled toward the strip.

"You okay?" he finally asked.

"A little intimidated by all this wilderness," she said.

"Don't be. The lodge is a very well-run operation. You'll like Cornelia, and the clientele there are more your crowd than mine."

She turned to look at him. "My crowd?"

"Millionaire city dwellers. They come here to get away from it all." He adjusted the flaps and the engine speed as they cruised their way toward the dusty landing a mile out back of the lodge.

WITH THE AIRPLANE NOW SILENT ON THE NARROW AIR-strip, Alaska felt enormous around Mia. She and Silas walked toward a little white shed at the edge of a thick forest. He had a box under his arm containing a computer component for an emergency repair.

"Is someone coming to meet us?" She wasn't crazy about standing out here completely defenseless.

There were wolves and bears lurking out in the woods, and Raven had told her more people were killed by moose than any other animal in Alaska. Raven had also said moose could weigh up to fifteen-hundred pounds.

Mia had no desire to meet a fifteen-hundred-pound moose.

"There'll be an ATV for us in the shed," Silas said as they arrived at the little building.

It wasn't locked, and he pulled up on the wide overhead door. It clattered its way open until it rocked to rest ten feet in the air.

There were three ATVs parked inside. One had a little trailer attached. Another was larger, with side-by-side seating and would transport six people. The third was just like the one at Galina, only bright blue with a long black seat and front and back racks. Silas headed for the third one.

"Can I drive it?" she asked, thinking this could be a chance for some extra practice.

Silas seemed hesitant as he fastened the computer package to the rack with a couple of stretchy black cords. "You took out a truck tire this morning."

"That was with a loader. ATVs have logical steering and stuff." She checked out the handlebar controls and saw they looked exactly like Galina's.

"And stuff?"

"Throttle. Brakes. Starter." She pointed them all out to him. "I know what I'm doing."

"Kill switch," he said and pointed. "In case it all goes bad."

"Ha-ha." She frowned at him then looped her leg over the seat, wrapping her hands around the handlebars and getting settled. The key was already in the ignition, and the ATV was facing the open door.

"So, we're doing this," he said as he straddled the seat behind her.

She started up the engine. "We're doing this."

She revved it up and pulled straight out of the shed, breathing a small sigh of relief when they were clear.

"Hold up," Silas called out.

She stopped smoothly and felt proud of herself. "What?"

"I need to shut the door."

"Oh. Right." Of course. She waited as he dismounted,

mentally reviewing the driving controls while he pulled the door closed behind them.

He returned and hopped back on the ATV, looping one arm around her waist, surprising a little gasp out of her.

"Ready?" she asked to cover up her reaction.

"Ready," he rumbled behind her ear. "You can pick up the access road at the south end of the strip. But check for air traffic before you start. Always check for incoming planes. This might be a quiet strip, but it's still an active runway."

Mia looked up, all around the sky. It was blue and clear. "Nothing up there."

"Then off we go." He settled himself on the seat behind her, the inside of his knees cradling her thighs and his chest brushing against her back.

"Off we go," she muttered under her breath, her skin tingling with awareness every place he touched.

They left the smooth airstrip for a rougher, narrow road. Mia tried her best to steer around the worst of the ruts and potholes, but the ATV still bounced beneath them, pushing Silas against her, or her against Silas. It was hard to tell which.

Tall trees shaded them from above while squirrels darted across the trail out front and birds flitted from branch to branch. They came up on a porcupine gnawing on a stick of wood. It looked up at the sound then sauntered away into the underbrush.

The bush felt alive around them.

Then she misjudged a maneuver and they dropped into a particularly deep pothole, sending a vibration up her arm, causing her to turn the handle, squeeze the throttle and fly sharply back against Silas.

She let the throttle go, and they coasted to a stop.

"You're doing fine," he said, his voice calm and soothing. "You can't miss them all."

"I'm just taking a breather." She didn't want to admit she

was unnerved, even though a couple more feet to the right and they'd have hit a tree.

"You want me to take over?"

"No, I'm good." She pushed the throttle again. She was not going to give up that easily.

The road smoothed out beneath them as they cruised into the yard of the resort. They passed some utilitarian outbuildings as well as several pretty log villas set back in the woods before coming up on what was obviously the main lodge. The building was bigger than it had looked from the air, built of massive smooth logs that gleamed with clear varnish.

Several people were outside on its giant deck, some sitting at tables under umbrellas, presumably guests, while servers were moving around in crisp white shirts, patterned green vests, black slacks and black bowties. The tables sported white tablecloths. Propane heaters dotted the area. And the seating looked plush and comfortable.

All gazes were on Mia as she drove closer.

"Pull out of the way," Silas told her. "Down past the gazebo."

A fit-looking fifty-something woman with a tidy, dark-haired bun spotted them and started her way down the grand staircase that was centered on the front of the building and ran next to the deck.

Ignoring the curious stares and focusing on parking the ATV, Mia pulled into a clear spot and shut off the engine.

Silas climbed off from behind her. As cool air swirled against the back of her thin, yellow and gray T-shirt, she realized how much she'd liked having him pressed up against her back. She should have thought to enjoy it more during the drive instead of concentrating so hard on controlling the ATV.

"Silas!" the woman exclaimed. She was wearing crisp black slacks and a meticulously ironed, button-up long-sleeved mottled shirt that coordinated with the vests of the other staff members. "I didn't know it would be you." She pulled him into a hug, and Mia noted her manicure, precise makeup and her classy little jade and gold stud earrings.

"I hate to miss a chance to come see you," he said, rocking her in the hug.

Mia was suddenly conscious of her own appearance. Her makeup was minimal. She'd fallen into that habit while working at Galina, deciding it was silly to spend an hour on her face in the morning, only to sweat it off. She was wearing a pair of Raven's khaki green workpants, the ones with seven different pockets. And her boots were scuffed and worn, with a patch of steel shining through one of the toes.

When she'd dressed this morning, she hadn't expected to see anyone except the staff at Galina. At least her high ponytail had held. If her hair had been loose, it would have been a rat's nest by the end of the ATV ride.

A few seconds later, Silas drew back and turned to include Mia in the conversation. "Cornelia, this is Mia, Raven's cousin from Los Angeles."

Cornelia stepped forward, sharing a wide, welcoming smile. "Very nice to meet you, Mia."

Mia held up her gritty-feeling palms. "I don't think we should shake. I didn't expect to be coming anywhere like this. Oh, and it's nice to meet you too."

Cornelia laughed and held out her hand. "I'm not afraid of a little dirt."

They shook, and Mia felt a bit better.

"You'll stay for dinner," Cornelia said to Silas. She linked an arm with his and turned him toward the lodge.

"Love to," he said, surprising Mia.

Cornelia looked back and motioned Mia up to her other side.

Mia quickly hopped up to catch them, moving from the gravel road to a cobblestone pathway that led to the wide staircase.

"I want you to make yourself at home," Cornelia said to

Mia. Then she switched back to Silas, taking in his flight suit. "You got anything decent under there?"

"Afraid not."

"Then off to the gift shop for both of you," she said cheerfully.

As they passed by the deck lounge, Mia saw how nicely the guests were dressed. The fashions were country club casual, but she recognized some fine labels, including two women wearing something from the Lafayette summer collection, one in a paint-spattered, cowl-neck tunic and scarf, the other in a pair of dark denim patch-pocket skinny jeans. The jeans were one of Mia's favorite styles.

Before she could catalogue the rest of the crowd, Cornelia had whisked them through a set of big coastal cedar and glass doors and into a bright, beam-ceilinged lobby with a polished reception desk and a smiling young attendant. The brunette woman looked to be in her early twenties with dark eyes, thick lashes and amazing cheekbones.

"Hi, Silas." The younger woman grinned. It was clear from her tone she found Silas attractive, but when her attention turned to Mia there was no jealousy or resentment in her expression.

"Piper will help you with anything you need," Cornelia said. She gave Silas's arm a final pat and smiled at Mia before turning for a hallway that led off from the right-hand side of the lobby.

"She wants us to dress for dinner," Silas elaborated to Piper.

"Are you staying the night?" Piper asked.

Silas seemed to consider the possibility. "I hadn't thought of it."

"The south creek villa is vacant," she said.

He lifted his brow and turned to Mia. "We could stay if you want."

The suggestion took her by surprise. "What? Spend the night here?" There'd been no plans for them to stay. She hadn't brought anything with her for overnight, and Raven was expecting her back.

"You heard Piper," Silas said easily. "The south creek villa is vacant."

Mia gave him a look that said his proposal was ridiculous. He thought the two of them should share a cozy little villa for the night?

"It has three bedrooms," Silas said, as if he was reading her mind.

"Each bedroom is self-contained," Piper added and held out a key. "At least take a look through it."

"Wildflower Lake Lodge loves to bribe West Slope Aviation," Silas said.

"It's how we get such good service," Piper said without missing a beat.

"This is a twofer," Silas said.

"How so?"

"Mia is Raven's cousin from Los Angeles."

Piper beamed at that. "Raven's fantastic."

"I agree with that," Mia said.

Piper held the key out farther. "Okay, now for sure you have to stay."

Silas took it. "I'll give her the grand tour."

Chapter Nine

SILAS WASN'T SURPRISED THE MIA LOVED THE SOUTH creek villa. It was much more her style than Raven's cabin.

Dominated by a spectacular great room, the villa's living area featured a massive stone fireplace. It had high, peaked windows overlooking the ocean, and an open maple-wood staircase leading to the rail of a sleeping loft. The kitchen, dining room and a library nook were tucked under the loft, bracketed by two bedrooms with doors off opposite sides of the great room.

After a visit to the gift shop, Silas was dressed in charcoal slacks, a white dress shirt and a jade-green tie. He'd paired them with a black sports jacket borrowed from Cornelia. His boots looked out of place, but at least they were black.

Piper had eagerly offered her own shoe collection for Mia to peruse. Silas hadn't yet seen what they'd found in Piper's closet, but it seemed like the two had become best friends within about an hour.

He'd given up watching Mia try things on in the gift shop.

She and Piper were clearly determined to analyze every single dress on the racks. So, instead, he'd wandered into the cigar bar and shared a scotch with two bankers from Boston who seemed eager to hear about Alaska in the winter.

By the time he'd made it back to the villa, Mia was already in her room, changing. He'd heard the shower running and changed for dinner himself. Now he heard the hum of a blow dryer and guessed it would be a while before she emerged. But the mini bar was stocked, so he dug into bag of chocolate almonds, pairing them with a bottle of club soda as he read his way through a recent fishing magazine.

When Mia's bedroom door finally opened, he glanced up to see how the process had all turned out. He froze at the sight. He swallowed and all but dropped the magazine.

Looking uncertain, she took a couple of steps into the great room. "I'm not sure about the neckline," she said, looking down.

The neckline was slashed straight across her chest and blended into short, dropped sleeves that left her creamy shoulders bare. The dress was snug over her breasts and waist, with a full skirt, the hem shorter in the front than the back showing off her long slender legs. It was deep burgundy, but the color couldn't have mattered less. To call it sexy was the understatement of the decade.

A wide silver choker encircled her graceful neck, and silver earrings dangled below her upswept, wispy hair. Everything about the outfit framed her, decorated her, celebrated her.

"I'm better with a cowl-neck," she said, but he barely heard.

He saw it now—the goddess who had the world infatuated.

He'd play poker for her. He'd walk through fire for her. Hell, he'd take on a grizzly a wolf pack or every man from here to California for her.

"Silas?" Her voice sounded far away but it brought him back to reality. She was waiting for his reaction.

"You look . . ." He wasn't about to say what he really thought.

She didn't seem to notice that his words had trailed off. She held out a foot and wiggled it back and forth as she studied the shoes. They were silver, sparkling, strappy with open toes and a narrow band around her ankle.

He had to stop looking at them.

"Good thing there's a walkway to the dining room with these heels," she said.

He came to his feet, spilling the remainder of almonds on the floor.

She laughed at his clumsiness. "Thank goodness somebody else finally messed something up."

He reached to the floor and crumpled the bag, scooping up the nuts then crossing to drop the whole mess in the kitchen wastebasket. He was less embarrassed about being clumsy than he was grateful to have something to distract himself from her.

He washed his hands in the sink and dried them on a towel. "Ready?" he asked, going back to the living area, determinedly fixing his focus on the front door.

She joined him there. "So, what do you think?"

"Of?"

"The dress." She sounded half annoyed, half perplexed.

"It's great," he said honestly, sneaking a sideways peek. "Terrific."

"Not too bad for a rush job, huh?" She adjusted the drop sleeves below her shoulders. "I'm lucky the shoes fit. My feet are big."

He tried to stop himself, but his gaze dropped to the uber-sexy shoes. Her feet couldn't have looked more perfect to him.

"The price of being tall," she said.

"You're not that tall." Even with her high shoes, he had several inches on her.

"I guess not for a model. But taller than average, bigger feet than average. It can be a problem."

As they stepped onto the porch, he reflexively offered his arm. The wood walkway was slightly uneven, and he'd feel like an absolute jerk if she stumbled.

She took it, and he couldn't stop the swell of pride that came up in his chest. Sure, he knew this wasn't a real date. But the people in the restaurant wouldn't know that. They'd get a load of Mia and think Silas was the luckiest man alive.

It was a three-minute winding walk along the trees and above the shoreline to the main lodge. There, they had to navigate the staircase, and Mia kept her hand on his arm as Piper showed them into the dining room.

Silas liked the way people looked at them—well, looked at Mia to be more precise, with admiration and longing.

Piper sat them at a table along the back wall. Their window looked out over the bay, the rocky shore and the forest in the background.

"This is nice," Mia said as she sat gracefully down on the padded, wraparound chair.

The white tablecloth, flickering candle, bone china and blown crystal were Wildflower's standard. The atmosphere was hushed beneath the beamed ceilings.

"They know how to do it right," Silas said with a smile. It wasn't his usual speed, but he could go high-end for a dinner occasionally, especially one with Mia.

"You come here often?" she asked, then smiled self-consciously at the phrasing.

"I don't often sit in the dining room or stay overnight, for that matter. There's lounge down the hall that's more casual, and the deck is nice when there's a breeze. It's too still out there tonight. The mosquitoes would be terrible."

"I'm all for staying out of the bugs," she said.

A waiter arrived offering drinks, but they decided on a bottle of wine instead. Silas asked Mia if she wanted to choose, and she stepped right up.

"Alastair was big into wine," Mia said as the waiter departed with their order. "We have a very large wine cellar back home."

"So, you're an expert?"

She gave a shake of her head and a pretty smile. "He was the expert. I mostly went along for the ride. But I recognize the label of the one I ordered. It's good."

"I wasn't worried."

"You drink much wine?"

"Beer in the fridge at the hanger. After flights only, of course. The guys like to hang out, compare notes, tell stories."

"Exciting stories?"

"Sometimes exciting, more often funny. Clients can be whacky, passengers amusing."

"Like the women who don't know enough to use the restroom before they get on the plane."

"I kept that to myself." Although he suspected the drillers would have shared their amusement at the mine.

"I didn't," Mia said.

Silas raised his brow, surprised she would tell a story where she looked foolish.

"I told Raven."

"Ah." That made sense.

"I also told her—" Mia pressed her lips together as if she was trying to keep herself from speaking up.

"What?" he prompted.

"Nothing."

"Oh no. That's not going to happen."

"It's embarrassing."

"I just spilled almonds all over the floor because—"

She pressed her lips tight together in a squelched grin. And he eyes lit up in a way that said she had him. "Because . . . ?"

"You first."

"No, you."

He leaned forward. "You."

"Okay, fine. I thought you were a serial killer."

He was baffled by the answer. "Because I sent you back to the restroom?"

She shook her head, her cheeks turning pink as squelched another smile. "When you took me to Raven's cabin. That's why I tried to drive away."

Silas's chest hitched in regret. "You were frightened?"

"Not for long."

He reached out to cover her hand, wondering what he could have done to make her feel that way. "I'm sorry I scared you."

"Don't be. It's funny now. It was funny right after too. At least to Raven."

"Got a minute, Silas?" Cornelia's adult son, Danny, appeared at their table.

Silas sent him a back-off look. The very last thing he wanted to do was leave Mia.

"We've got some cargo for your return trip," Danny said.

"Go ahead," Mia said to Silas, retrieving her hand. She didn't look at all annoyed by the interruption.

He was annoyed. Any moment away from Mia was a moment wasted.

It was on the tip of his tongue to refuse, but then he reminded himself that he was here on WSA business, and he'd given a pledge to Brodie to stay professional. It also occurred to him that Mia was probably used to business dinners. Given Alastair's position, interruptions must have happened to her all the time in LA.

"I'll just be a minute," he said as he rose, determined to make that true.

As he crossed with Danny to the end of the bar, he caught the many surreptitious looks being sent Mia's way, from women as well as men.

She was a knockout; there was no getting around that. He figured it was a classic case of all men wanting to date her and all women wanting to be her. Silas knew her life as an extraordinarily beautiful woman wasn't a living fantasy, but he could see it might look that way from the outside.

He took a barstool next to Danny. "What's up?"

"One of the XM6700 generators just quit on us. We can likely get warranty, but we have to ship it out. Can you fit it?"

Silas whistled under his breath, picturing the industrial generators that powered the lodge. "That'll be a squeeze into the beaver."

Danny nodded to that. "The rep said we can pull off the air intake and muffler ourselves without compromising the warranty coverage, if that'll help."

Silas cast his gaze over to Mia and saw she was in conversation with Piper, and the two were laughing. "Did you take some measurements?"

"We can."

"I'll need the weight too." Silas was most worried about the size. The beaver could handle a significant amount of weight, even considering the short Wildflower airstrip. But fitting the core of the industrial generator through the cargo door was going to be a challenge.

A woman's voice came up shrill behind them. "—and is *not* the level of responsiveness I expect from an establishment of this caliber."

Silas turned his head to see the older woman was talking to Cornelia—well, *at* Cornelia, while Cornelia looked to be sympathizing with the difficult customer. He wondered if maybe they'd changed chefs.

"We'll measure it up," Danny said.

"Send them to my phone," he said. "I'll let you know if it's going to work."

"Thanks, man."

"Did you by any chance change chefs?"

Danny looked puzzled. "No."

"Good. I was going to recommend the cherry duck breast." Silas was looking forward to Mia experiencing the fine cuisine at Wildflower Lake Lodge. He didn't care where else in the world she'd eaten, he'd bet she'd be impressed with this.

Danny grinned. "Still our feature dish."

"Great." Silas got to his feet.

But when he looked to their table, Mia was gone. He did a sweep of the dining room, wondering if she'd struck up a conversation with another diner. She hadn't.

He wandered back to the table, sat down and waited a minute, getting an odd feeling.

He scanned for Cornelia then, hoping she might know where Mia had gone, but Cornelia wasn't in the dining room either. He went to check in the lobby.

A woman emerged from the ladies' room, and Silas asked her if Mia was inside. But the woman said it was empty.

Baffled, Silas went outside to the porch. It was deserted, only a single propane torch flickering, warming the closest table. He could see partway up the boardwalk leading to their villa, but he didn't see Mia walking along it. He really hoped she hadn't headed back to the villa on her own. He was still worried about her tripping in her high shoes.

He took another pass through the restaurant before deciding to try the villa. Maybe she'd felt ill. He hoped not. He didn't want her evening to be ruined.

He picked up his pace along the walkway, turning into their villa and crossing the front porch to open the door.

"Mia?" He stopped short two steps inside.

She was there, on the sofa, shoes kicked off, her face flushed and her eyes shiny with tears.

He went to her, crouching down, disturbed by the dampness on her pink cheeks. "What happened?"

She shook her head, wiping her cheeks with the heel of her hand. "Nothing."

"Are you hurt?" He looked her up and down. "Sick?"

She shook her head again.

"Why did you leave? What's wrong?"

She gave herself a shake and sat up straighter. "I'm fine."

"You're not fine." That was completely obvious.

Her eyes lost focus for a second. "I will *not* let it get to me."

He couldn't tell if she was talking to him or to herself. "Let what get to you?"

"Nothing." She propped her hands on her knees, and he realized how close he was to touching her bare legs.

He eased back a little and ordered himself not to check them out. He didn't want to pry, so he didn't ask any more questions.

"You must be hungry," she finally said.

Yes, he was hungry. He stood and held his hand out to her, glad she seemed calmer now. "Let's go eat."

But Mia shook her head. "I can't."

"Sure, you can. It'll help you'll feel better."

She lifted her lashes to look at him. "Cornelia had to ask me to leave."

Silas didn't react because her words were preposterous.

Mia continued. "She was super nice about it, and I could tell she didn't want to do it. But—"

"Whoa, *what*?"

"Someone complained. I understand. They were a paying customer, and they're entitled to their opinion." Mia reached for a tissue, dabbed her nose, then crumpled it into her hand. "But I wasn't ready for it—mentally, I mean. I thought I could get away from it all here, you know?" Those vulnerable blue eyes of hers seemed to pierce his soul.

"It was that woman, the one at the other table," he guessed, things starting to come together in his head. He sat down on the sofa next to Mia. "That old bat recognized you."

"She'd heard all the stories, so she thought she knew me. Clearly she believed the part about me dancing on Alastair's grave."

"That's ridiculous."

"She was wearing a Lafayette dress, of all things. You probably didn't notice. It was from last year's spring collection. I sourced that print myself from Italy. She was wearing an out-of-date style and looking down her nose at me while she did."

"We're going back," he said with conviction. There was no way he was letting some judgmental old woman run Mia out of the restaurant.

"I'm fine."

"You're not fine. You need to eat."

Mia's expression turned stubborn while someone interrupted with a knock at the door.

"We're going back," Silas repeated.

"I don't want to."

He wasn't sure how to argue that, and the knock sounded again. He got up to answer.

It was a waiter from the dining room with a room service cart full of dishes.

"Cornelia asked me to convey her most sincere apologies," the man said, gesturing to a vase of flowers in the middle of covered table settings. "There's a card for the lady. She thought you'd enjoy the cherry duck breast, but if you'd prefer something else, the chef will prepare it right away."

It took Silas a moment to react. It was polite of Cornelia to apologize. And, yes, the duck was fine. But it couldn't simply end there. Mia had been bullied and insulted, and he wasn't about to stand for that.

"The duck sounds perfect," Mia said, appearing at Silas's side. "Please thank Cornelia for me."

"No," Silas barked out.

The waiter looked confused. "You'd prefer something else?"

"What we'd prefer—"

Mia touched his arm, effectively shutting him up. "This is all fine," she said.

The waiter gave her a smile. "Cornelia included another bottle of the wine you ordered. There's a corkscrew in your kitchen utensils, but I can open the bottle if you'd prefer."

"We don't have to eat here," Silas said to Mia.

"Here is better." She looked directly at him. "I'd rather it was here."

He realized then that she'd probably be uncomfortable going back, especially if the judgmental customer was still there. Who knew how many others in the restaurant recognized Mia?

"I'll open the bottle myself," he said to the waiter.

The waiter gave a nod of acknowledgment. "The chef included a baked brie appetizer, the melon prosciutto salad, and a selection of French pastries. Coffee is in the carafe, with brandy on the shelf below. Shall I set it up for you?" He looked past them to the dining area.

"We've got it," Silas said. He reached into his pocket for a bill and handed it to the man.

The waiter accepted the tip and wheeled the tray inside the doorway. "Please call down if you need anything else." With a final smile to Mia, the waiter withdrew.

Silas stared at the meal for a minute, not sure if Mia would rather talk it out some more or just move on.

"It smells really delicious," she said, and he decided to follow her lead.

MIA DIDN'T LIKE TO FIXATE ON HER TRIALS AND TRIBU-lations. They were what they were, and she was mostly a lucky person.

But Silas kept probing, and for the first time in forever she actually wanted to expand on her problems. It might have been the wine, or it might have been the brandy, or it might have been something about Silas himself. It was hard to know for sure.

"Gold-diggers are a dime a dozen," he was saying. "I mean, that's not a perfect metaphor . . . but you know what I mean."

From across the villa's round dining table, she couldn't

help but smile as he fumbled his way through consoling her. She rephrased for him. "You're asking why that woman resented me in particular."

"In a nutshell, yes. It's not a crime to marry for money. Not that I'm saying you married for money. I don't think that at all."

Mia chose a mini cream strawberry tart from the oblong silver plate that was set beside the wildflower bouquet. The meal had helped soothe her emotions.

"I'd guess it's because I've been more thoroughly vilified than your average gold-digger," she answered.

"Vilified how?"

"They've called me everything from trophy wife to jezebel and a murderer."

"*Murderer?*"

She responded in a mocking tone. "You don't think a fifty-year-old man spontaneously died on his own, do you?"

"You said he had a heart condition."

"A likely story." She took a bite of the tart. It was as delicious as everything else had been. The pastry was flaky and the vanilla cream sweet and smooth.

Silas considered for a moment. "Wouldn't there be records?"

She set the rest of the tart on her side plate. "I'm not about to release Alastair's medical records."

"I meant police records. If there was a murder investigation, there'd have to be a police record."

"Unless I was clever enough to get away scot-free."

"With murder? That's a stretch."

"You'd be amazed how many people believe I did. You'd be even more amazed by how many threaten revenge."

His gaze narrowed on that. "Revenge?"

"Some want me impoverished. Some want me jailed." She crumbled an edge of the pastry with her index finger. "Some want me killed. And some have suggested very colorful ways they would do it themselves." She caught Silas's expression and immediately regretted her words. She hadn't intended to be so graphic.

"That's why you're in Alaska." His tone had hardened. "You had death threats."

She was in the thick of it now and decided there was no point in holding back. "It was either hire round-the-clock security or get out of town. And there were these protesters at the end of our driveway. A tenacious group of about twenty of them with signs and cameras; reporters too." She shuddered, remembering. "You'd think people would have lives."

Silas reached across the table to hold her hand again. Crumbs clung to her fingertip, but he didn't seem to notice. Then, without letting go, he rose and moved around to her.

It was just a touch, she told herself, no more than a handshake, really. Yes, he was searching her eyes. But that was only a look.

"I can't believe they'd be so . . ." His tone was somber now, preoccupied. "What is *wrong* with people?"

"I've never figured it out." Her voice was huskier than she intended, more intimate as desire sizzled to life within her.

"They should be tracked down and arrested."

"That's not how the internet works."

Their gazes locked, his sky-blue eyes simmering with compassion.

She'd expected sharing a villa with Silas to be tough. The minute they'd agreed to stay, she'd known she'd have to fight her attraction to him. But she'd steeled herself against raw desire. She hadn't thought to mount a defense against his kindness. And that mistake let him slip right through.

"I thought you were delicate," he said in his deep, husky voice, drawing her to her feet so they were facing each other. He gazed a moment longer then brushed his thumb across her cheek. "Weak and pampered." He gave a ghost of a laugh. "But I was wrong about that. You're much tougher than you look."

Mia didn't feel tough. She felt soft as the pastry cream, her knees weak with longing to lean into his strength.

He read her mind and drew her close. One arm around her waist, the other enfolding her shoulders, a hug that was gentle, like he didn't want to break her. Their hearts beat together while he pressed her chest, hips and thighs to his own.

Their heat triggered her desire. She tilted her chin, looking for the kiss she knew was coming. It had to be coming.

And there it was, gentle, sweet and searching. His lips parted against hers, they firmed, delving deeper, drawing a moan from far within her.

In slow motions, she wound her arms around his neck, swept up once again by the power of their passion. It invaded her, engulfed her, demanded to be recognized and answered.

"You are *so* beautiful," he whispered, stroking her cheek. "Exquisite." He kissed her hair, the shell of her ear, the curve of her neck, sending shockwaves of pleasure skittering over her skin.

"Silas." She sighed. She couldn't be more specific than his name, his wonderful name, his amazing lips, his talented hands.

He touched his forehead to hers, his breathing deep. "I can't keep fighting this."

She didn't want him to fight. She didn't want him to stop. She wanted to keep going and going and going.

"Please don't fight." She took the initiative and kissed his lips. Then she molded her curves to his planes and angles, giving herself up to the moment.

He lifted her into his arms, carrying her to the bedroom he'd taken, the one with the bay window facing the thick forest that filtered the evening light, two armchairs bracketing the fireplace, and a plump, pillow-covered king-sized bed.

He set her bare feet on a plush rug.

"I do love this dress," he said, kissing her bare shoulder around the drop sleeve.

"This tie's okay," she responded with an impish smile as she tugged the knot free. Then she dropped the tie to the floor.

"Your hair . . ." he said, reaching behind her head and feeling the messy upsweep.

"Don't like it?" she asked.

"Better down."

She reached back to help him with the fastener, pulling it free, letting her hair fall around her shoulders.

"Sexy," he said, rubbing the ends between his fingertips.

"Not crazy about this shirt," she said, popping the top two buttons.

"The shirt's definitely got to go," he agreed, leaning into her neck and distracting her with another kiss.

She tipped her head to give him better access, letting the eroticism of his hot lips shimmer through her body.

He took over unbuttoning his shirt then stripped it off and tossed it to the floor.

"I've changed my mind about the dress," he said.

She gave a mock pout. "You don't like it?"

His kissed her lips, hard and long and deep. "It'll look better on the floor." He found the back zipper and dispatched the dress, leaving her standing in a pair of white lace panties.

"Those," he said, gazing down and pulling back a little. "Those, I love."

"They're from the Polar Collection."

"You're making that up."

She grinned. "I swear it's true."

"Well, welcome to the north." He smoothed his hands slowly over the silk and lace.

His smile disappeared, and he eased her close, skin to skin, chest to chest, desire and passion and pleasure arcing between them. He cradled her face and kissed her mouth again and again and again, all playfulness gone.

He kicked off his pants, and they fell to the bed, drawing together in slow motion, their limbs entwined as they shared kiss for kiss, caress for caress, cocooned in pleasure and surrounded by the wilds of the forest.

Afterward, Mia was floating. She knew she was still locked to the planet, but her spirit was on a different plane of existence. Sex had never been like that for her. It had never taken her to the clouds and back again. She'd never felt like another person, her life divided between before and after—before Silas and after Silas.

She was afraid to look at him now, afraid he didn't feel the same way, even more afraid he could tell how massively he'd rocked her world and would be amused by that.

They were both lying on their backs on the impossibly soft mattress, fan blades moving in slow motion above them beneath the red-hued cedar beams of the ceiling.

After a few minutes, he turned toward her and propped himself on his elbow. He brushed her hair from her cheek, his voice was low husky. "You good?"

She nodded, even though good didn't begin to describe it.

"You are—"

She waited, a coil of tension forming in the pit of her stomach.

"Amazing," he said. "But I think I said that already. I was trying for something more profound."

She chuckled a little, mostly at herself.

"What?" he asked.

"That's not what I thought you were going to say."

He inched a bit closer. "What did you think I was going to say?"

She shrugged.

"Come on, give."

She turned to face him, mirroring his posture, her head

on her own elbow. "I thought you were going to laugh at me."

He looked genuinely shocked. "Why would I do that?"

"I was . . . a little . . ." She flopped onto her back again to avoid looking at him. "Enthusiastic."

He shifted closer. After a minute, he walked his fingertips from her navel to a spot between her breasts. "You thought I'd find enthusiasm funny?"

She nodded.

He laid his hand flat, his forearm resting along the indent of her stomach. "Mia, that's the most ridiculous thing I've ever heard."

She checked out his expression. "You're laughing at me now."

"I'm smiling at you. You're delightful."

She felt an urge to bop him with a pillow, but they'd all been scattered to the floor.

"Thanks a lot," she deadpanned instead.

"I'm laughing at the idea that lovemaking enthusiasm could be a negative."

"I didn't say it was negative."

"Then what did you say?"

"I thought . . . I was afraid, that I was having more fun than you were."

He did laugh then, and he pulled her close, rolling over so that she was on top of him. "That," he growled in her ear, "is absolutely impossible. There are no levels of fun above what just happened to me."

"Seriously?"

"Yes."

"You're not just being nice?"

"I am not just being nice. Want me to prove it to you?"

She lifted her head to look at him. "How would you do that? You got a fun-o-meter strapped to your wrist or something?"

"No, but that's a very interesting idea. Look into my eyes."

She did. He had beautiful eyes. They were dusky blue in the filtered daylight, wide-set, and surrounded by thick lashes.

"What do you see?" he asked softly.

It was her turn to smooth his short hair from his forehead. "You have beautiful eyes."

"Satisfaction," he said. "You see satisfaction."

He was right. She did. She laid her head back down on his chest.

"How long will you stay?" he asked.

"Here? In bed?" She wanted to stay. She wanted to curl up in his arms and stay here all night long.

"In Alaska," he said.

"Oh. That." She squelched her disappointment, slipping off to the side. She would have moved away, but he held her fast against him. "The preliminary court date is three weeks from now."

"You have to go back for it?"

"I do. Marnie, my lawyer, is optimistic that Henry and Hannah will lose."

"It sounds like they will."

"So, you read that part of the story?" Mia hadn't gone into details about the court case itself.

"Some of the guys were talking the other day over dinner. They said—" He kissed the top of her shoulder. "It doesn't matter."

She could fill in the blanks. "Oh, how I *love* being a scandal."

He gently nudged her. "You're a whole lot more than a scandal."

"Well, I'm not sure how to take that." But she was joking and relaxed against him, crooking her knee onto his thigh.

He smoothed her hair. "What will you do once you win?"

"Figure out who's loyal." She hated the thought of undertaking a witch-hunt, but she couldn't run a company where people were secretly plotting against her.

"What about the threats?"

She was hoping they'd calm down once the estate was settled. According to Marnie, a few signs were pointing that way already, and surely having the law on her side would count for something.

"I hope the trolls will find something else to do. I might have to sell the house, move to a secret location."

"Would you do that?"

"Yes." She might think about it, anyway. "I don't need a house that big. I could buy a condo near the office; less upkeep. And I don't need a staff of seven."

"You have a staff of *seven*?"

"The house is big, and the gardens take a lot of maintenance. And there's the cooking and the cleaning, especially when we entertained. I shared Alastair's event manager."

"That must have been a sacrifice."

She pressed her elbow into his ribs. "Don't mock me."

"You have a staff of seven, how can I not mock you?"

"They're not *here*."

"Well, thank goodness for that." He nuzzled her neck. "I don't need help."

She smiled warmly at his joke.

"There's a very roomy shower in the ensuite," he said, his kisses meandering.

"Yeah?" The idea sounded interesting.

"Multiple nozzles, scented soaps, loads of hot water. You in?"

She was definitely in.

Chapter Ten

SILAS ACCEPTED THE MORNING DELIVERY OF COFFEE and waffles with all the trimmings. It was the least Cornelia could do. He tipped the waiter, closed the door behind the man and went first for the coffee urn and a white stoneware mug.

He intended to bring Mia a cup in bed, but she appeared in the doorway wrapped in a white fluffy robe. He knew it was her job to look gorgeous, but she still took his breath away. Her blond hair was prettily mussed, framing her face. Her cheeks were pink, lips red, eyes sparkling blue. You could snap a photo right here and now and put her straight on a magazine cover.

"Coffee?" he asked.

"Yum." She gave him a wide smile as she came forward. "Anything in it?"

"Just coffee." Their fingertips touched as he handed her the mug.

"Morning," she said, taking her time in drawing back her hands.

"Morning," he answered. He couldn't resist her mouth, so he gave her a gentle kiss.

"Thank you," she whispered.

"For a kiss?" He'd be happy to give her another. If they'd had time, he'd have been happy to give her a whole lot more than that.

"For the best night of my life."

Silas was stunned by the compliment. Last night had been spectacular for him too, off the charts amazing, and . . . well . . . yeah, he supposed it was probably the best night of his life.

"You are one sexy man," she said, running her fingertips down his chest. "Buff, fit, handsome and . . . well, you know."

"Say it anyway," he teased, liking her mood a whole lot.

"You first."

"Sure. You rocked my world."

"I, Captain Burke, was also rocked." She took a sip of her coffee. "And now I'm hungry."

"We have waffles," he said, moving to pour himself a cup of the fragrant coffee.

"Excellent. I didn't do many carbs before I came to Alaska. But now I'm a fan."

"Waffles have carbs?"

She curled into one of the dining chairs. "Waffles are *pure* carbs."

"Then I like carbs too." He set his coffee down and moved a big covered platter from the trolley to the center of the dining table.

Mia lifted off the cover to reveal half a dozen waffles, bacon, sausages and scrambled eggs while Silas set out their plates and napkin-wrapped utensils.

Orange juice, berries and whipped cream completed the meal.

She speared a waffle and spooned on some berries. "I seem to burn off more calories here."

He took two waffles and added a side of bacon. "I wouldn't know. I've never counted a calorie."

"I hate you, you know that."

He grinned at her. "I could tell."

"I guess when you've lived the outdoorsy lifestyle in Alaska and Colorado, it's easier to stay active."

"Are you saying I'm lucky to get my exercise naturally?" He went for both the berries and the whipped cream.

"I am. I wish there were more naturally fun ways to stay fit, instead of schlepping myself to the gym all the time. How long have you lived in Alaska?"

"Five years."

"Where'd you grow up?"

"At the base of Mount Mettridge, outside Salsa Springs."

"I've never heard of it."

"Neither has anyone else. I met Brodie when we both took a mountain flying course in the Rockies. At the end of it, he offered me a job."

"Did you hesitate, moving so far away?"

"I liked bush flying." Silas took a sip of his coffee. "As you can imagine, there wasn't much to leave behind in Salsa Springs."

"Your family?"

"Mom left when I was a kid. Dad, well, he eventually stopped caring about much beyond his next bottle of whiskey. He died a couple of years ago."

There was understanding in Mia's eyes. "Where was your mom?"

"I don't know. Salsa Springs wasn't her idea of a happening place, and my dad wasn't enough to keep her there."

The understanding in Mia's eyes turned to compassion.

But Silas wasn't looking for pity. "Don't do that."

"Do what? That's a sad story."

He wasn't going to let his history change the mood. "It was a long time ago, and it has a happy ending."

"It does?"

"Yes. Last night was the best night of my life."

She smiled at that, and his chest tightened in reaction.

"Plus these," she said, taking a slow bite of her waffle.

"You don't want to try the bacon?" He made a show of taking a bite of it and looking rapturously satisfied.

"You're the devil."

"Are there carbs in bacon too?"

"Not really; a little in the sugar cure, but they're mostly fat."

"Fat is bad?" He took another unrepentant bite.

"Not as bad as carbs." With a glint in her eyes she took a bite of waffle and berries.

"You have a perfect body, you know that?" he asked. If anyone could afford an extra carb or two it was Mia.

"I work pretty hard at it."

He was afraid he'd insulted her. "I didn't mean you—"

"It's part of the job." She didn't look offended. "But I'm thinking of giving it up."

"Giving up the perfect body?" It was totally up to her, of course.

"Modeling."

"Really?" He thought she was at the top of her game. It seemed like a very strange time to give up her career.

"Lafayette is going to take more of my attention now. Alastair did a lot of the work. I mean, I was there with him all the time. He took my advice and he shared all the details, even if people in the office didn't understand that. I've been a senior adviser in the company for years now, along with being a model."

"You've had enough of modeling?" Silas guessed it wasn't for everyone.

It looked glamorous. But being a jumbo-jet pilot on international flights looked glamorous too. That had never been his dream. He liked the challenges of small planes, VFR rules, short strips and rugged terrain.

"Management is a lot of planning and strategizing,

what's the mood of the consumer, the next color palette, which shoe designer will be impactful, how you build a relationship with retailers."

"I can see you'd be good at those things."

Her princess vibe had to be an asset in that world. Glitz and glamour were where she belonged, high-end hotels and star-studded parties.

It made him sad for a second, but then he stopped himself. Mia might be fleeting in his life, but that didn't mean he shouldn't enjoy this moment.

She ate only half her waffle, making him think she wasn't as cavalier about carbs as she pretended. He ate two, plus bacon and everything else. Then, much as he'd have loved to stay longer, they packed up their new clothes.

Danny and a couple of other staffers helped him fit the torn-down generator into the plane, and Cornelia offered a final apology to Mia.

Mia was gracious about it, but Silas could tell she didn't want to belabor the point. So, they headed to the plane and took off for the real world.

He waited until they were thirty minutes out, dreading the conversation he knew they had to have. But as they crossed the Yukon River and picked up the Chain Lakes, he knew he couldn't put it off any longer.

"Mia?" he said over the intercom.

"Something down there?" She perked up and looked out the windows, scanning the ground.

"When we get back," he continued.

She turned to look at him.

"What do you want to do?" He paused, switching his fingertip back and forth between them. "With this? With us?"

"What do you want to do?" she asked him back.

He didn't have an answer. What he wanted to do and what he ought to do were two completely different things.

"I get it," she said.

He didn't know how she could get it when he didn't get it himself. He opened his mouth to say so.

"What happened at Wildflower Lake stays at Wildflower Lake," she finished.

He took in the play of emotions on her face, trying to gauge her thoughts. "Is that what you want?"

"How about last night keeps the *best night* title, and we leave it at that?"

"That's not an answer, it's a question."

"I don't see that we have another choice. I'm leaving, and your boss is still . . . your boss."

"I can handle Brodie."

"I don't want to leave a mess behind."

There'd be a problem before she left too. Paradise was an incredibly small town.

"I don't want people gossiping about you," he said, reluctantly coming around to her way of thinking. "You've had enough of that in your life lately."

"And since this has to be temporary anyway . . ." She picked up the thread.

"It is a given," he said, hating that they were making the responsible choice. He'd love to take advantage of every single second of her visit, but that wouldn't be fair to her.

"It's fine." She waved a dismissive hand. "It's honestly fine, Silas. I mean, you and me?" This time it was her who pointed back and forth between them. "Are you kidding? No way it would have worked."

He tried to ignore the stab in his chest at her words. "You have your life," he said, instead of begging her to spend more time with him.

"And you have yours." She gave a nod that said the matter was settled.

Paradise came into view on the horizon, and he knew it had to stay settled. One night with Mia was all he was ever going to get. One single night.

* * *

ONLY TWO DAYS LATER AND MIA MISSED SILAS. SHE FELT like a chocoholic craving that next Belgian truffle or praline ganache. But it wasn't illicit cacao and sugar she wanted, it was Silas—the taste of his skin, the scent of his hair and the feel of his hands on her body.

She couldn't talk to Raven about Silas, but she desperately needed some girlfriend chat. Over the lunch break at Galina, she took her salad and iced tea onto Bear and Bar's deck for some privacy and a data connection.

She dialed Marnie.

"Hey, you," came Marnie's cheerful voice. It sounded like she was out on a busy street. The background traffic noise made Mia think of home.

"Hi, yourself," Mia said back with a smile.

"What's going on up there in the wild north?"

"Is this a bad time?"

"It's fine. I'm on my way back to the office. I couldn't move up the court date, so we're still nearly three weeks out on the docket."

Mia couldn't help but be disappointed. Not that she'd held out any real hope that things would suddenly turn her way.

"Everything okay with you?" Marnie asked.

"Mostly. Well, not exactly."

"Nobody found you up there, did they?" The background turned quieter, and Mia pictured Marnie entering the lobby of her office building.

"No, nothing like that." The woman at Wildflower Lake wasn't a stalker. And she wouldn't know Mia was in Paradise.

"Please don't tell me you wandered onto social media. You know you have to stay off there. It's only going to upset you, and those yahoos don't make any difference at all to your case."

"I haven't been on social media." That was one good thing about Paradise, it made staying unplugged a whole lot easier.

"Good. One little bright spot here, the crowd is much smaller at the end of your driveway. Just the diehards left since you're not giving them any fodder."

"That's good." Mia was encouraged to hear that, hopeful that she wouldn't be dodging stalkers for the rest of her life.

"So, what's the deal? What's going on up there?"

"There's a guy."

Marnie's voice perked up. "*Hello?* You buried the lede? What guy? Who is he? Tell me everything."

"He's a pilot," Mia said, feeling a huge sense of relief to finally share with someone. "He's sexy—like, off the charts sexy. Capable, I guess, is the best word for him. He's smart, kind of funny, nicer than he seems at first."

"And . . ." Marnie prompted.

"And, we went to this resort a couple of days ago, a five-star place out in the middle of nowhere, Alaska. You'd love it."

"Paint me a picture."

"A fancy villa overlooking this stunning green-blue lake, with huge-view windows, high ceilings, a stone fireplace, three bedrooms."

"Please tell me you only used one."

Mia grinned. "We only used one. Oversized tiled steam shower too."

"Okay, I'm getting hot just hearing about this."

"Thing is," Mia said, faltering.

"There's a thing? What thing? I don't want there to be a thing. He's not married, is he?"

"*No*, he's not married. He's got this boss who isn't my biggest fan, and I don't want to leave problems behind for him when I go. Plus, there's the whole temporary thing. I'm coming home soon, and he's staying here. And we couldn't be more opposite."

"But no harm, no foul in a great one-night stand," Marnie said.

"That's the problem."

"You feel guilty? There's nothing at all to feel guilty about."

"I really want to do it again."

Marnie took a beat to respond. "Oh. So, does hunky pilot man know this?"

"No, he doesn't. I haven't even seen him since—" Mia stopped speaking as Silas appeared in the doorway. She went hot with mortification thinking he might have overheard. "Gotta go."

"Why? What happened? I want to keep talking about your sex life."

"Can't."

"You sound funny. Wait, is it him?"

"Yes, gotta go."

"Call me later."

"Will do." Mia ended the call.

Silas crossed the deck, pulling back the chair across from Mia and sitting down at the table.

"Hi," she said, surprised he'd walk right up like this as if they were just two ordinary people at the Bear and Bar who hadn't slept together and agreed to leave it at that.

"I've been thinking," he said, drumming his fingertips rhythmically on the tabletop.

A surge of hope rose within her.

Did he feel like she did—that this was torture, that anything was better than suffering with this intense desire and longing? Was he going to ask her on a date or go on a tryst or to have a secret fling?

Her throat went dry and she swallowed. "About?"

"You working at Galina."

It took her a second to process his words, and she had to swiftly backpedal on her longing.

"It's dangerous," he said, his expression frank and no-nonsense.

Disappointment rose inside her, regret sharpening her tone. "I've taken all the safety training."

"A training course doesn't replace real experience."

"I've memorized the manuals."

"That's only the theoretical stuff, not the real-world stuff. And they don't need you; not really."

Well, there was a hit to her ego.

He wasn't here to pledge his undying passion. He was here to let her know she was useless.

"Who told you they didn't need me?"

"No one. This is me, Mia. I'm worried about you."

"Oh no, you don't." She leaned back and wagged her finger at him. "One night with me doesn't give you the right to—"

"This isn't about that."

"Then what's it about?"

"What's best for you."

To think, only moments ago she had been pining away for him, singing his praises to Marnie, wishing they could be together again.

She rose. "You don't get a say in what's best for me."

"Mia."

"No," she said sharply, turning to walk away.

"What if there was something else?" Silas called after her.

She kept walking.

"Mia, hear me out."

She slowed, curious despite herself.

"I came up with an idea," he said.

She stopped.

In a few strides he was next to her. "You don't have brute strength."

She cocked her head to look up at him. "This is your idea of a pep talk."

"But you're smart and articulate. You're a quick thinker. You're analytical."

She was clearly desperate for a compliment because she wanted to hear more.

"I was thinking I could teach you to operate the WSA radio," he said. "It's an important skill, a useful skill. WSA doesn't have a backup since Carol Sandor left town, and I'm sure you could learn quickly."

Mia had met Shannon Menzies a few times. She was clearly smart and held in high esteem by the pilots.

"What's Brodie going to think of that?" Mia couldn't help but ask.

"Don't worry about Brodie."

"But—"

"It's not like you'll be live on the air while you're learning. We can go in when the office is empty. You can practice and surprise everyone with your proficiency."

"Another secret?" she asked, not sure how she felt about that.

His expression changed, and his look jump-started her pulse. It was clear they were both remembering their first big secret.

"Yes," Silas said on a husky note. "Another secret."

MIA WATCHED RAVEN'S EXPRESSION CLOSELY AS SHE announced she was quitting Galina. Her cousin tried to cover it up, but she couldn't completely hide her relief, and Mia's heart sank a little bit further. Obviously, Silas had done her a favor by nudging her to leave.

She told herself to blow past the humbling experience. It wasn't like she didn't have a plan. She was going to take Silas up on his offer. She was going to dust herself off and learn something that was useful to Paradise. Quitting Galina didn't mean she would sit around while everyone else kept working.

She swallowed her pride and pretended she believed Raven when she said they'd miss her. But she couldn't quite let it go. "I'm really sorry I didn't do better."

"You did fine," Raven said heartily.

"You're relieved."

"I'm not relieved—"

Mia frowned. "I can see it in your eyes."

Raven perched herself on the arm of Mia's chair. "Okay, but you *were* dropped into a pretty well-oiled machine."

"And I screwed everything up." Mia should have known better than to barge her way in like that. She'd been so determined to learn her way around.

"The job is harder when you're a woman," Raven said.

"Because men are stronger and more coordinated?"

"No." Raven paused. "Well, muscles are good in the warehouse, since it is heavy-labor work. But I meant the guys aren't used to having pretty women around the place."

"They have you."

Raven rolled her eyes. "Glamorous, I am not. I'm also not so new and unique, so fresh and exciting."

Mia made a point of looking down at the work pants she still wore. "I was definitely not going for fresh and exciting."

"We don't get many women through town."

"Maybe you need to get more. Maybe then I wouldn't have caused such a stir and messed up your job."

"You didn't mess up my job."

Mia lifted her brow.

"Okay, maybe a little bit. But you tried. That shows character. And you've really stepped up around here. You baked chicken last night."

"I dehydrated chicken last night."

"My oven can be tricky. We'll grill the leftovers into sandwiches tonight, spice it up, add some mayo for moistness. It'll taste better."

"Alastair had a chef," Mia said to explain her lack of

cooking skills. "He was a French chef. I'm pretty sure Henri earned Michelin stars from somewhere."

"Hey, if I had a chef, I wouldn't be cooking my own chicken either."

Mia cracked a grin, glancing pointedly around the least-likely house to employ a chef.

"You should have brought him with you."

"He quit."

"The chef quit? Why?"

Mia followed Raven into the kitchen, feeling slightly better as the conversation ranged on. "There was no prestige in working for me. I wasn't going to host the same kinds of parties as Alastair. I don't have his social and business circle, at least not yet."

"Plus, you're not there."

"His assistant stayed on. I liked him better anyway."

"Any news on the court case?"

"Nothing good. I talked to Marnie earlier. The court date hasn't changed. But she did say the crowd is gone from my driveway. And last week she said negative social media is down twenty-five percent."

"At least that's encouraging."

Mia had been hoping for more than just encouraging.

Raven opened a bag of bread onto the wooden cutting board and located her slicing knife. "Has Marnie tried talking directly to Henry and Hannah? Maybe they'd negotiate out of court."

"Those two?" Mia almost laughed. "Not a chance. They want it all for themselves."

"Any chance they'll win?"

"Marnie says unlikely, but it's hard to predict the judge. It's crystal-clear from the wording of Alastair's will that he wanted me to have the business. The only thing they have to stand on is whether I manipulated or coerced him."

"Because you're young and pretty."

"Therefore, I can't be trusted."

Raven sliced her way through the bread while Mia went to the fridge for the chicken. "It's because you stand out."

"Stand out?" Mia opened the container.

"Your situation is unusual, not unheard-of, but still unusual: a stunning classy woman marrying an older, rather plain-looking man. You stand out, and it draws attention to itself. People start speculating. Same basic problem in the Galina warehouse."

"You lost me." Mia tore the chicken into strips.

Raven smeared some mayonnaise on the bread slices. "If there were a dozen drop-dead glamorous women working in the warehouse, the guys wouldn't look twice."

Washing her hands, Mia laughed, feeling lighter still. "Why didn't *I* think of that?"

"You should have brought along some friends." Raven licked a dollop of mayo from her fingertip.

"I should have. And then there wouldn't have been a poker game. And Brodie wouldn't resent me so much."

"Brodie doesn't resent you."

"Please."

"He . . . okay, he *notices* you because you stand out."

"I'm cutting my hair," Mia threatened, twisting her thick blond locks into her fist on top of her head.

"Won't work. It's your cheekbones and your eyes and your nose and chin."

"I can't exactly get rid of those. At least not without surgery."

"No respectable plastic surgeon anywhere is going to mess with your face."

"I wish there were a dozen city women here with me, so I wasn't so alone in this."

Raven struck up the stove beneath a heavy cast-iron frying pan and tossed some butter in to melt. "So does Zeke. He's bummed that he struck out with you."

Mia layered the chicken onto the bread slices, while Raven sliced up a tomato. "Zeke's a nice guy."

"He asked me if I could ship in another woman for him."

Mia paused as she added cheese to the sandwiches. "*Ship* a woman *in*? Do people think you shipped me in?"

"My own fault, really. I brag that I can find anything and ship it to anywhere. It's mostly true. I'm pretty good at my job, but that was a joke."

"Well, that doesn't sound half creepy."

"He didn't mean it to be creepy. He really is a nice guy."

Raven set the sandwiches into the sizzling butter, layered on the tomato and topped each with another slice of bread.

"Celeste would like him," Mia said, knowing it was true and thinking it would be a very fun match-up.

"Who's Celeste?"

"One of our designers. She's smart, pretty, laid-back and understated. She'd like Zeke's gentlemanly streak."

"He grew up in South Carolina. He gets it from there."

Sandwich sizzling in the background, the two women stared at each other. Mia wondered if Raven was thinking the same thing as her.

"You're going to burn them," Mia interjected.

Raven turned and quickly flipped the sandwiches over, adjusting the propane flame down.

Flipper in hand, she pivoted again. "We couldn't, could we?"

"No." Mia knew it was just a pipedream. "Celeste would have the same problem I do, standing out and causing a fuss. Brodie would really hate me then."

"Stop saying that. Brodie doesn't hate you."

Mia set two clean plates out on the counter. "Not yet."

"So what we need is . . ." Raven jiggled the flipper, clearly thinking through the problem.

"More women," Mia finished for her.

Raven pointed at her with the flipper. "That's *it*."

"I know plenty of women," Mia said, seriously warming to the idea. "And it's tough down there, and all the guys are arrogant assholes with zero chivalry. California women would love these guys—Zeke, Xavier, AJ, Dean. Cobra is too intimidating."

Raven laughed. "That's true."

"But Tristin and Tobias have that strapping Scandinavian look." Mia catalogued a few of the eligible men. "They could model outerwear if they wanted. All of these guys could, actually."

"And Silas?" Raven asked.

"Sure, yeah, and Silas." Mia couldn't not keep him to herself but then keep him to herself. That wasn't fair.

"How would we get them to come?" Raven asked.

"The bigger question is, how do we get them to stay away?" Mia could see it all now. "If I put out the offer of sexy, hardworking, principled Alaskan men, we'll have a stampede. The sandwiches."

Raven spun back and turned off the heat, transferring the grilled sandwiches from the pan to plates. "We curate them," she said.

"Sounding creepy again," Mia warned.

"I mean like a matchmaking service, only in bulk."

Mia grinned as they made their way to the kitchen table. "You do have a way with words."

"Pour us some wine," Raven said as she sat down. "Let's come up with a plan."

"You mean dispense us some wine from the little plastic spigot?" Mia altered her course to head back to the kitchen.

Raven responded to the teasing. "You *are* a princess."

Chapter Eleven

MIA FELT LIKE A COVERT OPERATIVE. THE FACT SHE'D slept with Silas was classified. That she was learning the WSA radio was classified. And the matchmaking project for the guys in Paradise was classified too—at least for now.

With the Bear and Bar her go-to place for internet access, she'd been reading up on Alaskan and international radio standards, including the phonetic alphabet. She was also working her way through the introductory pages of popular dating sites, seeing what kind of questions they asked and wondering how she and Raven could customize something for themselves.

Breena came by to refill Mia's soda.

Mia set down her phone then straightened and stretched out her shoulders. She was drinking diet cola to keep a little caffeine going through her system.

"Not too busy this morning," she said to Breena, glancing around the quiet café, hoping that meant Breena would have time to sit down for a chat.

"You look so focused," Breena said. "Your court case?"

"Tangentially related," Mia said feeling honor-bound to keep the matchmaking project under wraps.

"New husband?" Breena asked.

The question startled Mia.

"I couldn't help recognizing the Date-Deal logo," Breena explained. "It's pretty distinctive. Sorry, bad joke."

"Definitely not a new husband." It occurred to Mia that Breena could be a potential source of intelligence. "Do you use the site?"

Breena shook her head. "Guys are a dime a dozen down in Anchorage. But I have a few friends who've used dating sites."

Mia was interested. "What do they think of them?"

Breena slid into the chair next to Mia, obviously warming to the topic. "They tell me most of the guys on them are a bust."

"How so?"

"They're all looking for the perfect woman while bringing practically nothing to the table." Breena counted off on her fingers. "Low fitness, disorganized, little education, no money. There've been a few success stories among friends of friends, but it seems like you have to kiss a lot of frogs to get there."

Mia smiled at the joke.

"We made our own algorithm in one of my systems design courses. The good guys come in and go out really fast, while the losers' profiles hang around forever, so eventually your pool gets skewed. It's not your best bet for dating."

"I've never dated," Mia said. "I mean, I sort of dated Alastair. He took me to industry functions and events before we were married, but we were colleagues and friends long before any romance."

"So, not exactly the voice of experience," Breena joked.

"Alas, not."

Breena nodded to the phone screen. "So, if you're not dating, what are you doing?"

Mia looked from side to side, reconfirming they were beyond hearing distance of the few other diners.

Breena mimicked her action, chuckling softly and appreciatively as she leaned closer. "What's going on?"

"Can I bring you in on something?" Mia felt she could trust Breena, and was confident Raven would see the wisdom in asking for Breena's help since her computer skills would be such an asset.

"Well, yeah." Breena scooting closer still. "I'm dying to know now."

"Raven and I had an idea. You know, all this nonsense with the poker game."

"That was all in fun."

"I thought so at the time. But Brodie didn't like it."

Breena shrugged. "Brodie is Brodie. He can be a stick in the mud."

"But it's a real problem."

"Brodie?"

"No, women in Paradise. Well, the lack of women in Paradise compared to the number of men."

"That's sure true. A lot of the new guys hit on me. Not the ones who remember me from when I was fifteen; they stay away. But the last couple of summers, I've had a lot of guys come up to me."

"Do you date anyone in town?"

She shook her head. "I'd have to convince them to move to a big city with me when I leave. I think it makes more sense to find a guy once I get settled."

Mia knew would take a special kind of woman to settle down in rural Alaska. Which was why their curating process would be so important.

"We think we can find some," Mia said. "I know lots of women in California who have trouble meeting nice guys. The guys at WSA and Galina are a cut above."

"I'd agree with you there."

"Our plan—Raven's and mine—is to create an app to

identify California women who want a change of pace, a life outside the city, who might like it here. We'll bring them up for an event of some kind so they can mix and mingle."

"You're not going to match them one-on-one?"

"If the guys here wanted to use a dating site, they'd have already done it. We might not even tell them we're match-making, just have a bunch of friends swing by to visit."

"It would give the place more balance," Breena said. "More women's influence equals more progressive think-ing, in my opinion. I'll get my laptop. We're going to need data and an algorithm."

"You don't mind helping?"

"Are you kidding? Paradise is a sausage fest. This sounds like female empowerment to me." Breena pushed back her chair and came to her feet. "I am in!"

"In on what?" Zeke had arrived and wandered over without Mia noticing.

"Mia needs some help," Breena said. "Computer stuff for California."

Mia couldn't help but be impressed with both Breena's quick thinking and her apparent gift for misdirection. "How are you, Zeke?"

His attention switched to Mia. "Good. I'm good. How are things with you?"

"Do you want to sit down?" If they needed data on Par-adise men, Zeke seemed like as good a source as any.

He seemed surprised but pleased by her offer. He smiled as he sat across from her.

"Between flights?" she asked him, knowing that as a ground-crew rampie he had to be at the airport to load and unload airplanes.

"T-Two just left for a crew drop-off in the PC-12. Every-one's out now until about nine tonight."

"You work very odd hours," Mia said, thinking that was

common among the men in Paradise. She made a mental note of that.

"When the planes fly, they fly," Zeke said. "Twenty-four-seven. Well, not in the dark, unless it's an emergency and they're going into Fairbanks—lighted runway."

Breena returned with her laptop.

"Can I get a burger?" Zeke asked.

Her expression faltered as she sat down. "Sure." She set the laptop on the table and stood again. "I'll let the kitchen know you want one."

"Thanks," he said.

"What about in the winter?" Mia asked Zeke.

"Winters are quiet," Zeke said, helping himself to a couple of packs of sugar and turning over a coffee cup.

Catching his actions, Breena frowned, then deviated to the coffee station to pick up a pot.

Mia's sympathies were with her. It was hard to take a few minutes off in the restaurant.

"Does everyone leave town when it gets cold?" Mia asked Zeke.

"Some do," Zeke said. "You don't need all the pilots year-round, or the ground crew either. The guys take sun vacations or go home to their families."

"Families? You mean they have wives and children out of town?"

Breena filled Zeke's coffee cup.

"No. Not so much, at least the younger ones," he said, giving it a stir. "Parents or brothers and sisters for some. I spend January with my folks in Arizona. Dean's family has a ranch in Texas. T and T-Two usually take a fishing vacation off the California coast. Brodie stays, of course, and Silas stays. There's some work all year long, but the hours are really short in mid-winter."

Breena sat back down and opened her laptop. "Less than four hours of daylight on December twenty-first," she said.

"That short?" Mia said, slightly aghast.

"Dawn and dusk make it seem longer, and that's the very shortest day."

"That would take some getting used to," Mia said.

Breena began typing. "Important point, I'd say."

"Do you have hobbies?" Mia asked Zeke. "I mean, what do the guys like to do in Paradise when they're not working in the winter?"

"Snowmobiling is big," Zeke said. "The virgin powder up in the peaks is awesome. We play high mark on the hill. It's a betting game but for something silly, like a pizza or a beer. Brodie doesn't let us gamble for money. You have to be careful of avalanches if conditions are bad."

"Sounds exciting," Mia said, wondering which of her friends in California would be up for a mountain snowmobile adventure, in the dark, in the cold. Some of them surfed, so action sports weren't completely out of the question.

Breena typed some more.

"You staying that long?" Zeke asked, a hopeful note in his voice.

"Not me," Mia said, sneaking a glance at Breena to gauge how they were doing.

Breena's return look said she thought Mia's question were on the right track.

THE FIRST THING SILAS NOTICED IN THE BEAR AND BAR was Mia sitting across a table from Zeke. She looked stylish and tidy in snug jeans and a clingy bright blue top with flat lace at the neckline and cuffs. The two were engrossed in conversation, heads leaned forward, a laptop open beside Mia.

Silas wished he wasn't jealous of the way she was looking at Zeke, like she was absorbing every phrase he uttered. He told himself they were only talking. And even if it they weren't, Mia was perfectly entitled to hang out with any man she wanted.

They'd both agreed to leave their night of passion in the past, so he had no call on her now.

He shook off the aggravated feeling and headed their way. If Zeke could chat her up in the middle of the Bear and Bar, then Silas could do the same.

She glanced up as he arrived, looking surprised to see him and not in a good way. Guilt crossed her face, and she quickly shut the laptop, making Silas wonder if something more than talking was going on.

Still, he pulled up the chair next to Zeke, crowding him just a little bit. "How're you guys doing?" he asked, voice clipped as he sorted out his frame of mind.

Zeke seemed a little intimidated, but Silas didn't much care about that.

"Uh, fine," Zeke said. "I was just telling Mia about the trip to Eagle last winter."

"I've never been snowmobiling," Mia put in smoothly, clearly having recovered from whatever unease Silas had caused by breaking up the party.

"Can't go in July," Silas said, feeling twitchy, drumming his fingertips on the table.

Breena arrived. "Can I get you something, Silas?"

"Just a cola," he said. Then moderated his voice. "Please."

"Sure," she said. "Nothing to eat?"

He wasn't staying that long. "I'm good."

"Coming up," she said and left for the bar.

"You went on the trip?" Mia asked him.

"He's our first-aider," Zeke said. "When Brodie can't come. They both have their industrial tickets, and we need at least one person with that level just in case."

"Someone gets hurt," Mia responded to Zeke.

"Mostly someone gets stuck," Silas said.

"Guilty," Zeke said, his laugh a little nervous. "Silas

pulled me out of a ravine that time. His Hilltop Force, that's his snowmobile, has a lot of torque."

Silas might like the idea of impressing Mia, but he wasn't a braggart. "Everyone gets in trouble at some point. That's why you go as a group."

"Like when you're avoiding grizzly bears," Mia said with a smile.

Zeke laughed at that, a little too loudly since he wasn't in on the original joke.

"Groups are safer," Silas said, squelching his impatience with Zeke.

Sure, Silas would be happier if Mia wasn't having a cozy lunch with Zeke while doing some apparently secret thing on her laptop. But she hadn't expressed any romantic interest in him. And none of this was Zeke's fault.

"Are you ready to go, then?" Silas asked her, hoping she'd catch his meaning. "To the place."

Her change in expression signaled her comprehension along with a hint of amusement. "To see the thing? With the guy?"

"I'm the guy," he said. Then he caught Zeke's confusion and curiosity.

Mia seemed to see it too, and she sobered. "If now's a good time."

Breena dropped off Silas's cola and carried on to another table.

"Now's a good time." He swallowed half of the icy drink.

Mia focused her smile on Zeke. "Thanks for talking with me," she said. "I enjoyed your stories."

Zeke's cheeks flushed and his eyes went bright with infatuation. "Anytime."

With another quick drink, Silas pushed back his chair and dropped some money on the table.

Mia gathered up a brown leather tote bag. "See you soon," she said to Zeke.

Zeke stood with her. "Yeah. Absolutely."

"You shouldn't do that to him," Silas muttered to Mia as they walked away.

"Be polite?"

"Be so friendly."

"I'm not going to be rude. He was really nice."

Silas glanced back. "Hang on. You forgot your laptop."

"It's not mine. It's Breena's." Then she caught Breena's eye and gave her a cheery wave good-bye.

Breena grinned back and made a phone signal beside her ear.

"What's going on with you two?" Silas looked back and forth between the two women. He was clearly missing something here.

"Nothing."

"She's giving you hand signals."

Mia reached for the door handle, but Silas was quicker, opening it for them both.

"Yes," she said in a faux conspiratorial tone. "The super-secret CIA call-me-later signal. Nobody knows that one."

"Why's she calling you?"

"Did it occur to you that we could be friends?"

He pointed the way down the wooden sidewalk to his truck. "Okay, but what was with the laptop?"

"Is that a bear?"

"Don't change the—" But then Silas's saw it, and adrenaline kick-started his system. It was a bear that Mia spotted. And it was way too close for comfort.

He grabbed Mia around the waist and hustled her the few feet to his truck, hauling open the driver's door and unceremoniously shoving her inside. As he followed, he quickly scanned the street to make sure no one else was nearby.

He slammed the door shut as the sow and her two cubs sauntered past in the middle of the road, ignoring everything around them. He dialed the Bear and Bar, getting

Badger on the line. "The grizzly's right outside. Don't let anyone leave."

"Will do," Badger said. Then his voice went louder as he called to the room. "Bear's outside right now. Everybody stay put." He came back to Silas. "I can let Troy know."

"Thanks," Silas said.

Troy Corbett was the chief of police, the only paid police officer in Paradise. If the bears grew much bolder, they might have to consider calling in federal wildlife officers to trap them for relocation.

Silas hoped the animals would move off on their own. Relocation was stressful for them, and they often came back anyway, sometimes covering hundreds of miles to return to their own territory. For now, he twisted his neck to watch out the back window as the trio picked up their pace. They crossed Blue Crescent at a trot and loped off into the bush. By the time Troy arrived, there'd likely be no sign of them.

Mia was watching out the back window as well. "I almost forgot about them."

"There are always a few around, but these ones might turn into a problem."

She turned and settled into her seat, looking impressively calm and composed given their brief scare. "I'm guessing we're going to the WSA office?"

"There'll be a lull in traffic for the next few hours. Shannon will head home and come back later."

"Thanks for doing this," she said.

His chest grew warm. Clearly, he was a sucker for her gratitude. "Have you been studying?"

"Alpha, Bravo, Charlie, Delta, Echo." She recited the opening of the phonetic alphabet.

He smiled and nodded his approval as he started the truck. "Q?"

"Quebec."

"T"

"Tango."

He backed onto the street and turned north. "H?"

"Hotel."

"Z?"

"Zulu."

"You memorized the whole thing."

"I did."

"That was fast." He was impressed.

"Plus, I've downloaded the meteorology documents."

"I'll show you the aviation weather screen. We can't give official briefings, but it helps to be able to interpret what's coming."

He wanted to ask her about Zeke and Breena and the laptop again, but he didn't want to break the mood. And they were none of his business anyway. So, he focused on the drive, grateful for clear weather and calm winds, hoping they'd hold for a few days to come.

As Silas had hoped, the only trucks in the parking lot belonged to the pilots who were out flying and Cobra who would be working in the hangar. The office would be deserted now, and he could give Mia an initial tour of the radio room.

He parked close to the front door and they headed inside, straight to the radio room in the back. It was small and cramped with overloaded shelving along two of the walls. A wheeled chair sat at a small desk with two side tables, each at an angle to form a console.

"Have a seat." Silas pulled out the chair and got out of her way.

"Cozy," she said as she sat down.

"True. But it does stay warm in here through the winter." He rested his hands on the back of the chair and leaned down. "Radio is in the middle. This is the microphone; push to talk. You can set the radio frequency to anything with the dial. For example, Fairbanks approach and departure is 118.3. But you'll only need to use 120.1. That's WSA's private frequency. All the pilots will be on it."

As he rattled off the information, he could smell her shampoo. It was incredibly distracting. The scent took him back to their night together, and he had to fight the urge to close his hands over her shoulders. The lace on her shirt was sexy where it decorated her chest. It wasn't at all revealing, but he could imagine cleavage . . . and a whole lot more.

"What information do they need from me?" she asked, interrupting his fantasy.

"Let's start with the tracking screen." He pointed to the biggest computer screen on the left-hand table. "You can monitor the whole fleet from here, everyone who's out with their locator on. Each of those little plane shapes has a corresponding alphanumeric locator. It's their registration and call sign. For private company calls on the radio, you can abbreviate it, but it shows in full on the tracking screen."

"So, there's a plane here now?" She pointed to Viking Mine.

"Yes. That's T and T-Two in one of the otters. These dots and the line show their path while they were flying out. When they come back, you can watch where they are along the way."

"So, if anything bad happens?" She turned, and they were face to face. "Like when Hailey crashed."

"Landed," he corrected.

"Landed. This is how you knew where she was?"

"That's right. Shannon had her on the screen and talked to her on the radio until we lost the signal behind the mountains. It gave us as much information as possible to find her."

Concern crossed through Mia's eyes, making her looked sexier still. "That must have been scary for her, for all of you."

"It was." Silas hoped it was a long time before they had an incident like that again.

The emotion he felt that night came back for a moment, then it somehow blended with his attraction to Mia. An urgency surged inside him, a swell of desire had him wanting to hold her all over again, kiss her and—

"I can see where you'd have to keep your cool," she said.

He sure wasn't keeping his cool right now. His hands moved to her shoulders, feeling the heat of her skin through the thin fabric.

She closed her eyes, her head canting ever so slightly to one side.

Danger flashed in his mind, but the image of Mia was clearer: her eyes, her neck, her lips.

The outer door banged shut.

"Silas?" Cobra called.

Mia's eyes popped open in alarm.

"You here?" Cobra asked.

Silas let go of Mia's shoulders and moved swiftly through to the lunchroom. "Here in back."

Luckily, she didn't follow. Silas didn't know how he would have explained her if she had. He didn't want to advertise the fact that he was showing her the radio, but he didn't want Cobra to get the wrong idea about the two of them—or what was the right idea, if Silas was being honest with himself.

"Glad somebody's here," Cobra said. "Can you give me a hand with a cowling? I can't keep it in place without someone to balance the other end."

"Sure," Silas said, since there was nothing else he could say. He abandoned Mia and followed Cobra into the hangar.

AFTER SILAS LEFT, MIA HAD FOUND AN INSTRUCTION booklet for the MX-2000 radio and read it through. She was afraid to touch the tracking station, but the aviation weather application on the opposite table seemed to be running on a standard computer. So she entered the make and model of the tracking station and found a wealth of information from online sources.

The printer was easy to find, and by the time Silas came back, she had a stack of papers stuffed in her tote bag and a thousand questions for him.

"Sorry I had to leave." He seemed to expect her to be annoyed.

She wasn't annoyed. She was jazzed. "So, the signals use twenty-four satellites?"

"The . . . what?" He looked confused.

"I've been reading up on the GPS system." She patted her tote bag. "There's lots more to study, but I was wondering if you ever used the three-dimensional view. I couldn't think of a practical application in this case, but it would be exciting if you did."

"Mia?" Silas glanced around the room, suddenly looking wary. "What have you been doing?"

"I didn't touch anything." She held up her palms to show her innocence. "I wouldn't touch anything. Well, the printer, but that wasn't going to screw up any of WSA systems. So, you can tell lat and long, altitude, speed and direction all at the same time?"

"Yes."

"Wow."

"We should probably get going."

"Sure. Yeah." Shannon would probably be back soon since she clearly had important work to do here. Mia had read a paper list on the desktop. It showed the planned departure and arrival times for the aircraft that were out in the field. Some would be flying in soon.

She stood up and hiked her bag over her shoulder. "Can you pick up other air traffic?" she asked as they walked through the break room. "It was clear to me that you were set up to see all the WSA flights, but there seemed to be a process for interfacing with general aviation traffic. In bigger centers, it would just clutter up your screen. But up here, I have to think there's not too many people flying by."

"Commercial jetliners over the polar route," Silas said, giving her an odd look. He opened the front door and looked around the parking lot before walking outside.

"I guess there would be some of that." She hadn't thought of the polar route. "But they'd be at a way higher altitude."

"They would. Exactly how much did you read while I was gone?"

"The radio manual. I found it in on the shelf." That was another thing that she'd found interesting. Talking and listening were straightforward, but she had no idea what kinds of information Shannon would share with the pilots or what they shared with her.

"The whole thing?" he asked.

"You were gone for an entire hour."

"Did you miss me?" His cajoling tone and the twinkle in his eye made her smile.

"I didn't have time to miss you."

"Ouch." He nudged her with his shoulder, pressing against her.

Her mood shifted, her tone going soft and intimate, unable to pretend. "I didn't think I was allowed to miss you."

He paused at the door to the parking lot, turning to face her.

She looked at him, desire blooming anew inside her chest. She'd missed him every minute since Wildflower Lake. She'd been holding down her emotions these past days through sheer force of will.

"Tell me you felt it too." His tone was husky.

She tried to stall, tried to pretend it wasn't happening. "Felt what?"

He touched the bottom of her chin, his eyes softening. "You know what."

"Do you want me to say I'm attracted to you? Do I really have to say that after everything we did?" If she could have what she wanted, they'd be together. But reality was still reality.

She didn't want to sneak around on Raven or compromise Silas's relationship with Brodie.

"Nothing's changed," she forced herself to say.

He slowly dropped his hand to his side. "And here we are."

"Here we are."

They gazed at each other for another drawn-out moment.

He wrapped his hand around the back of his neck. "This is tougher than I expected."

It was tougher than Mia had expected too.

BREENA SHOWED UP AT RAVEN'S THAT EVENING, EX-cited to talk about the Paradise matchmaking project.

"It's too hot to make a big dinner," Raven said as Mia set three wineglasses out on the counter. "Let's do some loaded nachos."

The wine box was all but empty, giving Mia an excuse to open one of the more expensive bottles she'd picked up at the Co-op Grocery. She happily pulled a couple of her purchases out of a lower cupboard.

"Are we going with the good stuff?" Breena asked, coming over to take a look at the labels.

"Best I could find," Mia said. One was from a vineyard she recognized, although the bottle wasn't one of their premium labels. With the other, she'd based her decision on region, vintage and price, hoping for the best.

"She's a culinary princess," Raven said good-naturedly as she dumped a layer of tortilla chips onto a pan.

"I love drinking wine with culinary princesses," Breena said. "In fact, I prefer it. What can I do?" she asked Raven.

"Grate the cheese. It's in the bin in the fridge door."

Mia twisted the corkscrew. At home, the chef had usually opened the wine. Alastair did it on occasion if it was just the two of them. Mia had tried on her own a few times and broken the corks, but she was mastering new things every day here in Alaska.

She twisted the corkscrew in, and the cork popped out cleanly.

"Grater?" Breena asked.

"Bottom cupboard beside the oven," Raven answered as she pulled peppers and onions from the crisper drawer.

"This has nice legs," Mia said, swirling the first glass of wine before inhaling the aroma.

"Speaking of legs, we can't focus on supermodels," Breena said. "Most women with your . . . uh, *refined* lifestyle aren't going to like Alaska very much."

"My friends aren't supermodels," Mia said. "Okay, some of them are supermodels. But the models are only the public face of a fashion enterprise. Ninety percent of the people are behind the scenes, and they're mostly the ones I'm friends with. They're quite down-to-earth." She took a sip of the Cabernet Sauvignon and was impressed. "Nice. Smooth tannins, robust and fruit forward. Plum, I'd say and cherry, a hint of licorice, low on pepper. This should be good with the nachos."

Breena laughed at the grandiose description. "So, down-to-earth like you are?"

Raven laughed too. "Let's hope they're not all wine snobs."

"Damn. I still come off as snooty, don't I? I've been trying to work on that." The wine description had been out of long habit with Alastair.

"You're getting better," Raven said. "Maybe don't describe bottles of wine anymore."

"I can do that. And I can chop something, maybe the peppers." Mia stepped up to pitch in.

"I've only got one cutting board," Raven said.

"We're only teasing you," Breena said. "And you're doing great with the wine. Pouring it would be a good next step. I'm thirsty."

"On it," Mia said.

"I don't want you to change too much," Raven said as she chopped her way through the vegetables.

"We like you the way you are," Breena said with a teasing grin. "You know, mini loader–driving mishaps aside."

"I wish I had more useful skills." Mia sighed as she poured.

"I'm sure you have loads of talents."

"They don't appreciate her at Lafayette Fashion, and she's practically been running the place," Raven said with a wave of her chopping knife.

"I wouldn't go that far." Mia didn't want to take anything away from Alastair. He'd worked hard right up to the end. Then again, she could be fair to herself too.

She set a glass of wine in front of Raven and one in front of Breena. "I happen to have a good eye for predicting color palettes. You have to look nearly two years ahead to order the fabric, so if you guess wrong, you're in big, expensive trouble. It's super competitive, so the weaves and weights, color and patterns are closely guarded secrets. I talk to sources all over the world."

"You said you travel a lot?" Breena asked.

Mia nodded. "Less so as Alastair's health went downhill, but I've been to six out of seven continents."

"I've only left Alaska six times," Breena said as she finished grating a block of cheddar.

"Can you do some of the Havarti?" Raven asked Breena. "I never thought about it, but I haven't left Alaska in years. I haven't even left Paradise in months. But I might be going to Anchorage soon."

"You are?" That was news to Mia. "What for?"

"Brodie wants me to fly down for a dinner to seal the road deal with the commissioner."

Mia's antenna went up. "With Brodie?"

"Hugh Oberg's going to be there."

"Who's Hugh Oberg?" Mia asked.

"The owner," Breena said.

"Hugh owns Galina," Raven added. "I work for him."

"Really." Mia hadn't given any thought to who owned the company.

"They think I can help schmooze the transportation commissioner and get the road repairs moved up on the agenda." She gave a wry frown. "I'm supposed to soften the dinner, make it less official and more personal."

"You're going to add some beauty and class," Mia said.

Breena looked surprised by the statement.

Raven laughed as she sprinkled onions and peppers across the layer of chips. "Does that sound at all like me?"

"We'll put an outfit together. Do a nice makeup job." Mia moved a little closer to take a critical look. "This is *my* area of expertise . . . a little something with your hair. Oh, I have exactly the right shoes; not too frou-frou but not too utilitarian." She glanced at Raven's hands. "There's a sign in Yolanda's salon that says she does manicures." In fact, Mia had been thinking of getting her own nails done. "I quite desperately need an indulgent girls' day. We can go in together for a manicure and a trim."

"Count me in," Breena said. "Yolanda's assistant just finished an online facial course. She got one-hundred percent on the final."

"I don't need a manicure," Raven said, gazing at her nails.

"I'm looking at your hands right now," Mia countered. "I might suck at driving a loader, but I know a bad manicure when I see it."

"She's right," Breena said, bending forward to check out Raven's nails.

"Fine," Raven said with resignation. Then she switched on the oven. "Have we got enough cheese?"

"These are going to be awesome," Breena said, holding up a platter heaped with shredded cheese.

Mia had to agree with that. "It's been literally years since I had nachos."

Raven took a sip from her glass of wine. "And I've *never* had wine like this."

Breena grinned, giving Raven a mock toast before tasting her own wine. "Yum. So, what are you guys thinking for the dating app? How are we going to select our group?"

Chapter Twelve

"IS SOMETHING GOING ON BETWEEN YOU AND MIA?" Brodie asked Silas as the two men muscled bags of mineral core samples into the beaver at the Duncan Exploration camp. The Duncan airstrip was short and rough, and Brodie didn't trust anyone but the two of them to land or take off there, especially after the rain had taken its toll.

Sleeves rolled up, sweat dripping from their brows in the sunshine, they were most of the way done on the thousand-plus-pound load.

"What do you mean?" Silas asked, fishing for what Brodie might know before answering.

Brodie stopped and straightened. "I mean, do the two of you have a thing going?"

Silas straightened too, taking the opportunity to readjust his leather work gloves. "Why would you ask that?"

"Why won't you answer?"

"Because I don't understand the question. Do you want me to just say no?"

"I want you to tell the truth."

"Then no." Silas wished there was something going on between them. But there wasn't, not right now. And Brodie hadn't asked if anything had ever gone on between them.

"People keep seeing you together," Brodie said.

Silas silently cursed at the size of the town. "Where? When? Who?"

Brodie stopped working. "Well, that wasn't at all defensive."

"I just want to know what we're talking about here."

"AJ, Xavier, at the Bear and Bar, in your truck." Brodie waited.

"Everyone's always at the Bear and Bar. And she doesn't have her own car, so I was just giving her a ride."

Silas hopped in to secure the load. He covered the bags with a net then secured the tie-down strap to the floor, tightening it with the ratchet.

"So, that's all it is."

"That's all it is." Silas double-checked his work on the load then hopped down to close the cargo door.

"Cobra mentioned you brought Mia to the office."

Brodie had obviously saved that revelation for last. He had Silas trapped, and he knew it.

Silas paused, hoping for more specifics to help him frame an answer, but Brodie just waited him out.

Silas weighed the pros and cons of his admission. Did he tell Brodie he had a thing for Mia, or did he tell him she was learning to operate the radio?

"The longer you stall, the guiltier you look," Brodie said.

"I was showing her the radio," Silas blurted out.

"Uh-huh," Brodie looked suspicious. "And what did Mia think of *the radio*?"

"That wasn't a euphemism. I was literally showing her how to operate the radio."

Brodie's expression changed from suspicious to perplexed.

"I felt bad about how things went at Galina, so I offered to teach her the radio instead. It's a better fit for her. She's smart, articulate, quick on her feet."

Brodie held up a hand. "Hang on, hang on. You want to let *Mia* loose on the WSA radio?"

"I—"

"Are you *kidding* me? There are pilots in the sky depending on Shannon. I'm not letting some—"

"She's learning the skills, not taking over for Shannon." Silas secured the door, remembering Mia's enthusiasm that day. "I have to say, I'm surprised at how fast she's catching on. I thought it would take a lot longer."

Load ready, he headed for the pilot's seat.

Brodie had flown the left side on the way over, taking the landing on the camp strip while Silas helped spot the condition of the runway. Silas would do the takeoff and fly them back home.

"What I should have said was thanks," Brodie said as he buckled in.

The abrupt mood change confused Silas. "For?"

"Going the extra mile for Raven. Her stress level has dropped since Mia stopped working there."

"I know we need Raven in top form." Silas started his checklist. "The entire operation falls apart without her."

"My world falls apart without her," Brodie said, a reflective note in his voice.

Silas couldn't help but remember what Mia had said about Brodie having a thing for Raven. He'd thought the idea was crazy, but now he was curious.

"How so?" he asked.

"Well, for one, the dinner with the transportation commissioner. According to Hugh Oberg, I'm not enough to close the deal on my own."

"That's not how I picture Raven."

"Picture her?"

"As eye candy at a dinner meeting."

Brodie looked insulted on Raven's behalf. "She's not eye candy."

"I know. That's what I'm saying."

"Hugh wants it to have a personal feel, multigenerational Alaskan business owners who influence the vote and deserve government support."

Silas put on his headset. "It's not the worst idea in the world."

Brodie put his on as well, and they switched to intercom. "She could be eye candy if she wanted."

"Sure," Silas agreed, fighting a smile at Brodie's sudden defense of the multitalented Raven. "She can be anything she wants."

"WELL THAT'S THREE HOURS I'LL NEVER GET BACK," RAven said as she studied herself in the mirror.

"The girl does *not* know how to do a spa day," Breena said to Mia.

Mia grinned. Yolanda's beauty salon in the back of the Butterfly Boutique wasn't the most luxurious she'd seen, but it was more fun than she had expected, and the services were top-notch.

"My nails feel fantastic, Yolanda." She held out her hands to gaze at the new lilac shimmer. It was refreshing to have them redone. "They look great too."

Yolanda seemed pleased with the compliment.

Raven had gone with a sheer cashmere pink on her nails.

It didn't surprise Mia that she'd gone with something subtle. Unless she moved her hand under the light, you could barely tell it was there.

Raven's hair on the other hand, well you could definitely tell she'd changed her hair. It was the same color, mostly light brown. But the way Yolanda had combed and dried it, it looked thicker, sort of halo-like, and her natural auburn highlights were more pronounced.

"It's lighter since I took off an inch," Yolanda said, fluffing it up.

"I can't get used to my face," Raven said, wiggling her chin. "Hugh's not going to recognize me."

Mia smiled as she lifted her glass of wine. Everyone had seemed glad she brought a couple of bottles along for refreshments.

"You're still you," she said to Raven. "You've always been this gorgeous."

Raven tilted her face one way, then the other.

"She's right, you've got beautiful features," Breena said earnestly.

"You just needed to want it a bit," Mia said.

"I'm not the one who wanted it," Raven complained.

Mia stood and wrapped an arm around Raven's shoulders and gave her a squeeze. "Don't fuss so much. Just enjoy the girlie part of you for once."

Their gazes met in the mirror.

Raven's eyes looked darker than usual, bigger and a deeper blue. Her skin tones were perfectly even, with her cheeks ever so slightly bright. Her brows were perfectly shaped and her lips were a brick red, not too bright, just enough shine to make them more prominent.

"Hugh will be blown away," Mia finished. "And so will anyone else who gets a look at you."

Mia was happy with her own makeup as well. It was sharper than she did at home but more subtle than her look on the runway. Yolanda's assistant, Bette, had given them facials and brought an artistic flair to the makeup.

Breena seemed pleased too.

"Show us the full package," Breena said to Raven, taking down the gray plastic dress cover hanging on the wall.

Mia liked the idea, especially since she'd been the one

to pick the outfit. She didn't want to miss seeing the full effect. "Try it on. We've got half an hour."

"Fine," Raven agreed a little reluctantly, taking the outfit behind an opaque screen.

Mia had picked an all-purpose skirt, high-waisted and short, made from charcoal-colored fabric, with a slight flare. She'd combined it with mottled a burgundy and purple silk tank top with flat black lace on its scooped neck. A thin cropped burgundy cardigan with pushed-up sleeves would keep Raven's shoulders warm if the temperature dipped. And it all went on top of black leggings and high heeled ankle boots.

"Ta-da." Raven came out doing a pirouette in the outfit.

"That's killer," Breena said in awe.

"Why don't you dress like that all the time?" Bette asked.

"Are you kidding?" Raven asked. "It took a team of skilled professionals a whole afternoon to get me looking this way."

"You could easily learn how to do it." Mia took a look from several different angles. "I'd love to update your style while I'm here."

"My style's fine."

"Your style is early warehouse."

Breena laughed. "And you never know who might be visiting Paradise." She gave Mia a wag of her newly sculpted eyebrows.

Mia hadn't been thinking about the matchmaking women. She was excited about Raven's dinner with Brodie—more excited about it than Raven seemed to be. But that was okay. Mia was confident Brodie would be very excited . . . impressed . . . maybe in awe when he got a look at the updated Raven.

"Now we really are running late," Breena said, looking at the clock on the wall.

Raven hopped back into her jeans, and the three of them

raced for Breena's truck, Mia squeezing into the middle of the bench seat, Raven with the plastic-covered outfit on her lap.

"Are you excited?" Mia asked, fishing for information as they made their way out of town.

"Excited about dinner with the commissioner and Hugh?"

"And Brodie," Mia said. "It's a little bit like a date."

Raven snorted. "It's nothing like a date. We'll be talking about road repairs."

"While looking like a million bucks," Mia said.

"All they're going to care about are the facts and figures." She pointed to her temple. "I know all the details of Galina's business. I hope they give me a chance to rationalize spending taxpayer dollars on the haul road into one of the most important transportation points in central Alaska."

"Try to work in something fun," Mia said, hoping Brodie might know how to be a little less business-focused . . . it wasn't a really great hope.

They pulled into the parking lot to see Brodie doing a walkaround on a small plane. He was definitely a good-looking man, tall, strapping and confident. Mia could certainly see the appeal—so long as a woman wasn't sensitive to his scowls.

"Have fun," she called as Raven hopped out of the pickup truck.

"Do you think she knows?" Breena asked as Raven made her way toward Brodie.

"That Brodie's into her?"

"Yeah, that. I think he's been fighting it for a long time."

"I don't think she has a clue."

Breena cranked the wheel to turn the truck around in the parking lot. "Nice move, by the way, making her over like that."

"Yolanda and Bette did all the work."

"You got her into the chair."

Mia spread her fingers and held her nails out in front of herself. "It wasn't entirely altruistic. I feel more like myself now."

"You mind if I come to visit in LA some day? I'm guessing the spas there are off the charts."

"Oh, anytime," Mia said happily. "I know just the place."

MIA'S LATEST RADIO LESSON WAS FINISHED, AND SILAS was busy taking a customer call in the WSA office when her cell phone rang in her pocket.

She saw Marnie's name and quickly stepped outside, letting the door swing shut behind her. "Marnie, hi!" Her calls were infrequent enough these days that she was excited about getting one.

"How are you holding up?" Marnie asked.

"Good," Mia said, realizing it was true. She was good these days.

Raven might be mostly busy working; her trip to Anchorage tonight was just the latest thing. But Mia was keeping busy too. She and Breena had taken the opportunity to come up with some good ideas for the matchmaking event.

They planned to host a walking tour of the town, an afternoon hike through the meadows to the river bend, followed by a cocktail mixer, then a big barbecue on the Bear and Bar patio. No pressure, no matchups, just good fun for everyone involved.

"How about down there?" Mia asked. "What's the latest?"

"Well . . ." Marnie's voice turned somber and trailed off.

Mia's joy dipped a notch. "Uh-oh."

It took Marnie a moment to start talking. "I tried to reason with the judge. I really did. But I can't even get a meeting in chambers."

A sinking feeling hit Mia's stomach. "What happened? What did they do now?"

"It's not the twins this time. It's the management team."

"Lafayette's management team?"

"They cancelled Milan and London to attend São Paulo and Shanghai."

Mia took a few paces across the gravel, not believing she could have heard right. "They can't do that."

"I told them the decision went way beyond caretaking. That it was fundamental to the strategic direction of the company."

"It is."

"I *know*."

Mia turned so the sun wasn't shining directly in her eyes and kept walking. "So, what did they say?"

"That the strategic vision was archaic."

"That's insane. Alastair was a brilliant visionary. He's proven that year after year."

"I agree, and so do the company's balance sheets."

"Are they *trying* to ruin us?" Mia waved away a buzzing mosquito and walked a little faster. "How can they ignore Alastair's official plan?"

"Theresa's secretly behind it, I'm positive of that. But she must have Henry and Hannah's backing too."

Mia paused, figuring out exactly what was happening here. "If they can't have it, they'll burn it down."

"That could be it."

"What else could it be?"

"That they believe in their own vision."

"Those three don't know the first thing about the fashion business." The mosquitos started buzzing again, and one bit her on the back of the neck. Mia smacked it and started walking away from the forest, where the bugs were thick, and toward the open space of the runway access road.

"Agreed," Marnie said.

"Where have they even been for the last decade?"

"In high school and college," Marnie ventured.

"You're cracking jokes?"

"Sorry. Not funny. I'll keep trying with the judge."

"Do you think I should come back?" Mia asked, wondering if she could somehow pressure them into doing the right thing.

She heard footsteps on the gravel behind her and turned to see Silas striding her way, looking puzzled.

"No, it's safer if you stay there for now," Marnie said. "You run the risk of ramping up the protests again. And you being here won't help. You're the last person they'll listen to. I'll keep trying with the judge."

"We can't let them get away with this," Mia said as Silas grew closer.

"I'm on it. I'll do everything I can."

Mia wanted Marnie to be more reassuring—to say they would definitely stop the twins and the vice presidents, that they'd beat this, that the judge would have no choice but to see it their way. But Marnie wasn't being reassuring right now, and that told Mia they were in real trouble.

"I'll call you when I know something," Marnie said into the silence.

"Okay. Thanks." Feeling demoralized and defeated, Mia ended the call.

"What was that?" Silas asked, coming to a halt.

"Home. LA. My lawyer."

Taking in her expression, he sobered. "Something wrong?"

Mia waved her phone in the air. "Why, why do they have so little faith in me?"

"Who?"

"Everyone. Seriously, *everyone*."

"I have faith in you."

"Don't humor me."

"I'm not humoring you." He moved closer, his gaze intent. "You're smart, hardworking, committed."

She appreciated the effort, but it was too little too late. "You're trying a bit too hard here, Silas."

"I'm dead serious. You learned the phonetic alphabet in forty-eight hours."

"That's just memorization. I need to be analytical, strategic. I need to guess what people are going to do to thwart me and come up with a plan to fight back."

He covered her shoulder with his palm. "Tell me what happened."

"Henry and Hannah happened. The Lafayette vice presidents happened. Even the judge *happened*."

"Hey." He eased closer.

"They've tossed out Alastair's strategic plan. They're just making things up as they go along. Everyone is so convinced of my ineptitude that they're not even pretending."

"You're going to win, you know." Silas wrapped his comforting arms around her. "Before this is over, you're going to win."

"Maybe," she said, suddenly feeling more tired than angry.

"Not maybe. Be positive. Be confident." He smoothed her hair then drew back to meet her eyes. His lips curved into an unexpected smile. "In the meantime, want to do something fun?"

The question caught her off balance. "Fun?"

"Yes."

"What?" she asked, growing suspicious when a twinkle came into his eye.

But instead of suggesting something sexy, he nodded at a spot behind her. "Look."

She twisted her head. There was nothing behind her except the forest and a massive loader sitting twenty feet away.

"It's the six one five," he said. "Want to take it for a spin?"

"Very funny."

"I'm serious." He took her hand. "It'll be a confidence builder."

"You *know* my record with loaders."

He started forward, drawing her along. "Once you try this, the mini loader will feel like a toy. Plus, there's nothing to hit out here, and I'll be right beside you. Nothing can go wrong."

She craned her neck to look up at it, oddly warming to the idea. A distraction was exactly what she needed right now, something to take her mind completely off the problems at Lafayette. If she went back to Raven's, she was only going to sit and stew.

"There's no way I can drive this," she said, being realistic.

"I'll drive. You assist." He braced his hand on the ladder.

"It's sort of intimidating."

"That's the point." He cocked his head to the doorway above, giving her an encouraging waggle of his eyebrows.

"I can't believe I'm doing this." She reached up and grasped the cool metal, pulling herself onto the first rung.

"I'm right behind you," he said.

The door to the cab was wide open, and she climbed carefully inside. The square space was dusty and worn, and the floor scattered with grit, but she was a lot less sensitive to cleanliness these days. It had a single seat for the driver.

"Where do you want me?" she asked as he climbed in and hunched over behind her.

"Sit down for a minute."

"I told you, I'm not driving."

He chuckled. "I need to get the door shut."

She sat down on the bouncy seat. "It has joysticks," she said. "I've had bad experiences with joysticks."

"Those are levers," he said, securing the glass door. "Totally different thing."

"Very funny."

"Stand back up," he said, drawing back into the corner to give her room.

She rose and he slid past her into the seat. Then he patted his lap.

"I won't be in the way?"

"No. You're going to help me."

Feeling doubtful, she perched on his thigh. "Taking your life in my hands here, Captain Burke."

He reached around her to the ignition key. "You don't scare me, princess. First, we start it up. It's a diesel, so one click, then you wait about fifteen seconds for the glow plugs."

"Glow plugs?"

"The ignition system."

"Sure." She didn't have the slightest idea what he was talking about, but there wouldn't be a quiz on this at the end.

He started the engine, and it rumbled loudly beneath them, vibrating the cab.

"Pull the steering wheel down into place." He demonstrated, and she scooted back against his chest to get out of the way. "The levers are boom up and down and bucket tip up and down. Easy."

"That's what they said about the mini loader."

"Try it," he said. "Pull for up." He took her hand and placed it on the smooth black lever, covering it with his own and pulling.

The boom groaned in front of them, the bucket rising up in the air. After a minute, they pushed the level to move the bucket partway down.

"Duel brakes on the floor." Silas showed her the pedals. "And this takes it into forward."

The machine lurched, startling her, and she grabbed onto him. They trundled ahead toward the access road to the strip.

"Where are we going?"

"There's a pile of gravel at the end of the strip. We can take a few scoops."

"Are there planes up there?" She leaned forward to peer out, remembering what he'd told her at the Wildflower strip.

"Good question," he said. "We're staying off to the side, but you should always check anyway. Want to steer?"

"I'm not ready to—"

He put her hands on the wheel before she could protest. "Just like a car."

"A really *big* car."

"Try turning."

She did, carefully easing the wheel one way and then the other as they made their way up the access road.

They turned onto the runway, and she started to relax and take in the view.

"We're really high up in this."

"We are."

"I can see so much. Is that the river?"

"Falls Creek," he said. "It parallels the road then runs into the river. Water's really high now with all the rain and the runoff. Look up the mountain to the left there. In a minute, you'll see the falls in the distance."

The falls came into view, wide and frothy white, looking like they were falling twenty stories down the mountain. "It's gorgeous."

"Isn't it? There's a trail up if you ever want to hike it. It's steep, great exercise."

"Bear spray required," she guessed, thinking a hill climb would be a great workout.

"And a group of three or more."

She watched the falls as they drove farther along.

Silas's arm was loosely looped around her waist. His hand moved, brushing her thigh, and she was suddenly aware of everything—the warmth of his chest; the strength of his thighs; his musky, familiar scent.

She was on Silas's lap, and she was pressed tight up against him, like she'd hoped to be so many nights since Wildflower Lake. Since this was for a legitimate purpose, she didn't have to feel guilty; she could just enjoy the sensations.

"Stay at least twenty feet from the edge," he said, his voice a very sexy rumble in her ear.

He was controlling the accelerator, and he upped the speed, making her bounce a little.

"Oh," she said in surprise.

He tightened his hold, and desire soared to life, starting at the back of her thighs, sending the tingling warmth coursing upward.

"You're getting too close," he said, his breath tickling her neck. His hand covered hers on the steering wheel and he corrected the direction. "Perfect now. You're doing great."

Her muscles relaxed as they bounced along, and she felt like she was melting back into him. Her cheek came up against his chin, and she gasped in a breath, her heart thudding in time to the throb of the engine.

His hand flexed against her waist. Then his thumb moved in circles, higher and higher from her ribs to her breast.

Her eyes fluttered closed, and she tipped her head back.

He kissed her neck, his hand framing her cheek, easing her head around to give him access to her lips.

He swore then, and the loader took a sudden turn. He jammed his feet on the brakes and put it in park—whether for safety or from desire, she wasn't sure. But when he kissed her harder, swiftly turning her in his lap for a better angle and wrapping his arms tight around her, she knew it was desire.

"I've missed you so damn much," he said.

She nodded against his lips. She'd missed him too. She'd missed his lips, his touch, his scent, his taste, even the sound of his voice so close up and sexy.

"Say something," she said.

"What?"

"Anything. I don't care. I love the sound of your voice, especially when you're talking to me like that."

"It's been torture," he said between kisses. "I see you. I talk to you, and I want you in my arms. I think about you all the time. I think about *this* all the time."

Her skin came up in goose bumps, and passion throbbed deep in her core. She needed to feel more of him. She reached for the hem of her sweater and peeled it off, unhooking her bra and dropping it to the floor.

Silas's hand covered her bare breast.

"You're so beautiful," he said, his lips following in the wake of his fingertips.

She tipped her head back. "Don't stop."

"I'm not stopping." He peeled off his own shirt then released the snap of her jeans.

It took some fumbling, but soon they were naked, and she was facing him and kissing him, and their bodies finally meshed together.

She couldn't believe they'd held out this long.

With the diesel engine throbbing beneath them, and the wilds of Alaska all around them, currents of pleasure lifted them once more to unbelievable heights.

MIA COULDN'T KEEP HER SECRET ANY LONGER. IT FELT like a constant lie to sit here on the screen porch with Raven drinking wine when there was such a huge *thing* just hanging out there like a deadweight on her conscience.

"I slept with Silas," she blurted out, damn the torpedoes.

Raven stilled and then blinked. "I kissed Brodie."

"You *what*?" That news was even more earthshaking. Mia sat forward in her chair, all ears for the details. "When, where, how did it happen?"

Raven looked unhappy about it, but a little voice inside Mia couldn't help congratulating herself on orchestrating such a successful makeover. Plus, her sixth sense for relationships had been vindicated, and that boded well for their new matchmaking venture.

"In Anchorage," Raven said. "On an elevator. On the lips."

"It's not a kiss if it's not on the lips. At least, not one that counts."

"Well, this one didn't count anyway. We agreed on that." Raven's head began to nod as she seemed to warm up to the explanation. "It would totally have messed with our professionalism. We've built up a rhythm, Brodie and me; a rapport. It's important to both companies that nothing mess with that. So, we agreed. Nothing happened. It was a congratulatory gesture, and it doesn't count."

Mia watched her cousin's mental contortions with fascination. "I don't think it works that way. How long did it last?"

"About five floors, I think."

"That's a long congratulatory gesture."

"I know."

"And you're still thinking about it."

"I can't stop." Raven took a hefty swig of her wine. It was glass number three—probably why she was dishing so freely.

"Was it a good *congratulatory gesture*?" Mia asked.

"The best." Raven flopped back in her chair. "Ever." Then she abruptly sat up straight. "Hang on. Back the truck up. You slept with Silas?"

Mia was surprised it had taken her this long. "Twice."

"When? Where?" Raven made a rolling motion with her finger. "You know, all those questions."

"At Wildflower Lake."

Raven thought about it for a second. "So, Brodie was right."

"Brodie?"

"He thought you two were acting weird. But Silas told him it was the radio thing."

"The radio thing?"

"The lessons."

Mia was stunned to hear Silas had told Brodie. She was even more shocked he hadn't told her Brodie knew.

"You didn't have to keep it a secret," Raven said. "I think it's great."

"You know how Brodie is."

Raven looked puzzled. "How do you mean?"

"You saw his expression when I flattened the truck tire."

"He can be impatient," Raven allowed. "It can be hard to prove yourself to him."

"Was he mad about the radio lessons?" Mia asked, thinking that might be why had Silas kept quiet.

"He was mad," Raven said with a wry laugh. "But then Silas told him it was just for fun, something easier for you to learn."

Mia didn't understand. "For fun?"

"It doesn't matter if you're never going to use it," Raven carried on. "Expanding your skill set is admirable."

"Right," Mia said slowly as a simmer of anger rose inside her.

She'd worked her butt off learning the radio, learning about weather, terminology, air traffic control, flight tracking. She'd done it to help at WSA, not as an exercise in *fun*.

Silas had sworn he had faith in her, and then he made love to her, and all the while he was patronizing her.

"Silas says you're really good at it." Raven's carefree voice was jarring as she stood. "You surprised him. More wine?"

Mia's anger turned to humiliation and a cold sense of betrayal. She swallowed hard and rose to her feet, cobbling together the scraps of her pride as she followed Raven into the kitchen.

"It was a bit of a lark," she managed, setting down her glass. She was desperate to move on from her embarrassment. "Let's talk about the matchmaking project. That's far more exciting. I thought I'd go see Breena tomorrow to do some more planning. And we should talk about a budget. I'm happy to underwrite the costs."

"You can't spend your personal money on it," Raven protested as she poured from a bottle of Bordeaux.

Mia had taken over the wine buying, so it was in bottles now. "Sure, I can."

Raven handed her the refilled glass. "I thought we'd sell tickets or memberships or something."

"I think we have to make it free." Mia focused her mind and tamped down her emotions.

"Free? Are you kidding me?"

"How much could we possibly charge?" Mia grasped onto the project like a lifeline, blocking everything Silas-related. "Fifty bucks? A hundred? We're going to have to fly a couple dozen people to Alaska. There's the food and the venue, and wherever we're going to put them up. Hey, where can we put them up?"

The question seemed to stump Raven. "Mrs. France has three B&B rooms above the Bear and Bar, but they're pretty rustic. They share a bathroom."

Mia grimaced.

"Camping?" Raven tentatively offered. "Glamping?"

"We can't put the women up in tents."

"It would weed out the weak ones."

"It would weed out *all* of them. Plumbing and walls have to be our baseline."

"The only place big enough for that many people together is the WSA staff housing. It's very no-frills."

"Is there anything fancier? Another bed and breakfast? Or a big house we could rent?"

"You've seen the whole town," Raven said. "The only building of any size is the school."

"Cots on the gymnasium floor and communal showers? I don't think so."

"Are you saying we're dead in the water?"

Mia mentally shuffled through their options. "Could we maybe put the WSA guys in tents or something? Temporarily, of course. And would Brodie agree to an upgrade to the housing units?"

"You want Brodie to upgrade his staff residence for us while his guys are put in tents?"

"I'd pay for it—new linens, paint, a little wainscoting. You can do a lot with throw rugs and art. And lamps. The right lighting is pivotal to the ambiance. They can totally keep all that once the event is over."

Raven laughed. "Are you that rich?"

"I can swing this." There were many degrees of wealth. Mia wasn't even close to the top of the spectrum, but she wasn't at the bottom either. She could afford a pet project.

Raven sobered then. "I thought the kids were fighting you for the inheritance."

"That's just the business."

"There's money besides the business?"

"Oh yeah. Alastair was a prudent investor. And I kept my salary all those years. I put most of it away."

Raven gestured around the cabin. "And you're living *here*?"

"Visiting. And you swore this was one of the best places in Paradise."

Raven peered at Mia over the rim of her wineglass. "I can ask Brodie."

"Like I said, he's free to keep all the new stuff after we're done. Though I'm not sure the guys would consider my paint color an upgrade."

"No promises," Raven said.

"But we're not dead in the water."

"Not dead." Raven raised her glass to toast.

Chapter Thirteen

SILAS HAD NEVER SEEN THAT PARTICULAR EXPRESSION on Brodie's face—astonishment mixed with suspicion and a touch of revulsion.

He was standing thirty yards away in the open bay doorway of the WSA hangar, where Raven was talking fast, Mia was nodding enthusiastically and Brodie was staring at them if they'd just walked off a spaceship from Mars.

Curious, Silas picked up his pace.

"It would only last a couple of days," Raven said as Silas made it into hearing range.

Tristen and Hailey had just taken off in the caravan, and the sound of the engine faded into the morning sky. Cobra was working inside the shop, his impact gun intermittently clacking and echoing off the walls.

Brodie didn't say a word.

"Everything would be tasteful," Mia put in. "You'd be welcome to keep the upgrades. But it's all removable if somebody objected."

"Mrs. France is on board," Raven said. "And you know it would be super popular with the guys."

Silas came to a halt.

Mia fleetingly looked his way but didn't smile or greet him.

He wasn't particularly shocked by that. They were still keeping a low profile. But he hoped he could get her alone for a few minutes before his flight. He was surprised she hadn't told him she was coming out to the airstrip.

"Late September," Raven said.

"We're flexible on that," Mia said.

"As work winds down," Raven said.

"That would be best," Mia added.

Brodie's expression didn't change. "Is this a joke?"

Mia and Raven glanced at each other.

"No," Raven said.

"Because if it's a joke, it's a good one."

"Why would you think that?"

Silas couldn't keep quiet any longer. "What did I miss?"

They all looked his way.

"What?" he repeated.

"No," Brodie said to Raven.

"If you'll just think about—" she began.

"It's asinine."

"It's just a meet-and-greet."

"Is there something in particular—" Mia began, but Brodie shut her up with a glare.

Silas felt his hackles rise in Mia's defense. "What are we talking about?"

"Tell him," Brodie said, jutting his chin in Silas's direction.

Cobra's impact gun continued to punctuate the air.

"We want to invite some women to town," Raven said.

Silas looked at Mia, but she still wasn't making eye contact.

"A sort of meet-and-greet," Raven continued. "Just a few

women from California. Mia has a lot of contacts down there, and we thought—"

"The poker game on steroids," Brodie interjected.

Raven slid him a look of frustration. "It's hard for the men up here to meet new women, and it's hard for women down south to meet good men."

Silas was catching on to the general concept. What he didn't understand was Mia's interest in it. He tried to catch her eye again.

"We thought a group event would be more relaxed, low-key, give people a chance to mix and mingle without some of the awkwardness of a date," Raven said.

Brodie's tone was snide. "I can't even count the ways that could go wrong."

Silas didn't want to argue with his boss, but he wanted to support Mia. Plus, he didn't see what gave Brodie a veto.

"If they're just bringing a few friends to town," he ventured to Brodie.

"A few?" Brodie asked.

Silas looked to Mia. When that didn't get him anything, he looked to Raven instead.

"Twenty, twenty-five," Raven said.

The number astounded Silas. "Where are they going to—"

"Go ahead." Brodie gave a cold laugh. "Tell him where you want them to stay."

"WSA housing," Raven said.

Well, that explained Brodie's veto.

"With upgrades courtesy of Mia."

"Mia?" Silas asked, trying to force her to engage.

She looked at him, but her eyes were cold.

"If it's a no, it's a no," Raven said, her tone tight. "We'll figure out something else."

"Maybe that something could *not* include bringing twenty-five giggling city girls to Paradise to mess with business," Brodie said.

"*You,*" Raven said, pointing to his chest, "are a killjoy."

"Somebody's got to keep this town in check. The idea is ridiculous."

Silas had to admit, he could see Brodie's point. Were they supposed to evict the WSA staff and fill up the town for a party?

"We're doing this," Raven said, raising her chin in the air. "You can help us or not, but you can't stop us."

"How're you going to get them here?" Brodie asked mildly. "Who'll fly them in from Fairbanks?"

The question stumped Raven for a minute, but then she rallied. "I just made a deal on a refurbished haul road."

A muscle ticked in Brodie's cheek, but he didn't respond.

"There are other air charter companies," Mia said.

Even Raven looked surprised by that level of audacity. But again, she rallied. "Yeah."

Silas had to admire her self-assuredness. Then again, hostility between Brodie and Raven was a very bad thing for the town.

"Maybe we can come to a compromise," Silas offered.

"You mean, half the women?" Raven asked.

"Why would we do that?" Mia asked over top of Raven.

"To keep the peace," Silas said.

Mia didn't look remotely interested in keeping the peace.

He couldn't help feeling like he'd missed something more.

"I remain opposed," Brodie said.

"I remain supportive," Raven countered.

"Brodie?" Shannon called to him from the office doorway. "Fairbanks air operations is on the line."

"On my way." Brodie gave Raven a last stern look as he walked away.

Silas took the moment to move close to Mia. "Hey. What's going on?"

She looked puzzled. "What do you mean?"

He searched her expression. Gone were the bedroom eyes and the sly smile.

She was an ice-princess's ice-princess.

"I mean what's going on?" he repeated. "Is something wrong?"

"No. What would be wrong? Other than Brodie's attitude."

"Did *I* do something wrong?"

She gave a slightly brittle laugh. "I'm just busy. You know how it is."

He didn't.

"Ready to go, Raven?" she asked around him.

"Ready when you are," Raven said.

"Catch you later," Mia said to Silas and began walking away.

Oh no. It wasn't going to be that easy. He strode after her, touching her shoulder. "What the hell?"

She shrugged him off. "I really do have to go."

"Why are you mad?"

"I'm not mad."

Raven pulled ahead, walking toward her pickup.

"Something's clearly happened," he said to Mia.

"We're in different worlds, Silas."

"We were in different worlds two days ago, too." Neither of them had seemed to care then.

"We obviously had different expectations."

Maybe they had, but he still didn't understand. "Mia, *what* happened?"

She stopped and turned to face him. "Do I really need to spell it out?"

"*Yes.*"

"You lied."

"About what?"

"The radio, the lessons. You remember, the ones you

told Brodie were *just for fun*." Her eyes blazed, and regret cascaded over him. "Do you know how hard I worked? Was this just a joke to you?"

"Mia." He reached for her, but she recoiled.

"You *swore* you had faith in me."

"It wasn't like—"

"It was *exactly* like that," she snapped. Lips pressed together, she pivoted and marched away.

Raven was watching them from the truck, and Silas could only imagine what she thought of him.

"That's not good," Brodie said, coming up behind Silas.

"You told Raven?"

"I tried, but you heard her. She didn't exactly listen to my objections."

"I meant about the radio lessons."

"What about them?" Brodie asked, looking puzzled as he watched Raven's truck pull away in a spray of gravel and a cloud of dust.

"Did you tell Raven they were just for fun?"

"Well, I wasn't going to tell her they were only to keep Mia busy and out of her way."

"They weren't." That was part of it but not all of it.

Brodie frowned in obvious exasperation as he stared where the dust had settled on the driveway. "That's not really our biggest problem."

It was Silas's biggest problem. At least, it felt like Silas's biggest problem. He hadn't lied to Mia, but he wouldn't be able to convince her of that now.

"Twenty-five more city women," Brodie muttered.

"It might not—" Silas clamped his jaw. Things were far enough off the rails already.

"Spit it out," Brodie said.

"It might not be the worst idea in the world."

Brodie gave a curt nod. "Yes, yes, it might."

"The guys would love it. You'd be their hero."

"They love that fifth shot of whiskey, too."

Silas stifled his amusement at the comparison.

"And it always seems like a good idea at the time," Brodie continued in a resolute tone. "But it never ends well."

"Whatever," Silas said, realizing he was fighting for a cause he didn't even care about.

What he cared about was losing Mia. As the thought formed, he ruthlessly shut it down. He had it all wrong. He couldn't *lose* Mia because he'd never *had* Mia.

His dad had learned the hard way that women like her didn't stay with guys like him. Silas usually remembered that lesson. He remembered it now, and it had never been truer. But, man, it felt like a knife to the gut.

"I gotta get out of here," he said to Brodie.

"You and me both."

"I mean it. You mind if I swap trips with Xavier?"

"You want to stay up at Mile High Research camp for three days?" Brodie was clearly baffled.

"That's exactly what I want." The farther Silas could get away from Mia right now, the better. He had to work her out of his system, and cold turkey was his best shot.

Brodie shrugged. "No skin off my nose. Xavier will jump at the offer."

"Thanks, man."

SILAS HAD BEEN GONE NOW FOR MORE THAN TWO days.

Mia tried to convince herself it was a good thing. She didn't want to miss him. He didn't deserve to be missed.

He'd pretended to respect her, but he was just like all the rest—humoring her without having any real faith in her abilities.

"You sure you don't want to drop me off today and keep the truck?" Raven asked as she laced up her work boots.

Mia was sipping a strong pick-me-up coffee at the breakfast table. The sky was blue, the sun already high, and the robins were twittering happily in the trees outside. The world seemed to be fighting back against her sullen mood.

She wasn't going to buy into the world's cheerful outlook, but she would force herself into event-planning mode. "Breena finished the graphics on our information page. I promised her I'd put together the text today."

"You sure you want to keep working so hard on this? I hate to see you waste your effort."

"It won't be a waste." Mia lifted her chin, determination kicking in along with the caffeine.

"I can talk to him again," Raven said. "But you know Brodie's not a mind-changing kind of guy."

"Maybe you could lead with a kiss this time." It was clearer than ever that Brodie was vulnerable to his attraction to Raven.

But Raven gave her a stern frown. "The kiss was irrelevant. And he's not bribable."

Mia wasn't convinced the kiss was irrelevant, but she wasn't about to push. "If it has to be glamping, we'll make it glamping. I found a service that'll set up super-nice wall tents with wood floors."

"Expensive?" Raven polished off her coffee, set her mug in the sink and moved toward the door.

"Stop worrying about the money. My expenses this month have been negligible. I barely even pay for groceries."

"There's the wine."

"The most expensive bottle in town is thirty-eight dollars."

Raven shook her head and smiled as she stepped outside. "You're spoiling me."

"I have not yet begun to spoil," Mia said in a dramatic voice as Raven closed the door behind her.

The sun abruptly disappeared, dimming the sky and finally matching Mia's mood.

She topped up her coffee cup and moved to the screen

porch with Breena's laptop. The birds were still gamely singing, while the air was warm and fragrant from the pine trees.

As she settled into a chair, raindrops began clattering on the corrugated plastic roof. The sound was calming, and the ozone combined with the fresh scent of the forest.

Still determined to distract herself from memories of Silas, she opened the draft web page, gazing at the clean graphics and the beautiful scenery and Paradise photos Breena had put together. Impressed, Mia turned her mind to the questionnaire. They were looking for women with an adventurous spirit, possibly at a pivot point in their lives, open to a relationship, and with job skills or at least an aptitude they could use in Paradise. She didn't want anyone to end up with a repeat of her experience trying to work here.

She began typing then, framing, revising, moving text around. The rain gradually slowed and stopped, and the atmosphere brightened again.

Suddenly, a giant groaning roaring crash reverberated through the air. It jolted her upright as the earth vibrated beneath her. Her first thought was an earthquake, but she'd experienced plenty of those in LA.

But it was too loud for an earthquake. Plus, the vibrations felt wrong. Her next thought was more horrible—a plane crash. She leapt from her chair, dropping the laptop to rush outside.

She scanned the sky and the surrounding hills but didn't see any smoke rising up.

She went back inside and put on her shoes, trotting out to the road to look up and down. The clouds against the distant mountains were dark purple and black. She could see lightning flashing through them, but she couldn't hear the thunder. It wasn't thunder that shook the ground like that. But something had happened, and it was something big.

She had a choice. She could go south to town or north to

the airstrip. The airstrip was a lot closer, and her phone would work on their Wi-Fi. Plus, Silas was due back today. If there'd been a plane crash, it could have happened at the airstrip while someone was trying to land a plane. It could have been Silas.

Trying desperately not to consider that scenario, she ran back to the cabin for proper shoes and a few essentials then took off at a fast jog toward the airstrip. She hoped someone would drive up on the road. They'd likely have news and could give her a ride the rest of the way.

The creek beside the road was roaring high. She'd never seen it so high. In a few places, it lapped onto the roadbed and she had to detour around.

It hit her then. The bridge. A flash flood could have taken out the bridge. That would explain the strikingly high creek and the noise. She paused and considered turning back. Had Raven's cabin been cut off from town? What if someone had been on the bridge when it washed out? Did they need help?

The airstrip was less than a mile away. The bridge nearly four miles back. And Silas. She couldn't help thinking about Silas. Going toward the airstrip felt like she was going toward him.

She went with her instinct and started running again. The air was seeped with moisture. Rain trickled down on her, mingling with her sweat. The creek disappeared from the roadside and wound back into the bush, leaving only a puddle-strewn road.

She thought she spotted movement ahead, something just beyond the bend. Her heart lifted and her pace increased, looking for a pickup truck or an ATV to come zipping around the corner.

She swiped the dampness from her eyes and stared harder. Then her heart tripped, and panic flooded her system.

It was the bear. The *bears*. All three of them were staring straight at her.

She stopped, and they started toward her. Her instinct was to turn and run away, but Silas had told her in no uncertain terms to stand her ground.

But terror prickled her skin. It made her pulse race and her chest harden in pain.

She had to leave.

She had to get out of here before they got any closer.

She looked over her shoulder at the road stretching away. The brush was impenetrably thick in the forest. There was nowhere to run or hide.

The sow lowered her head. Her ears went back, and the cubs stopped still.

In a blinding moment of clarity, Mia remembered her bear spray. She reached to the back of her belt, past the water bottle to the mesh pouch. The Velcro sounded loud and she pulled the tab. The bear loped faster, its big paws eating up the ground between them. Time seemed to slow down as Mia jerked out the spray canister, peeled off the orange tab, double-checked the nozzle direction.

When she looked back up, the bear was at a full-on run. It was close, almost on her.

"No!" she shouted instinctively, but it didn't even break stride.

"Stay back!" she yelled at the top of her lungs.

It kept right on coming.

She guessed the distance, fifteen feet, ten, eight. She pointed the nozzle and pressed the trigger as hard as she could, holding it there.

The bear roared in anger, terrifyingly loud. It reared up.

Mia screamed and braced herself for impact.

But then the bear turned. It bolted into the forest, and the two cubs galloped after it.

Mia ran too. It was a sprint this time, definitely not a jog; but it was almost easy with the adrenaline running through her body.

She was afraid to look back over her shoulder. She told

herself to keep going, going, through the puddles in the straightest line possible until she spotted the parking lot.

That was the worst part, the hundred yards she had to run with safety in her sights and danger behind her. There were pickups in the parking lot, but most of the planes were gone.

She made it to the office door and threw it open, slamming it shut behind her and leaning back, gulping in breaths, holding back tears.

"Hello?" she finally managed. Her voice trembled, echoing back to her in the dim building. She tried again. "Hello?"

THE OFFICE WAS EMPTY, AND SHE DIDN'T FIND COBRA out in the hangar. It was eerily quiet with no one else around. She'd tried calling Raven, but her phone had gone to voice mail. Mia didn't know the main number for Galina.

Intensely thirsty from the exertion and the fear, she grabbed herself a bottle of water. She stood in the break room chugging it and wondering what to do next. Some of the pickups likely had keys left inside. Was she bold enough to borrow one and head for the bridge? It was an emergency, after all.

The radio crackled behind her. "WSA base, this is Three-Zero-alpha."

Mia whirled.

"WSA base, this is Three-Zero-Alpha. Come in WSA base." It was Hailey on the radio.

Mia set down the water bottle and crept to the doorway of the radio room. Why wasn't Shannon here if planes were coming in right now?

"WSA base? You there?"

A new voice came on, Silas this time. "Three-Zero-Alpha this is Echo-Sierra."

Mia gasped at the sound of Silas's voice, feeling its timbre to her bones.

"Hey, Silas. Roger that," Hailey said.

"I'm inbound over Clear Hills, weather's good to the north, crap to the south. What do you see?"

Mia moved to the desk and sat down at the radio, staring at the lights and switches.

"We're skirting the edge of it," Hailey said. "Should be able to make Paradise before it catches us. Shannon, you there?"

Mia's hand shook as she pressed the microphone button. "WSA base. It's, uh, Mia."

"Mia?" Silas's voice sounded shocked. "What are you doing there?"

"Shannon's not here," Mia said. "You guys should know the bridge may have washed out."

"Say again?" Hailey asked.

"The bridge. I didn't see it, but I heard it. I think it washed out. The creek's flooding the road."

"Did you check the strip?" Silas asked.

"I just got here."

"We need an airstrip condition report," Silas said.

Suddenly everything Mia had learned and read flooded into her brain. "Roger that," she said. "Stand by."

She hopped up from her chair and was halfway to the office door when she remembered the bears. She stumbled to a halt. There were grizzly bears outside. And they were mad at her. But Silas was up in the sky. The pilots needed her now.

She took a step forward, then another, then defiantly flung open the door and ran up the access road.

She took note of the windsock on the way, twelve knots, north, northeast. Then she came out on the strip and stopped to stare. Her heart sank all the way to her toes. It looked like the whole of Falls Creek had washed out onto the strip, leaving mud, rocks, tree branches and trunks, big uprooted trunks out in the middle.

Her hand went to her forehead in a moment of despair. Then she shook herself. It was what it was, and she had to focus. She turned to sprint back to the radio room.

Out of breath, she made the call. "WSA base here. Wind is twelve knots north, northeast. But the airstrip is compromised. Echo-Sierra, Thee-Zero-Alpha, reroute to your alternate airstrips."

"How bad?' Hailey asked.

"Mud and debris across the middle of the strip, one hundred feet west of the access road."

"Roger that," Hailey said. "Three-Zero-Alpha rerouting to Mulberry Trail. You have us on tracking."

Mia checked the tracking screen. "I've got you."

"We'll overnight and try to approach Paradise strip fifteen-hundred tomorrow. Three-Zero-Alpha out."

"Three-Zero-Alpha, approach Paradise strip fifteen-hundred tomorrow," Mia confirmed.

"WSA base, Echo-Sierra," Silas came back.

"Go ahead Echo-Sierra."

"Alternate airstrip is a no-go."

Mia's mind screamed *no*, and her hand trembled again. "Say again?"

"Alternate airstrip for Echo-Sierra is a no-go. Insufficient fuel to return to survey camp. Echo-Sierra is landing WSA strip in forty-five minutes. I'm in the PC-12. I need the whole strip."

"But . . ." She didn't know what else to say.

"Describe the debris."

"Mud, rocks, branches, tree trunks. They're big, Silas. I can't move them."

There was silence for a moment. "How far across?"

"All the way. All the way across."

"Mia."

"Yes."

"The loader."

She shook her head.

His voice was perfectly steady. "Start up the loader, use the bucket, and push whatever you can out of the middle of the strip."

She keyed the mic. "Silas, you know I can't . . ."

"You can do it. It doesn't have to be pretty. Just give me some space."

Her breathing turned shallow. She couldn't do this. She'd mess it up, like she'd messed everything else up.

"Mia?"

"What?" she asked on a gasp.

His tone turned gentle. "I do have faith in you."

She closed her eyes as her chest contracted with emotion. Then she willed the shaking from her hands to stop and swallowed, telling herself Silas needed her. She pressed the microphone button, keeping her voice strong. "Roger that, Echo-Sierra."

"Echo-Sierra forty-three minutes from WSA strip, coming in west, will do one fly-over and go-around. Echo-Sierra, out."

"Echo-Sierra, one fly over coming in west, WSA base, out."

Mia gave herself twenty seconds to breathe and get a grip. Then she marched into the break room, grabbed a pair of leather gloves and jogged to the loader in the corner of the parking lot.

She climbed the ladder and hoisted herself into the cab, wrestling the glass door shut behind her.

She took another breath, telling herself at least she was safe from the bears up here. She struggled to calm her mind and remember the lesson Silas had given her.

First, she buckled her seatbelt. Then she reached for the ignition key. She turned it one click and stopped herself. "Diesel. Glow plugs. Wait fifteen seconds." She waited.

Then she gritted her teeth and turned the key. The engine rumbled to life beneath her, vibrating the entire loader. She almost cheered in relief.

She used the lever to lift the bucket. Then she put the machine in forward and pressed on the accelerator. The giant beast inched its way ahead. She turned the steering wheel toward the access road, and it rumbled in the right direction.

"Just a big car," she muttered to herself. "Just a big ol' giant-ass car. There isn't even any other traffic."

She dared to press a little harder on the accelerator, and the loader sped up. The wheels bounced her up and down against the seatbelt and she hung on as she made her way to the strip.

The light was getting lower as the evening wore on, and the clouds were closing in darker above her. She glanced at the windsock to see that it hadn't changed. That was a good thing, since she had no way to contact Silas again.

She drove to the middle of the strip, then turned sharply right and aimed herself at the debris pile. She didn't know if the loader would push an entire tree, or if she should try one end at a time. So, she went straight on, lowering her speed and lowering the bucket.

She pressed into the debris, gritting her teeth as the bucket met with an eighteen-inch log and a pile of branches. To her surprise, the loader didn't even hesitate. It kept right on going as if there was nothing in the way.

She drove straight through the pile and pushed it off to the side.

Then she got bold, putting the loader into reverse to turn, she lined up for another pass.

Again, success. She pushed a significant amount of the debris out of the way and off to the side.

Six passes later, she was running out of time. She struggled to remember how wide the wingspan was on the PC-12, and how high the wings were off the ground. But she couldn't differentiate from plane to plane.

She wasn't positive, but she thought it looked like enough room for any of them.

The space she'd cleared was still scattered with bits of rubble, and she had ten minutes left. She pushed the bucket right down to the ground and made four more passes, doing her best to smooth out the muddy surface.

When she pulled out of the way, she could see Silas's plane, a dot in the distance.

He grew closer and larger then rumbled low over the strip, obviously checking her work. He circled back to the west and lined up to land.

She pushed the loader door open and leaned out to watch.

He came down on the strip at the far end. He slowed and cut through the center of the debris pile, coming to a stop about fifty feet past.

The pitch of the prop changed, and he turned to taxi.

Feeling fantastic at her success, she shut the door, re-buckled her seat belt and drove the loader down the access road, stopping in the middle of the parking lot and deciding it could stay right where it was. She shut off the engine as Silas climbed out of the plane.

Before she could even think, she was running his way. She was elated that he was safe and so incredibly happy to see him.

He wrapped her tight in his arms and held her there. "You did fantastic."

"You're okay," she said, as much to herself as to him. "You're safe."

"Thanks to you."

A new motor sound appeared in the silence, and they both looked to the road.

It was an ATV, Brodie with Raven on behind him, rip-ping their way into the parking lot.

Brodie slid to a stop and killed the engine. He looked around. "Hailey and Tobias?"

"Diverted to Mullberry Trail," Mia said. "They'll try coming in at fifteen-hundred tomorrow."

Brodie gave her a surprised look.

"Mia worked the radio," Silas said, giving her a one-armed hug, then leaving the arm around her.

Brodie looked stupefied now, but Raven was grinning as she dismounted the ATV.

"And the loader?" Brodie asked, seeing that it was sitting in the middle of the access road.

"That would be Mia again," Silas said with another squeeze. "Falls Creek washed out at the upper elbow, all the way across the strip. You should see what she did."

"That thing is amazing," Mia said. She was still feeling giddy from the power.

"You ran the loader?" Brodie asked, clearly baffled by the thought.

Raven nudged him in the shoulder with her elbow. "Quit asking stupid questions."

"I did," Mia said, meeting his gaze straight on.

"Saved my life," Silas said. "Not to mention your PC-12. Rough Hills strip was flooded. I had no alternate and not enough fuel to go back."

"I gotta see this," Raven said, and started hiking up the access road.

Mia quickly fell into step beside her. "Did you see the bridge?"

"The bridge is gone," Raven said. "Gone, gone. We had to ford the river down at the beaver pond."

"I heard it go out," Mia said. "At first I thought it was an earthquake."

Silas came up on her other side while Brodie walked next to Raven.

"How'd you get here?" Raven asked her.

"I wanted to call into town. So, I jogged up for the wireless. Saw the bears." The bear encounter had completely slipped her mind.

"On the road?" Raven asked.

"The big one charged at me."

All three of them swiveled their heads to stare.

"I bear sprayed it," she said. "And it ran away."

"The grizzly?" Silas asked.

Mia nodded.

"With the cubs?" Brodie asked, looking flabbergasted all over again.

"That's the one. I was dodging the puddles, then I looked up, and bam, there she was. And she was angry. So, I pulled out the bear spray, and when she got nice and close, I let her have it." Mia felt a guilty for making herself sound braver than she was, but she didn't want to admit she'd almost wet her pants. Well, maybe later she'd tell Raven that part of the story.

"Go, you," Raven said. "That should keep that old bear out of town for a while."

Brodie suddenly stopped in his tracks, staring at the strip ahead. "Wow."

"Wow," Raven echoed as she spotted the debris.

Staring from this angle at the giant hole she'd made in the pile, Mia's thoughts proudly echoed their words.

Chapter Fourteen

IT TOOK THREE DAYS TO GET THE TOWN AND THE AIR-
strip back to working order and to get a temporary Bailey
bridge set up over the river. But finally, Galina and WSA
were back in business.

Silas and Brodie stood in the front of the WSA hangar
watching the first Galina delivery trucks roll in.

"You're suspicious," Silas said to Brodie.

"I'm realistic," he said back.

"Mia didn't save your plane to use it as a bargaining chip
for their matchmaking scheme."

"That might not have been her plan. But the dust's settled now, and you know they're going to ask again. How do
I say no?"

"Maybe you can negotiate," Silas suggested, knowing
Brodie was probably right. Silas hadn't seen much of Mia
or Raven during the cleanup, but Breena had told him it was
still full steam ahead on the matchmaking plans. "They
seemed open to cutting the number of women in half.
Twelve? We could find a way to accommodate twelve."

Brodie frowned. "My main point's still the same."

"Their main argument's the same too. The guys *do* have trouble meeting women up here. And maybe it'll work. Maybe we'll get some new families started in Paradise."

"Or maybe the guys will follow the pretty women back to California. Women get tired of living like this. You know they do."

"Are you talking about my mother?" Silas's mother was a solid case in point for Brodie's side of the argument.

"I'm talking about women in general who, quite reasonably, like creature comforts."

Silas tried for optimism. "Carl and Shannon are happy here. Reece's wife, Kelly, came in from outside."

"Shannon grew up here and Kelly grew up on a ranch. They weren't city women to begin with. And you know the thing is going to distract everyone for days on end."

Another delivery truck pulled into the parking lot. Xavier and Zeke were on deck waiting to load up a beaver for a flight to Wildflower Lake.

"Change the timeframe," Silas suggested, wondering all over again why he was arguing Raven and Mia's side. "Put it into October. That way, the workload is way down, people are gearing up for their winter holidays anyway, and the visitors will get a better look at the reality of Paradise."

"There could be snow by then," Brodie said.

Silas shrugged. "Good. If you can't take the snow, you have no business dating an Alaskan bush pilot."

He couldn't stop his thoughts from shifting to Mia—the poster child for women who had no business dating an Alaskan bush pilot. Good thing she wasn't dating him.

"We could free up a few staff units in October," Brodie said.

Silas was surprised to hear the concession. "We could," he agreed in an even tone, purposefully not making a big deal out of Brodie's change of heart.

Kenneth and Xavier called out instructions to each other

from across the parking lot, while T taxied the caravan to the strip. Hailey and T-Two were methodically filling the big cargo space in an otter.

"If there's only twelve of them, we could make a single trip in the otter," Brodie added.

"You'd get major brownie points with Raven."

Brodie frowned. "Raven and I don't work that way."

"Oh. Okay. How do you two work?"

"She does her job. I do mine."

"With Mia and me, it's more of a free-for-all. Sometimes it's an argument, sometimes she saves my life, sometimes—"

Brodie reared back. "What do you mean, Mia and *you*? Tell me you're not one of those guys?"

"*Those* guys?"

"Guys who think they have something special going on with Mia . . . Zeke and Xavier, AJ, and who knows who all else."

"I'm not like those guys." Silas really did have something special going on with Mia. Or, at least, he had at one time. He had no idea what the status was now. "But we seem to wander into each other's orbits a lot."

"Just so long as you don't get too close to her gravitational field."

"It's not a big deal." Silas would prefer to be totally honest with Brodie about his feelings for Mia. But since nothing real was going on, it was better to just let it lie.

Brodie turned as another pickup entered the lot. "Is Raven psychic or what?"

It was Raven's truck with Mia in the passenger seat, and Silas's pulse kicked up at the sight of her.

Her shiny blond hair was bouncing in a ponytail. She wore a snug burgundy top with a colorful scarf around her neck. Her face was fresh and bright, and he could already picture her form-fitting jeans and sexy leather ankle boots.

His feet started moving, taking him toward the truck as it turned in and halted in front of the hangar.

Raven got out on their side. She grinned, looking perky and energized. "Feels good to be back in business."

"The pilots are raring to go," Brodie said.

With the exception of Brodie and Silas, everyone had a flight taking off in the next few hours. The entire ground crew and a few of the Galina workers were here loading up the planes.

Silas's attention went straight to Mia as she walked around the back of the pickup box. The view of her beat his expectations, and he had to fight with himself to keep from going straight over and pulling her into his arms, kissing her and more.

"Hey, Brodie," Xavier called out. Xavier, Kenneth and T-Two were all walking their way.

Brodie turned to the call.

"The tires for Wildflower are causing us grief," Xavier said. "Tobias says they can take them in the otter."

"That's one option," Brodie said and started to walk to meet them.

"Would it impact the delivery times?" Raven asked, going along with him.

"Hi," Silas said to Mia in an undertone, pulling her attention from the conversation.

She looked his way and he moved closer. "Haven't seen you for a couple of days."

"We've all been busy."

"I heard you were feeding the bridge workers."

She shrugged. "A few sandwiches is all. Raven's place was closest."

"No more heavy equipment operating?"

She smiled at that. "Turns out you need some kind of a license."

Her phone rang suddenly, interrupting them. "Ah, cell

service. I do love cell service." She put it to her ear. "Hey, Marnie."

Silas knew he should back off and give her some privacy, but he didn't want to go anywhere. He wanted her to finish the call so they could get past this awkward back-and-forth and have a real conversation about them and their relationship and where it might be now.

"How did that work?" Mia asked, sounding both shocked and happy. She listened again. "Just like that?" She shook her head. "I can't believe it." She laughed. "You sure earned your retainer today."

Mia's smile grew wide as she listened to Marnie. "I will. You bet. Later today, probably. Thanks, Marnie." She ended the call.

"Good news?" Silas asked.

"I won."

"Won?"

"Everything. The judge threw out the case. We're not even going to trial; Alastair's personal lawyer backed Marnie. The judge concluded Alastair was of sound mind when he wrote the will and that there was no evidence I had any undue influence on his decisions. An age gap alone is not grounds to contest a duly authorized will." She laughed again and all but squealed in happiness.

"That's great news." Silas tried to sound enthusiastic. He knew it was the best possible outcome. He also knew it meant Mia would be leaving Paradise.

She looked at him then, the real her, not the aloof acquaintance she'd pretended to be earlier. "So . . ."

"Yeah," he said. "So . . ."

"I'll be looking for a ride to the Fairbanks airport."

"Sure. You bet." He didn't want to know, but he made himself ask. "When?"

She bit her lip. "Today."

His disappointment was acute.

"Or tomorrow." Her gaze moved over to Raven. "I should probably leave time to say good-byes."

"That's a good idea." He wanted to slow her down, even if he had no right to do that.

Raven looked over at them then, and Mia waved her phone.

"What?" Raven asked as the little discussion group broke up and she headed back their way.

"We won."

Raven looked astonished. "The lawsuit?"

Mia nodded. "As of this minute, I am sole owner and CEO of Lafayette Fashion."

"That's fantastic!" Raven's reaction was honest and enthusiastic as she grabbed Mia for a hug.

Silas felt like a jerk for his lukewarm response. He also kicked himself for not using the moment as an excuse to hug her. His arms felt empty as he watched the two women embrace.

"Great news!" Even Brodie did a better job of it than Silas.

"I guess certain people are getting fired," Raven said with a gleam in her eyes.

"I can't fire the twins," Mia said. "But that's fair. Alastair wanted to take care of them. Besides, they're never around. I can't see them suddenly starting to meddle."

"What about their enablers?"

"I have to figure out who they are first," Mia said. "I don't want to be vindictive, but I don't want them sabotaging me either. Somebody signed the cancellation order for London and Milan. It won't take much of a detective to work that one out."

Silas couldn't help but be impressed by Mia's confidence and decisiveness. On the other hand, he'd really loved the uncertain, slightly klutzy Mia, the one who tried new things, made mistakes and tried again.

He didn't want her to change. He didn't want anything to change. He wanted Mia to stay here in Paradise, talk with him, laugh with him, make love with him. He wanted the impossible, but he knew better than to go after it.

Mia belonged in the fashion business, where she was accomplished and influential. She deserved her dream as much as anybody else. She belonged in city and she always would, just like Silas belonged in the skies.

MIA THANKED RAVEN PROFUSELY FOR TAKING HER IN and saving her sanity. She promised both Raven and Breena that she'd keep working on the matchmaking project from LA.

Brodie had had a sudden change of heart. He had some conditions, but they weren't unreasonable. And he'd offered to fly twelve women from Fairbanks into Paradise free of charge.

Mia was convinced he'd done it to keep peace with Raven. Brodie and Raven were an enduring team. Right now, it was professional because that was important to both of them, and neither of them wanted to mess it up. But Mia was sure their feelings went deeper, and she couldn't imagine Brodie would let a rift come between them.

She'd taken Silas up on his offer to fly her back to Fairbanks, and they lifted off the airstrip now, circling back over Paradise to head west.

She felt a hitch in her chest looking down at Raven's cabin, the new bridge, the Bear and Bar, the Co-op and everything else all nestled in the crisp green valley surrounded by burbling blue rivers, pockets of wildlife and craggy mountain peaks. She wondered for a minute where they grizzly bears had gone.

She caught sight of Silas then and remembered their lovemaking. In his headset, a WSA cap and smoky sunglasses, his profile was strong as ever, sexy as ever. She couldn't imagine ever meeting a man like him in Los Angeles.

She suddenly wanted to stop, to turn back, to land in Paradise and just spend the entire week with Silas. LA could wait. Lafayette could wait. They'd lasted these past few weeks without her. They'd last one more. She wasn't ready to say good-bye to Silas.

"You feeling okay?" he asked over the intercom, his voice making her want him more than ever. "Not airsick, are you?"

"I'm not airsick." She was lonely. She hadn't even said good-bye to him, and she already felt so alone.

She watched the rivers, mountains and glaciers disappear behind them one after the other. And far too soon, the city of Fairbanks came into view. Silas was on the radio with air traffic control. Then they were descending, gliding onto the runway amid the din of commercial airliners, private planes and service vehicles of all sizes.

She felt like she'd been dropped unceremoniously back into civilization.

Silas taxied swiftly and efficiently from the active runaway to the FBO parking.

He shut down the engine and ran through procedures, unbuckling his harness and removing his headset. When he opened the door, the rumble of motors and the shriek of jet engines filled the air. He hopped out and pushed up his seat to gain access to her bags in the back.

Mia unbuckled and hooked her headset above the doorway. She remembered how to unlatch the door and let herself out, firming her legs under her after the motion of the airplane, meeting Silas on the tarmac.

"Here we are," she said, gathering her hair against the wind.

"Don't forget your stored bags," he said as he turned, luggage in hand, for the FBO entrance.

She'd completely forgotten about her bag and was surprised he'd remembered. Her mind was far too full of Silas to leave room for anything else as each step brought her closer and closer to their final good-bye.

It was quiet and peaceful inside the FBO. Mia let out a breath of relief and released her hair, finger combing it back.

"Hey, Becky," Silas said with a nod.

It was the same young woman behind the counter.

"Your bags," she said, giving Mia a smile. "I'll be right back."

"Looks like this is where we came in," Silas said.

Mia met his blue-eyed gaze, thinking it might be for the last time. Her chest tightened and her heart hurt. "Silas, I don't want this to—"

"Don't," he said, putting two fingers gently across her lips. "It was great, I mean *great*, meeting you, Mia."

Excuse me? Meeting her? Was that how he summed it up?

He smoothed her windblown hair and stepped closer. "I'm going to miss you."

She relaxed then, anticipating his embrace.

But he cupped her shoulders instead and gave her a kiss on the cheek. On the *cheek*? "Have a good trip back."

No way. That couldn't be it. "What if I visit?"

He drew back. "Why would you do that?"

"Because that's what people do. You and me—"

He was shaking his head.

She didn't know what he meant. "You just said you'd miss me."

"I will."

"I'll miss you too."

He gave a sad smile then. "You know as soon as you get to LA, your real life is going to scoop you up like a tornado. You'll be far too busy to miss anyone."

But Silas wasn't just anyone. He was Silas. Silas, the sexiest, toughest, smartest, most exciting man she'd ever met. Her first real lover; she knew that now. What she'd had with him was beyond anything she could have imagined or dreamed.

"Just because I'll be busy doesn't mean I won't miss you," she said.

He looked like he didn't believe her, like he was humoring her.

"I'm coming back," she said with determination, knowing he couldn't stop her.

"Don't do that." He gave her a chaste kiss on the forehead this time. "Just let it be what it was."

"I don't want that. I want more."

"You think you do. You're an LA girl, Mia. It's what you know. It's where you thrive." He was saying she was soft. He was saying she was wimpy. He was saying she wasn't good enough for Alaska. Or maybe he just meant she wasn't good enough for him.

She was suddenly embarrassed.

He was politely brushing her off, and she was clinging to him like a lovesick teenager.

She straightened, her throat closing in. "You're right. You're you and I'm me, and that's that."

"Afraid so."

She gave him a nod, not trusting her voice any longer.

Becky reappeared behind the counter. "Two bags. One small roller bag, one garment bag."

"That's them," Mia said brightly.

Becky stacked them on a luggage cart. "Are you going over to the main terminal?"

Mia nodded.

"I'll call the shuttle driver."

Silas transferred her other bags to the luggage cart.

"You don't have to wait," she told him as he turned back to her.

"Okay. Good luck out there. I know you'll knock them dead."

She barely got a thank you out before he turned and headed back out the glass doors.

"Good-bye, Silas." she whispered to his back.

SILAS LANDED ON THE PARADISE STRIP, GLIDING OVER the newly smoothed patch from the creek washout before taxiing down the access road to park the Navajo. He shut things down and then sat there, staring at the trees.

He should have told Mia to come back for a visit. He should have begged her to come back for a visit. Cold turkey was a stupid idea. Most things in life were easier to give up if you weaned yourself off gradually, and Mia was easily the hardest thing he'd ever had to give up.

He delayed getting out of the plane, clinging to the scent of her perfume, which still lingered in the air. He spied the source: her multicolored scarf in the space beside her seat. It must have fallen from her tote bag somewhere along the trip.

His first instinct was to rush it back to her, use it as an excuse for a do-over of their good-bye. This time he'd hold her close, kiss her deeply and tell her yes, yes, come back to Paradise just as soon as she could.

But it was a ridiculous instinct. She was in the air by now on her way to Anchorage. The thought brought his mood down even further.

He tucked the scarf into his pocket and pushed open the airplane door. He climbed out and tied the Navajo down. The hangar's bay door was wide open, and Cobra was inside working on Papa-X-ray. Silas wandered that way.

"Problem?" he asked Cobra, nodding to the plane.

Cobra pulled back from the engine. "Nope. Hundred-hour service. Everything looks good. You can put it on the books for tomorrow."

"I'll tell Brodie."

"You dropped her off okay?"

Silas gave a nod. "She's on her way back to the big city."

Cobra chuckled. "I think the whole town is in mourning."

"Not you too." Silas hated to feel like just another guy in the crowd. He knew his relationship with Mia was special. Then again, according to Brodie, a lot of the guys felt that way.

"Nah," Cobra said. "I barely met her. Most of the other guys barely met her too. But that doesn't keep them from dreaming."

"I guess."

"Not like you," Cobra said.

"What about me?"

Cobra gave him a look that told him to quit bullshitting. "I practically live here, remember?"

Silas tried to figure out what Cobra might have seen.

And then it hit him. The day they'd come back from Wildflower Lake, he'd pretty much lifted Mia down from the airplane. He'd hugged her tight, hating the fact that their interlude was ending and trying to hold onto it a few moments longer.

And the ride in the loader. There was no way Cobra could have seen what had happened between them. They were too far away. But he might have seen them leave and seen them come back.

"Anybody else know?" Silas asked.

"Need-to-know basis," Cobra said, wiping down his ratchet handle with a cloth. "Nobody needed to know."

"Well, she's gone now," Silas said.

"Sucks, I'm sure."

"It really does." Silas was surprised at how much he wanted to talk about it. "I wish she'd come back."

"Will she?" Cobra placed the wrench back in the toolbox.

"I told her not to."

"Why?"

Silas shrugged. "Seemed like a bad idea . . . at the time."

"And now?"

"Now I wish I'd gone with her."

Cobra chuckled. "You? In LA? Man, you've got it bad."

"I've got it bad," Silas agreed, then considered Cobra's apparent empathy. "Ever happen to you?"

"Fall in love?"

"I'm not in love."

Cobra looked unconvinced. "Maybe not."

"We're talking about you now."

"Yeah," Cobra said. "I fell for someone."

Silas as intrigued. "And?"

"She fell for someone else. An investment banker. Well, in the end, he was an investment banker. We were all in high school at the time. I was taking shop classes. He was taking advanced calculus. They went off to college together, and I joined the air force two days after graduation."

"You regret losing her?" Silas asked.

"Not since high school. I wouldn't have made her happy in the long run."

"Same," Silas said, knowing it was true. He wasn't about to repeat his father's mistake.

"So, what next?" Cobra asked.

"I've got planes to fly." Silas might struggle to get over Mia, but at least he still had his life's passion.

"And I've got engines to make hum," Cobra said.

Silas clapped him on the shoulder. "Nobody appreciates your skills more than I do. Hey, you ever want to meet new women?"

Cobra didn't miss a beat. "Why? You got some?"

"Maybe," Silas said and chuckled. "It's a thing Mia and Raven were working on, coming out of that silly poker game."

"I'm not gambling for women."

"No, no. Nothing like that. Maybe a meet-and-greet, with some of Mia's friends from California."

"You are a sucker for punishment."

"No, I think it could really work."

Chapter Fifteen

MIA SAT BEHIND ALASTAIR'S BIG MAHOGANY DESK, feeling like she'd been swallowed by the size of the room and the furniture. The place needed a makeover before she'd feel at home here. She'd get rid of the heavy curtains, maybe go for sleek blinds. They'd take up less space, so she'd get natural light from the entire window instead of just the middle section.

The dark brown leather sofas were also on the hit list. She'd prefer armchairs; leather was okay, fabric even better, and a lighter color—cream, she thought. And the wood tones needed to be lightened up too.

There was a tap on her door.

"Yes?"

"Ms. Westberg?" Alastair's assistant, Veronica cautiously, opened the door.

It was clear Veronica was nervous. Everyone in the company was nervous, and for good reason. The lawsuit had failed spectacularly, so whatever Henry and Hannah had promised the senior managers was off the table. Mia was in charge now, and quite a few people seemed surprised by the turn of events.

"Here are the contracts you asked about." Veronica stepped in with a file folder.

Alastair had spoken glowingly of Veronica, but Mia didn't know her particularly well.

"Thanks," Mia said.

Veronica crossed to Mia's desk and set the folder down before turning to go.

"Veronica?"

She turned back. "Is there something else?"

"Can you sit down for a minute?"

Veronica hesitated and then swallowed. "Of course."

She sat in one of the guest chairs and smoothed the slim navy skirt of her Lafayette dress. The dress was one of Mia's favorites, with a square neckline and beige-stripe accents at the waist and shoulders. Mia had also taken note of Veronica's simple black and burgundy pumps. People weren't expected to dress exclusively in Lafayette wear, but Veronica was smart to show the corporate colors this week.

Mia got straight to the point. "What are your feelings on the outcome?"

Veronica hesitated.

"Me as the new CEO," Mia said, to be crystal-clear.

Veronica's fingers fidgeted together on her knee. "I feel fine. I mean, we don't know each other very well, but . . . you know . . . we can . . ." She paused.

"Get to know each other better?" Mia offered.

Veronica bobbed a rapid nod. "I'm sure you heard . . . I mean, some people thought . . ."

"That Henry and Hannah would take over?" Mia finished for her.

Veronica gave a slower, uneasy nod.

"I'm not going to ask who wanted that."

Veronica's shoulders settled in what looked like relief.

Mia reach out and slid the file toward herself. "I'm not

looking for blind loyalty. But I do need to know if you can be happy here under the changed circumstances."

Interacting with people from Galina and WSA these past weeks, even the staff of Bear and Bar, had been an eye-opening experience for Mia. She'd learned a lot about team dynamics. "It's important to me that you like your job and respect your team members."

"I do," Veronica said. "Respect you, I mean. I'm totally looking forward to working with you, and with Dara-Leigh too." She hesitated. "That is, if you want me to stay."

"I want you to stay if you're happy staying."

"I'm happy."

"Good. That's settled." Mia sat back and gazed around the office. "One thing to start, I want to freshen the decor in here. You think you could come up with some ideas to lighten it up?"

Veronica looked happily surprised. "Yes. Sure."

"Great. And can you get me the latest Boca and Rittenberg swatch samples? We're already behind on our fabric order."

"Of course."

"I'll need a presentation from the head designers for next year's winter collection, sometime tomorrow. Nothing fancy, just the broad strokes. Tell them whatever they have that's easy to put together."

Veronica rose. "Right away."

"Thank you."

As Veronica left the office, Mia tapped her fingers on the file folder. Inside were the contracts for the Shanghai and São Paulo shows. When she saw the signatures, she'd have her first traitor.

There was another knock on the door, sharper this time. Someone was in a hurry.

"Come in," Mia called out.

Geraldine Putts entered the room and closed the door behind herself.

"Hello, Geraldine."

"Good morning." Geraldine took a couple of careful steps forward, like Mia was a mother grizzly bear and Geraldine was prey. Her gaze dropped warily to the file folder.

It was obvious to Mia what that meant. "I take it your signature is on these contracts?"

"I didn't want to." Geraldine was clearly fearful. "They insisted. There was a study, facts and figures, data and statistics. The market is moving, and demographics are changing."

"But you knew I'd want to stick with Alastair's plan."

Geraldine slowly nodded.

Mia didn't know if Geraldine was a collaborator or merely a victim of circumstance, and she hated to jump to conclusions, since she'd had enough of that coming her way lately. It was no fun and utterly unfair to be the victim of assumptions.

She could fire Geraldine for signing the contracts, and she could fire Veronica for letting Geraldine know she'd asked for them. And then she could interrogate everyone on the senior management team and try to determine their loyalty, maybe fire them all.

The thought of it was exhausting.

"Are you happy here?" she asked Geraldine instead.

"Happy?" Geraldine seemed baffled by the question.

"In your job, working at Lafayette."

"Of course. Absolutely."

"And with me being in charge? Because I'm here, and that's just the way it is."

"Yes," Geraldine said eagerly.

"I don't know who to trust," Mia said.

Geraldine was silent for a minute. "We deserve that."

"But who wants to go on a witch-hunt?" Mia pushed the folder away. "I don't. Would you?"

The question seemed to stump Geraldine. Her answer was hesitant. "No."

"Good. I'm not making assumptions about anybody. Show me who you are and what you've got. And maybe you can do me the same courtesy."

"I will," she said, looking massively relieved. "Thank you."

"You can spread that around the gossip mill," Mia said.

Geraldine didn't seem to know how to respond.

Mia regretted the jab. "Veronica is setting up a design meeting for Thursday."

"I'll look forward to it." Geraldine's expression changed and her tone went softer. "Thank you, Mia."

After Geraldine left, Mia stared at the closed door, telling herself she was doing the right thing. She could trust her instincts here. As Silas had pointed out, this was her environment, the one where she would thrive.

She was in a supportive environment now, a place where her every whim would be respected and no one would challenge her anymore.

A car would pick her up tonight at five. The driver would deliver her to the house, where the assistant chef would have dinner prepared—maybe a salad, some salmon or halibut and maybe a nice Cabernet Sauvignon or Chablis to go with it. She wouldn't say no to dessert. Since that first cinnamon bun in Paradise, she'd embraced carbs and sugar, increasing her cardio to compensate.

She could work out in the basement gym tonight. No bears down there. No mosquitos either. Then, after a steam shower, she'd sleep in her custom-built Belgardi Luxury bed with the down pillows and silk comforter. Life here in LA was the best.

SILAS COULDN'T HELP BUT CHUCKLE AT RAVEN'S EF-forts over drinks at the Bear and Bar. He'd given her zero chance of Brodie agreeing to her latest idea, and it looked like he'd been right.

"I'm nobody's pilot poster boy," Brodie said.

"It'll be from a distance," Breena said. She was sitting next to Raven and across the table from Silas. It was late enough that there were only a few customers left in the restaurant.

Silas polished off his beer and checked his watch. It was more than thirteen hours until his flight tomorrow, so he was in good shape, alcoholwise.

"We don't want a close-up of your face or anything," Raven said.

"I'm not sure how to take that." Brodie sipped his whiskey.

"You two are the right size and shape," Breena said.

"What?" Silas gave them his full attention. It was the first anyone mentioned him being included. "Who?"

Brodie seemed amused that he wasn't being co-opted alone.

"Both of you," Raven said. She held her hands in a square like she was a movie producer. "In your flight suits, the caravan as a backdrop against the mountains. Green suits, red and white plane."

"It'll be perfect," Breena said. "You're both tall, rugged, dark hair, nice square shoulders."

"I don't know about you," Silas said to Brodie, "but I'm feeling objectified."

"That's because we're objectifying you." Breena gave a sly grin as she lifted her own frosty mug. Hers was full since she'd just joined the party.

Silas felt an urge for a whiskey nightcap, but he was trying not to slip into that habit. It had been three nights since Mia left. Three nights where he'd struggled to fall asleep, thinking about where she was, what she was doing and who she was with. He couldn't believe how badly he missed her.

"You want us to succeed, don't you?" Raven asked in a cajoling tone.

"I couldn't care less," Brodie said. "I'm humoring you; rewarding you, really."

"For what? I'll do it again if you'll be in the photo."

"I'm rewarding Mia."

Silas's chest contracted at the sound of her name, and her image bloomed even sharper in his mind. He pushed back his chair to head for the bar to get that whiskey.

"For saving my plane," Brodie continued. "And for saving Silas's life."

"Well, that means Silas has to be in the photo," Raven called out for Silas's benefit.

He didn't turn to acknowledge her, and the three of them chuckled from the table.

"A whiskey," he said to Badger. "Black Boar, neat. Make it a double."

"You got it," Badger said, flipping a cut-glass tumbler onto the bar then reaching for the bottle.

"For the record," Badger said as he poured, "I think you should do it."

"You overheard?" Silas asked.

"Little bit. And Breena told me earlier about their plans. Having Mia here was a breath of fresh air."

Silas looked at him sharply.

"Relax, man. Not like that. I saw the way you looked at her."

Silas took a swig of the whiskey. Was he that damn obvious?

"And she looked back at you the same way," Badger said. "But my point is, you and Brodie would make a good poster." Badger recapped the bottle and set it on the shelf. "You'd attract the ladies, and that would be a win for everybody."

"I'm not wild about being a male model." But he wondered if Mia would appreciate his effort. He wondered if it might give him an excuse to call her. Yeah, maybe he should call her to ask her advice on modeling.

It would be way too obvious, but he wanted to do it anyway.

"The guys will definitely bust your chops over it."

Silas gave a brief laugh, thinking about the teasing he and Brodie would endure.

"But do you care?" Badger asked. "If it's the right thing to do, do you care what the guys think?"

"Not really."

"Do you think she'll come back?"

"Mia?" Silas toyed with his glass, stalling.

"Yeah."

Silas shook his head. "Nothing for her here."

Badger was silent for a minute. "You sure about that?"

Silas looked up. "You met her. You saw her. She's not Paradise material."

"Maybe not."

There was no maybe about it.

"Then again, the planes go both ways," Badger said.

Silas had thought about that more than once. He could fly himself straight to Anchorage, hop a nonstop airliner and hit LAX within about five hours. But then what? A stolen weekend with Mia? If she'd even have him. Then he'd leave her all over again and it might hurt even worse.

"Why are you getting all bartender on me tonight?" he asked Badger.

"Because I know an unhappy man when I see one."

"You've got it wrong."

Badger smiled and tapped his hand on the bar as another customer arrived at the far end. "For your sake, I hope I do."

"Silas?" Breena called out to him.

He picked up his drink and turned back to the table.

"Brodie will do it if you will," Raven said.

Brodie looked aghast. "That's not what I—"

Silas cut him off. "Sure."

"You will?" Breena sounded delighted.

"Anything for the cause." Silas polished off the drink.

"What is *wrong* with you?" Brodie asked.

"Chill, man," Silas said. "If we're going to do this, we might as well do it right."

"Breena?" Badger called out. "Can you get these guys at the bar a quick burger before we close the kitchen?"

"On it." Breena grinned as she rose. "This is going to be awesome."

Raven dropped some money on the table. "I gotta run. Early morning tomorrow."

"Night." Brodie said.

"Later," Silas said.

"See you," Raven responded to both of them as she headed for the door.

Brodie watched until the door shut behind her. "What was that about?"

Silas shrugged, not ready to admit he was doing it for Mia. "They're working really hard."

"*We* don't need to be the sacrificial lambs."

"Where's your community spirit?"

"I'm lending them housing rooms and donating an otter flight." Brodie made a fair point.

Silas hadn't done much of anything to help so far. He wished he done more. In fact, he wished he done a lot of things differently. "I wasn't straight with you about Mia."

Brodie's brow went up in curiosity.

Silas rubbed his empty glass on the smooth table. "It *was* special. Me and her, I mean."

"Seriously? Come on."

"I slept with her."

Brodie went still this time, very still and very silent.

"Twice," Silas said. "We kept it quiet. Obviously, we kept it quiet."

"Does Raven know?"

Silas couldn't see how that was relevant. "I don't know. Mia wasn't planning to tell anyone."

"You should have said something."

"I know. Thing is, it hit me like a ground loop—my own

screw-up, embarrassing as hell, leaving destruction in its wake."

"You slept with her, Silas. You didn't marry her."

Silas thought of his father again, wondering if it could be a flaw in his genes. "Yeah, that's the thing."

"Don't say it."

"I wanted to keep her. I seriously thought about how it could work out for us."

MIA WAS HAPPY TO SEE RAVEN'S NAME COME UP ON her phone screen. She quickly accepted the call and sat back in Alastair's big desk chair. "Hey, you."

"We need your help," Raven said in a rush. "I'm here with Brodie."

Mia's interest immediately perked up. "You are?"

"In his room."

"Un-huh." Mia waited for details, hoping they were juicy, wondering exactly what kind of help they might need.

"I don't know the first thing about decorating."

"You're decorating?" Well, that was disappointing.

"Staff housing," Raven said. "For the women. Brodie wants me to pick out colors and stuff."

Mia laughed at the idea of Raven as a decorator.

Her cabin had been done in *early practical*. As far as Mia could tell, her cousin had randomly hung her paintings where she found existing hooks. The paintings themselves seemed equally random, gifts Raven said she'd gathered over the years. Her furniture was functional—some used, some floor models she said she bought on sale. And she'd confessed her bedroom linens had come as a set from a discount place, in a giant bag, sheets, blankets even curtains.

Mia doubted Raven had ever chosen an item for its aesthetics.

"There's no way I'm doing all of that," Brodie's voice came on. "It's your project."

"You've got the speakerphone on?" Mia asked.

"You've got us both here," Raven answered.

"What do you want to know?" Mia asked.

"Do you want the rooms together?" Brodie asked.

"Yes, we do."

"I don't suppose we could double people up."

Mia frowned. "I don't suppose we could. We're trying to impress the women, make them like the town, not have some sort of college dorm roomie situation."

"You know this isn't going to work," he said. "Not in the long run."

"We're curating the right type of women. I know both worlds, and we've come up with a questionnaire."

"It's a whole lot easier to answer a questionnaire than survive forty below." Brodie changed his voice to soprano, mimicking a woman. "*Yes, I like skiing, pretty snowflakes and sipping hot chocolate in front of the fire on cold winter nights.*"

Mia laughed out loud. She'd never, not even once, seen Brodie make a silly joke.

"That was terrible," Raven said, laughing along with Mia.

"You should be asking them if they know how to chop firewood, shovel snow, fuel a generator or stoke a fire," he said.

"Chop firewood? Be serious," Raven said.

"You chop your own firewood."

"You know I have an electric log splitter. Anybody can run one of those."

"No, not just *anyone* can do that," he countered. It was pretty obvious he meant Mia.

"Mia ran the loader," Rave pointed out.

It warmed Mia's heart to have Raven immediately defend her like that.

Brodie didn't rebut.

That part made Mia happy too.

"You want the units closest to the Bear and Bar?" he asked, moving on.

"The shorter the walk the better," Mia said. "They might wear heels."

"Heels. Perfect." Brodie said, sarcasm clear in his tone.

"I've sent you pictures of Brodie's unit," Raven said as Mia's phone pinged to signal their arrival.

The room was basic—a single bed, two chairs, beige walls and a small bathroom. On the upside, there was oil heat and indoor plumbing. Mia knew the units were a cut above wall tents.

"They're all pretty much the same," Raven said.

"What color do you want them?" Brodie asked.

"I was thinking maybe blue?" Raven said. "Or a soft yellow might be warmer and brighter, like sunshine inside."

"Dusty rose," Mia said. "It's warm but not too bright. It'll make the rooms feel bigger."

"Dusty rose?" Brodie echoed. "Seriously?"

"I'll send up some art for the walls. And some linens."

Mia's assistant, Dara-Leigh, had been disappointed when Veronica was assigned to decorate the office. So Mia had offered the matchmaking project décor as a consolation prize. To Mia's surprise, Dara-Leigh had been thrilled and was already shopping for ideas.

"I'll give your contact information to my assistant down here," Mia said. "Dara-Leigh's offered to help, and she's got a good flare."

"You don't mean mine," Brodie said.

"Mine?" Raven echoed, sounding doubtful.

"I was thinking Breena's," Mia said.

"Good choice," Raven said, relieved.

"Is this going to be all frilly?" Brodie asked.

Mia chuckled. "You'll just have to wait and see."

Brodie's heavy sigh came through loud and clear. "Well, won't that be popular with the guys."

AS MIA ENDED THE CALL, SILAS BLOOMED IN HER MIND. She was catapulted back to the town, back to his arms, back to every single thing they'd done together.

She missed him desperately, and she missed Paradise too. Dealing with it at work was bad enough, but at least there she had distractions. Home was even worse. Her house seemed so empty now, hollowly opulent, ridiculously large. Her own voice echoed back from her in every gilded room.

She couldn't even picture Alastair anymore. When she tried, Silas filled the frame. Not that she could imagine Silas in his work boots, flight suit and WSA cap traipsing through that meticulously decorated monument to fine art.

He'd hate it.

She pretty much hated it now too. She knew she had to move out, buy something smaller, a condo or a penthouse closer to the office. But her days were busy, and at night she couldn't seem to muster up the energy to look for new places.

Restless, she left her office and headed down the hall.

A movement caught her eye, and she drew up short. Hannah was inside her office, sitting at the meeting table deep in conversation with Henry. The pair had been in the office only a handful of times over the past three years, so Mia's suspicions immediately rose.

She may have decided against purging the staff, but that didn't mean Henry and Hannah were free to continue meddling in the company. No chance of that. And she was setting the ground rules right here and now.

She gave a sharp courtesy rap and opened the office door to walk in.

They both stopped talking and looked up in surprise.

"I didn't expect to see you here." Mia shut the door behind her for privacy and strode to the middle of the office.

They exchanged glances.

"We need to get a few things straight," Mia said.

"Would you like to sit down?" Hannah asked.

The offer took Mia by surprise and temporarily pushed her off her game. "No, thank you. First, I'd appreciate it if you let me know when you planned to visit the office. Second, I want a heads up on any meetings you have with the vice presidents or the department managers. Third, if you're attending any event on behalf of Lafayette Fashion, I want a chance to discuss it in advance."

"Mia," Hannah said.

"Fourth," Mia said, letting her tone tell them she was annoyed by the interruption. "Although I'm not purging the senior staff—no thanks to you two—I will be watching. Some of them are on probation for a while."

"We're not here to get in your way." Henry's tone was deferential, not the least bit combative.

Mia wasn't buying it. "Right."

Hannah rose. "We accept the judge's decision."

Henry rose too.

Mia looked from one to the other, trying to interpret their expressions. They looked sincere, but that didn't mean much. She'd lived through years of the twins' and their mother's conniving ways.

"We just want to be involved," Hannah said.

"Involved how?" Mia asked.

This wasn't making sense. The twins had never shown an interest in the company before. They just took their salaries and ran. They had to be up to something here.

"Supply chain management," Henry said. "I'm no designer, but I've watched Dad stick with the same old suppliers year after year, never even considering what else was out there that might be an improvement or a cost savings, India, for example."

"You've *watched*?" Mia was completely baffled now.

"We have access to the entire company computer system," Hannah said.

"You made use of it?" Mia asked, trying to wrap her head around the idea that the two had done anything other than travel and party since college.

"We've stuck with the same target demographic forever," Hannah said. "Our customers are getting older. Older people buy fewer clothes."

"Lafayette is a classic designer." Mia didn't know why she was explaining, except maybe that they'd taken her by surprise.

"That's a pathway to oblivion," Hannah said. "Whereas Shanghai and São Paulo—"

"I *knew* that was you two."

"Are up and coming," Hannah continued, ignoring the interruption. The enthusiasm level in her voice increased with every sentence. "I've been watching them for years. We have a new designer on staff, Emille Castille. She's a perfect match for São Paulo, and—"

"What?" Mia looked back and forth between them, wondering if this was some kind of a practical joke.

"Emille works under Jo Bouvier, but I think she'd do better with a young adult focus."

Mia reached for the back of a chair and pulled it out to sit down.

Hannah sat too. "There's another designer, Werner Faux. He's freelancing, but his work has been so phenomenal that I'd like to make him an offer. I can show you his portfolio."

"It's not just the fabric and designs," Henry jumped in as he sat down too. "It's the subcontracting, the store locations and setup, the web interface, even the packaging. There are huge improvements to be made. Have you analyzed the sales channels recently?"

"Have you?" Mia asked.

Henry nodded. "If we make some changes, I'm conservatively projecting a thirty percent increase in business over the next two years. I can show you the numbers."

"You two are serious." It was obvious to Mia they were more than just serious. They were keeners. They reminded her of Raven.

"Completely," Henry said while Hannah nodded.

"Why haven't you said anything before now? Why didn't you talk to Alastair?"

They exchanged another look.

"What?" Mia asked.

"We did," Hannah said.

Mia knew Alastair would have been thrilled to have them involved. "And what did he say?"

"That us being here would upset you."

Mia's chest hitched with guilt. "He *did*?" She'd never meant to keep Alastair from his children.

"He . . . uh . . ." Henry began haltingly. "He told us he talked to you about it."

"But—" Mia stopped herself. She didn't want to admit Alastair had lied to them.

"He never even asked you," Henry said with conviction.

"I guess we deserved that," Hannah said.

"We were pretty nasty," Henry said.

"I don't hold that against you," Mia quickly put in. Oddly, she didn't. She had for a lot of years, but somehow the resentment had faded.

She realized they'd been kids back then, naturally hostile against the teenager their father was marrying. And she'd been so defensive, so busy trying to hide her insecurities and pretend she was perfect that she hadn't let anyone know the real her, not even Alastair.

Ironically, almost amusingly, and out of necessity really,

Raven had come closest to seeing the true Mia, the flawed and awkward Mia. Well, Raven and Silas. Silas had gotten to know her better than anyone ever had.

He bloomed in her mind again, amused by her, patient with her, forcing his way past her veneer to reveal her flaws. And then he'd laugh at them and they wouldn't seem so bad.

And he'd had faith. That one last time on the radio when the chips were down and his life hung in the balance, he'd truly put his faith in her.

She felt an urge to run to him now, to hop on the next plane and fling herself into his arms. She wouldn't even care if she never came back. Her old life was gone.

"Do you want the house?" she asked the twins.

They both stilled and pasted her with identical looks of stupefaction.

"What did you say?" Henry asked.

"You want it? You grew up there—well, at first anyway—and it's way too big for me." As soon as the words were out, she knew it was the right thing to do.

She wanted a simpler life. In fact, the simpler life she thought she wanted was beginning to frighten her.

Chapter Sixteen

LYING IN HIS BED, SILAS COULD STILL FEEL MIA IN HIS arms. In his truck, he could hear her voice. And in the air, he could see her smiling profile as she gazed down at the majesty of Alaska's valleys. He couldn't get away from her—not at the airstrip, not at Galina, and definitely not in the Bear and Bar.

So, when he couldn't avoid a trip to Wildflower Lake Lodge, he prepared himself for the worst. And he got it. Standing on the boardwalk gazing at the chalets, their entire night together replayed in his mind.

She'd liked here. She'd fit better in the luxury chalet than she had anywhere else in Alaska. Then, because he was feeling particularly masochistic, he walked all the way to the south creek villa.

The door to it was open, the screen door shut. And there were two towels on the front porch loungers. Obviously someone was staying there.

He didn't want to be rude, so he didn't stop. But he slowed his pace, pictured her in the big shower, in that white bathrobe, curled up on the sofa. Then he rounded a curve and the villa went out of sight.

He heard a compressor running and the distinctive bang-bang of a nail gun. Around the corner he came across the wood building frame of a new villa.

"Hey, Silas," Danny called from across the construction site. Hardhat on his head, he picked his way through the lumber, gravel piles, sawhorses and power tools. "Didn't expect you today."

"Tristen cut his finger. I had to sub in."

"Hope it's not bad."

"Nurse was giving him a couple of stitches. He'll be fine."

"Good to hear." Danny gazed up at the frame with Silas.

"Will this be the same as the others?" Silas asked.

"A tried-and-true design," Danny said. "Good for shedding snow, efficient to heat, and my guy's built so many of them, he and his crew have it down to an art. You staying?"

"No, not tonight."

"You alone?" Danny peered past Silas to look down the boardwalk.

"Sorry to say, I am."

"I bet you're sorry," Danny said with a grin. "Mia was too good for you."

"She was," Silas agreed. He nodded at the wood frame. "What do these things run you?"

"Out here?" Danny blew out a breath. "They cost a small fortune."

"What about in town?" An idea was formulating in Silas's mind. It was just an idea, not something he was seriously contemplating; at least not yet. But it was an idea.

"In Paradise? For you?"

"Yeah. The staff housing feels cramped in the winter."

"You're probably looking at a couple hundred per square foot, more depending on the finishing. You want a stone fireplace and lots of glazing?"

"Probably," Silas said. Since it was only a dream, he might as well go for broke. "What's the square footage on your plan?"

"Just under twenty-four hundred. That's with the expanded kitchen and nook. You serious?"

"I'm thinking about it."

"I can give you the plans, no problem. You want to talk to Michael?"

"Not yet." Silas didn't want to waste the builder's time.

Danny reached into his shirt pocket. "Take his card. You can call if you have questions."

Silas accepted. "Thanks. Better take off."

"See you." Danny gave a wave as he started back to the villa.

Silas walked past the south creek villa once more, took the trail up to the airstrip and climbed into the plane, all the while thinking about Mia. He tried to imagine her expression if he asked her to live in Paradise. Would she smile, frown, laugh, assume he was joking?

Probably. If he was her, he'd assumed it was a joke. The thought of her leaving her perfect LA life, along with the successful fashion business she'd just fought tooth and nail to keep, was ludicrous.

By the time he landed at WSA, he knew his dream was just that: a ludicrous pipedream. Mia wasn't coming back to Alaska. If Silas wanted to be with her, he'd have to go to LA. But that idea was almost as absurd as Mia coming here.

Almost.

He tied down the plane and crossed the parking lot, trying to imagine what a bush pilot would do in downtown Los Angeles. Wait tables, probably.

"No thank-you bottle of wine this time?" Brodie asked as Silas walked into the office.

"She didn't even offer," Silas said, crossing to the fridge for a bottle of beer.

"She must not need anything from us," Brodie said, straightening away from the reception desk, where he'd been leaning while reading an invoice. "That right tire hold air okay?"

"I checked after landing. It's good." Silas kept going, grabbed the beer and straddled a chair at one of the lounge tables.

Brodie followed and took a seat across from him. "Raven says WSA guys can use four of the rooms in the Galina housing. T and T-Two offered to share."

"You're being very helpful all of a sudden."

Brodie's attitude had done a one-eighty.

He shrugged. "Mia's got us painting the units dusty rose. But don't worry, we're not taking over your place."

Mia again.

"Is she coming up?" Silas asked, trying not to sound hopeful.

"Mia?" Brodie played dumb.

Silas tilted his bottle as if to ask *who else?*

"Don't think so."

Silas let his disappointment settle for a moment. "I don't know how this is going to work."

Brodie got up for a beer. "I told you, we're not using your room."

"I mean with Mia."

"Mia's not coming." Brodie popped the cap.

"That's the problem." It didn't matter how many ways Silas came at this, he couldn't accept having Mia out of his life completely and forever. "I don't see how this works."

Brodie swung back into his seat. "Women come to Paradise, the guys meet them. After that, it's pretty much up to biology or fate or whatever."

"I mean Mia."

Brodie took a drink, obviously waiting for more information.

"I can't stop thinking about her."

"It hasn't been that long."

"The more time that goes by, the worse it gets." Silas was too embarrassed to tell Brodie about his house-building fantasy. "Thing is, I don't know if I can let her go."

"You want to go get her and bring her back?"

"I think she'd have to be willing."

"I can lend you a plane. But it's illegal to bring her unwillingly across state lines."

Silas chuckled. "Probably not our best plan."

"Nope. You want me to get Raven to help?"

Silas shook his head. "I can't see Mia staying long-term in Alaska."

Brodie was contemplative. "That would be . . . surprising."

"Yeah." Silas took a beat. "But I also don't think I can let her go."

"You just said—" Brodie sat up straight. "Oh no. Oh no you don't."

"I haven't figured out how it could work. I mean, a bush pilot, in LA?"

"That's nut, Silas."

"They have, like, national forests and things around there, right?"

"I need you here."

"She's there." Silas took a drink. He'd feel terrible leaving Brodie, but he couldn't see another way.

"You can't up and follow a woman to California."

"I thought about building her a house here in town. Danny offered me the plans for a three-bedroom villa. They're nice. Mia would like it."

"There you go." Brodie gestured with his beer bottle.

"It would still be in Paradise, though, where there's nothing for her. No restaurants."

"The Bear and Bar."

"No clubs."

"You can dance on the deck."

"No nightlife."

"Aurora Borealis."

Silas frowned. "You know what I mean."

"Not all women are like your mom."

Silas shook his head. "Most of them are."

Brodie didn't argue. "You've lost your mind."

"What if I haven't?" Silas was seriously considering that possibility. What if it turned out Mia was more important to him than his bush-flying career? What did he do then?

"I tell you what," Brodie said decisively. "Take the new Cessna down. Take the weekend; make it a long weekend. Feel her out. See what you think. Enjoy the noise and the crowds and the commercialism."

"You can spare me for a long weekend?"

"Xavier can step up. I'll make it work."

"What if I'm right? What if I'm in love with her?"

Brodie plunked his beer on the table and shook his head. "I guess the heart wants what the heart wants."

"Seriously? You're going poetic?"

"No, I'm mocking you." Then Brodie frowned. "Ah hell, I'd sure hate to lose you."

Silas hated the thought too. "This is the best job I've ever had."

"But she's the best woman you've ever had."

Silas couldn't help but smile thinking about her. "By far."

MIA'S BAGS WERE PACKED AND WAITING FOR HER driver to arrive. Nine years ago, she'd moved in with all of Alastair's things. Now she was leaving them here for Henry and Hannah. Her closet was full of more clothes than she'd ever wear, plus she chose new Lafayette outfits every season. So, she'd been very selective, taking things that were comfortable more than glamorous. If she needed a killer outfit, she could always get something from the warehouse. She was a standard size and easy to fit.

She had a one-month reservation at the Waldorf to give herself time to condo shop.

"As your lawyer, I have to seriously advise against this," Marnie said, where they sat in the formal great room under the huge portrait of Alastair's father that hung above the ornate stone fireplace. The fireplace hadn't seen a fire in decades.

The mantel was covered in expensive sculptures, including two golden candlesticks. The candles never burned either. Mia hadn't given that a single thought, at least until she stayed in Alaska. In Paradise, fireplaces were for heating and candles were for making light. In Raven's cabin, anyway, nothing was for show.

"Your objection is noted." Mia took a sip of her final bottle of Chateau Garrant. It had been Alastair's favorite.

"The house I can see," Marnie said. "But I busted my butt to get you sole control of Lafayette Fashion."

"They're his kids, Marnie."

"They're his little terrors."

"They're not as bad as we thought."

"But two-thirds—*two-thirds* of the company to them?"

"There are three of us. That seemed fair. I didn't give any of it to Theresa."

"I'd have had you committed it you'd tried to bring her into the mix."

Mia laughed at Marnie's scowl.

"Can we at least take a few bottles of this with us?" Marnie asked.

Mia waved a hand. "Take as many as you like."

"Seriously?"

"Sure."

"I'm really going to," Marnie warned, coming to her feet.

"You know the way to the wine cellar."

"I do." Marnie paused. "You're sure?"

"Have at it."

Marnie grinned then and headed for the basement stairs.

The doorbell rang, and Mia rose to meet the driver. This evening was her final good-bye to the house, and it felt even better than she'd expected to leave the past behind.

She opened the door and staggered to a halt, finding Silas standing on the porch. She blinked for a moment, unable to believe what she was seeing.

Her heart lifted with joy before astonishment settled in. "*What* are you doing here?"

He gave a self-conscious half-smile. "I was in the neighborhood." He paused. "Well, by neighborhood, I mean Los Angeles generally, not this particular street." He looked past her into the foyer. "So, *this* is the place."

"Come in." She realized she didn't much care why he was here; she was just thrilled to see him, really thrilled, grab-him-and-kiss-him-hard-and-deep thrilled.

He moved past her, gazing with interest at the high ceiling, the formal staircase and the rich mahogany walls. "It's like a palace in here."

"It is grand," she said, closing the door behind him.

"Raven's place must have been a shock to your system. No wonder you thought it was a joke."

"I got used to it," she said, still fighting the urge to kiss him.

"I doubt that." He walked into the great room. "Paradise can't compete with this."

"It's not a competition," she said, reluctantly accepting the fact that he wasn't here to kiss her.

It was strange to see him in these surroundings. He didn't fit, not by any stretch. It wasn't his clothes, the black work pants, the leather boots or the T-shirt delineating his broad shoulders and bulging biceps. It might have been his rangy build. But she thought it was the contained wildness, the power that didn't seem to belong among all the elaborate trimmings.

Another knock sounded on the door, and Mia went back, knowing this had to be her driver.

It was.

"Come in," she told the uniformed man. She could feel Silas watching her. "The bags are upstairs in the master bedroom." She pointed to the staircase. "Turn left at the top. It's the double doors at the end of the hall."

"How many bags?" he asked.

"Six. They're on the bed and on the floor, burgundy plaid."

"I'll get them loaded up right away," the man said. He gave Silas a nod and headed up the stairs.

"Going someplace?" Silas asked. He was frowning as he watched the driver disappear.

"The Waldorf."

"Which one?"

"LA. Here."

Now he looked confused. "Why? Fumigating or something?"

She recoiled at the thought. "No. Really?"

He shrugged. "Bugs happen."

"Not here, they don't."

He scanned the room. "I suppose they wouldn't dare breach an inner sanctum like this."

"Plus, we have great cleaning staff and groundskeepers."

"As one does. So, why are you going to a hotel?"

She wandered her way toward him, wanting to be near him. "I'm moving."

His expression flattened. "To where?"

"The Waldorf, for starters."

"You're going to live in a five-star hotel?"

"Temporarily. I'm looking for a condo . . . or something. Smaller than this, anyway."

"You're selling." Now he looked like he approved of the decision.

"I'm giving the house to Alastair's kids."

The statement obviously surprised him. "I thought they were your enemies."

Before Mia could answer, Marnie strode through the hall into the great room.

She had an armload of wine bottles. "At least these ones won't go to waste." She stopped short when she saw Silas.

Mia stepped in with introductions. "Marnie, this is Silas Burke from Alaska. Silas, this is my lawyer, Marnie Anton."

Marnie looked him up and down and a smile grew on her face. "*This* is the guy?"

"This is the guy," Mia admitted, flicking a self-conscious glance Silas's way. There was no denying Marnie knew they'd slept together.

But Silas didn't miss a beat. "Great to meet you, Marnie." He stepped up, hand extended.

She quickly set the five bottles on a side table and shook his hand. "Just raiding the wine cellar. With Mia's permission, of course."

"I didn't think you were stealing it." His good-humored tone strummed over Mia like a soothing balm.

She'd missed him so much. "You want to pick out a few to take back with you?" she asked him.

"Oh, you definitely do," Marnie said. "Alastair was quite the collector."

"Tempting," Silas said. "But no thanks."

The driver made his way down the stairs, three of the six bags in hand.

"Am I holding you up?" Silas asked.

Mia was suddenly afraid he would leave just as suddenly as he'd arrived. "No, not at all."

Marnie retrieved her tote bag and began gathering up the wine, putting two of the bottles inside it. "I'll review the real estate deal tomorrow and start drafting the other contract." Her look to Mia was stern. "But my legal advice stands. We'll talk more *before* you sign."

"You need some help with those?" Silas asked Marnie, making a motion toward the wine bottles.

She gave him a grin. "I only took what I could carry. But

you could get the door for me." She hit a button on her car key fob and heard a double beep.

Silas went for the door and met the driver coming back in. The driver headed back up the stairs while Silas waited for Marnie.

"Thanks," Mia said to Marnie, giving her a pat on the shoulder in lieu of an awkward hug around the bottles.

"Call me if you have questions, ideas, any second thoughts."

"I won't have second thoughts." Seeing Silas here in the house made Mia even more convinced she'd made the right decision on all fronts. "But I'll call."

"Second thoughts?" Silas asked as he closed the door behind Marnie.

The driver's muffled footsteps sounded on the staircase. "This is all of them?"

"That's the lot," she said.

He glanced at Silas. "I'll be outside whenever you're ready. Take your time."

"I've got a car here," Silas said to Mia. "I can drive you over."

The driver stopped halfway out the door to wait for Mia's decision.

"Sure," she said, more than happy to prolong their visit, still hoping a hug and a kiss from him would be somewhere in the mix. She'd been dreaming of his arms night after night.

"I'll leave the bags with the bellhop," the driver said.

"Thank you."

Silas was quick on the draw and tucked some money into the man's pocket. "Appreciate that."

SILAS STOPPED HIS RENTAL CAR IN FRONT OF THE lighted gardens of the Waldorf entrance. He didn't know what he'd expected to find in LA, but it wasn't Mia moving out of her mansion—a mansion that was about ten times bigger than he'd expected.

He'd known she had money, that Alastair's company had been successful, but he hadn't expected a palace sitting in the middle of a meticulously groomed park. No wonder she had a staff of seven. His vague plan to win her back seemed patently ridiculous right now.

"Have you had dinner?" she asked as the valet approached the driver's side and Silas unrolled the window.

Silas shook his head.

"Then come in and have something. I'm hungry too."

Silas looked down at his clothes. "I doubt they'll serve me dressed like this."

She seemed to consider the problem.

"Checking in, sir?" the valet asked.

"We can go up to the rooftop lounge," she said to Silas. "It's casual."

"There's casual, and then there's casual." Silas didn't know why he was hesitating. The very last thing he wanted to do was drop Mia off at the front door and leave.

"Sir?" the valet asked.

"Yes," Silas answered, opening his door to get out.

A bellhop opened the door on Mia's side.

"Can we assist with the luggage?" the bellhop asked Silas over the roof of the car.

"We sent the bags ahead," Mia answered the man.

"If you let the front desk know, they'll get them to your room right away."

The valet handed Silas a ticket.

"Check-in is this way." The bellhop took the lead, gesturing them through a set of glass doors.

"Your name?" he asked Silas.

"Mia Westberg," Silas answered.

The man smoothly turned his attention to Mia, obviously realizing his error. "I'll let the front desk know you've arrived."

Once the check-in clerk was given Mia's name, a flurry of activity ensued. Another man in a suit jacket who looked to be a manager hustled around the end of the front desk to personally present her with a room key and assure her that her bags had already been taken upstairs. And when she mentioned they wanted to dine on the rooftop, an assistant hovering near the manager produced a cell phone and confirmed a reservation with the urgency, speed and precision of a well-run fire department.

"I take it they know you here?" Silas whispered in her ear.

"My assistant must have booked a fancy suite," she whispered back.

"The gold elevator at the south end will take you to the penthouse floor," the manager told Mia, pointing the way. "If you'd like to go directly to the roof top, take the black elevator straight across. There's a sign above it."

"Is my outfit a problem?" Silas asked, gesturing to his pants and T-shirt. Better to get the embarrassment over with down here than get kicked out once they were upstairs.

"No, sir. That's not a problem at all."

"I told you not to worry," Mia said, standing there in dangling diamond earrings, a sparkling silver blouse topped with a cropped, leather accented jacket, slim black dress pants and killer shoes. Really sexy, sexy shoes.

"I didn't want to run into a problem upstairs."

"You're anticipating contingencies again, aren't you?"

"They'll probably think I'm your driver."

"You're my pilot." She looked at the manager with a grin. "He's my pilot."

Silas gave her a gentle squeeze on the arm.

He didn't care what the hotel staff thought of him.

The manager handed her a key card. "Very good, ma'am. I'm Armond Hanover. Please call down if you need anything, anything at all."

"Thank you so much, Armond."

They took the elevator straight to the outdoor rooftop lounge and were shown to a table with a view of the sunset.

A waitress was by their side a moment later offering cocktails. Mia asked for a martini, Silas went for a whiskey.

The light breeze lifted her blond hair in the waning sunshine, and she reached into her bag for a tie, raking the hair back into a ponytail that left just enough of the strands loose to frame her face.

"I'm sorry," he said.

The apology took her by surprise. "For what?"

"For the way I left things the day you left. 'It was great meeting you.' Not my finest line."

"I wasn't looking for a good line."

"I know." His tone was full of regret. "You deserved honesty. But what I wanted was to beg you to stay, and I knew I couldn't do that. What I should have said was this: You were so far beyond the best night of my life. You were the best . . . everything in my life."

Her heart warmed. "Thanks for saying it now."

He paused and seemed to drink her in. "You are incredibly beautiful."

She gave a self-conscious smile. "Well, you are incredibly handsome."

He chuckled at that, rubbing his chin and feeling the few days' stubble.

"It's rakish," she said.

"Is rakish good?"

"Rakish is sexy."

"Are you going to sleep with me?" He clamped his jaw, not believing he'd blurted his thought out so bluntly. He braced himself for her reaction. Whatever it was, he deserved it.

She leaned forward. She didn't look angry. She looked intrigued. "Is that an invitation?"

He leaned as close as he dared. "It's a standing invitation. Has been since Wildflower Lake."

"Then, I accept." She sat back in her chair, grinning as their drinks arrived and Silas absorbed his incredible good fortune at this unexpected turn of events.

They snacked on samosas, beef skewers, guacamole and cherry tarts. Then they headed down to Mia's suite and made leisurely love in a luxury bed, with the patio doors open and the warm Pacific breeze billowing over diaphanous curtains.

Mia slept in his arms, while Silas laid awake willing the sunrise away.

Then she turned onto her back, and he suddenly realized the sun was full up.

"Morning," she said, meeting his eyes with a beautiful smile.

He kissed her tenderly. "Morning."

"You sleep well?"

"Yes." He had when he'd finally given in to it.

"Me too." She stretched. "Hungry?"

"Whatever you want."

"Coffee," she said, reaching for the phone beside the bed.

"I can make it." There was a coffee machine in the little kitchen.

"No." She put her arm across his stomach. "Don't leave yet."

"No problem." He'd stay in her bed just as long as she liked.

After a short conversation with room service, she hung up the phone. She nestled her head back against his shoulder and he held her close, trailing his fingertips over the curve of her hip.

"Tell me why," she said.

"Because you're beautiful and I'm very into you." He could feel her smile.

"Not why you made love to me. Why you're here." She

twisted her head so she could look up at him in the bright sunshine.

"I'm picking up a thing," he lied.

After last night, seeing her mansion, seeing her life, he knew he'd been crazy to think he could be a part of it. "For Brodie. It's an electronic thing, a computer . . . piece."

She sobered. "Why are you lying to me?"

He struggled to squelch his guilt so that it wouldn't show on his face. "I'm not."

She sat up. "Silas? What's going on?"

He gave up. There was no way he was getting out of this with his pride intact. "Fine." He sat up beside her. "I had a stupid idea."

"What?"

"You're going to make me do this, aren't you?"

"Tell me the truth? Yes, I am."

"I thought . . ." He told himself to get it over with. "I thought I'd come here, see you, confirm what I was feeling."

"Did you?" she asked.

"Yes." He'd confirmed it beyond a shadow of a doubt. He was in love with Mia.

"So, why lie?"

"I thought I could maybe find a job down here. Not right in LA but, you know, in the area, maybe in the national forest."

"You were going to find a job in LA?"

"Yes." It sounded crazier the more he said it out loud.

"And what, move here?"

"Yes." There was no point in dancing around it any longer. "Move here to be with you."

She looked angry then, angrier than he'd expected.

His back went up over that. All she had to do was say no—tell him no, and he'd be on his way.

"You'd hate LA," she exclaimed.

He didn't have an answer for that, since she was likely right.

"And I'm insulted," she said in the same angry tone.

Insulted? She was insulted that he was in love with her? Great. He started to move off the bed.

"What about Alaska?" she said, stopping him.

He looked back, vaguely hearing the outer door open to the living room.

"Did you even consider Alaska?" she asked. "Do you still think I'm not good enough for Alaska?"

For a moment he was distracted knowing a waiter was in the suite. Then her words penetrated.

"Maybe I didn't fit in at first," she continued. "Okay, I'll grant you that. I made loads of mistakes. But I learned the WSA radio. I mastered Raven's kooky shower. I drove a loader. I fought off a damn grizzly bear. What more do I have to do, Silas? Exactly how much more do I have to do to prove myself to you?"

"*What?*" he asked, too stupefied to come up with something more intelligible. He was grateful to hear the door click closed and know the waiter had left.

"I *am* good enough for Alaska." She huffed.

He reached for her, but she pulled away. "You've got this all wrong, so wrong."

"And if I'm not, I can learn."

He took her shoulder then, shifting closer. "There's nothing for you to learn."

Her eyes were glassy with unshed tears. Her voice was small. "Don't give up on me so soon."

"I'm not giving up on you." He could see he was botching this big time. He drew her into his arms. "I was afraid." He rocked her, smoothed her hair, kissed her temple. "Afraid that Alaska wasn't good enough for you."

She swallowed. "Why?"

"I love you, Mia. I'm head over heels in love with you, and I've been racking my brain trying to come up with a way for us to be together."

She drew back. "You came here to be with me?"

He nodded, smoothing her messy hair back from her face.

"That was your plan?" she continued.

"Yes."

"Well, that was stupid."

He grinned.

"You'd hate it here."

"I thought you'd hate it in Paradise."

"I can't wait to get back to Paradise." She searched his expression. "I love you, Silas. I don't love this." She waved her arm around the room. "I don't even love Lafayette, not really, not the way Henry and Hannah seem to love it."

"Henry and Hannah? Why are we talking about them?"

"I gave them Lafayette. Well, I split it with them. But they've got controlling shares."

Silas's brain scrambled to keep up. "I thought you gave them the house."

"That too." She came up on her knees and cradled his face in her hands. "There's nothing holding me here, Silas."

"So . . ." He couldn't bring himself to believe it. "You'll come to Paradise."

She nodded, and his chest all but burst with emotion.

"I'm building you a house," he said, drawing her into his arms again.

"Yeah? Something like Raven's?"

"*No*, not like Raven's. I wouldn't ask you to live like Raven." He made a point of gazing around the opulent room. "Plus, there are certain elements of your lifestyle I'm coming to like. Danny's offered me the plans for a villa—just like the one we had at Wildflower Lake. We can buy a lot near the river if you want. Or we can do something else."

"I'd love a villa by the river. That sounds perfect."

"I never should have let you go."

"I had to come back here to find out what mattered," she said gently. "I think we both knew that."

"I mean, I should have come back with you. I should

have known enough to figure this out with you by my side. I made so many mistakes."

She chuckled at that. "You? Seriously? I'm the super-klutz."

"No, you're wrong about that. I took one look at your classy clothes, your beautiful hair, your elegant manners and made assumptions. I was wrong to do that, and I'm sorry."

She shook her head. "We're both guilty. I took a look at you and thought you were a serial killer."

"I'm still sorry that I scared you." He shook his head with a chuckle.

"A sexy one," she said in a husky voice. "But I took one look at your stature, your height, your shoulders—" She rubbed his bare shoulder with her palm. "Your rakish beard and rugged chin, and I thought you were dangerous."

"I'm not dangerous." He paused. "Well, not to you. Maybe to some of those yahoos who've been trolling you on social media."

"They've stopped. Well, mostly stopped. But they're never going to find me in Paradise."

"You're coming to Paradise." He repeated it because he couldn't quite believe it was real.

"I'm coming to Paradise," she said on a sight, her lithe body molding against him.

"I love you so much." He kissed her mouth, her tender, sweet mouth, gathering her as close as he could, holding her tight as he dared, determined never to let her go.

Chapter Seventeen

MIA WANTED SILAS TO ENJOY THE BEST OF LA, SO SHE made reservations at the Hamburg Room, a private club overlooking the Malibu shore. It was one of her favorite spots, where waves crashed up on the rock shore, splashing over the ground lights and against the glass wall. The lighting inside was more muted, yellow-toned and romantic.

She'd dressed in a midnight-blue off-the-shoulder, chiffon-column sheath, with a sweetheart neckline and an asymmetrical hemline. It looked great with diamonds, and she'd worn them on her ears and around her neck. She'd had her favorite hairdresser put her hair up, going with an elaborate style, since she wouldn't be coming back to the salon again. The night was also a not-so-fond farewell to a barely-there pair of black stilettoes with ankle bands. They'd looked fabulous, but they were the most uncomfortable pair of shoes she'd ever bought.

She wanted to have a final night out to remember.

Silas had only brought along jeans and a dark blazer, but he'd paired them with a white dress shirt and a burgundy tie. He looked fantastic, turning the heads of several women as they were shown to a prime table beside the window. The white tablecloth was crisp and the crystal stemware sparkled over the polished silver.

"What do you think?" she asked as they took their seats.

"It sure isn't the Bear and Bar," he said, glancing around.

"The food is fabulous. You should try the scallop and citrus salad."

"You think?" An odd expression pulled at his face.

She hadn't meant to push her preferences on him. "Or whatever you want. They have a nice filet mignon. I like it with the blue cheese crumble."

He glanced pensively around the room again, and Mia followed his gaze—the party of businessmen laughing at a large table with a couple of them surreptitiously glancing her way, the staid-looking older couple near the rock feature, the young lovers in the alcove booth gazing into each other's eyes.

"Do people recognize you when you're out like this?" he asked.

She suspected he'd seen the businessmen looking. "Sometimes," she said. "But they're not nearly so hostile lately."

His frown deepened.

"Is something wrong?" she asked him.

"No," he said, switching his frown to a faux smile. "Nothing."

She drew back. "You're lying to me again, Silas Burke. Why are you lying to me?"

His smile turned sheepish. "Okay, total honesty. This isn't exactly my kind of place."

"You don't like frou-frou food," she guessed. She could understand that. The portions here were quite small, and they did tend to doll them up with garnishes and exotic sauces.

He shook his head. "It's more the atmosphere." He gave

a little shudder. "It's not exactly the kind of place where you kick back and relax."

She gathered her purse.

"What are you doing?"

"We're leaving."

He reached out and covered her hand. "No, that's not what I meant. If this is your favorite place, we'll eat here. I really don't mind."

The waitress arrived with a beaming smile. "Can I offer either of you a cocktail tonight?"

"We've had a change of plans," Mia told her with an apologetic smile.

The waitresses smile disappeared. "Is something not right? Would you like to change tables? Something a little quieter, perhaps?"

"It's not the table," Mia said.

"We can stay," Silas said.

"Nothing's wrong," she said to the waitress. "We've just changed our plans."

"All right." The waitress withdrew. "Have a great evening."

"I didn't mean for us to leave," Silas said. "This is not exactly a hardship. Let's order drinks."

Mia rose from her chair. "LA has about five thousand restaurants; it's really no big deal. What did you have in mind?"

Silas quickly stood.

"No lying," she admonished.

He grinned sheepishly then, looking like his usual self. "Burger. Maybe nachos. Someplace with comfortable chairs where your fancy dress won't fit in and I can take off my tie."

"You okay with a water view?" she asked, thinking she knew just the place.

"I've got nothing against the ocean."

They grabbed a cab and moved a few miles down the road toward Santa Monica.

Mia showed Silas into a laid-back bistro with wide open windows, bare wood tables and lively chatter.

He stripped off his jacket and tie as the waitress showed them to a table.

"Better?" she asked as they got seated.

"Perfect," he said, draping his jacket over the chair and pocketing the tie. He looked over at her with a smile and squeezed her hand. "Thank you."

She smiled back at him, happy that he looked more relaxed. The evening was about both of them enjoying the city, and she loved this little bistro.

The sun had set, and the lights in the garden below illuminated the shrubbery and the palm trees.

"Beer?" she asked as the waitress approached.

"Whatever you've got on tap," Silas said to the woman.

"Light or red?" she asked.

"Red."

"Same," Mia said.

Silas looked at her in surprise.

"I'm having French fries too."

The waitress gave them a grin as she walked away.

Mia opened the menu, flipping through all the pages, not just the salads. Everything looked delicious.

"Mia?"

"Hmm?" The pulled pork wrap looked very tempting. But so did the bacon burger.

"Mia?" he repeated.

She looked up and gasped, all thoughts of food forgotten.

Silas had reached across the table. He was holding out a small box—a ring box.

Her heart skipped a beat as she took in the recessed round diamond nestled in a swirl of diamond chips set on a woven band.

She was speechless for a moment.

"Mia, you are my everything. I love you so much. . . . Will you marry me?" he asked, his deep tone totally sexy and romantic.

She looked into his eyes that were peering hopefully at her. "You . . ."

He cocked his head.

The waitress approached with their beer, saw what was happening and abruptly backed away.

"It's a yes-or-no question, Mia." But he didn't look worried. He looked happy. He was glowing.

She was glowing too, everything from her skin to her eyes to her heart. "Yes. Absolutely yes."

He took the ring from the box.

"It's perfect," she said as he slid it onto her finger.

"I asked for something low-profile. LA elegant meets Alaska practical." He kissed her ring finger. "We're going to make this thing work, Mia. I promise."

"We will," she said. "Oh, I know we will."

MIA WORE A LOOSE-FITTING SOFT COTTON BLEND T-shirt, steel gray with short sleeves, tucked into a pair of khaki cargo pants. Overtop, she'd layered a breathable cotton black-and-white-checkerboard shirt, buttoned and tied at her waist, the cuffed sleeves rolled up to her elbows. She and Silas had stopped in Anchorage to pick up a few necessities, so she had practical weatherproof leather boots laced on her feet. They were super comfortable for walking in the woods.

Her hair was up in a ponytail, threaded through the back of a WSA baseball cap. No need for a handbag. Bear spray was strapped to her belt, and her phone was in a pocket of the cargo pants. Silas's truck keys dangled in the ignition where they'd parked it on the road between the airstrip and Paradise.

"This is where I was thinking," Silas said as the pathway lead them to a grass-and-wildflower-strewn meadow on a bend in the river.

Mia paused and smiled, breathing the fresh, fragrant air and feeling the sunshine on her face. Wind whispered softly through the trees, and birds chirped all around them. The river rolled past with an understated rumble, while the mountains rose sharp against the sky beyond.

"It's nice," she said, thinking the view was spectacular.

He took her hand and they started walking again. "The bank's high enough that we wouldn't need to worry about floods."

"Live and learn," she said, liking the idea of the precaution.

"We can build the deck right out over the water, get the morning sun, glass part of it in if we want to extend the season. If we take down a few of those trees over there, our bedroom will have views out two sides."

"You've really thought this through, haven't you?"

He pulled her close to his side. "What do you think?"

"I love it."

"You sure? It doesn't have to be here."

"We'd practically be neighbors with Raven. Of course it has to be here."

A smile curved his lips. "There's a footpath to her place. It's a ten-minute walk, but we can bring in a machine and widen it for the ATV."

"We're getting an ATV?"

"I have an ATV."

"Aren't you just full of surprises."

"I have a boat, too. We can build a dock and a boathouse right out front, and we can tour up the river whenever the mood strikes us."

"It's perfect," she said, gazing around.

He leaned in and kissed her hairline. "We can put in a lawn, or we can keep the meadow."

She turned to face him, tilting her chin and looping her arms around his neck. "Anything sounds good to me."

"We can decide later."

"Let's decide later." Right now, she just wanted to enjoy the moment.

He bent his head to kiss her lips, the sweetest, most earthy kiss, making her wish the villa was already built so they could rush to the bedroom.

"There you are!" Raven's voiced called out from a distance.

They broke their kiss, and Mia looked toward the sound and saw her cousin emerge from the trees.

"That path needs some work," Raven said as she approached.

Mia smirked. "I'd be happy to widen it out with the mini loader."

"Oh no you don't." There was a mock warning in Raven's tone.

Silas kept his arm looped around Mia's waist, resting loosely on her hip. "I can vouch for her. She's pretty good with the heavy equipment."

"I can see why you picked this spot." Raven shaded her eyes and gazed around.

"We're building the deck out over the river," Mia said. In her mind's eye, she could already see their villa blending into the natural setting.

"That'll be Brodie," Silas said as they heard a truck engine stop.

"He owes me twenty bucks," Raven said. "I bet him you'd come back."

"He probably thought that was a safe bet." Three weeks ago, Mia herself would have put a lot more than twenty bucks on her staying in LA.

"He bet Silas would move to LA."

Mia looked up at Silas, his profile in relief against the Alaskan wilderness. "That was never going to happen."

"It might have happened," Silas said as Brodie cleared the trees.

They watched him stride across the meadow.

"Welcome back," he said to Mia as he approached. He smiled at her without a trace of reluctance, no suspicion or caution.

It warmed her heart to be accepted by him. "Thanks, Brodie."

"So, this is the place," he said, sounding like he approved.

"This is the place," Silas responded. "Danny's guy says he can double up on the crew and get it built before the snow flies."

"While they're here, maybe they can do some work on Raven's house," Brodie said, nudging her shoulder teasingly.

"Hey," she protested. "Quit picking on my cabin. It's got a great roof now."

"Plumbing," Brodie suggested with an arch of his brow.

"Oh, do the bathroom," Mia added with enthusiasm. "Get yourself a real shower. Go wild, girl."

Raven laughed. "Fine. The bathroom." She paused. "Maybe the countertops too."

"Welcome to the dark side, cousin."

"Where are you staying while they build?" Raven asked her.

Mia looked at Silas, and he looked back. She couldn't imagine sharing his single bed in WSA housing, but she didn't want them to live apart either.

"Glamping?" she suggested. "They can set up a really nice wall tent. Right out here on the meadow."

"Without plumbing?" Silas asked her in clear amazement.

Mia couldn't say she loved the idea.

"You can take my place," Raven said. "I'll take Silas's room until the construction's complete."

"Seriously?" Brodie said to Raven, his amazement rivaling Silas's. "After all this time, you'll move into WSA housing?"

Raven responded with a long-suffering sigh. "I think it's my destiny."

Brodie reached out and gave her ponytail a tug. "In that case, welcome to the neighborhood."

"Are you sure?" Mia asked. She didn't want to put Raven out for weeks.

"It's not as bad as she thinks," Brodie said. "The food's good, and it's walking distance to the Galina warehouse."

"It's only temporary," Raven warned him.

Brodie seemed to be savoring her capitulation. But after a minute, he turned his attention to Mia. He rubbed his hands together. "So, Mia, while this is all going on, you think you'll be super busy?"

"With the housebuilding?" she asked.

"Don't forget the matchmaking," Raven said.

"As if any of us could," Brodie shot back.

"Why?" Mia asked, curious as to why he would care.

"Shannon has to go out on medical for a couple of weeks. I'm looking for a radio operator."

Mia couldn't believe what he was asking.

Silas gave her shoulder an encouraging squeeze.

She pointed to her chest. "You want *me*?"

"I want you. You proved yourself, and I'd be grateful for the help."

She nodded, feeling elated. "Okay."

He reached out to shake on it, his broad hand, enclosing hers. "Then welcome to WSA." He turned to Raven then, cocking his head. "Let's do it. I'll help you pack."

"Right now?"

"These two need somewhere to sleep tonight."

"It doesn't have to be right away," Mia quickly put in.

"No. It makes sense," Raven said with a backward step. "No reason to wait. I'll go make room."

Raven and Brodie turned and left, walking side by side.

"I still think they're going to be a thing," Mia said as she watched the pair approach the forest fringe. Their voices faded, but it was clear they were continuing an animated conversation.

Silas stepped around to face her, blocking her view. He cradled her cheeks with his palms and his low sexy voice rumbled. "Maybe so. But you and me? We're going to be the best thing."

She felt instantly weightless with love and joy. "Yes." She nodded. "We're going to be fantastic. You and me. Right here, together, in Paradise."

He kissed her lips. "Forever."

ACKNOWLEDGMENTS

I owe this series to my hard-working agent, Laura Bradford, and my fabulous editor, Angela Kim, who believed in me and supported me in multiple ways from conception to publication.

My everlasting love and gratitude to my wonderful husband, Gordon Dunlop, bush pilot, technician and outdoorsman—he's every hero a woman could want.

And finally, a huge thank you and a debt of gratitude to the authors who inspired, supported and cheered my writing efforts and continue doing so to this day: Jane Porter, Jane Graves, C.J. Carmichael and Lorraine Heath— fantastically successful authors and dearly valued friends.

Keep reading for a special preview of
the next novel in Barbara Dunlop's
Paradise, Alaska, series

Finding Paradise

Coming soon from Berkley Jove!

ENJOYING THE LAST SIP OF A BUBBLY 2006 DE Beauchene from her blown crystal flute, Marnie Anton paused beneath the vaulted ceilings of LA's Lafayette mansion to ponder irony and the twists of fate.

"I see you need more champagne," Hannah Lafayette observed, her voice light and cheerful as she approached Marnie in the great room. She gave a discreet wave to a nearby waiter who was standing at the ready.

Hannah had grown up in the mansion and was completely comfortable in its grandeur and opulence.

Marnie, on the other hand, had grown up behind an auto shop in Merganser, Kansas.

A crisp-dressed, white-shirted man refilled her glass with the dry, deeply flavored golden champagne that foamed partway up to the rim. In a town full of entertainment power brokers, the late Alastair Lafayette still had an unbeatable wine cellar.

"Thank you." Marnie gave the waiter a truly grateful smile. She might have grown up playing in a wheel alignment pit instead of a wine cellar, but that didn't mean she couldn't appreciate a great vintage.

"I can feel the excitement from here." Hannah gestured to the dozen women chatting and laughing over drinks and hors d'oeuvres in scattered groups around the gracious room.

"You didn't have to do all this." Marnie had been surprised when Hannah and her twin brother Henry so whole-heartedly embraced supporting the Finding Paradise Alaskan match-making venture. They were hosting a launch party tonight, giving the selected women a chance to get to know each other before tomorrow's flight to Anchorage then Fairbanks, then on to the small, rural town of Paradise.

"We're more than happy to help out," Hannah said with what sounded like sincerity. "I know Mia transferred own-ership of the house to us, but we still consider it hers too." She paused for a moment, a thread of humor coming into her voice. "And Henry wouldn't have it any other way. He got a haircut, picked up a new suit and shaved at four o'clock this afternoon."

Marnie couldn't help but smile at Henry's eagerness to meet the young, eligible women who were participating in the endeavor.

Her legal client and close friend Mia Westberg was a driving force behind the Alaska matchmaking project. At twenty-seven, Mia was only two years older than her step-children Hannah and Henry, and over the past few months, they'd battled each other in a drawn-out court case over Mia's husband Alastair's estate. By rights, Marnie and Hannah should still be adversaries.

Marnie had successfully argued for the fashion empire and mansion to go to Mia—as Alastair had directed. But Mia had promptly shared ownership of the company with the twins, handed over the family mansion to them, then ceded control of the company and moved to Paradise, Alaska.

Having met bush pilot Silas Burke and having seen the diamond ring he put on Mia's finger, Marnie didn't blame her friend for falling in love. But Mia had turned a clear court case win into what felt like a partial loss. It was hard for the competitive streak in Marnie to accept the final outcome.

"Scarlett Kensington seems particularly amped up," Hannah continued the conversation like she and Marnie were old friends, nodding to one particular group of women.

Marnie took in Scarlett's flushed cheeks and her brisk hand gestures where she chatted with Olivia Axler and Willow Hale in front of the wide stone fireplace that soared to the ceiling—a portrait of Grandfather Lafayette gazing down from its face. Scarlett was twenty-two and worked as a production assistant in the film industry.

Mia and her cousin Raven, who also lived in Paradise, had carefully selected each applicant, choosing women they thought might fit in best in small town Alaska. There were plenty of robust, hard-working men in Paradise who were eager to meet new women. And the women here were eager to meet honorable men.

"Scarlett's into surfboarding and parasailing," Marnie said to Hannah, having studied the background on each of the successful applicants. "She also said she likes to hike in the San Gabriel Mountains."

"I guess that's that kind of thing you'd be looking for."

"Willow hang-glides, and Olivia's been fly fishing with her grandfather. We built outdoor sports into the algorithm."

"That seems smart," Hannah said, tilting her head to study another of the conversation groups. "From the pictures Mia sent, Paradise is nothing but mountains, trees and rivers. You'd have to be outdoorsy to put up with that."

Marnie had seen those same pictures. "They have a café, a bar, housing—well cabins and camp trailers mostly. But

there's the health center, the school, Galina Expediting's
warehouse and West Slope Aviation at the airstrip."

Galina and WSA, were the main employers in the town,
its reason for existing, in fact.

Hannah pouted her pretty red lips. "Not a single designer boutique, no fine dining, no beach-front, never mind
a country club."

Marnie cracked a smile at the justified criticism. "Plus,
the bugs and the bears. Definitely not my idea of paradise."

"Whose was it, do you think?" Hannah looked perplexed, giving her champagne flute a small wave of emphasis. "Who got there, looked around and said, ahh, Paradise,
that's the right name?"

Marnie's grin widened. It felt strange to chat amicably
with Hannah after the bitterness of the court case.

Marnie had later learned that Hannah's mother, Alastair's
ex-wife Theresa, had been the driving force behind the hostility. Still, it was unsettling to have Hannah's attitude turn
on a dime like this. Marnie kept expecting Hannah to voice
some sharp disagreement or have an angry outburst liked
she'd done a couple of time in the courtroom.

"Silas is picking them up in Fairbanks?" Hannah asked
after a moment of silence.

Marnie nodded. "I'm not sure he's thrilled to be dropped
into the middle of the whole undertaking. But he can't say
no to Mia."

Hannah took a sip of her own champagne. "Mia made it
sound like his boss was the real grouch."

"Most of the guys can't wait to mix and mingle. The
entire town is in desperate need of more estrogen. But his
boss Brodie thinks it'll be disruptive to his airline's operations."

"It probably will."

"True, and he's skeptical that any of the women will
settle down in Alaska."

"Even if they do meet their perfect match?" Hannah asked.

"Even then."

"What do you think?"

Marnie had to agree with Brodie—even though they'd chosen women who skewed toward outdoor pursuits. "Would *you* leave LA for Paradise, Alaska, population four-hundred?"

"With gravel roads, a single restaurant and an average winter temperature of ten-below?" Hannah grimaced.

Marnie lifted her flute in mock toast to their evident agreement. "Exactly."

They both drank then pondered for a moment.

"I hear the guys are super sexy," Hannah ventured.

"I suppose they'd keep you warm at night," Marnie allowed.

Hannah stretched out her fingers and gazed at her perfect coral manicure. "I'd miss Celeste's esthetics talents . . . and my friends at the club . . . and where would you even wear your Castille or your Faux?"

Marnie couldn't afford either of those fashion designers, but she understood the point. "I have a dozen pairs of perfectly good shoes that would *not* survive gravel roads and muddy pathways."

Hannah's sculpted brows furrowed. "Mia's been wearing those brown leather boots all the time up there, water-proofed, I think."

"Barely a heel." Marnie had seen them in pictures, splattered in mud. They looked tragically practical, reminding her of a time in her life she preferred to forget.

"No calf elongation whatsoever." Hannah glanced down at her own shapely legs beneath the shimmer of her slim, steel blue cocktail dress. Her stiletto peep-toes had obviously been dyed to match the dress, and they looked terrific.

"I'm only five-feet-two." Marnie needed all the help she could get in the heel department.

Hannah stepped back to take in Marnie's four-inch t-straps. "Those are really nice."

Marnie turned her ankle sideways. "A little platform under the toe helps. Keeps the arches more comfortable when you're standing." She'd learned back in law school that she needed to add to her height if she wanted anyone to take her seriously.

In front of a judge, she always wore slacks to help camouflage the lift of her shoes. She tied her hair back too. The bright copper color seemed to distract male judges, also male opposing attorneys. She'd never figured out why. It was just hair, and plenty of people had hair that color.

"I take it Alaska's not on your bucket list?" Hannah asked.

"My bucket list includes places like London and the Mediterranean."

As for Alaska, Marnie would see the women safely to LAX tomorrow morning and onto the plane. Then she planned to take a little time for herself to recover from the flurry of activity. She hadn't booked any client appointments for tomorrow or for Friday either, planning to extend the weekend, kick back and relax.

Thinking about it, she could use a new manicure herself, maybe a pedicure too. Maybe she'd do an entire spa day.

"I guess we leave the outdoorsy stuff to the hang-gliders and the parasailers."

"I've played beach volleyball," Marnie offered with a thread of humor.

She could also navigate by the stars and survive a week in the wilderness with nothing but a pocketknife and a pound of dried beans, but she didn't say so. And she'd sure as hell never do it for fun.

"Tennis for me," Hannah said. "But that's mostly because the Turquoise Racket Club serves such a great brunch."

"I feel like an underachiever," Marnie said.

"You? You're one of the best lawyers in LA!" Hannah paused. "I mean, you beat us without breaking a sweat."

Marnie sent her a sidelong glance, wondering if this was it, if Hannah was about to express her hidden hostility.

"And we had ourselves a top-notch team," Hannah continued offhandedly. "Brettan LaCroix spared no expense."

"There wasn't much they could do with an iron-clad will." Marnie was still tense, still on alert for an argument.

"Mia was a highly flawed defendant. Half the city hated her. The rest thought she was a shameless gold-digger."

"She wasn't." Marnie reflexively defended her friend.

"Turns out not. And you never gave up on her. And you represented her brilliantly. So, I'm saying, you're not an underachiever."

"Oh." Marnie sorted through the conversation in her mind. It didn't seem like Hannah was going to get hostile after all.

"You should come and see us next week," Hannah said.

"For what?" Had Marnie missed something in the exchange?

"To look at giving us some legal advice. You worked with Mia for years, so you know our business."

After a stunned moment, Marnie gathered her wits. "I specialize in family law."

"And it's a family business."

Marnie supposed you could frame it that way.

"So, will you take us on?" Hannah asked.

"Uh, sure, yeah, I'll come by next week." Who would say no to a new client who owned a mansion and a fashion empire? Not Marnie, that was for sure.

Hannah raised her glass again, and Marnie silently toasted to the most unlikely business relationship in the city.

"I'VE SAID IT ALL ALONG—DISTRACTION, DISRUPTION then fallout." Brodie Seaton, owner of West Slope Aviation ended his sentence on a firm note of conviction. Then, obviously confident his message had been delivered, he leaned back against the workbench of the airplane hangar in Paradise, Alaska, his arms crossed over his chest.

Aircraft Maintenance Engineer Cobra Stanford didn't disagree with his boss. He'd been skeptical about the Finding Paradise matchmaking scheme from the beginning. But it was above his paygrade and none of his business, so he'd kept his thoughts mostly to himself.

"I'm planning to keep my distance," he said now.

"Wise," Brodie said with a nod. "I wish there were more like you around."

Cobra swung the engine cowl shut on the twin otter bush plane—one of the largest in the fleet—secured it and stepped down off the ladder. The aircraft was fit and ready to make the run to Fairbanks tomorrow to pick up the twelve LA women.

The light dimmed to dark orange through the high hangar windows as the sun set behind the mountains in the late September evening, making the fluorescent ceiling lights appear brighter.

"Are the pilots drawing lots to see who takes the Viking Mine run?" he asked. Whoever took the lengthy flight to Viking was sure to miss the women's big arrival.

"I'm assigning T-Two and Xavier."

Cobra gave an ironic grin. "That's going to go over well."

T-Two, Tobias Erikson, was a laid-back guy, but Xavier O'Keefe was as excited about the LA women's visit as anyone in town.

"They're up in the rotation," Brodie said. "Business is not going to be interrupted by this."

Cobra moved to the bench and took a clean shop rag from the pile to wipe his hands. "I can take the right seat if that helps."

Cobra had trained as a pilot in the military. Although he didn't keep his hours current enough to serve as pilot in command, he could take the first officer's seat when needed.

"You're just trying to get out of town."

Cobra gave a shrug. "Maybe."

Brodie grinned. "Nice of you to offer, but I'm not making concessions to this madness."

"You let them take over half your staff housing." Cobra turned to rest his hips against the workbench, matching Brodie's posture.

The air compressor finished chugging and hissed to silence and the fluorescent's buzz above them filled the space.

"Mia saved my PC-12 from crashing," Brodie said, referring to the time Mia Westberg had cleared airstrip debris in the middle of a flood.

"Plus, Raven wanted this," Cobra added.

Brodie's eyes narrowed as he sent Cobra a sidelong glance. "Keeping the peace between Raven and me is important to the town."

That was true enough. Raven was operations manager at Galina Expediting. Together with Brodie's company West Slope Aviation, they supplied outlying mining, scientific and wilderness tourism operations all across central Alaska. The two companies made up the majority of Paradise's economy.

"They redecorated half of your housing units—girlified them, according to Peter."

"That wasn't Raven."

Cobra knew Brodie had a soft spot for Raven. He also knew enough to let that particular subject drop. "Mia?"

WSA's chief pilot Silas Burke's new fiancée Mia was a former supermodel and had a flare for the artistic. She'd first come to town in June, and she was behind the matchmaking project. She'd also had an impact on the décor over at the Bear and Bar Café, and now she had Silas building her a swanky new house beside the river.

"Who else?" Brodie asked with an arch of his brow. "Dusty rose. My walls are *dusty rose*."

"Is that a real color?" Cobra moved a few steps to the refreshment fridge at the end of the workbench. Since he

was off the clock now, he pulled out a couple of beers holding one up to Brodie as a question.

Brodie nodded, and Cobra tossed him the can.

"You should see the curtains," Brodie said, sounding
like he was in pain. "Watercolor paintings and frilly curtains and something called wainscoting."

"What's wainscoting?" A picture was forming in Cobra's mind. He'd heard sawing and hammering next door to
his own WSA staff housing unit for weeks now. He'd never
been inclined to check out what Peter and the construction
crew were doing.

"It's trim, fancy wooden trim."

"Does it add any structural value?" Cobra popped the
top of his beer can.

"A little, maybe, I suppose. But it's white and . . . you
know . . . dusty rose."

"So, white and pink?"

Brodie grimaced.

"Like a little girl's bedroom." Cobra covered his smirk
with a chug of his beer. It tasted good going down, crisp,
cold and refreshing. He realized how long it had been since
he'd taken a break. He stretched out his neck and shoulders.

"Sure." Brodie took a drink himself. "Kick a man when
he's down."

Cobra's grin broadened. "There is one upside."

Brodie gestured with the can. "I don't want to hear any
optimism from you."

"Okay."

It took Brodie less than a minute to crack. "Alright. Give
it to me."

"Pretty women."

Brodie frowned. "That's not the upside. It's the downside."

"Potato, Potahto."

"No. All downside for me. I'm not interested in any of
that, but all of my pilots are."

Cobra guessed Brodie was only interested in Raven—

who was pretty herself in a not-so-flashy, down-to-earth way. But he wasn't going to bring her up again.

"Don't tell me you're interested now," Brodie said with mock disgust. "You're the only other guy on Team This-is-Stupid."

"Not my thing," Cobra said.

Brodie gave him an odd look.

"Short term," Cobra elaborated. "I have zero interest in getting to know a woman who's only sticking around for seventy-two hours. Plus, they're lower-forty-eight, big-city. Could you have found any less likely group of women for this?"

"*I* didn't find them," Brodie pointed out.

"Why not from Anchorage or Wyoming?" Targeting LA had struck Cobra as flawed from the beginning.

"Wyoming?"

"Rural women who don't expect five-star dining and maybe know their way around a shovel or a well-pump."

Brodie straightened away from the workbench. "I said that weeks ago. I suggested some perfectly practical screening questions, but I was shouted down. It's pointless to let people think Paradise is all sipping brandy in front of an open fire."

"It's not an easy life up here."

"It's a great life." Brodie pointed around with his beer can for emphasis. "But it's not cushy by any stretch. And did you see the website they built?"

"I did not." Cobra was surprised that Brodie had.

"All vistas and bonfires, snowmobiles and fun. They showed the France's house, like that's typical of where people live around here."

Mrs. France owned the Bear and Bar Café, and the France family had the fanciest house in town.

"They dressed up a section of the Bear and Bar for a photoshoot." Brodie was clearly on a roll, and Cobra settled back to sip his beer and listen. "Tablecloths and silverware

and flowers. It's false advertising, I tell you. And Mia—
they used Silas and Mia's happily-ever-after story, set him
all combed and clean shaven in his flight suit in the sunshine in front of a freshly washed bush plane, Mia holding
his hand all uber citified, like anyone from LA would naturally fit in up here. Do they show the mud? No. Do they
show the mosquitoes? No. Mia barely escaped a bear at-
tack. Do they mention that? No."

Cobra was sympathetic but also entertained by how
worked up Brodie was getting over the whole crazy idea.
He quickly raised his beer to hide his grin.

Brodie caught the expression anyway and scowled.
"This isn't a joke."

"I know. But you're headed off the deep end there."

Brodie jabbed his thumb against his chest. "I'm the rare
voice of reason."

Cobra polished off the beer then dropped his empty into
the recycle bin. "Here's the thing about these women, Brodie. They're small. They're slow. They'll probably wear
high heels. I'm liking our chances of a clean escape."

Brodie cracked a smile then too.

Cobra clapped him on the shoulder. "Bob and weave, Brodie. Bob and weave. We'll make it through the weekend."

Ready to find
your next great read?

Let us help.

Visit prh.com/nextread

Penguin
Random
House